NON SANZ DROICT.

William Shakespeare

The History of
TROILUS
and
CRESSIDA

Edited by Daniel Seltzer

The Signet Classic Shakespeare
GENERAL EDITOR: SYLVAN BARNET

Revised and Updated Bibliography

A SIGNET CLASSIC

NEW AMERICAN LIBRARY

NEW YORK AND SCARBOROUGH, ONTARIO

SIGNET CLASSIC TRADEMARK REG. U.S. PAT. OFF. AND FOREIGN COUNTRIES
REGISTERED TRADEMARK—MARCA REGISTRADA
HECHO EN WINNIPEG, CANADA

SIGNET, SIGNET CLASSIC, MENTOR, ONYX, PLUME, MERIDIAN AND
NAL BOOKS are published *in the United States* by
NAL PENGUIN INC.,
1633 Broadway, New York, New York 10019,
in Canada by The New American Library of Canada Limited,
81 Mack Avenue, Scarborough, Ontario M1L 1M8

First Printing, September, 1963

12   13   14   15   16   17   18   19   20

PRINTED IN CANADA

Contents

Shakespeare: Prefatory Remarks

Between the record of his baptism in Stratford on 26 April 1564 and the record of his burial in Stratford on 25 April 1616, some forty documents name Shakespeare, and many others name his parents, his children, and his grandchildren. More facts are known about William Shakespeare than about any other playwright of the period except Ben Jonson. The facts should, however, be distinguished from the legends. The latter, inevitably more engaging and better known, tell us that the Stratford boy killed a calf in high style, poached deer and rabbits, and was forced to flee to London, where he held horses outside a playhouse. These traditions are only traditions; they may be true, but no evidence supports them, and it is well to stick to the facts.

Mary Arden, the dramatist's mother, was the daughter of a substantial landowner; about 1557 she married John Shakespeare, who was a glove-maker and trader in various farm commodities. In 1557 John Shakespeare was a member of the Council (the governing body of Stratford), in 1558 a constable of the borough, in 1561 one of the two town chamberlains, in 1565 an alderman (entitling him to the appellation "Mr."), in 1568 high bailiff—the town's highest political office, equivalent to mayor. After 1577, for an unknown reason he drops out of local politics. The birthday of William Shakespeare, the eldest son of this locally prominent man, is unrecorded; but the Stratford parish register records that the infant was baptized on 26 April 1564. (It is quite possible that he was born on 23 April, but this date has probably been assigned by tradition because it is the date on which, fifty-two years later, he died.) The attendance records of the Stratford grammar school of the period are not extant, but it is reasonable to assume that the son of a local official attended the school and received substantial training in Latin. The masters of the school from Shakespeare's seventh to fifteenth years held Oxford degrees; the Elizabethan curriculum excluded mathematics and the natural sciences but taught a good deal of Latin rhetoric, logic, and literature. On 27 November 1582 a marriage license was issued to Shakespeare and Anne Hathaway, eight years his senior. The couple had a child in May, 1583. Perhaps the marriage was necessary, but perhaps the couple had earlier engaged in a formal "troth plight" which would render their children legitimate even if no further ceremony were performed. In 1585 Anne Hathaway bore Shakespeare twins.

That Shakespeare was born is excellent; that he married and had children is pleasant; but that we know nothing about his departure from Stratford to London, or about the beginning of his theatrical career, is lamentable and must be admitted. We would gladly sacrifice details about his children's baptism for details about his earliest days on the stage. Perhaps the poaching episode is true (but it is first reported almost a century after Shakespeare's death), or perhaps he first left Stratford to be a schoolteacher, as another tradition holds; perhaps he was moved by

> Such wind as scatters young men through the world,
> To seek their fortunes further than at home
> Where small experience grows.

In 1592, thanks to the cantankerousness of Robert Greene, a rival playwright and a pamphleteer, we have our first reference, a snarling one, to Shakespeare as an actor and playwright. Greene warns those of his own educated friends who wrote for the theater against an actor who has presumed to turn playwright:

> There is an upstart crow, beautified with our feathers, that with his *tiger's heart wrapped in a player's hide* supposes he is as well able to bombast out a blank verse as the best of you, and being an absolute Johannes-factotum is in his own conceit the only Shake-scene in a country.

The reference to the player, as well as the allusion to Aesop's crow (who strutted in borrowed plumage, as an actor struts in fine words not his own), makes it clear that by this date Shakespeare had both acted and written. That Shakespeare is meant is indicated not only by "Shake-scene" but by the parody of a line from one of Shakespeare's plays, *3 Henry VI:* "O, tiger's heart wrapped in a woman's hide." If Shakespeare in 1592 was prominent enough to be attacked by an envious dramatist, he probably had served an apprenticeship in the theater for at least a few years.

In any case, by 1592 Shakespeare had acted and written, and there are a number of subsequent references to him as an actor: documents indicate that in 1598 he is a "principal comedian," in 1603 a "principal tragedian," in 1608 he is one of the "men players." The profession of actor was not for a gentleman, and it occasionally drew the scorn of university men who resented writing speeches for persons less educated than themselves, but it was respectable enough: players, if prosperous, were in effect members of the bourgeoisie, and there is nothing to suggest that Stratford considered William Shakespeare less than a solid citizen. When, in 1596, the Shakespeares were granted a coat of arms, the grant was made to Shakespeare's father, but probably William Shakespeare (who the next year bought the second-largest house in town) had arranged the matter on his own behalf. In subsequent transactions he is occasionally styled a gentleman.

Although in 1593 and 1594 Shakespeare published two narrative poems dedicated to the Earl of Southampton, *Venus and Adonis* and *The Rape of Lucrece,* and may well have written most or all of his sonnets in the middle nineties, Shakespeare's literary activity seems to have been almost entirely devoted to the theater. (It may be significant that the two narrative poems were written in years when the plague closed the theaters for several months.) In 1594 he was a charter member of a theatrical company called the Chamberlain's Men (which in 1603 changed its name to the King's Men); until he retired to Stratford (about 1611, apparently), he was with this remarkably stable company. From 1599 the company acted primarily at the Globe Theatre, in which Shakespeare held a one-tenth interest. Other Elizabethan dramatists are known to have acted, but no other is known also to have been entitled to a share in the profits of the playhouse.

Shakespeare's first eight published plays did not have his name on them, but this is not remarkable; the most popular play of the sixteenth century, Thomas Kyd's *The Spanish Tragedy,* went through many editions without naming Kyd, and Kyd's authorship is known only because a book on the profession of acting happens to quote (and attribute to Kyd) some lines on the interest of Roman emperors in the drama. What is remarkable is that after 1598 Shakespeare's name commonly appears on printed plays—some of which are not his. Another indication of his popularity comes from Francis Meres, author of *Palladis Tamia: Wit's Treasury* (1598): in this anthology of snippets accompanied by an essay on literature, many playwrights are mentioned, but Shakespear's name occurs more often than any other, and Shakespeare is the only playwright whose plays are listed.

From his acting, playwriting, and share in a theater, Shakespeare seems to have made considerable money. He put it to work, making substantial investments in Stratford real estate. When he made his will (less than a month before he died), he sought to leave his property intact to his descendants. Of small bequests to relatives and to friends (including three actors, Richard Burbage, John Heminges, and Henry Condell), that to his wife of the second-best bed has provoked the most comment;

perhaps it was the bed the couple had slept in, the best being reserved for visitors. In any case, had Shakespeare not excepted it, the bed would have gone (with the rest of his household possessions) to his daughter and her husband. On 25 April 1616 he was buried within the chancel of the church at Stratford. An unattractive monument to his memory, placed on a wall near the grave, says he died on 23 April. Over the grave itself are the lines, perhaps by Shakespeare, that (more than his literary fame) have kept his bones undisturbed in the crowded burial ground where old bones were often dislodged to make way for new:

> Good friend, for Jesus' sake forbear
> To dig the dust enclosèd here.
> Blessed be the man that spares these stones
> And cursed be he that moves my bones.

Thirty-seven plays, as well as some nondramatic poems, are held to constitute the Shakespeare canon. The dates of composition of most of the works are highly uncertain, but there is often evidence of a *terminus a quo* (starting point) and/or a *terminus ad quem* (terminal point) that provides a framework for intelligent guessing. For example, *Richard II* cannot be earlier than 1595, the publication date of some material to which it is indebted; *The Merchant of Venice* cannot be later than 1598, the year Francis Meres mentioned it. Sometimes arguments for a date hang on an alleged topical allusion, such as the lines about the unseasonable weather in *A Midsummer Night's Dream*, II.i.81–117, but such an allusion (if indeed it is an allusion) can be variously interpreted, and in any case there is always the possibility that a topical allusion was inserted during a revision, years after the composition of a play. Dates are often attributed on the basis of style, and although conjectures about style usually rest on other conjectures, sooner or later one must rely on one's literary sense. There is no real proof, for example, that *Othello* is not as early as *Romeo and Juliet*, but one feels *Othello* is later, and because the first record of its performance is 1604, one is glad enough to set its composition at that date and not push it back into Shakespeare's early years. The following chronology, then, is as much indebted to informed guesswork and sensitivity as it is to fact. The dates, necessarily imprecise, indicate something like a scholarly consensus.

PLAYS

1588–93	*The Comedy of Errors*
1588–94	*Love's Labor's Lost*
1590–91	*2 Henry VI*
1590–91	*3 Henry VI*
1591–92	*1 Henry VI*
1592–93	*Richard III*
1592–94	*Titus Andronicus*
1593–94	*The Taming of the Shrew*
1593–95	*The Two Gentlemen of Verona*
1594–96	*Romeo and Juliet*
1595	*Richard II*
1594–96	*A Midsummer Night's Dream*
1596–97	*King John*
1596–97	*The Merchant of Venice*
1597	*1 Henry IV*
1597–98	*2 Henry IV*
1598–1600	*Much Ado About Nothing*
1598–99	*Henry V*
1599–1600	*Julius Caesar*
1599–1600	*As You Like It*
1599–1600	*Twelfth Night*
1600–01	*Hamlet*
1597–1601	*The Merry Wives of Windsor*
1601–02	*Troilus and Cressida*
1602–04	*All's Well That Ends Well*
1603–04	*Othello*
1604–05	*Measure for Measure*
1605–06	*King Lear*
1605–06	*Macbeth*

1606–07	*Antony and Cleopatra*
1605–08	*Timon of Athens*
1607–09	*Coriolanus*
1608–09	*Pericles*
1609–10	*Cymbeline*
1610–11	*The Winter's Tale*
1611–12	*The Tempest*
1612–13	*Henry VIII*

POEMS

1592	*Venus and Adonis*
1593–94	*The Rape of Lucrece*
1593–1600	*Sonnets*
1600–01	*The Phoenix and the Turtle*

Shakespeare's Theater

In Shakespeare's infancy, Elizabethan actors performed wherever they could—in great halls, at court, in the courtyards of inns. The innyards must have made rather unsatisfactory theaters: on some days they were unavailable because carters bringing goods to London used them as depots; when available, they had to be rented from the innkeeper; perhaps most important, London inns were subject to the Common Council of London, which was not well disposed toward theatricals. In 1574 the Common Council required that plays and playing places in London be licensed. It asserted that

sundry great disorders and inconveniences have been found to ensue to this city by the inordinate haunting of great multitudes of people, specially youth, to plays, interludes, and shows, namely occasion of frays and quarrels, evil practices of incontinency in great inns having chambers and secret places adjoining to their open stages and galleries, and ordered that innkeepers who wished licenses to hold performances put up a bond and make contributions to the poor.

The requirement that plays and innyard theaters be licensed, along with the other drawbacks of playing at inns, probably drove James Burbage (a carpenter-turned-actor) to rent in 1576 a plot of land northeast of the city walls and to build here—on property outside the jurisdiction of the city—England's first permanent construction designed for plays. He called it simply the Theatre. About all that is known of its construction is that it was wood. It soon had imitators, the most famous being the Globe (1599), built across the Thames (again outside the city's jurisdiction), out of timbers of the Theatre, which had been dismantled when Burbage's lease ran out.

There are three important sources of information about the structure of Elizabethan playhouses—drawings, a contract, and stage directions in plays. Of drawings, only the so-called De Witt drawing (c. 1596) of the Swan—really a friend's copy of De Witt's drawing—is of much significance. It shows a building of three tiers, with a stage jutting from a wall into the yard or center of the building. The tiers are roofed, and part of the stage is covered by a roof that projects from the rear and is supported at its front on two posts, but the groundlings, who paid a penny to stand in front of the stage, were exposed to the sky. (Performances in such a playhouse were held only in the daytime; artificial illumination was not used.) At the rear of the stage are two doors; above the stage is a gallery. The second major source of information, the contract for the Fortune, specifies that although the Globe is to be the model, the Fortune is to be square, eighty feet outside and fifty-five inside. The stage is to be forty-three feet broad, and is to extend into the middle of the yard (i.e., it is twenty-seven and a half feet deep). For patrons willing to pay more than the general admission charged of the groundlings, there were to be three galleries provided with seats. From the third chief source, stage directions, one learns that entrance to the stage was by doors, presumably spaced widely apart at the rear ("Enter one citizen at one door, and another at the other"), and that in addition to the platform stage there was occasionally some sort of curtained booth or alcove allowing for "discovery" scenes, and some sort of playing space "aloft" or "above" to represent (for example) the top of a city's walls or a room above the street. Doubtless each theater had its own peculiarities, but perhaps we can talk about a "typical" Elizabethan theater if we realize that no theater need exactly have fit the description, just as no father is the typical father with 3.7 children. This hypothetical theater is wooden, round or polygonal (in *Henry V* Shakespeare calls it a "wooden O"), capable of holding some eight hundred spectators standing in the yard around the projecting elevated stage and some fifteen hundred additional spectators seated in the three roofed galleries. The stage, protected by a "shadow" or "heavens" or roof, is entered by two doors; behind the doors is the "tiring house" (attiring house, i.e., dressing room), and above the doors is some sort of gallery that may sometimes hold spectators but that can be used (for example) as the bedroom from which Romeo—according to a stage direction in one text—"goeth down." Some evidence suggests that a throne can be lowered onto the platform stage, perhaps from the "shadow": certainly characters can descend from the stage through a trap or traps into the cellar or "hell." Sometimes this space beneath the platform accommodates a sound-effects man or musician (in *Antony and Cleopatra* "music of the hautboys is under the stage") or an actor (in *Hamlet* the "Ghost cries under the stage"). Most characters simply walk on and off, but because there is no curtain in front of the platform, corpses will have to be carried off (Hamlet must lug Polonius' guts into the neighbor room), or will have to fall at the rear, where the curtain on the alcove or booth can be drawn to conceal them.

Such may have been the so-called "public theater." Another kind of theater, called the "private theater" because its much greater admission charge limited its audience to the wealthy or the prodigal, must be briefly mentioned. The private theater was basically a large room, entirely roofed and therefore artificially illuminated, with a stage at one end. In 1576 one such theater was established in Blackfriars, a Dominican priory in London that had been suppressed in 1538 and confiscated by the Crown and thus was not under the city's jurisdiction. All the actors in the Blackfriars theater were boys about eight to thirteen years old (in the public theaters similar boys played female parts; a boy Lady Macbeth played to a man Macbeth). This private theater had a precarious existence, and ceased operations in 1584. In 1596 James Burbage, who had already made theatrical history by building the Theater, began to construct a second Blackfriars theater. He died in 1597, and for several years this second Blackfriars theater was used by a troupe of boys, but in 1608 two of Burbage's sons and five other actors (including Shakespeare) became joint operators of the theater, using it in the winter when the open-air Globe was unsuitable. Perhaps such a smaller theater, roofed, artificially illuminated, and with a tradition of a courtly audience, exerted an influence on Shakespeare's late plays.

Performances in the private theaters may well have had intermissions during which music was played, but in the public theaters the action was probably uninterrupted, flowing from scene to scene almost without a break. Actors would enter, speak, exit, and others would immediately enter and establish (if necessary) the new locale by a few properties and by words and gestures. Here are some samples of Shakespeare's scene painting:

> This is Illyria, lady.
>
> Well, this is the Forest of Arden.
>
> This castle hath a pleasant seat; the air
> Nimbly and sweetly recommends itself
> Unto our gentle senses.

On the other hand, it is a mistake to conceive of the Elizabethan stage as bare. Although Shakespeare's Chorus in *Henry V* calls the stage an "unworthy scaffold" and urges the spectators to "eke out our performance with your mind," there was considerable spectacle. The last act of *Macbeth*, for example, has five stage directions calling for "drum and colors," and another sort of appeal to the eye is indicated by the stage direction "Enter Macduff, with Macbeth's head." Some scenery and properties may have been substantial; doubtless a throne was used, and in one play of the period we encounter this direction: "Hector takes up a great piece of rock and casts at Ajax, who tears up a young tree by the roots and assails Hector." The matter is of some importance, and will be glanced at again in the next section.

The Texts of Shakespeare

Though eighteen of his plays were published during his lifetime, Shakespeare seems never to have supervised their publication. There is nothing unusual here; when a playwright sold a play to a theatrical company he surrendered his ownership of it. Normally a company would not publish the play, because to publish it meant to allow competitors to acquire the piece. Some plays, however, did get published: apparently treacherous actors sometimes pieced together a play for a publisher, sometimes a company in need of money sold a play, and sometimes a company allowed a play to be published that no longer drew audiences. That Shakespeare did not concern himself with publication, then, is scarcely remarkable; of his contemporaries only Ben Jonson carefully supervised the publication of his own plays. In 1623, seven years after Shakespeare's death, John Heminges and Henry Condell (two senior members of Shakespeare's company, who had performed with him for about twenty years) collected his plays—published and unpublished—into a large volume, commonly called the First Folio. (A folio is a volume consisting of sheets that have been folded once, each sheet thus making two leaves, or four pages. The eighteen plays published during Shakespeare's lifetime had been issued one play per volume in small books called quartos. Each sheet in a quarto has been folded twice, making four leaves, or eight pages.) The First Folio contains thirty-six plays; a thirty-seventh, *Pericles,* though not in the Folio is regarded as canonical. Heminges and Condell suggest in an address "To the great variety of readers" that the republished plays are presented in better form than in the quartos: "Before you were abused with diverse stolen and surreptitious copies, maimed and deformed by the frauds and stealths of injurious impostors that exposed them; even those, are now offered to your view cured and perfect of their limbs, and all the rest absolute in their numbers, as he [i.e., Shakespeare] conceived them."

Whoever was assigned to prepare the texts for publication in the First Folio seems to have taken his job seriously and yet not to have performed it with uniform care. The sources of the texts seem to have been, in general, good unpublished copies or the best published copies. The first play in the collection, *The Tempest,* is divided into acts and scenes, has unusually full stage directions and descriptions of spectacle, and concludes with a list of the characters, but the editor was not able (or willing) to present all of the succeeding texts so fully dressed. Later texts occasionally show signs of carelessness: in one scene of *Much Ado About Nothing* the names of actors, instead of characters, appear as speech prefixes, as they had in the quarto, which the Folio reprints; proofreading throughout the Folio is spotty and apparently was done without reference to the printer's copy; the pagination of *Hamlet* jumps from 156 to 257.

A modern editor of Shakespeare must first select his copy; no problem if the play exists only in the Folio, but a considerable problem if the relationship between a quarto and the Folio—or an early quarto and a later one—is unclear. When an editor has chosen what seems to him to be the most authoritative text or texts for his copy, he has not done with making decisions. First of all, he must reckon with Elizabethan spelling. If he is not producing a facsimile, he probably modernizes it, but ought he to preserve the old form of words that apparently were pronounced quite unlike their modern forms —"lanthorn," "alablaster"? If he preserves these forms, is he really preserving Shakespeare's forms or perhaps those of a compositor in the printing house? What is one to do when one finds "lanthorn" and "lantern" in adjacent lines? (The editors of this series in general, but not invariably, assume that words should be spelled in their modern form.) Elizabethan punctuation, too, presents problems. For example in the First Folio, the only text for the play, Macbeth rejects his wife's idea that he can wash the blood from his hand:

> no: this my Hand will rather
> The multitudinous Seas incarnardine,
> Making the Greene one, Red.

Obviously an editor will remove the superfluous capitals, and he will probably alter the spelling to "incarnadine," but will he leave the comma before "red," letting Macbeth speak of the sea as "the green one," or will he (like most modern editors) remove the comma and thus have Macbeth say that his hand will make the ocean *uniformly* red?

An editor will sometimes have to change more than spelling or punctuation. Macbeth says to his wife:

> I dare do all that may become a man,
> Who dares no more, is none.

For two centuries editors have agreed that the second line is unsatisfactory, and have emended "no" to "do": "Who dares do more is none." But when in the same play Ross says that fearful persons

> floate vpon a wilde and violent Sea
> Each way, and moue.

need "move" be emended to "none," as it often is, on the hunch that the compositor misread the manuscript? The editors of the Signet Classic Shakespeare have restrained themselves from making abundant emendations. In their minds they hear Dr. Johnson on the dangers of emending: "I have adopted the Roman sentiment, that it is more honorable to save a citizen than to kill an enemy." Some departures (in addition to spelling, punctuation, and lineation) from the copy text have of course been made, but the original readings are listed in a note following the play, so that the reader can evaluate them for himself.

The editors of the Signet Classic Shakespeare, following tradition, have added line numbers and in many cases act and scene divisions as well as indications of locale at the beginning of scenes. The Folio divided most of the plays into acts and some into scenes. Early eighteenth-century editors increased the divisions. These divisions, which provide a convenient way of referring to passages in the plays, have been retained, but when not in the text chosen as the basis for the Signet Classic text they are enclosed in square brackets [ ] to indicate that they are editorial additions. Similarly, although no play of Shakespeare's published during his lifetime was equipped with indications of locale at the heads of scene divisions, locales have here been added in square brackets for the convenience of the reader, who lacks the information afforded to spectators by costumes, properties, and gestures. The spectator can tell at a glance he is in the throne room, but without an editorial indication the reader may be puzzled for a while. It should be mentioned, incidentally, that there are a few authentic stage directions—perhaps Shakespeare's, perhaps a prompter's —that suggest locales: for example, "Enter Brutus in his orchard," and "They go up into the Senate house." It is hoped that the bracketed additions provide the reader with the sort of help provided in these two authentic directions, but it is equally hoped that the reader will remember that the stage was not loaded with scenery.

No editor during the course of his work can fail to

recollect some words Heminges and Condell prefixed to the Folio:

> It had been a thing, we confess, worthy to have been wished, that the author himself had lived to have set forth and overseen his own writings. But since it hath been ordained otherwise, and he by death departed from that right, we pray you do not envy his friends the office of their care and pain to have collected and published them.

Nor can an editor, after he has done his best, forget Heminges and Condell's final words: "And so we leave you to other of his friends, whom if you need can be your guides. If you need them not, you can lead yourselves, and others. And such readers we wish him."

SYLVAN BARNET
Tufts University

Introduction

The modern student of *Troilus and Cressida*—reader, spectator, or actor—is faced with complex problems of staging, character, and moral ideas. The challenge of the play has been complicated (in many instances, unnecessarily) by a critical history full of dissension. Some of the insolubles connected with *Troilus* concern the auspices of its first performances, or, indeed, whether it was acted at all before it was printed. Others stem from a consideration of the nature of the play itself, because critics have always felt that it is strange and untypical, and somehow flawed, expounding an approach to life which Shakespeare found uncongenial even as he set it forth. It may be helpful, therefore, to review some basic facts, to indicate those questions that can never be settled with the documentation at our disposal, and then to move on to an appraisal of the work itself and its place in Shakespeare's career. Ultimately, we should try to see in the play the attempt Shakespeare was making to solve certain ethical questions in dramatic form.

The history of the play's first production is inextricably bound up in its early textual history. Literary critics as well as bibliographical historians have been interested in the latter for some years, perhaps because it seems unlikely that so strange a play should be accompanied only accidentally by a curious textual provenance. Believing that the tastes of its first audience might help explain the problematic nature of the play, critics have wanted to know where and for whom it was first performed. Certain aspects of the textual history of *Troilus and Cressida* seem to offer answers; this has led to great speculation, some of which has tended to obscure the facts.

The facts are these. In February of 1603, the permission of the Stationers' Company was granted to James Roberts to print, "when he hath gotten sufficient aucthority, the booke of Troilus and Cressida, as yt is acted by my Lord Chamberlens men." From whom Roberts had yet to secure "aucthority" is not immediately apparent; presumably it was from the actors themselves, who wanted to block publication for the time being. Nevertheless, the entry clearly documents the existence and performance of *Troilus and Cressida* by Shakespeare's company, probably during the winter of 1602–03. Roberts, for whatever reason, did not print the play. The first edition of *Troilus* did not appear until almost six years later, when two newcomers to the printing business, Richard Bonian and Henry Walley, published a quarto of the text in January, 1609. While the book was still in the press, Bonian and Walley altered its title page and added an extra leaf, which carried an epistle to the reader. The first title page announced the play: "As it was acted by the Kings Maiesties seruants at the Globe." The new title page of the quarto, the same as the first in other particulars, replaced this acknowledgment with the phrase: "Excellently expressing the beginning of their [Troilus and Cressida's] loues, with the conceited wooing of Pandarus Prince of Licia." Following the altered title page appeared the epistle to the reader, unsigned, claiming that the play was "neuer stal'd with the Stage, neuer clapper-clawd with the palmes of the vulger . . . not . . . sullied, with the smoaky breath of the multitude." Finally, in 1623, *Troilus* was printed by Heminges and Condell in their great folio collection of Shakespeare's plays, in a text occasionally fuller than that of the 1609 quarto, but also containing many errors (see note on the text of this edition). *Troilus* appears in the section of the Folio containing the tragedies, although its position in this section was altered after printing had begun. The alteration used to be grounds for an inference by some critics that even Shakespeare's editors and colleagues were not certain about the type of play with which they were dealing. More recently, however, textual critics have shown that the change was probably due only to the reluctance of Walley, the surviving publisher of the quarto, to give up his rights to the printer of the Folio—the delay meanwhile causing the latter to withdraw *Troilus* after three pages of it had been set up in type, and to reinsert it later when permission was granted. Thus, although Heminges and Condell apparently classified *Troilus and Cressida* as a "Tragedy," and although the writer of the 1609 epistle called it a "Comedy," its position in the Folio has nothing to do with the ambiguous nature of the play itself; after all, both title pages of the 1609 quarto call it a "History." Nothing is really proved by this contradictory nomenclature except how casual the Elizabethan and Jacobean vocabulary was when it came to naming genres.

Although unnecessary problems raised by the play's position in the Folio have been removed, the earlier printer's claim that *Troilus* had never been applauded "with the palmes of the vulger" has elicited various and conflicting interpretations: the play, indeed, was never acted; it entered rehearsals, proved too difficult, and was withdrawn; it was acted not for the "vulger" at the public theater, but for an audience of sophisticated and cynical wits at the Inns of Court; it was actually produced at the Globe but was a failure with the "multitude," therefore "neuer clapper-clawd." We should note that all these conjectures are possible only because of the altered title page and printer's epistle in the quarto; but neither of these bibliographical facts should obscure the evidence of the original entry in the Stationers' Register (that Shakespeare's company had acted the play by the beginning of 1603), nor that of the first 1609 title page (which tells us specifically that the play "was acted by the Kings Maiesties seruants at the Globe"). Any further suggestions about the theatrical provenance of the play are clearly conjectural. More important, interpretations of characters, mood, and general intention of *Troilus and Cressida* that are based on such conjecture should be considered with great caution.

One such interpretation that has attained considerable currency is that the play was acted by Shakespeare's company for the young lawyers at one of the Inns of Court, and that it was especially written and rehearsed for this occasion. Such circumstances, the theory maintains, would not only be in keeping with the cynical mood and legalistic rhetoric of the drama, but with the claims of the epistle, whose author is careful to state only that the play was never performed for the "vulger," and not that it had never been performed at all. If this is the case, however, it represents the only example during Shakespeare's career of any play actually subsidized for a special production in this manner. To purchase a single performance for a play already in the public repertory was something else entirely—Elizabeth's court did this frequently—but it was very costly to do so. Moreover, although much in the play would delight the ears of a cynic, and although some of the language in it is drawn (very generally) from legal vocabulary, the fact remains that the bitterness of this drama runs deeper than the self-conscious sneer which often accompanies sarcasm. There is metaphor drawn from the law in many other Shakespearean plays, and one should ask, in reading or seeing *Troilus,* whether some of its abstractions and overblown circumlocutions may not have a more general purpose than the pleasure of some law students attending a theatrical charade.

To suggest that Shakespeare wrote the play for the students to act themselves is even more unlikely. *Troilus and Cressida* is extremely difficult for amateurs to perform, even if they are very talented and very cynical. Pandarus' allusions to prostitutes and others employed in the "hold-door trade" would have been absurd in a performance for one of the Inns; illogical, indeed, before any audience except that of the public theater. This epilogue is as unsavory and ugly as anything in Thersites' "mastic" harangues, and although we may not like to think so, it, and the action preceding it, must have been spoken in a public theater by actors in Shakespeare's company.

Whether the public audience applauded it is another matter. *Troilus* may not have been performed more than once or twice, and it is very possible that Bonian and Walley, as they prepared the first title page for their 1609 quarto, knew only that the play was by an extremely successful dramatist and that it had once been acted at the Globe. Details of failures, even today, are not often remembered after seven or eight years. Whatever made them decide to alter the title page, deleting the acknowledgment to Shakespeare's company and inserting the epistle to the reader, we can never know. We must keep in mind, however, that possibly their correction was itself a mistake. In any case, the inserted phrase about the "conceited wooing of Pandarus Prince of Licia" was an easy line filler for the deleted acknowledgment, and no publisher has ever shrunk from a descriptive phrase which might promote sales of his book. The tone of the epistle indicates that Bonian and Walley knew a good thing when they saw it, and they were delighted to have in their possession a play by Shakespeare which six years earlier his own company apparently had tried to withhold from publication, and which had been in the repertory but was not generally known.

Our only positive evidence dates *Troilus* before February 1603, in performance at the Globe Theatre by the King's Men (then the Lord Chamberlain's Men). Although it is probably impossible to solve the riddle of this play's textual history, it is important to keep that mystery separate from the enigma of the play itself. There is no doubt that the peculiar strengths and failings of *Troilus and Cressida* are unique in the Shakespearean canon; even when compared to the other so-called "problem plays" (*Measure for Measure, All's Well That Ends Well*), it stands by itself. *Troilus* contains speeches that illuminate difficult portions of other plays, but seem somehow incongruous in this one; most of its cast of characters were traditionally associated with ideals of romance and chivalry, but even as they describe heroic emotions and speak the old ringing epithets, these figures appear addicted to long-winded gossip, petty projects, morbid preoccupations, and selfishly narrow ambitions. Such incongruities remind us of the intentions and methods of satire, and it has been suggested that *Troilus and Cressida* was Shakespeare's specific attempt to write in the currently popular vein of "comical satire." But human depravity obviously saddened Shakespeare infinitely more than it angered Marston, Jonson, or Chapman, and the satirical elements of the play have ultimately very little to do with the final impression it makes in reading, or with its overall effect in the theater. If the play has a satirical spokesman, it is Thersites, but Thersites' corrosive voice hardly speaks for balance or good sense, and, if the actor is brave enough to play him correctly, no audience smiles upon him except in embarrassment. At first, one may suspect satirical intention behind such incongruous components as Ulysses' eloquent perceptions and the insignificant use made of them, but much of the pathos of the play occurs in just those scenes that would be mercilessly satirical if Shakespeare were being consistent. It has been proposed, with good logic, that in *Troilus and Cressida* Shakespeare consciously imitated or unconsciously assimilated certain elements of cynicism and satire from the plays then being performed by child actors with great success at Blackfriars and Paul's. Perhaps less than a year before the composition of *Troilus,* Shakespeare allowed Hamlet himself to express surprise that these children should "carry it away," even in competition with "Hercules and his load, too." Always alert to the economic problems of his profession as well as to the artistic ones, Shakespeare was inevitably influenced by the issues that the war of the theaters expressed, but although this influence surely affected some aspects of *Troilus and Cressida,* it can never be held accountable for the play as a whole.

In the problems that the drama presents for directors, actors, and stage designers, one may find, perhaps, a clue to its mystery, a way to understand why some parts of it are so emotionally and intellectually satisfying, others so flat and ill-conceived. Problems of modern production often reveal with lucidity the answers to many questions that a purely literary approach cannot solve. Although probably no modern production of this play can make a satisfactory theatrical experience (as much may have been said of the script in 1602), one quality that does emerge in production tells us much about the development of Shakespeare's ideas around the time *Troilus* was written. That quality is one of energetic experimentation—experimentation not of the amateur, unsure of his materials, nor of the craftsman temporarily exhausted and therefore forgetting for the moment the almost automatic use of his tools. Rather, *Troilus* reminds one of a study by Michelangelo, boldly and completely rendered in some places, lightly blocked in elsewhere—the whole cartoon groping with line and space to build a conception that seems to develop before us, sometimes obscure but never tentative, and that will require ultimately another form, perhaps even a different medium, for its perfect expression.

In producing *Troilus and Cressida* for the stage, this quality of experimentation, of searching for form, comes to the director when he first tries to develop an overall conception of the action and the general style that should guide him when rehearsals begin, but he is likely to discover early in his efforts that this play defies such an attempt. This is why *Troilus and Cressida,* perhaps more frequently than any other play by Shakespeare, succumbs in preparation to that last effort of the desperate director, a striking form of modern dress. The modern theater has seen *Troilus* in Edwardian dress, modish evening clothes, Wild West costumes, and the uniforms of the American Civil War; and there is little doubt that such aberrations occur (invariably in the name of originality or "significance to the modern audience") because the director, in forgivable despair, has begun to mistrust the text itself.

A setting for this play usually presents problems. Perhaps the original plan of the director and his designer is to use a three-sided apron stage, approximating the projection of the platform in the Elizabethan public theaters;

hey have envisioned the dramatic potentials of certain
peeches delivered from different parts of this remarkable
cting area: the oaths of the two lovers, for example,
ust before Pandarus packs them off to bed; Ulysses' two
great addresses, the first of which seems especially to
equire the magnificent plenitude of space provided by
he apron stage; the great quintet near the end of the
play, when Troilus, Ulysses, and Thersites watch and
comment upon the surrender of Cressida to Diomedes;
he last chaotic battle exchanges, which require maximum
fluidity of movement. If, however, on the basis of such
scenes, a setting is provided that utilizes the large, even
epic proportions of the open platform, the director and
actors will soon discover that in other portions of the
play so much space becomes a burden instead of an
advantage. Even scenes that begin with the promise of
pomp and procession become, within twenty or thirty
lines, scenes of intimate discussion. The Trojan princes
marching over the stage (I.ii.191–248) are much less
important to the progress of the play than the innuendos
and small talk of Cressida and Pandarus; nor is there suspense built in anticipation of the entrance of Troilus himself, for we have already seen him, and, having heard
Cressida's replies to Pandarus' gossip, we are even prepared for her coy response when he appears. The combat between Hector and Ajax (IV.v.113) is a red herring
for the director, because this combat, when it finally
happens, is dramatically uninteresting compared to other
portions of the scene—Ulysses' enthusiastic praise of
Troilus, for example, or Troilus and Ulysses' short exchange, which ends the episode; the combat is especially
pale compared to the byplay between Achilles and Hector.
If the director plans the moves of his actors to emphasize
the apparent climax of the episode, he will find that the
real interest of the scene has shifted elsewhere, that the
point of the action is not what he thought it was, and that
whatever this scene should be, it is not a scene of
pageantry.

The actors themselves will face problems of characterization comparable to the vocal difficulties of an

operatic baritone who, while studying his role, com
suddenly upon an aria written in the range of a tenc
If, for example, Hector is as sharply intelligent as ?
appears throughout the debate with Troilus and Par
(II.ii), the actor playing him will have difficulty portra
ing the hero's flabby and illogical surrender at the end
the scene. It is true that men commit themselves eve
day to causes in which they do not believe, but this iror
does not impregnate Hector's

> I am yours,
> You valiant offspring of great Priamus.
> I have a roisting challenge sent amongst
> The dull and factious nobles of the Greeks
> Will strike amazement to their drowsy spirits.
> I was advertised their great general slept
> Whilst emulation in the army crept;
> This, I presume, will wake him.
>
> (II.ii.206–1?)

These lines neither satirize Hector nor (as has been sug
gested) reveal ironically the fate of reason in a situatic
of uncontrolled passion. Moreover, they do not contai
the sort of formalized change of motivation that occur
frequently in Elizabethan plays, and which an actor mu
cope with as best he can. These lines are simply a man
festation of the history to which Shakespeare was boun
and to which his previous development of Hector's intell
gence and viewpoint was inimicable.

Experimentation with motive and personality that re
sults in inconsistent characterization presents difficultie
for actors in other roles. The actress playing Cressid
appears on stage only twice after she has been exchange
by the Trojans for Antenor; earlier (III.ii.63–197 an
IV.ii.101–03) she has managed somehow the character'
unrealistic anticipation of her own treachery, but, afte
her tearful leave-taking of Troilus, in which his repeate
cry, "Be true," has touched her own fears, Cressida mus
parade happily among the Grecian generals, who kiss he
"in general," and receive Ulysses' coldly perceptive insult

Whatever the actress has made of Cressida earlier, she is now the brassy and degraded slut the Elizabethans had been taught to expect. She appears only once more, to fall to Diomedes, and the actress must decide how to effect this transition of character. Once again, the problem is not so much one of an unfamiliar convention, but of unreconciled strands of development.

Such difficulties of production, and others similar to them, suggest that one of Shakespeare's major problems in composing *Troilus* was not only consistency of character in the normal sense, but the nature of constancy itself, whether in politics or in love. Each of the troublesome matters noted above concerns the continuity of some factor pertinent to all parts of the text, whether that factor is stage setting or characterization. In IV.v. Hector's dialogue with Achilles assumes more importance than his short fight with Ajax, because it is Achilles and not Ajax who should have entered the lists against the Trojan champion. It would be in keeping with Elizabethan ideas of order and degree for Achilles to maintain the identity of an active hero, and Ulysses wishes to goad him on toward his proper role. But more important, we listen eagerly to the talk between Hector and Achilles because so much in the play concerns sentiments identical to those motivating these men: Hector's faith in the principles that define what is right and good, and Achilles' surrender to the "one touch of nature" that can make all human beings blind and selfish. The confrontation of these men demands full use of the open stage, with the other actors distributed so as to emphasize it, but the machinery of Ajax's exhibition bout still hangs fire, and Shakespeare, almost as though he were working out the problem before our eyes, develops his main line of interest without bothering to erase false starts and unnecessary detail.

There is no need to examine in every character the way in which inconstancy, as a thematic concern, vitiates dramatic consistency. One final example is provided importantly by the heroine of the play. In the first half of the action Cressida is full and varied, yet her later fall from constancy is so baldly unqualified that Shakespeare's interest seems to have been attracted more to the violence of the metamorphosis than to maintaining the credibility of the character. No simple reliance upon the Elizabethan rumor of Cressida's harlotry can explain her sudden and complete degeneration.

The nature of that constancy which can preserve felicity in love and stability in politics had concerned Shakespeare since he began writing plays, and it was to remain a fundamental concern throughout his career. *Troilus and Cressida* is a pivotal play in the canon because it looks forward and backward simultaneously, indicating the ways in which Shakespeare's view of constancy was developing, and the dramatic forms which eventually would have to be employed to render that development effectively. From the beginning, he had found great dramatic potential in the stability that can be maintained only by the king who mirrors in himself an ordered nation, and in the fidelity of love that can overcome laughable folly or dangerous misunderstanding. By far the greater part of his writing had been, consequently, in varying forms of romantic comedy and patriotic chronicle-histories (the latter a theatrical form that may actually have been Shakespeare's own conception). He had also dramatized, though with less frequency, that form of constancy within the individual which forces him to be so energetically true to himself in love or even in crime that he can no longer be tolerated in the world of living men. In the lives of those tortured kings whose stories had added the aspect of tragedy to some of the history plays, Shakespeare had found that the world of politics could serve as background to the story of an individual whose mind demanded isolation from his surroundings, and whose actions would effect a downfall as inevitable as his virtues were magnificent. The two years preceding *Troilus* saw Shakespeare's utilization of Roman politics for the scene of Brutus' individual tragedy. The fall of Julius Caesar, finished by the middle of the play, is patterned after the simple downward movement of Fortune's wheel—the pattern of almost all late medieval and early Tudor tragedies. But Shakespeare intended that his exploration of Brutus' constancy should hold the center of the drama; in *Julius Caesar* his refining hand turned attention in upon the mind of the hero himself. Roughly contemporary with this play were the romantic comedies *As You Like It* and *Twelfth Night,* each touched with a pervasive melancholy, each in its own way implying that only the truth of love can survive the vicissitudes of the world, the "rain [that] raineth every day." Perhaps a year before *Troilus* came *Hamlet,* in which the public and private responsibilities of the mind are probed with a range and precision that elude comment. It may be helpful to observe, however, that many of the problems that challenge Hamlet's mind are paralleled by those that confuse the Trojan princes and the Greek generals. In both *Hamlet* and *Troilus and Cressida,* the authority of law is opposed by individual desire or private principle; in both, the ultimate canon of morality is set against the honor, real or supposed, of the individual; and in both, the definition of honor, "rightly to be great," is strenuously argued by those who have most at stake.

In *Troilus and Cressida* Shakespeare tried for the first time to combine in dramatic terms a story of love with a story of public affairs. It is worth noting that in the major tragedies that follow, the personal fate of the hero is inextricably bound up in the world of the state, and that in *Troilus* Shakespeare made his first real study of the relationship between the pressures of the public world and the survival of love. Hamlet's uncle believed that "within the very flame of love" there lived a power which would destroy it, that, like goodness itself, it could not remain constant, but would grow "to a plurisy" and die in its own excess (*Hamlet,* IV.vii)—a metaphor very similar to Ulysses' description of passion, the "universal wolf" that would "last eat up himself" (I.iii.121, 124). Whatever Claudius' opinion, however, Shakespeare clearly believed that true love, untainted with destructive appetite, would not alter "when it alteration finds. . . . But [bear] it out even to the edge of doom" (Sonnet 116). These two statements articulate extremes that became the foundations for much of Shakespeare's thinking in the second half of his professional career; again and again he concerned himself with those forms of love that would survive all trials or succumb to the snares of the world. Always the process involved a growth of self-knowledge, and in *King Lear,* his most inclusive tragic statement, Shakespeare was able to show that after the greatest suffering might come the greatest achievement—a perception of constancy more powerful than any worldly reward or punishment; and that after such perception, death could come almost as a reward, as the final felicity.

Naturally, the creation of dramatic situations capable of sustaining this sort of action required a gradual revision of forms in which to work, and Shakespeare searched continually for the most appropriate modes of expression. That he moved from romantic comedy and history to tragedy, and from tragedy to romance, indicates a developing view of life and art; this development should not be divided into sharply limited chronological "periods," each one represented by a different kind of play. Nothing could be more misleading, for even in Shakespeare's earliest plays are individual lines and scenes as typical of his mature outlook as anything in the last romances. His metamorphosis of dramatic forms is more like Beethoven's progress toward the last piano sonatas and string quartets —a steady growth, a long series of experiments and finished monuments, none actually exclusive of the others, but attaining finally an absolute correspondence between idea and expression. Coming where it does in Shakespeare's development, *Troilus and Cressida* contains within it all the components of the playwright's most typical tragic pattern, but arranged in such a way as to prohibit the achievement possible in that form.

In 1601, probably about a year before the first performances of *Troilus,* Shakespeare's poem "The Phoenix and Turtle" was published in *Love's Martyr,* a collection of allegorical and emblematic verse. The subject matter of this poem clarifies the nature of Shakespeare's thematic concerns in his play, and it is no accident that in both poem and play one senses the author's effort to shape difficult materials to his purpose. "The Phoenix and the Turtle" describes the remarkable union of the mythical Phoenix and the Turtledove, in which love was so complete that even Reason stands amazed at the sight. In this mating, we are told, "number . . . in love was slain," for two separate lovers became one, and "Property" itself —the defining essence of the individual thing—was "appalled."

> Property was thus appalled,
> That the self was not the same;
> Single nature's double name
> Neither two nor one was called.
>
> (37–40)

These two lovers, in themselves all "Beauty, truth, and rarity," do not survive their own union, but are consumed "In a mutual flame," even as each finds absolute perfection in the other. The implication is that such absolute love cannot survive its own assault upon reason; its achievement is set forth as admirable and its inevitable passing as wonderful, but the poem also articulates the great sadness of such an event. It is a funeral dirge in which Reason, personified as the voice of admiration, composes the closing hymn of praise—a hymn, Shakespeare says specifically, "As chorus to their tragic scene."

Claudius' "too-much" of love, drowning itself in a "plurisy," may be equated with the self-cannibalism of appetite, as described by Ulysses; but these are a far cry from the admirable, yet sadly "tragic scene," which Shakespeare paints in "The Phoenix and the Turtle." Shakespeare articulated in this poem—perhaps for the first time in his career—what was to become his most powerful dramatic irony in plays still to come: that the purity of love in "the marriage of true minds," while stronger than any other human achievement, cannot survive in the material world; and, as he demonstrated about five years after *Troilus,* in the glorious conclusion to *Antony and Cleopatra,* such an achievement in love is inimical to that earthly order which must control the reasonable state. In this sense, the coolly efficient Octavius Caesar, in *Antony,* and the personified Reason, in "The Phoenix and the Turtle," both observe the same qualities of constancy in the dead lovers before them. The possession of these qualities was a basic criterion for tragedy, as Shakespeare must have understood the form at this time. The pure strains of love of Troilus for Cressida and of Antony for Cleopatra are, speaking quantitatively, the same; but a tragedy is the result of Antony's love, because he is as constant as Cleopatra's beauty is felicitous. However, "Property" in *Troilus and Cressida* cannot be "appalled" by "simple . . . so well compounded"; in this play no miraculous marriage of "Truth and Beauty" deserves the repose of death.

In its structural position in the play, Troilus' sight of Cressida, as she gives in to Diomedes, corresponds to the insight that carries the truly tragic hero toward his death; but what Troilus sees, though the truth, runs counter to his ideal, and to this ideal he is as constant as any genuinely tragic hero. His vocabulary, as he tries to convince both himself and Ulysses that what he has seen cannot actually have taken place, is very similar to that of "The Phoenix and the Turtle." "If there be rule in unity itself," he cries, "This was not she" (V.ii. 138–39)— recalling the paradox in the poem that "number" (i.e., that "one" cannot be "two") "was slain," that the lovers merged into one entity, yet preserved their distinct essences. Building upon the conceit that there must be two Cressidas—his own, faithfully waiting in Troy, and this one, who is Diomedes'—he elaborates the most painful truth in the play: that what has seemed glorious and admirable, is not so.

> This she? No, this is Diomed's Cressida.
> If beauty have a soul, this is not she;
> If souls guide vows, if vows be sanctimonies,
> If sanctimonies be the gods' delight,
> If there be rule in unity itself,
> This was not she. O madness of discourse,
> That cause sets up with and against itself:
> Bifold authority, where reason can revolt

Without perdition, and loss assume all reason
Without revolt. This is, and is not, Cressid.

(V.ii.134–43)

Shakespeare wanted to show the disruption of constancy in both streams of action in the play—that of the love affair, and that of the famous war. Troilus' view of Cressida in Diomedes' arms does not give him that sublime lucidity of the tragic hero, but tempts him instead toward nihilism; his prayer, as the play closes, is that Troy's destruction be swift, that the gods show their mercy by sending "brief plagues." Similarly, the great order of government which is Ulysses' ideal, and in which all men must assume their proper degree, is shown to elude the Greek generals. Shakespeare never maligns the ideal itself (it would be absurd to imagine that the author of the English histories would do so!), but he allows Thersites to remark how "that stale old mouse-eaten dry cheese, Nestor, and that same dog-fox, Ulysses" have failed it:

O'the t'other side, the policy of those crafty swearing rascals . . . is not proved worth a blackberry. They set me up, in policy, that mongrel cur, Ajax, against that dog of as bad a kind, Achilles; and now is the cur Ajax prouder than the cur Achilles, and will not arm today. Whereupon the Grecians begin to proclaim barbarism, and policy grows into an ill opinion.

(V.iv.9–18)

Many of the difficulties of this play in performance, as we have seen, occur because the dramatic rendering of inconstancy in love and in the state actually forces an inconstancy of character and a jarring sequence of events: To make the metamorphoses of love and political honor as striking as possible, Shakespeare first had to set forth both in their admirable condition. That Troilus' love and Ulysses' ideal polity come to nothing is not the result of satirical intention, but rather the requirement of the particular history Shakespeare chose to render dramatically.

He always chose his plots carefully, and must have realized that the story of the lovers and the war contained the potential for tragedy, as he was beginning to understand it, but never achieved it. In *Antony and Cleopatra*, after all, he was to demonstrate how a "marriage of true minds," violently drawn together with physical and spiritual joy, would admit no impediments, even that of the Roman state; in *Troilus and Cressida*, he chose a plot full of impediments which are appallingly effective. The Trojan lover dotes upon his own ideal of faith as much as he dotes upon his faithless woman, and is blinded to a true perception of worth. His ringing question, "What's aught but as 'tis valued?" implies assessment by only one of two parties in love, for whatever price Troilus puts upon Cressida, he has yet to learn that she holds herself cheap. Similarly, that "policy grows into an ill opinion" in the Greek camp shows that its leaders have been insufficient to Ulysses' early description of divine and earthly order; and they, and Ulysses himself, have substituted machination—Thersites' "policy"—for true statecraft. On stage, what begins as divine intelligence ends as a practical joke.

We must not forget that Shakespeare's Elizabethan audiences (public or private) probably would not have found the inconsistencies of *Troilus and Cressida* where we find them. In the retelling of a story so familiar, they would have been surprised, for example, that so much hope is engendered in the first part of the play for Cressida's constancy, and not that she proves unfaithful. Ulysses' "degree" speech, perhaps the *locus classicus* in modern study of the Elizabethan conception of the "Great Chain of Being," is the sort of speech ordinarily suggestive in Shakespeare of a different dramatic decorum; it explicitly defines an ideal which this play never renders in action.

All this Shakespeare must have realized. The incidents of the Troy story chosen for dramatization predicated disappointment in the love plot and a shambles of order in the story of the war; even if he planned to carry forward the story of Troy in the sequel, which many critics infer from Pandarus' epilogue, surely he knew that in this drama the materials he had chosen demanded an ending in which no realization of the ideal was possible. Moreover, he knew that although the sequence of events and partial characterizations of his history were basically appropriate to the "tragic scene," he would be dealing as well with incongruities of folly and affectation suggestive of comic decorum. Since his audience would be familiar with his fable, he could count on their awareness of traditional characters and events; but even though he did not strive for novelty, he must have wondered how the implicit ethical significance of his rendering would be received. Moreover, since the public nature of the state was the background for the action, he would have realized that he was combining, for the first time with equal importance, a romantic story with a historical story. Clearly he desired to indicate a parallel between the betrayal of love that ends the former and the disintegration of heroism that ends the latter. Shakespeare may have anticipated the intractable nature of some of his materials, and it is quite possible that, during its composition, he knew that *Troilus and Cressida* might turn out to be an imperfect play—but the experiment fascinated him, and it was necessary.

The dangers that can prevent the triumph of love— both external to it and within it—occupied his mind henceforth, but his genius as a practical man of the theater did not always prevent this interest from assuming proportions inappropriate to the play at hand. Just as Shylock's monstrous faith in himself had almost swamped the romantic action of *The Merchant of Venice,* Angelo's morbidly distorted concept of law and love in *Measure for Measure* (written three or four years after *Troilus*) was disproportionate to the romantic action surrounding it. Ultimately—but not until *Antony and Cleopatra* had shown him the way—Shakespeare discovered the dramatic form in which the persistent faith necessary for tragic achievement could be preserved in the living world, in which the ideal is made part of reality. The dying life in *Troilus and Cressida* is far from the world of romance, but the qualities of humanity and the grace of nature required to revivify men are so violently excluded from the fabric of the play, that these healing powers become more explicit for their absence. The characters of *Troilus* are unable to achieve them, but by implication we know what they must be.

Following an earlier formula for tragical action, Shakespeare created, in *Romeo and Juliet,* a hero and heroine whose hopes seem almost mechanically doomed; the truth and beauty of their faith stand no chance against the external accidents of the world, although their love never alters in purity. After *Romeo and Juliet,* Shakespeare slowly shifted his emphasis; the character's inner strength to withstand external impediments became more important than an arbitrary caprice of fate, and the cause of disaster or tragic achievement was shown thereafter to reside within the human personality itself. Such causes were never again only partially articulated. In *Troilus and Cressida* they are frighteningly explicit, and because of the experimental form of the play they appear to us brutal and even cynical. But Thersites' view of the world was never Shakespeare's. Never again was he to allow his audiences to witness such despair in the ability of men to achieve grace in love or death.

DANIEL SELTZER
Harvard University

A Never Writer, to an Ever Reader.
News.

Eternal reader, you have here a new play, never staled with the stage, never clapperclawed with the palms of the vulgar, and yet passing full of the palm comical; for it is a birth of your brain°[1] that never undertook anything comical vainly. And were but the vain names of comedies changed for the titles of commodities, or of plays for pleas, you should see all those grand censors, that now style them such vanities, flock to them for the main grace of their gravities—especially this author's comedies, that are so framed to the life that they serve for the most common commentaries of all the actions of our lives, showing such a dexterity and power of wit that the most displeased with plays are pleased with his comedies. And all such dull and heavy-witted worldlings as were never capable of the wit of a comedy, coming by report of them to his representations, have found that wit there that they never found in themselves and have parted better witted than they came, feeling an edge of wit set upon them more than ever they dreamed they had brain to grind it on. So much and such savored salt of wit is in his comedies that they seem, for their height of pleasure, to be born in that sea that brought forth Venus.° Amongst all there is none more witty than this; and had I time I would comment upon it, though I know it needs not, for so much as will make you think your testern° well bestowed, but for so much worth as even poor I know to be stuffed in it. It deserves such a labor as well as

---

[1] The degree sign ° indicates a footnote, which is keyed to the text by line number. Text references are printed in *italic* type; the annotation follows in roman type.

4 *your brain* i.e., Shakespeare's brain   23 *Venus* (the Greek goddess Aphrodite, who, according to Hesiod, was born in ocean foam) 26 *testern* sixpence (slang)

the best comedy in Terence or Plautus. And believe
30 this, that when he is gone and his comedies out of sale,
you will scramble for them and set up a new English
Inquisition. Take this for a warning, and at the peril of
your pleasure's loss, and judgment's, refuse not, nor
like this the less for not being sullied with the smoky
35 breath of the multitude; but thank fortune for the
'scape it hath made amongst you, since by the grand
possessors'° wills I believe you should have prayed for
them rather than been prayed. And so I leave all such
to be prayed for, for the state of their wits' healths,
40 that will not praise it. *Vale.*

---

37 *grand possessors* (presumably, the actor-sharers of the King's
Men, who may have tried to stop publication)

The History of
Troilus and Cressida

The History of
Troilus and Cressida

THE PROLOGUE

[Enter the Prologue, armed for battle.]

In Troy there lies the scene. From isles of Greece
The princes orgulous,° their high blood chafed,
Have to the port of Athens sent their ships,
Fraught with the ministers and instruments
Of cruel war. Sixty and nine, that wore   5
Their crownets regal, from th' Athenian bay
Put forth toward Phrygia;° and their vow is made
To ransack Troy, within whose strong immures°
The ravished Helen, Menelaus' queen,
With wanton Paris sleeps—and that's the quarrel.   10
To Tenedos° they come,
And the deep-drawing barks do there disgorge
Their warlike fraughtage.° Now on Dardan° plains
The fresh and yet unbruisèd Greeks do pitch

Prologue 2 *orgulous* proud   7 *Phrygia* western Asia Minor   8 *immures* walls   11 *Tenedos* the port of Troy   13 *fraughtage* freight, i.e., soldiers   13 *Dardan* Trojan (after Dardanus, son of Zeus and the Pleiad Electra, and ancestor of Priam)

15   Their brave pavilions. Priam's six-gated city,
        Dardan, and Timbria, Helias, Chetas, Troien,
        And Antenonidus,° with massy staples
        And correspensive and fulfilling° bolts,
        Sperr up° the sons of Troy.
20   Now expectation, tickling skittish° spirits,
        On one and other side, Troyan and Greek,
        Sets all on hazard. And hither am I come,
        A prologue armed,° but not in confidence
        Of author's pen or actor's voice, but suited°
25   In like conditions as our argument,°
        To tell you, fair beholders, that our play
        Leaps o'er the vaunt° and firstlings of those broils,
        Beginning in the middle, starting thence away
        To what may be digested in a play.
30   Like or find fault; do as your pleasures are;
        Now good or bad, 'tis but the chance of war.

16–17 *Dardan . . . Antenonidus* (names of the gates of Troy)
18 *fulfilling* filling tightly   19 *Sperr up* shut up   20 *skittish* nervous
23 *armed* equipped for fight   24 *suited* dressed   25 *argument* subject   27 *vaunt* beginning

[ACT I

Scene I. *Within Troy.*]

Enter Pandarus and Troilus.

Troilus. Call here my varlet,° I'll unarm again.
   Why should I war without° the walls of Troy
   That find such cruel battle here within?
   Each Troyan that is master of his heart,
   Let him to field; Troilus, alas, hath none.   *5*

Pandarus. Will this gear° ne'er be mended?

Troilus. The Greeks are strong, and skillful to° their
     strength,
   Fierce to their skill, and to their fierceness valiant;
   But I am weaker than a woman's tear,
   Tamer than sleep, fonder° than ignorance,   *10*
   Less valiant than the virgin in the night,
   And skilless° as unpracticed infancy.

Pandarus. Well, I have told you enough of this. For
   my part, I'll not meddle nor make no farther. He
   that will have a cake out of the wheat must tarry   *15*
   the grinding.

I.i.1 *varlet* servant 2 *without* outside 6 *gear* business 7 *to* in
addition to, in proportion to 10 *fonder* more unsophisticated,
simpler 12 *skilless* inept, naïve

47

Troilus. Have I not tarried?

Pandarus. Ay, the grinding; but you must tarry the bolting.°

20 *Troilus.* Have I not tarried?

Pandarus. Ay, the bolting; but you must tarry the leavening.

Troilus. Still have I tarried.

Pandarus. Ay, to the leavening; but here's yet in the
25   word "hereafter" the kneading, the making of the cake, the heating the oven, and the baking. Nay, you must stay the cooling too, or ye may chance burn your lips.

Troilus. Patience herself, what goddess e'er she be,
30   Doth lesser blench° at suff'rance than I do.
       At Priam's royal table do I sit,
       And when fair Cressid comes into my thoughts—
       So, traitor,° then she comes when she is thence.°

Pandarus. Well, she looked yesternight fairer than
35   ever I saw her look, or any woman else.

Troilus. I was about to tell thee, when my heart,
       As wedgèd with a sigh, would rive° in twain,
       Lest Hector or my father should perceive me—
       I have, as when the sun doth light a-scorn,°
40   Buried this sigh in wrinkle of a smile;
       But sorrow, that is couched in seeming gladness,
       Is like that mirth fate turns to sudden sadness.

Pandarus. An° her hair were not somewhat darker
       than Helen's—well, go to—there were no more
45   comparison between the women; but, for my part,
       she is my kinswoman: I would not, as they term it,
       praise her, but I would somebody had heard her

19 *bolting* sifting   30 *blench* flinch   33 *traitor* (a self-rebuke, for suggesting that she is sometimes absent)   33 *then she comes when she is thence* i.e., she returns immediately whenever she is absent 37 *rive* split   39 *a-scorn* mockingly (?), grudgingly (?)   43 *An* if

talk yesterday, as I did. I will not dispraise your
sister Cassandra's wit, but——

Troilus. O Pandarus! I tell thee, Pandarus,   50
  When I do tell thee, there my hopes lie drowned,
  Reply not in how many fathoms deep
  They lie indrenched. I tell thee I am mad
  In Cressid's love; thou answer'st she is fair,
  Pour'st in the open ulcer of my heart   55
  Her eyes, her hair, her cheek, her gait, her voice;
  Handlest in thy discourse, O, that her hand°
  In whose comparison all whites are ink,
  Writing their own reproach; to whose soft seizure°
  The cygnet's° down is harsh, and spirit° of sense   60
  Hard as the palm of plowman. This thou tell'st me,
  As true thou tell'st me, when I say I love her;
  But, saying thus, instead of oil and balm,
  Thou lay'st in every gash that love hath given me
  The knife that made it.   65

Pandarus. I speak no more than truth.

Troilus. Thou dost not speak so much.

Pandarus. Faith, I'll not meddle in it; let her be as
  she is. If she be fair, 'tis the better for her; and she
  be not, she has the mends° in her own hands.   70

Troilus. Good Pandarus, how now, Pandarus?

Pandarus. I have had my labor for my travail;° ill
  thought on of her, and ill thought of you; gone between and between, but small thanks for my labor.

Troilus. What, art thou angry, Pandarus? What, with   75
  me?

Pandarus. Because she's kin to me, therefore she's
  not so fair as Helen. An she were not kin to me,

---

57 *that her hand* that hand of hers   59 *seizure* grasp   60 *cygnet's*
young swan's   60 *spirit* (the thin bodily substance believed to trans-
mit sense impressions through the nerves)   70 *mends* (1) remedies
(2) cosmetics   72 *travail* (punning on "travel" ["gone between and
between"])

she would be as fair a'° Friday as Helen is on Sun-
80   day.° But what care I? I care not aL she were a
blackamoor; 'tis all one to me.

Troilus. Say I she is not fair?

Pandarus. I do not care whether you do or no. She's
a fool to stay behind her father.° Let her to the
85   Greeks, and so I'll tell her the next time I see her.
For my part, I'll meddle nor make no more i' th'
matter.

Troilus. Pandarus——

Pandarus. Not I.

90   *Troilus.* Sweet Pandarus——

Pandarus. Pray you, speak no more to me. I will leave
all as I found it, and there an end.

                              Exit. Sound alarum.

Troilus. Peace, you ungracious clamors! Peace, rude
sounds!
Fools on both sides! Helen must needs be fair,
When with your blood you daily paint her thus.
I cannot fight upon this argument;°
It is too starved a subject for my sword.
But Pandarus—O gods, how do you plague me!
I cannot come to Cressid but by Pandar;
100   And he's as tetchy° to be wooed to woo
As she is stubborn, chaste, against all suit.
Tell me, Apollo, for thy Daphne's° love,
What Cressid is, what Pandar, and what we.
Her bed is India; there she lies, a pearl.
105   Between our Ilium° and where she resides
Let it be called the wild and wand'ring flood,
Ourself the merchant, and this sailing Pandar

79 *a'* on   79–80 *on Sunday* i.e., in her Sunday best   84 *father*
(Calchas, who had deserted to the Greeks)   96 *argument* theme
100 *tetchy* peevish   102 *Daphne* (the nymph who was changed into
a bay tree as she ran to escape Apollo)   105 *Ilium* (here, Priam's
palace; generally, Troy [for Ilus, founder of the city, Priam's
grandfather])

Our doubtful hope, our convoy and our bark.

Alarum. Enter Aeneas.

Aeneas. How now, Prince Troilus, wherefore not
    afield?

Troilus. Because not there. This woman's answer
    sorts,°   110
    For womanish it is to be from thence.
    What news, Aeneas, from the field today?

Aeneas. That Paris is returnèd home, and hurt.

Troilus. By whom, Aeneas?

Aeneas.   Troilus, by Menelaus.

Troilus. Let Paris bleed; 'tis but a scar to scorn:°   115
    Paris is gored with Menelaus' horn.°   *Alarum.*

Aeneas. Hark what good sport is out of town today!

Troilus. Better at home, if "would I might" were
    "may."
    But to the sport abroad; are you bound thither?

Aeneas. In all swift haste.

Troilus.   Come, go we then together.   120
                                        Exeunt.

---

110 *sorts* is appropriate   115 *but a scar to scorn* i.e., considering
its source, the kind of scar to be scorned   116 *horn* (of a cuckold)

[Scene II. *Within Troy.*]

Enter Cressida and [Alexander,] her man.

Cressida. Who were those went by?

Man.   Queen Hecuba and Helen.

Cressida. And whither go they?

Man.   Up to the eastern tower,
   Whose height commands as subject all the vale,
   To see the battle. Hector, whose patience
5   Is as a virtue fixed, today was moved.
   He chid Andromache, and struck his armorer,
   And, like as there were husbandry° in war,
   Before the sun rose he was harnessed° light,
   And to the field goes he, where every flower
10   Did, as a prophet, weep what it foresaw
   In Hector's wrath.

Cressida.   What was his cause of anger?

Man. The noise goes, this: there is among the Greeks
   A lord of Troyan blood, nephew to Hector;
   They call him Ajax.

Cressida.   Good; and what of him?

15 *Man.* They say he is a very man per se
   And stands alone.

Cressida. So do all men unless they are drunk, sick,
   or have no legs.

Man. This man, lady, hath robbed many beasts of
20   their particular additions.° He is as valiant as the

I.ii.7 *husbandry* good management, thrift   8 *harnessed* armored
20 *additions* distinctive qualities, characteristics

lion, churlish as the bear, slow as the elephant; a
man into whom nature hath so crowded humors°
that his valor is crushed into folly, his folly sauced
with discretion. There is no man hath a virtue that
he hath not a glimpse° of, nor any man an attaint°   25
but he carries some stain of it. He is melancholy
without cause and merry against the hair.° He hath
the joints of everything, but everything so out of
joint that he is a gouty Briareus,° many hands and
no use, or purblind Argus,° all eyes and no sight.   30

Cressida. But how should this man that makes me
smile make Hector angry?

Man. They say he yesterday coped° Hector in the
battle and struck him down, the disdain and shame
whereof hath ever since kept Hector fasting and   35
waking.

Enter Pandarus.

Cressida. Who comes here?

Man. Madam, your uncle Pandarus.

Cressida. Hector's a gallant man.

Man. As may be in the world, lady.   40

Pandarus. What's that? What's that?

Cressida. Good morrow, uncle Pandarus.

Pandarus. Good morrow, cousin° Cressid. What do
you talk of? Good morrow, Alexander. How do
you, cousin? When were you at Ilium?   45

Cressida. This morning, uncle.

---

22 *humors* (bodily fluids which, in excess, were thought to cause
emotional disorder)   25 *glimpse* momentary shining   25 *attaint*
imputation of dishonor   27 *against the hair* contrary to natural
tendency (cf. "against the grain")   29 *Briareus* (a hundred-handed
giant)   30 *Argus* (a herdsman with eyes covering his body)   33
coped engaged, encountered   43 *cousin* (a term of familiarity; here,
niece)

Pandarus. What were you talking of when I came? Was Hector armed and gone ere ye came to Ilium? Helen was not up, was she?

50 *Cressida.* Hector was gone, but Helen was not up.

Pandarus. E'en so, Hector was stirring early.

Cressida. That were we talking of, and of his anger.

Pandarus. Was he angry?

Cressida. So he says here.

55 *Pandarus.* True, he was so; I know the cause too. He'll lay about him today, I can tell them that; and there's Troilus will not come far behind him. Let them take heed of Troilus, I can tell them that too.

60 *Cressida.* What, is he angry too?

Pandarus. Who, Troilus? Troilus is the better man of the two.

Cressida. O Jupiter! There's no comparison.

Pandarus. What, not between Troilus and Hector? Do
65   you know a man if you see him?

Cressida. Ay, if I ever saw him before and knew him.

Pandarus. Well, I say Troilus is Troilus.

Cressida. Then you say as I say, for I am sure he is not Hector.

70 *Pandarus.* No, nor Hector is not Troilus in some degrees.°

Cressida. 'Tis just to each of them; he is himself.

Pandarus. Himself? Alas, poor Troilus, I would he were.°

70–71 *in some degrees* by some distance; in some (specific) ways (?)   73–74 *I would he were* i.e., I wish he were himself, and not in love

Cressida. So he is.   75

Pandarus. Condition,° I had gone barefoot to India.

Cressida. He is not Hector.

Pandarus. Himself? No, he's not himself. Would 'a°
were himself. Well, the gods are above; time must
friend or end. Well, Troilus, well, I would my heart   80
were in her body. No, Hector is not a better man
than Troilus.

Cressida. Excuse me.

Pandarus. He is elder.

Cressida. Pardon me, pardon me.   85

Pandarus. Th'other's not come to't;° you shall tell me
another tale when th' other's come to't. Hector shall
not have his will° this year.

Cressida. He shall not need it if he have his own.

Pandarus. Nor his qualities.   90

Cressida. No matter.

Pandarus. Nor his beauty.

Cressida. 'Twould not become him. His own's better.

Pandarus. You have no judgment, niece. Helen herself swore th' other day that Troilus, for a brown   95
favor°—for so 'tis, I must confess—not brown
neither——

Cressida. No, but brown.

Pandarus. Faith, to say truth, brown and not brown.

Cressida. To say the truth, true and not true.   100

Pandarus. She praised his complexion above Paris.

Cressida. Why, Paris hath color enough.

---

76 *Condition* i.e., even if to bring that about   **78** *'a* he   **86** *come to't* reached manhood   **88** *will* (some editors emend to *wit*, i.e., intelligence)   **95–96** *brown favor* dark complexion

Pandarus. So he has.

105 *Cressida.* Then Troilus should have too much. If she praised him above, his complexion is higher than his. He having color enough, and the other higher, is too flaming a praise for a good complexion. I had as lief Helen's golden tongue had commended Troilus for a copper nose.

110 *Pandarus.* I swear to you, I think Helen loves him better than Paris.

Cressida. Then she's a merry Greek° indeed.

Pandarus. Nay, I am sure she does. She came to him th' other day into the compassed° window—and, 115 you know, he has not past three or four hairs on his chin——

Cressida. Indeed, a tapster's arithmetic may soon bring his particulars therein to a total.

Pandarus. Why, he is very young; and yet will he, 120 within three pound, lift as much as his brother Hector.

Cressida. Is he so young a man, and so old a lifter?°

Pandarus. But to prove to you that Helen loves him, she came and puts me her white hand to his cloven 125 chin——

Cressida. Juno have mercy; how came it cloven?

Pandarus. Why, you know 'tis dimpled; I think his smiling becomes him better than any man in all Phrygia.

130 *Cressida.* O, he smiles valiantly.

Pandarus. Does he not?

Cressida. O, yes, an 'twere a cloud in autumn.

---

112 *a merry Greek* i.e., one of frivolous or loose behavior (slang)
114 *compassed* bay   122 *so old a lifter* so experienced a thief
(cf. "shoplifter")

Pandarus. Why, go to then. But to prove to you that Helen loves Troilus——

Cressida. Troilus will stand° to the proof if you'll prove it so.   135

Pandarus. Troilus? Why, he esteems her no more than I esteem an addle° egg.

Cressida. If you love an addle egg as well as you love an idle head, you would eat chickens i' the shell.   140

Pandarus. I cannot choose but laugh to think how she tickled his chin. Indeed, she has a marvel's° white hand, I must needs confess.

Cressida. Without the rack.°

Pandarus. And she takes upon her to spy a white hair   145
on his chin.

Cressida. Alas poor chin, many a wart is richer.

Pandarus. But there was such laughing. Queen Hecuba laughed that her eyes ran o'er.

Cressida. With millstones.   150

Pandarus. And Cassandra laughed.

Cressida. But there was a more temperate fire under the pot of her eyes. Did her eyes run o'er too?

Pandarus. And Hector laughed.

Cressida. At what was all this laughing?   155

Pandarus. Marry,° at the white hair that Helen spied on Troilus' chin.

Cressida. An't had been a green hair, I should have laughed too.

Pandarus. They laughed not so much at the hair as at   160
his pretty answer.

135 *stand* (a bawdy pun; cf. Sonnet 151)   138 *addle* rotten
142 *marvel's* marvelous   144 *rack* torture   156 *Marry* (an interjection, from the oath, "By the Virgin Mary")

Cressida. What was his answer?

Pandarus. Quoth she, "Here's but two-and-fifty hairs
on your chin, and one of them is white."

165 *Cressida.* This is her question.

Pandarus. That's true, make no question of that.
"Two-and-fifty hairs," quoth he, "and one white.
That white hair is my father, and all the rest are
his sons." "Jupiter!" quoth she, "which of these
170   hairs is Paris, my husband?" "The forked° one,"
quoth he; "pluck't out, and give it him." But there
was such laughing, and Helen so blushed, and
Paris so chafed, and all the rest so laughed, that
it passed.

175 *Cressida.* So let it now, for it has been a great while
going by.

Pandarus. Well, cousin, I told you a thing yesterday;
think on't.

Cressida. So I do.

180 *Pandarus.* I'll be sworn 'tis true; he will weep you,
an° 'twere a man born in April.   *Sound a retreat.*

Cressida. And I'll spring up in his tears, an 'twere a
nettle against° May.

Pandarus. Hark, they are coming from the field. Shall
185   we stand up here and see them as they pass toward
Ilium? Good niece, do; sweet niece, Cressida.

Cressida. At your pleasure.

Pandarus. Here, here, here's an excellent place; here
we may see most bravely.° I'll tell you them all by
190   their names as they pass by, but mark Troilus above
the rest.

Enter Aeneas [and passes across the stage].

170 *forked* (resembling a cuckold's horns [?])   181 *an* as if   183
against in advance of   189 *bravely* excellently

Cressida. Speak not so loud.

Pandarus. That's Aeneas. Is not that a brave° man?
He's one of the flowers of Troy, I can tell you. But
mark Troilus; you shall see anon.   195

   Enter Antenor [and passes across the stage].

Cressida. Who's that?

Pandarus. That's Antenor. He has a shrewd wit, I can
tell you; and he's man good enough—he's one o'
the soundest judgments in Troy whosoever, and a
proper° man of person. When comes Troilus? I'll   200
show you Troilus anon. If he see me, you shall see
him nod at me.

Cressida. Will he give you the nod?°

Pandarus. You shall see.

Cressida. If he do, the rich shall have more.°   205

   Enter Hector [and passes across the stage].

Pandarus. That's Hector, that, that, look you, that;
there's a fellow! Go thy way, Hector! There's a
brave man, niece. O brave Hector! Look how he
looks; there's a countenance! Is't not a brave man?

Cressida. O, a brave man.   210

Pandarus. Is 'a not? It does a man's heart good. Look
you what hacks are on his helmet. Look you yonder, do you see? Look you there. There's no jesting;
there's laying on, take't off who will,° as they say.
There be hacks!   215

Cressida. Be those with swords?

---

193 *brave* fine   200 *proper* handsome   203 *nod* (play on "noddy,"
simpleton)   205 *the rich shall have more* i.e., the fool shall become
more foolish   214 *take't off who will* i.e., whoever cares to say
otherwise (to "lay on" and "take off" were common colloquial tags)

Pandarus. Swords, anything, he cares not; an the
    devil come to him, it's all one. By God's lid, it
    does one's heart good.

Enter Paris [and passes across the stage].

220   Yonder comes Paris, yonder comes Paris. Look ye
      yonder, niece. Is't not a gallant° man too, is't not?
      Why, this is brave now. Who said he came hurt
      home today? He's not hurt. Why, this will do
      Helen's heart good now, ha? Would I could see
225   Troilus now. You shall see Troilus anon.

Cressida. Who's that?

Enter Helenus [and passes across the stage].

Pandarus. That's Helenus. I marvel where Troilus is.
    That's Helenus. I think he went not forth today.
    That's Helenus.

230   *Cressida.* Can Helenus fight, uncle?

Pandarus. Helenus? No. Yes, he'll fight indifferent
    well. I marvel where Troilus is. Hark, do you not
    hear the people cry "Troilus"? Helenus is a priest.

Cressida. What sneaking fellow comes yonder?

Enter Troilus [and passes across the stage].

235   *Pandarus.* Where? Yonder? That's Deiphobus. 'Tis
      Troilus! There's a man, niece, hem? Brave Troilus,
      the prince of chivalry!

Cressida. Peace, for shame, peace!

Pandarus. Mark him, note him. O brave Troilus!
240   Look well upon him, niece. Look you how his
      sword is bloodied, and his helm more hacked than
      Hector's—and how he looks, and how he goes. O

221 *gallant* (general term of praise, as "brave")

admirable youth! He never saw three-and-twenty.
Go thy way, Troilus, go thy way! Had I a sister
were a grace,° or a daughter a goddess, he should   *245*
take his choice. O admirable man! Paris? Paris is
dirt to him; and I warrant Helen, to change, would
give an eye to boot.

Enter Common Soldiers.

Cressida. Here comes more.

Pandarus. Asses, fools, dolts; chaff and bran, chaff   *250*
and bran; porridge after meat. I could live and die
in the eyes of Troilus. Ne'er look, ne'er look. The
eagles are gone; crows and daws, crows and daws.
I had rather be such a man as Troilus than Agamemnon and all Greece.   *255*

Cressida. There is amongst the Greeks Achilles, a
better man than Troilus.

Pandarus. Achilles? A drayman,° a porter, a very
camel.°

Cressida. Well, well.   *260*

Pandarus. "Well, well"? Why, have you any discretion, have you any eyes, do you know what a man
is? Is not birth, beauty, good shape, discourse,
manhood, learning, gentleness, virtue, youth, lib-
erality, and such like, the spice and salt that season   *265*
a man?

Cressida. Ay, a minced° man; and then to be baked
with no date in the pie, for then the man's date is
out.°

---

245 *grace* attendant goddess   258 *drayman* one who draws a cart
259 *camel* i.e., beast of burden   267 *minced* (1) mincing, affected
(2) overspiced (3) divided into parts beyond recognition   267–69
then to be baked . . . out (dates were a common ingredient
in most pastries; Cressida's pun implies that Troilus, as Pandarus
compounds him, could contain no substance and be of no interest,
out of date)

270 *Pandarus.* You are such a woman a man knows n◌
at what ward° you lie.

Cressida. Upon my back, to defend my belly; upo◌
my wit, to defend my wiles; upon my secrecy, ◌
defend mine honesty;° my mask, to defend m◌
275 beauty; and you, to defend all these. And at all thes◌
wards I lie, at a thousand watches.°

Pandarus. Say one of your watches.

Cressida. Nay, I'll watch you for that; and that's on◌
of the chiefest of them too. If I cannot ward wha◌
280 I would not have hit, I can watch you for telling◌
how I took the blow; unless it swell past hiding,◌
and then it's past watching.

Pandarus. You are such another!

Enter [Troilus'] Boy.

Boy. Sir, my lord would instantly speak with you.

285 *Pandarus.* Where?

Boy. At your own house. There he unarms him.

Pandarus. Good boy, tell him I come.   [*Exit Boy.*]
I doubt° he be hurt. Fare ye well, good niece.

Cressida. Adieu, uncle.

290 *Pandarus.* I will be with you, niece, by and by.

Cressida. To bring,° uncle.

Pandarus. Ay, a token from Troilus.

---

271 *ward* position of defense in swordplay   274 *honesty* chastity
276 *watches* periods of the night   280 *watch you for telling* i.e.,
to make certain you do not tell   281 *swell past hiding* (Cressida
thus completes her ribald play on words)   288 *doubt* suspect
that, fear that   291 *To bring* (an idiomatic intensifier, now obsolete,
meaning roughly, "indeed" or "with a vengeance"; Cressida says,
with mild sarcasm, "yes, I am sure you will," although Pandarus
picks up the word in its normal verbal sense)

Cressida. By the same token, you are a bawd.

                                        Exit Pandarus.

Words, vows, gifts, tears, and love's full sacrifice
He offers in another's enterprise;   295
But more in Troilus thousandfold I see
Than in the glass of Pandar's praise may be.
Yet hold I off. Women are angels, wooing;°
Things won are done, joy's soul lies in the doing.
That she° beloved knows nought that knows not   300
    this:
Men prize the thing ungained more than it is;°
That she was never yet, that ever knew
Love got° so sweet as when desire did sue.
Therefore this maxim out of love° I teach:
Achievement is command; ungained, beseech.°   305
Then, though my heart's content firm love doth
    bear,
Nothing of that shall from mine eyes appear. *Exit.*

[Scene III.   *The Greek camp.*]

*Sennet.° Enter Agamemnon, Nester, Ulysses, Dio-
        medes, Menelaus, with others.*

Agamemnon. Princes,
    What grief hath set these jaundies° o'er your
        cheeks?
    The ample proposition that hope makes
    In all designs begun on earth below
    Fails in the promised largeness. Checks and disas-   5
        ters

298 *wooing* while being wooed   300 *That she* that woman   301 *it
is* its value   303 *got* i.e., by men   304 *out of love* from love's
teaching   305 *Achievement . . . beseech* when men achieve love,
they command; while still trying to gain it, they will beg   I.iii.s.d.
Sennet (a trumpet call announcing specific personages in a procession)   2 *jaundies* jaundice (an obsolete plural)

Grow in the veins of actions highest reared,
As knots, by the conflux° of meeting sap,
Infects the sound pine and diverts his grain
Tortive and errant° from his course of growth.
10 Nor, princes, is it matter new to us
That we come short of our suppose° so far
That after seven years' siege yet Troy walls stand;
Sith every action that hath gone before,
Whereof we have record, trial did draw
15 Bias and thwart,° not answering the aim
And that unbodied figure of the thought
That gave't surmisèd shape. Why then, you princes,
Do you with cheeks abashed° behold our works
And call them shames, which are indeed nought
      else
20 But the protractive° trials of great Jove
To find persistive constancy in men?
The fineness of which metal is not found
In Fortune's love; for then, the bold and coward,
The wise and fool, the artist° and unread,
25 The hard and soft, seem all affined° and kin.
But, in the wind and tempest of her frown,
Distinction, with a broad and powerful fan,
Puffing at all, winnows the light away,
And what hath mass or matter by itself
30 Lies rich in virtue and unmingled.°

Nestor. With due observance of thy godlike seat,
Great Agamemnon, Nestor shall apply°
Thy latest words. In the reproof° of chance
Lies the true proof of men. The sea being smooth,
35 How many shallow bauble boats dare sail
Upon her patient breast, making their way
With those of nobler bulk?

---

7 *conflux* flowing together 9 *Tortive and errant* twisted and
wandering 11 *suppose* anticipation 15 *Bias and thwart* to one
side and crosswise 18 *cheeks abashed* i.e., faces turned aside in
confusion and shame 20 *protractive* extended 24 *artist* scholar
25 *affined* in affinity, related 30 *unmingled* unmixed with other
essences 32 *apply* show examples of (as in a rhetorical exercise)
33 *reproof* rebuff

But let the ruffian Boreas° once enrage
The gentle Thetis,° and anon behold
The strong-ribbed bark through liquid mountains   *40*
     cut,
Bounding between the two moist elements
Like Perseus' horse,° where's then the saucy boat,
Whose weak untimbered sides but even now
Corrivaled greatness? Either to harbor fled,
Or made a toast° for Neptune. Even so   *45*
Doth valor's show° and valor's worth divide
In storms of fortune. For in her ray and brightness
The herd hath more annoyance by the breese°
Than by the tiger; but when the splitting wind
Makes flexible the knees of knotted oaks,   *50*
And flies fled under shade, why then the thing of
     courage,
As roused with rage, with rage doth sympathize,°
And with an accent tuned in selfsame key
Returns° to chiding fortune.

Ulysses.   Agamemnon,
Thou great commander, nerves° and bone of   *55*
     Greece,
Heart of our numbers, soul and only sprite,°
In whom the tempers and the minds of all
Should be shut up,° hear what Ulysses speaks.
Besides th' applause and approbation
The which [*to Agamemnon*], most mighty for thy   *60*
     place and sway,
[*to Nestor*] And thou most reverend for thy
     stretched-out life,
I give to both your speeches—which were such
As Agamemnon and the hand of Greece
Should hold up high in brass; and such again

38 *Boreas* (the north wind) 39 *Thetis* (a sea maiden, Achilles'
mother, but here personifying the sea) 42 *Perseus' horse* (Pegasus,
the winged horse) 45 *toast* (a piece of toast was usually soaked
in wine) 46 *show* outward appearance 48 *breese* gadfly 52 *sympathize* becomes similar to 54 *Returns* replies 55 *nerves* sinews
56 *sprite* spirit 58 *shut up* gathered in

65   As venerable Nestor, hatched in silver,°
       Should with a bond of air, strong as the axletree
       On which heaven rides, knit all the Greekish ears
       To his experienced tongue—yet let it please both,
       Thou great, and wise, to hear Ulysses speak.

70   *Agamemnon.* Speak, Prince of Ithaca; and be't of less
           expect
       That matter needless, of importless burden,
       Divide thy lips than we are confident,
       When rank Thersites opes his mastic° jaws,
       We shall hear music, wit, and oracle.

75 .   *Ulysses.* Troy, yet upon his basis, had been down,
       And the great Hector's sword had lacked a master,
       But for these instances.°
       The specialty of rule° hath been neglected;
       And look, how many Grecian tents do stand
80   Hollow upon this plain, so many hollow factions.
       When that the general is not like the hive
       To whom the foragers shall all repair,
       What honey is expected?° Degree being vizarded,°
       Th' unworthiest shows as fairly in the mask.
85   The heavens themselves, the planets, and this center
       Observe degree, priority, and place,
       Insisture,° course, proportion, season, form,
       Office, and custom, in all line of order.
       And therefore is the glorious planet Sol°
90   In noble eminence enthroned and sphered
       Amidst the other;° whose med'cinable eye
       Corrects the influence° of evil planets,

65 *hatched in silver* (referring to the silver lines in his hair)   73
mastic abusive, scourging (sometimes emended to "mastiff")   77
instances reasons   78 *The speciality of rule* the particular organiza-
tion of ruling, the distinction of rights in a chain of authority
81–83 *When . . . expected* i.e., when the endeavors of the general
populace are not similar to those of the agent which rules them,
and to which they are responsible, what profit can be expected?
(?); when the ruling general is dissimilar in kind to the soldiers in
his army, what profit, etc. (?)   83 *Degree being vizarded* the
hierarchy of authority being hidden   87 *Insisture* regularity of
position   89 *Sol* the sun   91 *other* others   92 *influence* astrological
effect

And posts, like the commandment of a king,
Sans check, to good and bad. But when the planets
In evil mixture° to disorder wander,   95
What plagues, and what portents, what mutiny,
What raging of the sea, shaking of earth,
Commotion in the winds, frights, changes, horrors,
Divert and crack, rend and deracinate°
The unity and married calm of states   100
Quite from their fixure? O, when degree is shaked,
Which is the ladder of all high designs,
The enterprise is sick. How could communities,
Degrees in schools, and brotherhoods in cities,
Peaceful commerce from dividable shores,   105
The primogenity° and due of birth,
Prerogative of age, crowns, scepters, laurels,
But by degree, stand in authentic place?
Take but degree away, untune that string,
And hark what discord follows. Each thing meets   110
In mere oppugnancy.° The bounded waters
Should lift their bosoms higher than the shores
And make a sop° of all this solid globe;
Strength should be lord of imbecility,°
And the rude son should strike his father dead;   115
Force should be right, or rather right and wrong—
Between whose endless jar° justice resides—
Should lose their names, and so should justice too.
Then everything include itself in power,°
Power into will, will into appetite,   120
And appetite, an universal wolf,
So doubly seconded with will and power,
Must make perforce an universal prey
And last eat up himself. Great Agamemnon,
This chaos, when degree is suffocate,   125
Follows the choking.
And this neglection of degree it is

95 *evil mixture* unlucky or malignant relationship (astrological)
99 *deracinate* uproot   106 *primogenity* right of the eldest son to
succeed to his father's estate   111 *mere oppugnancy* total strife
113 *sop* pulp   114 *imbecility* i.e., weakness   117 *jar* discord   119
include itself in power enclose itself within power, i.e., become
power

That by a pace goes backward with a purpose
It hath to climb.° The general's disdained
130   By him one step below, he by the next,
That next by him beneath; so every step,
Exampled by the first pace that is sick
Of his superior, grows to an envious fever
Of pale and bloodless emulation;°
135   And 'tis this fever that keeps Troy on foot,
Not her own sinews. To end a tale of length,
Troy in our weakness stands, not in her strength.

Nestor. Most wisely hath Ulysses here discovered
The fever whereof all our power is sick.

Agamemnon. The nature of the sickness found,
140   Ulysses,
What is the remedy?

Ulysses. The great Achilles, whom opinion crowns
The sinew and the forehand of our host,
Having his ear full of his airy fame,
145   Grows dainty of° his worth, and in his tent
Lies mocking our designs. With him Patroclus
Upon a lazy bed the livelong day
Breaks scurril jests,
And with ridiculous and silly action
150   (Which, slanderer, he imitation° calls)
He pageants° us. Sometime, great Agamemnon,
Thy topless deputation° he puts on,
And, like a strutting player, whose conceit
Lies in his hamstring,° and doth think it rich
155   To hear the wooden dialogue° and sound
'Twixt his stretched footing° and the scaffoldage,°

127–29 *And this neglection . . . climb* this neglect of hierarchy
causes a step toward disintegration each time an attempt is made
to climb upward   134 *emulation* rivalry   145 *dainty of* finicky
about   149–50 *silly action . . . imitation* (Ulysses contrasts such
charades with true imitation to the life, presumably the goal of the
excellent   actor)   151 *pageants* mimics   152 *topless deputation*
unlimited office   153–54 *conceit Lies in his hamstring* imagination
lies in the tendon of his leg   155 *wooden dialogue* i.e., the thumps
of heavy footfalls on the wooden stage floor   156 *stretched footing*
absurdly long strides   156 *scaffoldage* scaffold, stage

Such to-be-pitied and o'erwrested seeming°
He acts thy greatness in; and when he speaks,
'Tis like a chime a-mending,° with terms un-
    squared,°
Which, from the tongue of roaring Typhon° drop-
    ped,   160
Would seem hyperboles. At this fusty° stuff
The large Achilles, on his pressed bed lolling,
From his deep chest laughs out a loud applause,
Cries, "Excellent! 'tis Agamemnon right.
Now play me Nestor; hem, and stroke thy beard,   165
As he being drest° to some oration."
That's done, as near as the extremest ends
Of parallels, as like as Vulcan and his wife,°
Yet god Achilles still cries, "Excellent!
'Tis Nestor right. Now play him me,° Patroclus,   170
Arming to answer in a night alarm."
And then, forsooth, the faint defects of age
Must be the scene of mirth; to cough and spit,
And with a palsy fumbling on his gorget,°
Shake in and out the rivet. And at this sport   175
Sir Valor dies; cries, "O, enough, Patroclus,
Or give me ribs of steel; I shall split all
In pleasure of my spleen!"° And in this fashion
All our abilities, gifts, natures, shapes,
Severals and generals° of grace exact,   180
Achievements, plots, orders, preventions,
Excitements to the field or speech for truce,
Success or loss, what is or is not, serves
As stuff for these two to make paradoxes.°

157 *o'erwrested seeming* overstrained impersonation   159 *chime
a-mending* (1) chime being repaired (2) dissonant combination
of sounds just following the ringing of many chimes (?)   159 *unsquared* inappropriate   160 *roaring Typhon* (a monster with
serpents' heads and a tremendous voice)   161 *fusty* stale, second-
rate   166 *drest* carefully prepared for, addressed   168 *Vulcan and
his wife* (Vulcan, god of the smithy and forge, was depicted as
sooty, and was lame besides; his "wife" was Venus, who cuckolded
him with Mars)   170 *me* i.e., for me   174 *gorget* throat armor
178 *spleen* (supposed the seat of the emotions of anger and
hilarity)   180 *Severals and generals* individual and general qualities
184 *paradoxes* absurdities

185 *Nestor*. And in the imitation of these twain,
          Who, as Ulysses says, opinion crowns
          With an imperial voice, many are infect.
          Ajax is grown self-willed, and bears his head
          In such a rein,° in full as proud a place
190   As broad Achilles; keeps his tent like him;
          Makes factious feasts; rails on our state of war,
          Bold as an oracle, and sets Thersites,
          A slave whose gall° coins slanders like a mint,
          To match us in comparisons with dirt,
195   To weaken and discredit our exposure,
          How rank° soever rounded in with danger.

        Ulysses. They tax° our policy and call it cowardice,
          Count wisdom as no member of the war,
          Forestall prescience,° and esteem no act
200   But that of hand. The still and mental parts
          That do contrive how many hands shall strike
          When fitness° calls them on, and know by measure
          Of their observant toil the enemies' weight—
          Why, this hath not a finger's dignity.
205   They call this bed-work, mapp'ry,° closet war;
          So that the ram that batters down the wall,
          For the great swinge° and rudeness of his poise,
          They place before his hand that made the engine,
          Or those that with the fineness of their souls
210   By reason guide his execution.

        Nestor. Let this be granted, and Achilles' horse°
          Makes many Thetis' sons.   *Tucket.*°

        Agamemnon. What trumpet? Look, Menelaus.

        Menelaus. From Troy.

---

189 *In such a rein* i.e., so high   193 *gall* (the source of bile, which
was thought to produce rancor and abuse)   196 *rank* densely,
abundantly   197 *tax* criticize   199 *Forestall prescience* discount
foresight   202 *fitness* readiness   205 *mapp'ry* map work   207
swinge impetus, whirling force   211 *Achilles' horse* (either literally, or collectively, for his soldiers, the Myrmidons)   212 s.d.
Tucket trumpet call

Enter Aeneas.

Agamemnon. What would you 'fore our tent?   215

Aeneas. Is this great Agamemnon's tent, I pray you?

Agamemnon. Even this.

Aeneas. May one that is a herald and a prince
  Do a fair message to his kingly eyes?°

Agamemnon. With surety stronger than Achilles' arm   220
  'Fore all the Greekish heads, which with one voice
  Call Agamemnon head and general.

Aeneas. Fair leave and large security. How may
  A stranger to those most imperial looks
  Know them from eyes of other mortals?

Agamemnon.   How?   225

Aeneas. Ay.
  I ask, that I might waken reverence,
  And bid the cheek be ready with a blush
  Modest as morning when she coldly eyes
  The youthful Phoebus.°   230
  Which is that god in office, guiding men?
  Which is the high and mighty Agamemnon?

Agamemnon. This Troyan scorns us, or the men of
    Troy
  Are ceremonious courtiers.

Aeneas. Courtiers as free, as debonair, unarmed,   235
  As bending° angels; that's their fame in peace.
  But when they would seem soldiers, they have galls,
  Good arms, strong joints, true swords—and, great
    Jove's accord,°
  Nothing so full of heart. But peace, Aeneas;
  Peace, Troyan; lay thy finger on thy lips.   240
  The worthiness of praise distains° his worth,

219 *to his kingly eyes* i.e., in his presence   230 *Phoebus* Phoebus
Apollo (the sun god)   236 *bending* bowing   238 *Jove's accord*
i.e., with Jove on their side   241 *distains* sullies

If that the praised himself bring the praise forth.
But what the repining enemy commends,
That breath fame blows; that praise, sole pure, transcends.

Agamemnon. Sir, you of Troy, call you yourself
245   Aeneas?

Aeneas. Ay, Greek, that is my name.

Agamemnon. What's your affair, I pray you?

Aeneas. Sir, pardon; 'tis for Agamemnon's ears.

Agamemnon. He hears nought privately that comes
    from Troy.

250 *Aeneas.* Nor I from Troy come not to whisper him.
I bring a trumpet to awake his ear,
To set his seat on the attentive bent,°
And then to speak.

Agamemnon.   Speak frankly as the wind;
It is not Agamemnon's sleeping hour.
255 That thou shalt know, Troyan, he is awake,
He tells thee so himself.

Aeneas.   Trumpet, blow loud,
Send thy brass voice through all these lazy tents;
And every Greek of mettle, let him know,
What Troy means fairly shall be spoke aloud.
                  Sound trumpet.
260 We have, great Agamemnon, here in Troy
A prince called Hector—Priam is his father—
Who in this dull and long-continued truce
Is rusty grown. He bade me take a trumpet,°
And to this purpose speak: kings, princes, lords,
265 If there be one among the fair'st of Greece
That holds his honor higher than his ease,
That seeks his praise more than he fears his peril,
That knows his valor and knows not his fear,
That loves his mistress more than in confession

252 *To . . . bent* i.e., to make him, and his place of government,
pay attention 263 *trumpet* i.e., a trumpeter in attendance

With truant vows to her own lips he loves,°   270
And dare avow her beauty and her worth
In other arms than hers°—to him this challenge;
Hector, in view of Troyans and of Greeks,
Shall make it good, or do his best to do it;
He hath a lady wiser, fairer, truer,   275
Than ever Greek did compass in his arms;
And will tomorrow with his trumpet call,
Midway between your tents and walls of Troy,
To rouse a Grecian that is true in love.
If any come, Hector shall honor him;   280
If none, he'll say in Troy when he retires,
The Grecian dames are sunburnt° and not worth
The splinter of a lance. Even so much.

Agamemnon. This shall be told our lovers, Lord
     Aeneas;
If none of them have soul in such a kind,   285
We left them all at home. But we are soldiers;
And may that soldier a mere recreant prove,
That means not, hath not, or is not in love!
If then one is, or hath, or means to be,
That one meets Hector; if none else, I am he.   290

Nestor. Tell him of Nestor, one that was a man
When Hector's grandsire sucked. He is old now,
But if there be not in our Grecian host
A nobleman that hath one spark of fire
To answer for his love, tell him from me,   295
I'll hide my silver beard in a gold beaver,°
And in my vantbrace° put my withered brawns,°
And, meeting him, will tell him that my lady
Was fairer than his grandam, and as chaste
As may be in the world. His youth in flood,   300
I'll prove this truth with my three drops of blood.

269–70 *That loves . . . lips he loves,* i.e., one that loves his mistress
even more than the false oaths of lip service (?); more than enough
to swear false vows that he loves her (?)   272 *In other arms than
hers* i.e., with weapons   282 *sunburnt* dark (for the Elizabethans,
ugly)   296 *beaver* movable face guard of a helmet   297 *vantbrace*
armor fitting the forearm   297 *brawns* arm (or leg) muscles (an
obsolete plural)

Aeneas. Now heavens forfend such scarcity of youth!

Ulysses. Amen.

[*Agamemnon.*] Fair Lord Aeneas, let me touch your
    hand;
305 To our pavilion shall I lead you first.
    Achilles shall have word of this intent;
    So shall each lord of Greece, from tent to tent.
    Yourself shall feast with us before you go,
    And find the welcome of a noble foe.
                Exeunt. Manent° Ulysses and Nestor.

310 *Ulysses.* Nestor.

Nestor. What says Ulysses?

Ulysses. I have a young conception in my brain;
    Be you my time to bring it to some shape.°

Nestor. What is't?

315 *Ulysses.* This 'tis:
    Blunt wedges rive hard knots; the seeded pride
    That hath to this maturity blown up
    In rank Achilles, must or now be cropped
    Or, shedding,° breed a nursery of like evil
320 To overbulk us all.

Nestor.   Well, and how?

Ulysses. This challenge that the gallant Hector sends,
    However it is spread in general name,
    Relates in purpose only to Achilles.

Nestor. True, the purpose is perspicuous as substance
325 Whose grossness little characters sum up;°
    And, in the publication, make no strain°
    But that Achilles, were his brain as barren
    As banks of Libya—though, Apollo knows,
    'Tis dry enough—will with great speed of judgment,

309 s.d. *Manent* (they) remain   312–13 *I have . . . some shape* i.e.,
I have the beginning of an idea; let me develop it as you listen
319 *shedding* i.e., scattering seed   325 *Whose grossness . . . sum up*
whose large size can be defined by small figures   326 *make no
strain* you may be sure

Ay with celerity, find Hector's purpose   330
Pointing on him.

Ulysses. And wake him to the answer, think you?

Nestor. Why, 'tis most meet. Who may you else oppose
    That can from Hector bring his honor off,
    If not Achilles? Though't be a sportful combat,   335
    Yet in the trial much opinion° dwells;
    For here the Troyans taste our dear'st repute
    With their fin'st palate;° and trust to me, Ulysses,
    Our imputation shall be oddly poised
    In this vild action.° For the success,   340
    Although particular, shall give a scantling°
    Of good or bad unto the general;°
    And in such indexes, although small pricks
    To their subsequent volumes,° there is seen
    The baby figure of the giant mass   345
    Of things to come at large. It is supposed
    He that meets Hector issues from our choice;
    And choice, being mutual act of all our souls,
    Makes merit her election,° and doth boil,
    As 'twere from forth us all, a man distilled   350
    Out of our virtues—who miscarrying,
    What heart receives from hence a conquering part,
    To steel a strong opinion to themselves;
    Which entertained, limbs are his° instruments,
    In no less working than are swords and bows   355
    Directive by the limbs.

Ulysses. Give pardon to my speech. Therefore 'tis meet
    Achilles meet not Hector. Let us, like merchants,
    First show foul wares, and think perchance they'll sell;

336 *opinion* reputation   337–38 *taste . . . palate* put our most valued
reputation to the test of their most careful, sensitive observation
339–40 *Our . . . action* our reputation shall be unequally balanced
in this trivial action   341 *scantling* sample   342 *general* (1) general view (2) entire army   343–44 *small . . . volumes* small markings compared to the great significance to follow   349 *election*
criteria for choice   354 *his* i.e., of the strong opinion

360 If not, the luster of the better shall exceed
By showing the worse first. Do not consent
That ever Hector and Achilles meet;
For both our honor and our shame in this
Are dogged with two strange followers.°

Nestor. I see them not with my old eyes; what are
365   they?

Ulysses. What glory our Achilles shares from Hector,
Were he not proud, we all should share with him.
But he already is too insolent,
And it were better parch in Afric sun
370 Than in the pride and salt° scorn of his eyes,
Should he 'scape Hector fair. If he were foiled,
Why then we do our main opinion° crush
In taint of° our best man. No, make a lott'ry;
And by device let blockish Ajax draw
375 The sort° to fight with Hector; among ourselves
Give him allowance for the better man,
For that will physic the great Myrmidon°
Who broils° in loud applause, and make him fall
His crest that prouder than blue Iris° bends.
380 If the dull brainless Ajax comes safe off,
We'll dress him up in voices; if he fail,
Yet go we under our opinion still
That we have better men. But, hit or miss,
Our project's life this shape of sense assumes:
385 Ajax employed plucks down Achilles' plumes.
Nestor. Now, Ulysses, I begin to relish thy advice,
And I will give a taste thereof forthwith
To Agamemnon. Go we to him straight.
Two curs shall tame each other; pride alone
390 Must tarre° the mastiffs on, as 'twere a bone.

Exeunt.

---

364 *followers* consequences   370 *salt* bitter   372 *our main opinion*
the mainstay of our reputation   373 *In taint of* to the loss of,
with the shame of   375 *sort* lot   377 *the great Myrmidon* (Achilles,
whose father, Peleus, had subjects called Myrmidons)   378 *broils*
bakes; i.e., suns himself   379 *Iris* (the rainbow)   390 *tarre* incite,
provoke

[ACT II

Scene I.   *The Greek camp.*]

Enter Ajax and Thersites.

Ajax. Thersites!

Thersites. Agamemnon, how if he had boils—full, all over, generally?

Ajax. Thersites!

Thersites. And those boils did run?—say so—did not   5
the general run then? Were not that a botchy core?°

Ajax. Dog!

Thersites. Then would come some matter from him. I see none now.

Ajax. Thou bitch-wolf's son, canst thou not hear?   10
Feel then.   *Strikes him.*

Thersites. The plague of Greece upon thee, thou mongrel beef-witted lord!

Ajax. Speak then, thou vinewed'st leaven,° speak. I will beat thee into handsomeness.   15

II.i.6 *botchy core* erupted boil   14 *vinewed'st leaven* most mildewed dough

Thersites. I shall sooner rail thee into wit and holiness; but I think thy horse will sooner con° an oration than thou learn a prayer without book.°
20 Thou canst strike, canst thou? A red murrain° o' thy jade's° tricks!

Ajax. Toadstool, learn me° the proclamation.

Thersites. Dost thou think I have no sense, thou strikest me thus?

Ajax. The proclamation!

25 *Thersites.* Thou art proclaimed fool, I think.

Ajax. Do not, porpentine,° do not; my fingers itch.

Thersites. I would thou didst itch from head to foot; an I had the scratching of thee, I would make thee the loathsomest scab in Greece. When thou art
30 forth in the incursions,° thou strikest as slow as another.

Ajax. I say, the proclamation!

Thersites. Thou grumblest and railest every hour on Achilles, and thou art as full of envy at his greatness as Cerberus° is at Proserpina's° beauty, ay,
35 that thou bark'st at him.

Ajax. Mistress Thersites!

Thersites. Thou shouldst strike him.

Ajax. Cobloaf!°

40 *Thersites.* He would pun° thee into shivers with his fist, as a sailor breaks a biscuit.

Ajax. You whoreson cur!   [*Beating him.*]

17 *con* memorize   18 *without book* by heart   19 *red murrain* (form of plague manifested in red skin eruptions)   20 *jade's* nag's   21 *learn me* find out for me   26 *porpentine* porcupine   30 *incursions* battle raids, attacks   35 *Cerberus* (the monstrous watchdog of Hades)   35 *Proserpina* (a beautiful goddess carried off by Pluto to the underworld)   39 *Cobloaf* a badly baked, crusty loaf of bread   40 *pun* pound

Thersites. Do, do.

Ajax. Thou stool for a witch!

Thersites. Ay, do, do, thou sodden-witted lord! thou 45
   hast no more brain than I have in mine elbows;
   an asinico° may tutor thee. Thou scurvy-valiant
   ass, thou art here but to thrash Troyans, and thou
   art bought and sold° among those of any wit like
   a barbarian slave. If thou use to beat me, I will 50
   begin at thy heel, and tell what thou art by inches,
   thou thing of no bowels,° thou!

Ajax. You dog!

Thersites. You scurvy lord!

Ajax. You cur!   [*Beating him.*] 55

Thersites. Mars his° idiot! Do, rudeness; do, camel;
   do, do.

Enter Achilles and Patroclus.

Achilles. Why, how now, Ajax, wherefore do you
   thus? How now, Thersites, what's the matter, man?

Thersites. You see him there? Do you?   60

Achilles. Ay, what's the matter?

Thersites. Nay, look upon him.

Achilles. So I do. What's the matter?

Thersites. Nay, but regard him well.

Achilles. "Well"—why so I do.   65

Thersites. But yet you look not well upon him; for,
   whosomever° you take him to be, he is Ajax.

Achilles. I know that, fool.

---

47 *asinico* ass, simpleton   49 *bought and sold* i.e., made fun of
52 *bowels* mercy (the bowels were thought to be the source of com-
passion)   56 *Mars his* Mars's   67 *whosomever* whomsoever

Thersites. Ay, but that fool° knows not himself.

70   *Ajax.* Therefore I beat thee.

Thersites. Lo, lo, lo, lo, what modicums of wit he ut-
      ters! His evasions have ears thus long.° I have
      bobbed his brain more than he has beat my bones.
      I will buy nine sparrows for a penny, and his pia
75   mater° is not worth the ninth part of a sparrow.
      This lord, Achilles, Ajax, who wears his wit in his
      belly and his guts in his head, I'll tell you what I
      say of him.

Achilles. What?

80   *Thersites.* I say, this Ajax——
                    [*Ajax threatens to strike him.*]

Achilles. Nay, good Ajax.

Thersites. Has not so much wit——
                    [*Ajax threatens again to strike him.*]

Achilles. Nay, I must hold you.

Thersites. As will stop the eye of Helen's needle, for
85   whom he comes to fight.

Achilles. Peace, fool!

Thersites. I would have peace and quietness, but the
      fool will not—he there, that he. Look you there.

Ajax. O thou damned cur, I shall——

90   *Achilles.* Will you set° your wit to a fool's?

Thersites. No, I warrant you; the fool's will shame it.

Patroclus. Good words, Thersites.

Achilles. What's the quarrel?

---

69 *that fool* (as though Achilles had said "I know that fool")
72 *thus long* i.e., as long as those of an ass   74–75 *pia mater* i.e.,
brain (literally, the membrane covering the brain)   90 *set* match

Ajax. I bade the vile owl go learn me the tenor of the proclamation, and he rails upon me. 95

Thersites. I serve thee not.

Ajax. Well, go to, go to.

Thersites. I serve here voluntary.

Achilles. Your last service was suff'rance, 'twas not voluntary; no man is beaten voluntary. Ajax was 100 here the voluntary, and you as under an impress.°

Thersites. E'en so. A great deal of your wit, too, lies in your sinews, or else there be liars. Hector shall have a great catch if he knock out either of your brains. 'A were as good crack a fusty nut with no 105 kernel.

Achilles. What, with me too, Thersites?

Thersites. There's Ulysses and old Nestor, whose wit was moldy ere your grandsires had nails on their toes, yoke you like draft oxen and make you plow 110 up the wars.

Achilles. What, what?

Thersites. Yes, good sooth. To, Achilles! To, Ajax! To——°

Ajax. I shall cut out your tongue. 115

Thersites. 'Tis no matter, I shall speak as much as thou afterwards.

Patroclus. No more words, Thersites; peace!

Thersites. I will hold my peace when Achilles' brach° bids me, shall I? 120

Achilles. There's for you, Patroclus.

Thersites. I will see you hanged like clotpoles,° ere

101 *impress* (pun on impressment, compulsory military service) 113–114 *To, Achilles! To, Ajax! To* (imitation of the shouts of a driver, urging on his horses) 119 *brach* bitch 122 *clotpoles* blockheads

I come any more to your tents. I will keep where
there is wit stirring and leave the faction of fools.
                                                Exit.

125 *Patroclus.* A good riddance.

Achilles. Marry, this, sir, is proclaimed through all
    our host:
That Hector, by the fifth hour° of the sun,
Will, with a trumpet, 'twixt our tents and Troy
Tomorrow morning call some knight to arms
130 That hath a stomach,° and such a one that dare
Maintain—I know not what; 'tis trash. Farewell.

Ajax. Farewell? Who shall answer him?

Achilles. I know not. 'Tis put to lott'ry. Otherwise,
He knew his man.
                            [*Exeunt Achilles and Patroclus.*]

135 *Ajax.* O, meaning you? I will go learn more of it.
                                                Exit.

            [Scene II.   *Troy; Priam's palace.*]

    Enter Priam, Hector, Troilus, Paris, and Helenus.

Priam. After so many hours, lives, speeches spent,
    Thus once again says Nestor from the Greeks:
    "Deliver Helen, and all damage else,
    As honor, loss of time, travail, expense,
    Wounds, friends, and what else dear that is con-
        sumed
    In hot digestion of this cormorant° war,
    Shall be struck off." Hector, what say you to't?

127 *fifth hour* i.e., eleven in the morning   130 *stomach* temperament or relish (here, for chivalric achievement)   II.ii.6 *cormorant*
ravenous, rapacious

Hector. Though no man lesser fears the Greeks than
   I,
  As far as toucheth my particular,°
  Yet, dread Priam,   10
  There is no lady of more softer bowels,°
  More spongy to suck in the sense of fear,
  More ready to cry out, "Who knows what follows?"
  Than Hector is. The wound of peace is surety,°
  Surety secure; but modest doubt is called   15
  The beacon of the wise, the tent° that searches
  To the bottom of the worst. Let Helen go.
  Since the first sword was drawn about this question,
  Every tithe soul, 'mongst many thousand dismes,°
  Hath been as dear as Helen. I mean, of ours.   20
  If we have lost so many tenths of ours
  To guard a thing not ours nor worth to us,
  Had it our name, the value of one ten,°
  What merit's in that reason which denies
  The yielding of her up?

Troilus.   Fie, fie, my brother!   25
  Weigh you the worth and honor of a king
  So great as our dread father in a scale
  Of common ounces? Will you with counters° sum
  The past proportion of his infinite,°
  And buckle in a waist most fathomless°   30
  With spans° and inches so diminutive
  As fears and reasons? Fie, for godly shame!

Helenus. No marvel, though you bite so sharp at reasons,
  You are so empty of them. Should not our father

---

9 *my particular* me, personally   11 *of more softer bowels* more
averse to violence   14 *The wound of peace is surety* peace is en-
dangered by a sense of safety   16 *tent* (roll of absorbent material,
for cleaning or probing wounds)   19 *Every . . . dismes* every
tenth soul, among many thousand tens (?); every soul taken by war
as its tenth among many thousand such tenths (?)   23 *one ten*
i.e., one in ten   28 *counters* pieces of worthless metal used for
computation   29 *The past . . . infinite* i.e., his infinite greatness
which is past all measurement   30 *fathomless* i.e., immeasurable
31 *spans* (units of measure averaging nine inches)

35   Bear the great sway of his affairs with reason,
      Because your speech hath none that tell him so?

Troilus. You are for dreams and slumbers, brother
      priest;
      You fur your gloves with reason.° Here are your
      reasons:
      You know an enemy intends you harm;
40   You know a sword employed is perilous,
      And reason flies the object° of all harm.
      Who marvels then, when Helenus beholds
      A Grecian and his sword, if he do set
      The very wings of reason to his heels
45   And fly like chidden Mercury from Jove,
      Or like a star disorbed?° Nay, if we talk of reason,
      Let's shut our gates and sleep! Manhood and honor
      Should have hare-hearts, would they but fat their
      thoughts
      With this crammed° reason. Reason and respect
50   Make livers° pale and lustihood deject.

Hector. Brother, she is not worth what she doth cost
      The keeping.

Troilus.   What's aught but as 'tis valued?

Hector. But value dwells not in particular will.°
      It holds his° estimate and dignity°
55   As well wherein 'tis precious of itself
      As in the prizer.° 'Tis mad idolatry
      To make the service greater than the god;
      And the will dotes that is attributive°
      To what infectiously itself affects,
60   Without some image of th' affected merit.°

---

38 *You fur your gloves with reason* i.e., you use reason as a comfortable word with which to decorate your speech, much as fur lines gloves 41 *object* (here, presentation, sight) 46 *disorbed* thrown from its sphere 49 *crammed* filled to excess, doughy 50 *livers* (thought to be the seats of passions) 53 *particular will* the individual's inclination 54 *his* its 54 *dignity* value 56 *prizer* appraiser 58 *attributive* dependent, subservient 59–60 *To what . . . merit* to what it, to its own infection, desires, with no objective perception of the worth of the thing desired

Troilus. I take today a wife, and my election
   Is led on in the conduct of my will—°
   My will enkindled by mine eyes and ears,
   Two traded° pilots 'twixt the dangerous shores
   Of will and judgment. How may I avoid,   65
   Although my will distaste what it elected,
   The wife I chose? There can be no evasion
   To blench° from this and to stand firm by honor.
   We turn not back the silks upon the merchant
   When we have soiled them, nor the remainder
      viands   70
   We do not throw in unrespective sieve°
   Because we now are full. It was thought meet
   Paris should do some vengeance on the Greeks.
   Your breath with full consent bellied his sails;
   The seas and winds, old wranglers, took a truce   75
   And did him service; he touched the ports desired,
   And for an old aunt° whom the Greeks held captive
   He brought a Grecian queen, whose youth and
      freshness
   Wrinkles Apollo's and makes pale the morning.
   Why keep we her? The Grecians keep our aunt.   80
   Is she worth keeping? Why, she is a pearl
   Whose price hath launched above a thousand ships
   And turned crowned kings to merchants.
   If you'll avouch 'twas wisdom Paris went—
   As you must needs, for you all cried, "Go, go"—   85
   If you'll confess he brought home worthy prize—
   As you must needs, for you all clapped your hands
   And cried, "Inestimable!"—why do you now
   The issue of your proper wisdoms rate,°
   And do a deed that never Fortune did: 90
   Beggar the estimation° which you prized

61–62 *I take . . . my will*—(Troilus is setting forth, rhetorically,
an example to prove his point; whatever he may be thinking, he
is not announcing, of course, his approaching liaison with Cressida)
64 *traded* experienced   68 *blench* shrink   71 *unrespective sieve*
common receptacle   77 *aunt* (Hesione, Priam's sister and Ajax's
mother, married to Telamon; another son was Teucer, greatest
archer among the Greeks)   89 *The issue . . . rate* condemn the
result of your own judgments   91 *estimation* thing esteemed

Richer than sea and land? O theft most base,
That we have stol'n what we do fear to keep!
But thieves unworthy of a thing so stol'n,
95   That in their country did them that disgrace°
We fear to warrant° in our native place.

Enter Cassandra raving with her hair about her ears.

Cassandra. Cry, Troyans, cry!

Priam.   What noise? What shriek
     is this?

Troilus. 'Tis our mad sister.° I do know her voice.

Cassandra. Cry, Troyans!

100 *Hector.* It is Cassandra.

Cassandra. Cry, Troyans, cry! Lend me ten thousand
     eyes,
     And I will fill them with prophetic tears.

Hector. Peace, sister, peace!

Cassandra. Virgins and boys, mid-age and wrinkled
     eld,
105   Soft infancy, that nothing canst but cry,
     Add to my clamors! Let us pay betimes
     A moiety° of that mass of moan to come.
     Cry, Troyans, cry! Practice your eyes with tears!
     Troy must not be, nor goodly Ilion stand;
110   Our firebrand° brother, Paris, burns us all.
     Cry, Troyans, cry! A Helen and a woe!
     Cry, cry! Troy burns, or else let Helen go.   *Exit.*

Hector. Now, youthful Troilus, do not these high
     strains
     Of divination in our sister work
115   Some touches of remorse? Or is your blood

95 *disgrace* i.e., the abduction of Helen 96 *warrant* justify by
defense 98 *our mad sister* (when Cassandra refused Apollo's love,
he destroyed his former gift of prophecy by causing her never to
be believed) 107 *moiety* part 110 *firebrand* (Hecuba dreamed
she was delivered of a firebrand when Paris was born)

So madly hot that no discourse of reason,
Nor fear of bad success in a bad cause,
Can qualify° the same?

Troilus.   Why, brother Hector,
We may not think the justness of each act
Such and no other than event° doth form it,   *120*
Nor once deject the courage of our minds
Because Cassandra's mad. Her brainsick raptures°
Cannot distaste° the goodness of a quarrel
Which hath our several honors all engaged
To make it gracious. For my private part,   *125*
I am no more touched than all Priam's sons;
And Jove forbid there should be done amongst us
Such things as might offend the weakest spleen°
To fight for and maintain.

Paris. Else might the world convince° of levity   *130*
As well my undertakings as your counsels;
But I attest the gods, your full consent
Gave wings to my propension° and cut off
All fears attending on so dire a project.
For what, alas, can these my single arms?   *135*
What propugnation° is in one man's valor
To stand the push and enmity of those
This quarrel would excite? Yet, I protest,
Were I alone to pass° the difficulties,
And had as ample power as I have will,   *140*
Paris should ne'er retract what he hath done
Nor faint in the pursuit.

Priam.   Paris, you speak
Like one besotted on your sweet delights.
You have the honey still, but these the gall;
So to be valiant is no praise at all.   *145*

Paris. Sir, I propose not merely to myself

---

118 *qualify* moderate   120 *event* outcome   122 *brainsick raptures*
fits of prophecy   123 *distaste* make distasteful   128 *spleen* temper,
temperament   130 *convince* convict   133 *propension* inclination
136 *propugnation* defense   139 *pass* suffer, undergo

The pleasure such a beauty brings with it;
But I would have the soil of her fair rape°
Wiped off in honorable keeping her.
150   What treason were it to the ransacked° queen,
Disgrace to your great worths, and shame to me,
Now to deliver her possession up
On terms of base compulsion! Can it be
That so degenerate a strain as this
155   Should once set footing in your generous° bosoms?
There's not the meanest spirit on our party
Without a heart to dare or sword to draw
When Helen is defended, nor none so noble
Whose life were ill bestowed or death unfamed
160   Where Helen is the subject. Then, I say,
Well may we fight for her whom we know well
The world's large spaces cannot parallel.

Hector. Paris and Troilus, you have both said well,
And on the cause and question now in hand
165   Have glozed°—but superficially: not much
Unlike young men, whom Aristotle thought
Unfit to hear moral° philosophy.
The reasons you allege do more conduce
To the hot passion of distempered blood
170   Than to make up a free determination
'Twixt right and wrong; for pleasure and revenge
Have ears more deaf than adders° to the voice
Of any true decision. Nature craves
All dues be rendered to their owners. Now,
175   What nearer debt in all humanity
Than wife is to the husband? If this law
Of nature be corrupted through affection,°
And that great minds, of partial° indulgence

148 *rape* carrying off   150 *ransacked* carried off   155 *generous*
nobly born (therefore magnanimous)   165 *glozed* commented,
glossed   167 *moral* (Aristotle wrote "political" [*Nicomachean
Ethics,* I.3], but the use of "moral" here is paralleled in Erasmus,
Bacon, and many other contemporary translations and commentaries; the two words were roughly interchangeable in sixteenth-
century terminology)   172 *more deaf than adders* (cf. Psalm
58:4–5)   177 *affection* appetite   178 *partial* biased, favoring

To their benumbèd° wills, resist the same,
There is a law in each well-ordered nation   180
To curb those raging appetites that are
Most disobedient and refractory.
If Helen, then, be wife to Sparta's king,
As it is known she is, these moral laws
Of nature and of nations speak aloud   185
To have her back returned. Thus to persist
In doing wrong extenuates° not wrong,
But makes it much more heavy. Hector's opinion
Is this in way of truth. Yet ne'ertheless,
My spritely° brethren, I propend° to you   190
In resolution to keep Helen still;
For 'tis a cause that hath no mean dependence
Upon our joint and several° dignities.

Troilus. Why, there you touched the life of our design!
Were it not glory that we more affected   195
Than the performance of our heaving spleens,°
I would not wish a drop of Troyan blood
Spent more in her defense. But, worthy Hector,
She is a theme of honor and renown,
A spur to valiant and magnanimous deeds,   200
Whose present courage may beat down our foes
And fame in time to come canonize us;
For I presume brave Hector would not lose
So rich advantage of a promised glory
As smiles upon the forehead of this action   205
For the wide world's revenue.

Hector.   I am yours,
You valiant offspring of great Priamus.
I have a roisting° challenge sent amongst
The dull and factious nobles of the Greeks
Will strike amazement to their drowsy spirits.   210
I was advertised° their great general slept

---

179 *benumbèd* paralyzed (by affection and appetite)   187 *extenu-ates* lessens   190 *spritely* spirited   190 *propend* incline   193 *joint and several* collective and individual   196 *heaving spleens* angry passions   208 *roisting* noisy, clamorous   211 *advertised* informed

Whilst emulation° in the army crept;
This, I presume, will wake him.   *Exeunt.*

[Scene III.   *The Greek camp; near Achilles' tent.*]

Enter Thersites solus.

Thersites. How now, Thersites? What, lost in the
labyrinth of thy fury? Shall the elephant Ajax carry
it° thus? He beats me, and I rail at him. O worthy
satisfaction! Would it were otherwise—that I could
5   beat him, whilst he railed at me. 'Sfoot,° I'll learn
to conjure and raise devils, but I'll see° some issue
of my spiteful execrations. Then there's Achilles, a
rare enginer.° If Troy be not taken till these two
undermine it, the walls will stand till they fall of
10   themselves. O thou great thunder-darter of Olym-
pus, forget that thou art Jove, the king of gods;
and, Mercury, lose all the serpentine craft of thy
caduceus,° if ye take not that little, little, less than
little wit from them that they have; which short-
15   armed ignorance itself knows is so abundant scarce
it will not in circumvention deliver a fly from a
spider, without drawing their massy irons and
cutting the web. After this, the vengeance on the
whole camp! Or, rather, the Neapolitan bone-ache,°
20   for that, methinks, is the curse depending on those
that war for a placket.° I have said my prayers,
and devil Envy say "Amen." What ho, my Lord
Achilles!

212 *emulation* envious rivalry (see I.iii.134) II.iii.2–3 *carry it*
carry it off, come out on top   5 *'Sfoot* (an oath; "God's foot")
6 *but I'll see* rather than not see   8 *enginer* (a soldier in a
company used for ditch digging, tunneling, and otherwise under-
mining the battlements of an enemy camp)   13 *caduceus* (Mercury's staff, twined with serpents)   19 *Neapolitan bone-ache*
syphilis   21 *placket* opening in a petticoat (used obscenely, with
anatomical suggestion)

Enter Patroclus.

Patroclus. Who's there? Thersites? Good Thersites, come in and rail.   25

Thersites. If I could 'a' rememb'red a gilt counterfeit, thou wouldst not have slipped° out of my contemplation. But it is no matter; thyself upon thyself! The common curse of mankind, folly and ignorance, be thine in great revenue. Heaven bless° thee from a tutor, and discipline come not near thee. Let thy blood° be thy direction till thy death. Then, if she that lays thee out says thou art a fair corse,° I'll be sworn and sworn upon't she never shrouded any but lazars.° Amen. Where's Achilles?   30   35

Patroclus. What, art thou devout? Wast thou in prayer?

Thersites. Ay, the heavens hear me!

Patroclus. Amen.

Enter Achilles.

Achilles. Who's there?   40

Patroclus. Thersites, my lord.

Achilles. Where? Where? O, where? Art thou come? Why, my cheese, my digestion,° why hast thou not served thyself in to my table so many meals? Come, what's Agamemnon?   45

Thersites. Thy commander, Achilles. Then tell me, Patroclus, what's Achilles?

Patroclus. Thy lord, Thersites. Then tell me, I pray thee, what's thyself?

---

27 *slipped* (pun on "slip," a counterfeit coin of brass, covered with silver or gold)   30 *bless* i.e., save   32 *blood* passion   34 *corse* corpse   35 *lazars* lepers (with decayed bodies)   43 *my cheese, my digestion* (cheese served as the final course of a meal was thought to aid digestion)

50   *Thersites.* Thy knower, Patroclus. Then tell me, Pa-
     troclus, what art thou?

     Patroclus. Thou must tell that knowest.

     Achilles. O tell, tell.

     Thersites. I'll decline° the whole question. Agamem-
55   non commands Achilles, Achilles is my lord, I am
     Patroclus' knower, and Patroclus is a fool.

     Patroclus. You rascal!

     Thersites. Peace, fool! I have not done.

     Achilles. He is a privileged man.° Proceed, Thersites.

60   *Thersites.* Agamemnon is a fool, Achilles is a fool,
     Thersites is a fool, and, as aforesaid, Patroclus is a
     fool.

     Achilles. Derive this; come.

     Thersites. Agamemnon is a fool to offer° to command
65   Achilles, Achilles is a fool to be commanded of
     Agamemnon, Thersites is a fool to serve such a
     fool, and this Patroclus is a fool positive.

     Patroclus. Why am I a fool?

     Thersites. Make that demand of the Creator; it suffices
70   me thou art. Look you, who comes here?

     *Enter Agamemnon, Ulysses, Nestor, Diomedes, Ajax,
     and Calchas.*

     Achilles. Patroclus, I'll speak with nobody. Come in
     with me, Thersites.   *Exit.*

     Thersites. Here is such patchery,° such juggling, and
     such knavery. All the argument is a whore and a
75   cuckold, a good quarrel to draw emulous° factions

     ───────────────────────────────
     54 *decline* run through (in the grammatical sense, as to decline
     a noun)   59 *He is a privileged man* (in the sense that the railing
     of a professional jester or fool was "allowed")   64 *offer* attempt
     73 *patchery* roguery   75 *emulous* jealous

and bleed to death upon. Now, the dry serpigo° on
the subject, and war and lechery confound all!
[Exit.]

Agamemnon. Where is Achilles?

Patroclus. Within his tent, but ill-disposed, my lord.

Agamemnon. Let it be known to him that we are here.   80
He shent° our messengers, and we lay by
Our appertainments,° visiting of him.
Let him be told so, lest perchance he think
We dare not move° the question of our place
Or know not what we are.   85

Patroclus.   I shall so say to him.
[Exit.]

Ulysses. We saw him at the opening of his tent. He is
not sick.

Ajax. Yes, lion-sick, sick of proud heart. You may
call it melancholy if you will favor the man; but,
by my head, 'tis pride. But why, why? Let him show   90
us a cause. A word, my lord.
[Takes Agamemnon aside.]

Nestor. What moves Ajax thus to bay at him?

Ulysses. Achilles hath inveigled his fool from him.

Nestor. Who, Thersites?

Ulysses. He.   95

Nestor. Then will Ajax lack matter, if he have lost his
argument.°

Ulysses. No, you see, he is his argument that has his
argument, Achilles.

Nestor. All the better. Their fraction° is more our   100

---

76 *serpigo* a quickly spreading skin disease, with eruptions   81
shent rebuked   82 *appertainments* rights of rank   84 *move* raise
97 *argument* subject matter   100 *fraction* fracture, break

wish than their faction.° But it was a strong com-
posure° a fool could disunite.

Ulysses. The amity that wisdom knits not, folly may
easily untie.

Enter Patroclus.

105   Here comes Patroclus.

Nestor. No Achilles with him?

Ulysses. The elephant hath joints, but none for courtesy. His legs are legs for necessity, not for flexure.°

Patroclus. Achilles bids me say he is much sorry
110   If anything more than your sport and pleasure
Did move your greatness and this noble state°
To call upon him. He hopes it is no other
But, for your health and your digestion sake,
An after-dinner's breath.°

Agamemnon.   Hear you, Patroclus.
115   We are too well acquainted with these answers;
But his evasion, winged thus swift with scorn,
Cannot outfly our apprehensions.°
Much attribute he hath, and much the reason
Why we ascribe it to him; yet all his virtues,
120   Not virtuously on his own part beheld,°
Do in our eyes begin to lose their gloss—
Yea, like fair fruit in an unwholesome dish,
Are like to rot untasted. Go and tell him
We come to speak with him; and you shall not sin
125   If you do say we think him overproud
And underhonest,° in self-assumption greater
Than in the note of judgment,° and worthier than
    himself

---

101 *faction* union   101–02 *composure* union   108 *flexure* bending
111 *noble state* assemblage of noblemen   114 *breath* exercise
117 *apprehensions* perceptions   120 *Not . . . beheld* not carried
with modesty   126 *underhonest* calculating, not open   127 *the note
of judgment* the opinion of men of judgment

Here tend the savage strangeness° he puts on,
Disguise the holy strength of their command,
And underwrite in an observing kind   130
His humorous predominance;° yea, watch
His pettish lunes,° his ebbs and flows, as if
The passage and whole carriage of this action
Rode on his tide. Go tell him this; and add
That, if he overhold° his price so much,   135
We'll none of him; but let him, like an engine°
Not portable, lie under this report:
"Bring action hither, this cannot go to war."
A stirring dwarf we do allowance° give
Before a sleeping giant. Tell him so.   140

Patroclus. I shall, and bring his answer presently.
                                        [*Exit.*]

Agamemnon. In second voice we'll not be satisfied;
We come to speak with him. Ulysses, enter you.
                                Exit Ulysses.

Ajax. What is he more than another?

Agamemnon. No more than what he thinks he is.   145

Ajax. Is he so much? Do you not think he thinks
himself a better man than I am?

Agamemnon. No question.

Ajax. Will you subscribe his thought, and say he is?

Agamemnon. No, noble Ajax; you are as strong, as   150
valiant, as wise, no less noble, much more gentle,
and altogether more tractable.

Ajax. Why should a man be proud? How doth pride
grow? I know not what pride is.

---

128 *tend the savage strangeness* wait upon the rude aloofness
129–31 *Disguise . . . predominance* allow to be hidden the divine
authority of their command, and, in a form of acquiescence,
subscribe to his eccentric notion of superiority   132 *pettish lunes*
capricious variations (like the changes of the moon)   135 *overhold*
overvalue   136 *engine* mechanical contrivance (here, military)
139 *allowance* praise

¹⁵⁵ *Agamemnon.* Your mind is the clearer and your vir-
    tues the fairer. He that is proud eats up himself.
    Pride is his own glass,° his own trumpet, his own
    chronicle; and whatever praises itself but in the
    deed, devours the deed in the praise.

Enter Ulysses.

¹⁶⁰ *Ajax.* I do hate a proud man as I hate the engend'r-
    ing of toads.

Nestor. [*Aside*] And yet he loves himself. Is't not
    strange?

Ulysses. Achilles will not to the field tomorrow.

Agamemnon. What's his excuse?

¹⁶⁵ *Ulysses.*   He doth rely on none,
    But carries on the stream of his dispose°
    Without observance or respect of any,
    In will peculiar and in self-admission.°

Agamemnon. Why will he not upon our fair request
¹⁷⁰   Untent his person and share th'air with us?

Ulysses. Things small as nothing, for request's sake
        only,°
    He makes important. Possessed he is with great-
        ness,
    And speaks not to himself but with a pride
    That quarrels at self-breath.° Imagined worth
¹⁷⁵ Holds in his blood such swoln and hot discourse
    That 'twixt his mental and his active parts
    Kingdomed° Achilles in commotion rages
    And batters down himself. What should I say?

---

157 *glass* mirror   166 *dispose* inclination   168 *In . . . self-admission*
i.e., with will exclusively his own and with self-approval   171 *for
request's sake only* only because requested   174 *That quarrels at
self-breath* that quarrels with speech itself   177 *Kingdomed* i.e.,
as though Achilles were himself a kingdom engaged in civil
strife

He is so plaguy proud that the death-tokens° of it
Cry "No recovery."

Agamemnon.   Let Ajax go to him.   180
  Dear lord, go you and greet him in his tent;
  'Tis said he holds you well, and will be led
  At your request a little from himself.

Ulysses. O Agamemnon, let it not be so!
  We'll consecrate the steps that Ajax makes   185
  When they go from Achilles. Shall the proud lord
  That bastes his arrogance with his own seam°
  And never suffers matter of the world
 ⁻Enter his thoughts, save such as doth revolve
  And ruminate himself—shall he be worshiped   190
  Of that we hold an idol more than he?
  No, this thrice-worthy and right valiant lord
  Shall not so stale his palm,° nobly acquired,
  Nor, by my will, assubjugate° his merit,
  As amply titled as Achilles' is,   195
  By going to Achilles.
  That were to enlard his fat-already pride,
  And add more coals to Cancer° when he burns
  With entertaining great Hyperion.°
  This lord go to him! Jupiter forbid,   200
  And say in thunder, "Achilles, go to him."

Nestor. [*Aside*] O, this is well. He rubs the vein° of
  him.

Diomedes. [*Aside*] And how his silence drinks up his
  applause!

Ajax. If I go to him, with my armèd fist
  I'll pash° him o'er the face.   205

Agamemnon. O, no! You shall not go.

---

179 *death-tokens* external symptoms of the plague preceding death
187 *seam* grease, fat 193 *stale his palm* detract from his glory
194 *assubjugate* debase 198 *Cancer* i.e., summer, which begins
under this sign of the zodiac 199 *Hyperion* the sun 202 *vein*
mood 205 *pash* bash

Ajax. An he be proud with me, I'll pheese° his pride. Let me go to him.

Ulysses. Not for the worth that hangs upon our quarrel.

210 *Ajax.* A paltry, insolent fellow!

Nestor. [*Aside*] How he describes himself!

Ajax. Can he not be sociable?

Ulysses. [*Aside*] The raven chides blackness.

Ajax. I'll let his humor's blood.°

215 *Agamemnon.* [*Aside*] He will be the physician that should be the patient.

Ajax. An all men were of my mind——

Ulysses. [*Aside*] Wit would be out of fashion.

Ajax. 'A° should not bear it so, 'a should eat swords
220   first! Shall pride carry it?

Nestor. [*Aside*] An 'twould, you'd carry half.

Ulysses. [*Aside*] 'A would have ten shares.

Ajax. I will knead him; I'll make him supple.

Nestor. [*Aside*] He's not yet through° warm. Force°
225   him with praises; pour in, pour, his ambition is dry.

Ulysses. [*To Agamemnon*] My lord, you feed too much on this dislike.

Nestor. Our noble general, do not do so.

Diomedes. You must prepare to fight without Achilles.

Ulysses. Why, 'tis this naming of him does him harm.
230   Here is a man—but 'tis before his face;
     I will be silent.

---

207 *pheese* settle the business of   214 *let his humor's blood* i.e., cure him by letting blood, thus decreasing the strength of Achilles' humor, his mood of pride   219 *'A* he   224 *through* thoroughly 224 *Force* stuff

Nestor. Wherefore should you so?
  He is not emulous,° as Achilles is.

Ulysses. Know the whole world, he is as valiant——

Ajax. A whoreson dog, that shall palter° with us thus!
  Would he were a Troyan!   235

Nestor. What a vice were it in Ajax now——

Ulysses. If he were proud——

Diomedes. Or covetous of praise——

Ulysses. Ay, or surly borne——

Diomedes. Or strange, or self-affected!°   240

Ulysses. Thank the heavens, lord, thou art of sweet
      composure;
  Praise him that gat° thee, she that gave thee suck;
  Famed be thy tutor, and thy parts of nature
  Thrice-famed beyond, beyond all erudition;°
  But he that disciplined thine arms to fight,   245
  Let Mars divide eternity in twain
  And give him half; and, for thy vigor,
  Bull-bearing Milo° his addition° yield
  To sinewy Ajax. I will not praise thy wisdom,
  Which, like a bourn, a pale,° a shore, confines   250
  Thy spacious and dilated parts. Here's Nestor,
  Instructed by the antiquary times,°
  He must, he is, he cannot but be wise;
  But pardon, father Nestor, were your days
  As green as Ajax, and your brain so tempered,   255
  You should not have the eminence of him,
  But be as Ajax.

---

232 *emulous* jealously competitive 234 *palter* play shifty games,
dodge 240 *strange, or self-affected* haughty, or self-centered
242 *gat* begat 243–44 *thy parts ... erudition* your natural attributes
three times more famous (i.e., than your tutor), even more famous
than all learning itself 248 *Milo* (a famous Greek athlete, said
to have carried a bull upon his shoulders for forty yards) 248
addition title, i.e., "Bull-bearing" 250 *a bourn, a pale* a boundary,
a fence 252 *Instructed by the antiquary times* i.e., his wisdom
learned from olden times, all the years of his old age

Ajax.   Shall I call you father?

Nestor. Ay, my good son.

Diomedes.   Be ruled by him, Lord Ajax.

Ulysses. There is no tarrying here; the hart Achilles
260   Keeps thicket. Please it our great general
To call together all his state° of war;
Fresh kings are come to Troy. Tomorrow,
We must with all our main° of power stand fast.
And here's a lord—come knights from east to west,
265   And cull their flower, Ajax shall cope the best.

Agamemnon. Go we to council. Let Achilles sleep;
Light boats sail swift, though greater hulks draw
    deep.   *Exeunt.*

261 *state* noblemen in council   263 *main* might

[ACT III

Scene I. *Troy; Priam's palace.*]

Music sounds within. Enter Pandarus and a Servant.

Pandarus. Friend you, pray you a word. Do you not
follow the young Lord Paris?

Servant. Ay, sir, when he goes before me.

Pandarus. You depend° upon him, I mean.

Servant. Sir, I do depend upon the Lord.   5

Pandarus. You depend upon a notable gentleman; I
must needs praise him.

Servant. The Lord be praised!

Pandarus. You know me, do you not?

Servant. Faith, sir, superficially.   10

Pandarus. Friend, know me better. I am the Lord
Pandarus.

Servant. I hope I shall know your honor better.

Pandarus. I do desire it.

III.i.4 *depend* i.e., serve, in a position of dependence

15 *Servant.* You are in the state of grace.°

Pandarus. Grace?° Not so, friend. Honor and lord-
ship are my titles. What music is this?

Servant. I do but partly know, sir. It is music in
parts.°

20 *Pandarus.* Know you the musicians?

Servant. Wholly, sir.

Pandarus. Who play they to?

Servant. To the hearers, sir.

Pandarus. At whose pleasure, friend?

5 *Servant.* At mine, sir, and theirs that love music.

Pandarus. Command, I mean, friend.

Servant. Who shall I command, sir?

Pandarus. Friend, we understand not one another. I
am too courtly, and thou too cunning. At whose
30   request do these men play?

Servant. That's to't, indeed, sir. Marry, sir, at the request of Paris, my lord, who is there in person;
with him the mortal Venus, the heartblood of
beauty, love's invisible soul.

35 *Pandarus.* Who? My cousin Cressida?

Servant. No, sir, Helen. Could not you find out that
by her attributes?

Pandarus. It should seem, fellow, that thou hast not
seen the Lady Cressid. I come to speak with
40   Paris from the Prince Troilus. I will make a com-

---

15 *You . . . grace* (pretending that Pandarus meant that he desired
his own honor to be better; also, perhaps, the servant is hinting
for a gratuity) 16 *Grace* (the courtly title of a duke, etc.)
18–19 *music in parts* music containing several vocal or instrumental
parts in counterpoint

plimental assault upon him, for my business
seethes.°

Servant. Sodden business! There's a stewed° phrase,
indeed.

Enter Paris and Helen [with courtiers].

Pandarus. Fair be to you, my lord, and to all this fair   45
company. Fair desires in all fair measure fairly
guide them. Especially to you, fair queen, fair
thoughts be your fair pillow.

Helen. Dear lord, you are full of fair words.

Pandarus. You speak your fair pleasure, sweet queen.   50
Fair prince, here is good broken music.°

Paris. You have broke it, cousin; and, by my life, you
shall make it whole again; you shall piece it out
with a piece of your performance. Nell, he is full
of harmony.   55

Pandarus. Truly, lady, no.

Helen. O, sir!

Pandarus. Rude,° in sooth; in good sooth, very rude.

Paris. Well said, my lord. Well, you say so in fits.°

Pandarus. I have business to my lord, dear queen. My   60
lord, will you vouchsafe me a word?

Helen. Nay, this shall not hedge us out. We'll hear you
sing, certainly.

Pandarus. Well, sweet queen, you are pleasant with
me. But, marry, thus, my lord: my dear lord and   65
most esteemed friend, your brother Troilus——

42 *seethes* boils, i.e., demands immediate attention   43 *stewed*
(1) boiled (2) pertaining to stews, or brothels (?)   51 *broken
music* music the parts for which are written for different solo
instruments, or groups of different instruments   58 *Rude* unpol-
ished, rough   59 *fits* sections or divisions of a song (perhaps
Paris means, "you say so only at times")

Helen. My Lord Pandarus, honey-sweet lord——

Pandarus. Go to, sweet queen, go to——commends himself most affectionately to you.

70 *Helen.* You shall not bob° us out of our melody. If
you do, our melancholy upon your head!

Pandarus. Sweet queen, sweet queen, that's a sweet
queen, i' faith.

Helen. And to make a sweet lady sad is a sour offense.

75 *Pandarus.* Nay, that shall not serve your turn; that
shall it not, in truth, la. Nay, I care not for such
words; no, no. And, my lord, he desires you that,
if the king call for him at supper, you will make his
excuse.

80 *Helen.* My Lord Pandarus——

Pandarus. What says my sweet queen, my very, very
sweet queen?

Paris. What exploit's in hand? Where sups he tonight?

Helen. Nay, but my Lord——

85 *Pandarus.* What says my sweet queen? My cousin will
fall out with you.°

Helen. You must not know where he sups.

Paris. I'll lay my life, with my disposer° Cressida.

Pandarus. No, no; no such matter; you are wide.°
90 Come, your disposer is sick.

Paris. Well, I'll make excuse.

Pandarus. Ay, good my lord. Why should you say
Cressida? No, your poor disposer's sick.

Paris. I spy.

70 *bob* cheat   85–86 *My cousin . . . you* (Pandarus lightly pretends
that Paris, his "cousin," will become jealous if Helen continues
to flirt with him, Pandarus)   88 *disposer* i.e., she who rules him
(Paris jokingly uses an excessively gallant term)   89 *wide* wide
of the mark

Pandarus. You spy? What do you spy? Come, give 95
me an instrument now, sweet queen.

Helen. Why, this is kindly done.

Pandarus. My niece is horribly in love with a thing
you have, sweet queen.°

Helen. She shall have it, my lord, if it be not my Lord 100
Paris.

Pandarus. He? No, she'll none of him; they two are
twain.°

Helen. Falling in, after falling out, may make them
three.° 105

Pandarus. Come, come, I'll hear no more of this. I'll
sing you a song now.

Helen. Ay, ay, prithee. Now by my troth, sweet lord,
thou hast a fine forehead.

Pandarus. Ay, you may, you may.° 110

Helen. Let thy song be love. This love will undo us all.
O Cupid, Cupid, Cupid!

Pandarus. Love! Ay, that it shall, i' faith.

Paris. Ay, good now, "Love, love, nothing but love."

Pandarus. In good troth, it begins so: [*Sings.*] 115
Love, love, nothing but love, still love still more!
For, O, love's bow shoots buck and doe.
The shaft confounds not that° it wounds,
But tickles still the sore.°
These lovers cry, O ho! they die! 120
Yet that which seems the wound to kill

98–99 *My niece is . . . sweet queen* i.e., Cressida loves, or would
love to have, a sexual partner such as Paris is to Helen   103 *twain*
at odds, have nothing in common   104–105 *Falling in . . . them
three* (Helen's bawdy joke picks up the train of thought begun
by Pandarus)   110 *you may*, i.e., have your joke   118 *confounds
not that* does not distress because   119 *sore* wound (perhaps a
pun on the term for a buck in his fourth year)

Doth turn O ho! to Ha, ha, he!
So dying love lives still.
O ho! a while, but Ha, ha, ha!
125   O ho! groans out for Ha, ha, ha!—Heigh ho!

Helen. In love, i' faith, to the very tip of the nose.

Paris. He eats nothing but doves, love, and that breeds
hot blood, and hot blood begets hot thoughts, and
hot thoughts beget hot deeds, and hot deeds is love.

130   *Pandarus.* Is this the generation of love—hot blood,
hot thoughts, and hot deeds? Why, they are vipers.
Is love a generation of vipers?° Sweet lord, who's
a-field today?

Paris. Hector, Deiphobus, Helenus, Antenor, and all
135   the gallantry of Troy. I would fain have armed
today, but my Nell would not have it so. How
chance my brother Troilus went not?

Helen. He hangs the lip at something. You know all,
Lord Pandarus.

140   *Pandarus.* Not I, honey-sweet queen. I long to hear
how they sped° today. You'll remember your
brother's excuse?

Paris. To a hair.°

Pandarus. Farewell, sweet queen.

145   *Helen.* Commend me to your niece.

Pandarus. I will, sweet queen. [*Exit.*] *Sound a retreat.*

Paris. They're come from the field. Let us to Priam's
hall
To greet the warriors. Sweet Helen, I must woo you
To help unarm our Hector. His stubborn buckles,
150   With these your white enchanting fingers touched,
Shall more obey than to the edge of steel

132 *a generation of vipers* (cf. Matthew 3:7) 141 *how they
sped* i.e., the results of their action 143 *To a hair* (does Paris
jokingly recall Troilus' "pretty answer" about the hairs on his
chin [see I.ii.169–71?])

   Or force of Greekish sinews. You shall do more
   Than all the island kings°—disarm great Hector.

Helen. 'Twill make us proud to be his servant, Paris;
   Yea, what he shall receive of us in duty   *155*
   Gives us more palm in beauty than we have,
   Yea, overshines ourself.

Paris. Sweet, above thought I love thee.   *Exeunt.*

[Scene II. *Within Troy.*]

Enter Pandarus and Troilus' Man.

Pandarus. How now, where's thy master? At my
   cousin Cressida's?

Man. No, sir; he stays for you to conduct him thither.

Enter Troilus.

Pandarus. O, here he comes. How now, how now?

Troilus. Sirrah, walk off.   [*Exit Man.*]   *5*

Pandarus. Have you seen my cousin?

Troilus. No, Pandarus. I stalk about her door
   Like a strange soul upon the Stygian° banks
   Staying for waftage.° O, be thou my Charon,°
   And give me swift transportation to those fields   *10*
   Where I may wallow in the lily beds
   Proposed° for the deserver. O gentle Pandar,
   From Cupid's shoulder pluck his painted wings,
   And fly with me to Cressid.

153 *island kings* i.e., kings of the Grecian islands III.ii.8 *Stygian*
(from Styx, the principal river of the underworld) 9 *waftage* passage
across water 9 *Charon* (ferryman of the dead, across the Styx
to Hades) 12 *Proposed* promised

15 *Pandarus.* Walk here i' th' orchard. I'll bring her
       straight.   *Exit Pandarus.*

    Troilus. I am giddy; expectation whirls me round.
       Th' imaginary relish is so sweet
       That it enchants my sense. What will it be
20   When that the wat'ry° palates taste indeed
       Love's thrice-repurèd° nectar? Death, I fear me,
       Sounding° destruction, or some joy too fine,
       Too subtle, potent, tuned too sharp in sweetness
       For the capacity of my ruder° powers.
25   I fear it much; and I do fear besides
       That I shall lose distinction° in my joys,
       As doth a battle, when they charge on heaps
       The enemy flying.

                      Enter Pandarus.

    Pandarus. She's making her ready; she'll come
30   straight; you must be witty° now. She does so blush,
       and fetches her wind so short as if she were frayed
       with a spirit.° I'll fetch her. It is the prettiest vil-
       lain;° she fetches her breath as short as a new-
       ta'en sparrow.   *Exit Pandarus.*

35 *Troilus.* Even such a passion doth embrace my bosom.
       My heart beats thicker than a feverous pulse,
       And all my powers do their bestowing° lose,
       Like vassalage° at unawares encount'ring
       The eye of majesty.

                 Enter Pandarus and Cressida.

40 *Pandarus.* Come, come, what need you blush? Shame's
       a baby. Here she is now; swear the oaths now to

    20 *wat'ry* watering (cf. mouth "watering" with appetite)   21 *thrice-
    repurèd* distilled again and again (i.e., to extract the purest
    essence)   22 *Sounding* swooning   24 *ruder* physical   26 *distinc-
    tion* ability to distinguish   30 *be witty* be alert, have your wits
    about you   31–32 *frayed with a spirit* frightened by a ghost   33
    villain (here a term of endearment)   37 *bestowing* proper use
    38 *vassalage* vassals

her that you have sworn to me. What! Are you
gone again? You must be watched ere you be made
tame,° must you? Come your ways, come your
ways; an you draw backward, we'll put you i' the   45
fills.° Why do you not speak to her? Come, draw
this curtain,° and let's see your picture. Alas the
day, how loath you are to offend daylight! An
'twere dark, you'd close° sooner. So, so; rub on,
and kiss the mistress.° How now, a kiss in fee-   50
farm!° Build there, carpenter; the air is sweet.
Nay, you shall fight your hearts out ere I part you.
The falcon as the tercel, for all the ducks i' the
river.° Go to, go to.

Troilus. You have bereft me of all words, lady.   55

Pandarus. Words pay no debts, give her deeds; but
she'll bereave you o' the deeds too if she call your
activity in question. What, billing again? Here's "In
witness whereof the parties interchangeably"°—
Come in, come in. I'll go get a fire.   [*Exit.*]   60

Cressida. Will you walk in, my lord?

Troilus. O Cressid, how often have I wished me thus!

Cressida. Wished, my lord? The gods grant—O my
lord!

Troilus. What should they grant? What makes this   65
pretty abruption?° What too curious° dreg espies
my sweet lady in the fountain of our love?

43–44 *watched ere you be made tame* i.e., prodded on until made
submissive (a hawk was tamed by "watching" it, i.e., keeping it constantly awake) 46 *fills* shafts (of a cart) 47 *curtain* i.e., her
veil 49 *close* move together 49–50 *rub . . . mistress* (terms from
bowling, where "to rub" was to meet obstacles in the way of the
small object-ball, called the "mistress"; bowls are still said "to
kiss" when they touch gently) 50–51 *a kiss in fee-farm* i.e., a
long kiss (a fee-farm was a grant of lands in perpetuity) 53–54
The falcon . . . river i.e., I will bet on the falcon (the term applied
only to the female of the species) against the tercel (the male)
to bring down any game 58–59 *"In witness . . . interchangeably"*
(a legal formula, usually ending with the words "have set their
hands and seals") 66 *abruption* breaking off 66 *too curious*
overly cautious, anxious, or inquisitive

Cressida. More dregs than water, if my fears have
eyes.

70 *Troilus.* Fears make devils of cherubins; they never
see truly.

Cressida. Blind fear, that seeing reason leads, finds
safer footing than blind reason stumbling without
fear. To fear the worst oft cures the worse.

75 *Troilus.* O, let my lady apprehend no fear; in all
Cupid's pageant there is presented no monster.°

Cressida. Nor nothing monstrous neither?

Troilus. Nothing but our undertakings when we vow
to weep seas, live in fire, eat rocks, tame tigers,
80 thinking it harder for our mistress to devise imposi-
tion enough than for us to undergo any difficulty
imposed. This is the monstruosity in love, lady,
that the will is infinite and the execution confined;
that the desire is boundless and the act a slave to
85 limit.

Cressida. They say all lovers swear more performance than they are able, and yet reserve an ability
that they never perform, vowing more than the
perfection of ten and discharging less than the
90 tenth part of one. They that have the voice of
lions and the act of hares—are they not monsters?

Troilus. Are there such? Such are not we. Praise us
as we are tasted,° allow us as we prove; our head
shall go bare till merit crown it. No perfection in
95 reversion° shall have a praise in present; we will
not name desert before his birth, and, being born,
his addition shall be humble.° Few words to fair
faith. Troilus shall be such to Cressid, as what envy

75–76 *apprehend . . . no monster* (Troilus refers to some type of
dramatic allegory such as Cupid might be depicted as "presenting,"
or the emblematic characters, such as Fear, in pageants or court
masques)   93 *tasted* tested   95 *reversion* right or anticipation of
future possession   97 *his addition shall be humble* it shall be
given no high or pompous titles

can say worst shall be a mock for his truth, and
what truth can speak truest not truer than Troilus.° 100

Cressida. Will you walk in, my lord?

Enter Pandarus.

Pandarus. What, blushing still? Have you not done
talking yet?

Cressida. Well, uncle, what folly I commit, I dedicate
to you.   105

Pandarus. I thank you for that. If my lord get a boy
of you, you'll give him me. Be true to my lord;
if he flinch, chide me for it.

Troilus. You know now your hostages: your uncle's
word and my firm faith.   110

Pandarus. Nay, I'll give my word for her too. Our
kindred, though they be long ere they be wooed,
they are constant being won. They are burrs, I can
tell you; they'll stick where they are thrown.

Cressida. Boldness comes to me now and brings me
heart.   115
    Prince Troilus, I have loved you night and day
    For many weary months.

Troilus. Why was my Cressid then so hard to win?

Cressida. Hard to seem won; but I was won, my lord,
    With the first glance that ever—pardon me;   120
    If I confess much you will play the tyrant.
    I love you now, but, till now, not so much
    But I might master it. In faith, I lie;
    My thoughts were like unbridled children grown
    Too headstrong for their mother. See, we fools!   125
    Why have I blabbed? Who shall be true to us
    When we are so unsecret to ourselves?

98-100 *as what envy . . . Troilus* so that the worst malice can do
is sneer at his constancy, and even the best truth that truth can
speak will not be truer than Troilus

But, though I loved you well, I wooed you not;
And yet, good faith, I wished myself a man,
130   Or that we women had men's privilege
Of speaking first. Sweet, bid me hold my tongue,
For in this rapture I shall surely speak
The thing I shall repent. See, see! Your silence,
Cunning in dumbness, from my weakness draws
135   My very soul of counsel.° Stop my mouth.

Troilus. And shall, albeit sweet music issues thence.

Pandarus. Pretty, i'faith.

Cressida. My lord, I do beseech you, pardon me;
'Twas not my purpose thus to beg a kiss.
140   I am ashamed. O heavens, what have I done?
For this time will I take my leave, my lord.

Troilus. Your leave, sweet Cressid?

Pandarus. Leave! An you take leave till tomorrow
morning——

Cressida. Pray you, content you.

145   *Troilus.*   What offends you, lady?

Cressida. Sir, mine own company.

Troilus. You cannot shun yourself.

Cressida. Let me go and try.
I have a kind of self resides with you;
150   But an unkind self, that itself will leave
To be another's fool.° I would be gone.
Where is my wit? I know not what I speak.

Troilus. Well know they what they speak that speak
so wisely.

Cressida. Perchance, my lord, I show more craft than
love,
155   And fell so roundly° to a large° confession

135 *very soul of counsel* inmost thoughts and secrets   151 *fool*
dupe   155 *roundly* frankly, openly   155 *large* unrestrained

To angle for your thoughts. But you are wise,
Or else you love not, for to be wise and love
Exceeds man's might;° that dwells with gods above.

Troilus. O that I thought it could be in a woman—
As, if it can, I will presume in you—   160
To feed for aye her lamp and flames of love;
To keep her constancy in plight and youth,°
Outliving beauty's outward,° with a mind
That doth renew swifter than blood decays;
Or that persuasion could but thus convince me   165
That my integrity and truth to you
Might be affronted° with the match and weight
Of such a winnowed° purity in love:
How were I then uplifted! But, alas,
I am as true as truth's simplicity,   170
And simpler than the infancy of truth.

Cressida. In that I'll war with you.

Troilus.   O virtuous fight,
When right with right wars who shall be most right!
True swains in love shall in the world to come
Approve° their truth by Troilus. When their
     rhymes,   175
Full of protest, of oath and big compare,
Wants similes, truth tired with iteration,
"As true as steel, as plantage to the moon,°
As sun to day, as turtle° to her mate,
As iron to adamant,° as earth to the center,"   180
Yet, after all comparisons of truth,
As truth's authentic author to be cited,
"As true as Troilus" shall crown up the verse
And sanctify the numbers.°

156–58 *But you are wise . . . man's might* i.e., you are reasonable,
which means you are not in love, for no man can follow reason
and love at the same time   162 *in plight and youth* as it was
when it was plighted, and as fresh   163 *beauty's outward* external,
transitory beauty   167 *affronted* confronted, i.e., equaled   168
winnowed i.e., distilled   175 *Approve* attest   178 *plantage to the
moon* (the moon was thought to influence plantage, or vegetation)
179 *turtle* turtledove (an emblem of eternally faithful love)   180
adamant the loadstone (magnetic)   184 *numbers* metrical verses

Cressida.   Prophet may you be!
185 If I be false or swerve a hair from truth,
When time is old and hath forgot itself,
When waterdrops have worn the stones of Troy,
And blind oblivion swallowed cities up,
And mighty states characterless° are grated
190 To dusty nothing, yet let memory,
From false to false among false maids in love,
Upbraid my falsehood! When they've said, "As false
As air, as water, wind or sandy earth,
As fox to lamb, as wolf to heifer's calf,
195 Pard to the hind,° or stepdame to her son,"
Yea, let them say, to stick the heart of falsehood,
"As false as Cressid."

Pandarus. Go to, a bargain made. Seal it, seal it; I'll
be the witness. Here I hold your hand, here my
200 cousin's. If ever you prove false one to another,
since I have taken such pains to bring you together, let all pitiful goers-between be called to the
world's end after my name; call them all Pandars.
Let all constant men be Troiluses, all false women
205 Cressids, and all brokers-between Pandars! Say,
"Amen."

Troilus. Amen.

Cressida. Amen.

Pandarus. Amen. Whereupon I will show you a cham-
210 ber which bed,° because° it shall not speak of your
pretty encounters, press it to death. Away!
                    Exeunt [Troilus and Cressida].
And Cupid grant all tongue-tied maidens here
Bed, chamber, Pandar to provide this gear!   *Exit.*

---

189 *characterless* without an identifying mark   195 *Pard to the hind* leopard to the doe   210 *which bed* the bed in which   210 *because* (1) for the reason that (normal usage) (2) in order that (?)

[Scene III.   *The Greek camp.*]

Enter Ulysses, Diomedes, Nestor, Agamemnon,
[*Menelaus, Ajax, and*] *Calchas. Flourish* [*of trumpets.*]

Calchas. Now, princes, for the service I have done,
　Th' advantage of the time prompts me aloud
　To call for recompense. Appear it to mind
　That through the sight° I bear in things to come,
　I have abandoned Troy, left my possession,　　　　　5
　Incurred a traitor's name, exposed myself,
　From certain and possessed conveniences,
　To doubtful fortunes, sequest'ring° from me all
　That time, acquaintance, custom, and condition
　Made tame° and most familiar to my nature;　　　10
　And here, to do you service, am become
　As new into the world, strange, unacquainted.
　I do beseech you, as in way of taste,°
　To give me now a little benefit
　Out of those many registered in promise,　　　　15
　Which, you say, live to come in my behalf.

Agamemnon. What wouldst thou of us, Troyan? Make
　demand.

Calchas. You have a Troyan prisoner, called Antenor,
　Yesterday took; Troy holds him very dear.
　Oft have you—often have you thanks therefor—　　20
　Desired my Cressid in right great exchange,°
　Whom Troy hath still° denied; but this Antenor

III.iii.4 *sight* i.e., foresight　8 *sequest'ring* putting aside　10 *tame*
familiar, comfortable　13 *taste* foretaste　21 *right great exchange*
exchange for someone sufficiently great　22 *still* always

I know is such a wrest° in their affairs
That their negotiations all must slack,
25 Wanting his manage; and they will almost
Give us a prince of blood, a son of Priam,
In change of him. Let him be sent, great princes,
And he shall buy my daughter; and her presence
Shall quite strike off all service I have done
In most accepted° pain.

30 *Agamemnon.*   Let Diomedes bear him,
And bring us Cressid hither; Calchas shall have
What he requests of us. Good Diomed,
Furnish you fairly, for this interchange.
Withal bring word if Hector will tomorrow
35 Be answered in his challenge. Ajax is ready.

Diomedes. This shall I undertake, and 'tis a burden
Which I am proud to bear.   *Exit [with Calchas].*

          Achilles and Patroclus stand in their tent.°

Ulysses. Achilles stands i' th' entrance of his tent.
Please it our general pass strangely° by him,
40 As if he were forgot; and, princes all,
Lay negligent and loose regard upon him.
I will come last. 'Tis like he'll question me
Why such unplausive° eyes are bent, why turned,
     on him.
If so, I have derision medicinable
45 To use between your strangeness and his pride,
Which his own will shall have desire to drink.
It may do good; pride hath no other glass
To show° itself but pride, for supple knees
Feed arrogance and are the proud man's fees.

50 *Agamemnon.* We'll execute your purpose, and put on
A form of strangeness as we pass along.
So do each lord, and either greet him not

23 *wrest* a key used for tuning stringed instruments (i.e., the influence of harmony in Trojan discussions)   30 *accepted* cheer-
fully endured   37 s.d. *stand in their tent* i.e., appear and stand
in the entrance of their tent   39 *strangely* aloofly   43 *unplausive*
disapproving   48 *show* mirror

    Or else disdainfully, which shall shake him more
    Than if not looked on. I will lead the way.

Achilles. What comes the general to speak with me?   55
    You know my mind; I'll fight no more 'gainst Troy.

Agamemnon. What says Achilles? Would he aught
    with us?

Nestor. Would you, my lord, aught with the general?

Achilles. No.

Nestor. Nothing, my lord.   60

Agamemnon. The better.

Achilles. Good day, good day.

Menelaus. How do you? How do you?

Achilles. What, does the cuckold scorn me?

Ajax. How now, Patroclus?   65

Achilles. Good morrow, Ajax.

Ajax. Ha?

Achilles. Good morrow.

Ajax. Ay, and good next day too.   *Exeunt.*

Achilles. What mean these fellows? Know they not
    Achilles?   70

Patroclus. They pass by strangely. They were used to
    bend,
    To send their smiles before them to Achilles,
    To come as humbly as they used to creep
    To holy altars.

Achilles.   What, am I poor of late?
    'Tis certain, greatness, once fall'n out with fortune,   75
    Must fall out with men too. What the declined is
    He shall as soon read in the eyes of others
    As feel in his own fall; for men, like butterflies,

      Show not their mealy° wings but to the summer,
80   And not a man, for being simply man,
      Hath any honor, but honor for those honors
      That are without° him, as place, riches, and favor,
      Prizes of accident as oft as merit;
      Which when they fall, as being slippery standers,
85   The love that leaned on them as slippery too,
      Doth one pluck down another, and together
      Die in the fall. But 'tis not so with me;
      Fortune and I are friends. I do enjoy
      At ample point° all that I did possess,
90   Save these men's looks—who do, methinks, find out
      Something not worth in me such rich beholding
      As they have often given. Here is Ulysses;
      I'll interrupt his reading.
      How now, Ulysses.

Ulysses.   Now, great Thetis' son.

Achilles. What are you reading?

95 *Ulysses.*   A strange fellow here
      Writes me that man, how dearly ever parted,°
      How much in having, or without or in,°
      Cannot make boast to have that which he hath,
      Nor feels not what he owes but by reflection;°
100 As when his virtues aiming upon others
      Heat them, and they retort that heat again
      To the first giver.

Achilles.   This is not strange, Ulysses.
      The beauty that is borne here in the face
      The bearer knows not, but commends itself
105 To others' eyes; nor doth the eye itself,
      That most pure spirit of sense, behold itself,
      Not going from itself; but eye to eye opposed

---

79 *mealy* powdery   82 *without* external to   89 *At ample point* in full measure, in every way   96 *how dearly ever parted* however excellently endowed by nature   97 *How much . . . or in* however much in possession, whether externally or internally   99 *Nor feels . . . by reflection* and understands what he himself possesses (*owes* = "owns") only as it is reflected

Salutes each other with each other's form;
For speculation° turns not to itself
Till it hath traveled and is married there   110
Where it may see itself. This is not strange at all.

Ulysses. I do not strain at the position°—
    It is familiar—but at the author's drift;
    Who in his circumstance° expressly proves
    That no man is the lord of anything—   115
    Though in and of him there be much consisting°—
    Till he communicate his parts to others.
    Nor doth he of himself know them for aught
    Till he behold them formèd in th' applause
    Where they're extended;° who,° like an arch, rever-   120
        b'rate
    The voice again, or, like a gate of steel
    Fronting the sun, receives and renders back
    His figure and his heat. I was much rapt in this,
    And apprehended here immediately   125
    Th' unknown Ajax.
    Heavens, what a man is there! A very horse,
    That has he knows not what. Nature, what things
        there are
    Most abject in regard and dear in use!°
    What things again most dear in the esteem
    And poor in worth! Now shall we see tomorrow,   130
    An act that very chance doth throw upon him:
    Ajax renowned. O heavens, what some men do,
    While some men leave to do!
    How some men creep in° skittish° Fortune's hall,
    Whiles others play the idiots in her eyes!   135
    How one man eats into another's pride,
    While pride is fasting in his wantonness!°
    To see these Grecian lords—why, even already

---

109 *speculation* power of sight   112 *position* i.e., that of the writer whom Ulysses paraphrases above   114 *circumstance* detailed discussion   116 *Though . . . consisting* although much exists in him and also because of him   120 *Where they're extended* in which his natural attributes are noised abroad   120 *who* which   128 *Most . . . use* most despised and yet invaluable   134 *in* into   134 *skittish* i.e., unreliable   137 *his wantonness* its own self-satisfaction

          They clap the lubber Ajax on the shoulder,
140   As if his foot were on brave Hector's breast,
          And great Troy shrinking.

      Achilles. I do believe it; for they passed by me
          As misers do by beggars, neither gave to me
          Good word nor look. What, are my deeds forgot?

145 *Ulysses.* Time hath, my lord, a wallet at his back,
          Wherein he puts alms for oblivion,
          A great-sized monster of ingratitudes.
          Those scraps are good deeds past, which are de-
              voured
          As fast as they are made, forgot as soon
150   As done. Perseverance, dear my lord,
          Keeps honor bright. To have done, is to hang
          Quite out of fashion, like a rusty mail°
          In monumental mock'ry. Take the instant° way;
          For honor travels in a strait so narrow
155   Where one but goes abreast. Keep, then, the path;
          For emulation hath a thousand sons
          That one by one pursue. If you give way,
          Or hedge aside from the direct forthright,°
          Like to an ent'red tide they all rush by
160   And leave you hindmost;
          Or, like a gallant horse fall'n in first rank,
          Lie there for pavement to the abject rear,°
          O'errun and trampled on. Then what they do in
              present,
          Though less than yours in past, must o'ertop yours.
165   For time is like a fashionable host,
          That slightly shakes his parting guest by the hand,
          And with his arms outstretched, as he would fly,
          Grasps in the comer. The welcome ever smiles,
          And farewell goes out sighing. Let not virtue seek
170   Remuneration for the thing it was. For beauty, wit,
          High birth, vigor of bone, desert in service,

---

152 *mail* piece of armor   153 *instant* most immediate   158 *direct
forthright* course of action clearly at hand, the path straight ahead
162 *the abject rear* the miserable, degraded members of the rear (as
in a military charge or parade)

Love, friendship, charity, are subjects all
To envious and calumniating time.
One touch of nature° makes the whole world kin,
That all with one consent praise newborn gauds,°   175
Though they are made and molded of things past,
And give to dust that is a little gilt
More laud than gilt o'erdusted.°
The present eye praises the present object.
Then marvel not, thou great and complete man,   180
That all the Greeks begin to worship Ajax;
Since things in motion sooner catch the eye
Than what stirs not. The cry° went once on thee,
And still it might, and yet it may again,
If thou wouldst not entomb thyself alive   185
And case° thy reputation in thy tent;
Whose glorious deeds, but in these fields of late,
Made emulous missions° 'mongst the gods them-
       selves
And drave great Mars to faction.°

Achilles.   Of this my privacy
I have strong reasons.

Ulysses.   But 'gainst your privacy   190
The reasons are more potent and heroical.
'Tis known, Achilles, that you are in love
With one of Priam's daughters.°

Achilles. Ha! Known!

Ulysses. Is that a wonder?   195
The providence° that's in a watchful state
Knows almost every grain of Pluto's° gold
Finds bottom in th' uncomprehensive° deeps,

174 *One touch of nature* a natural inclination, common to all men
(to praise according to superficial values)   175 *gauds* toys, trifles
178 *More laud than gilt o'erdusted* more praise than gold covered
with dust   183 *cry* public opinion   186 *case* encase   188 *emulous
missions* competitive and jealous warfare (the gods took sides in
the Trojan war, fighting among themselves)   189 *to faction* to
become a partisan   193 *one of Priam's daughters* (Polyxena)   196
providence careful and timely understanding   197 *Pluto's* (Shakespeare's error for Plutus, god of wealth; Pluto was god of the underworld)   198 *uncomprehensive* unfathomable

Keeps place° with thought, and almost, like the
    gods,
200 Do thoughts unveil in their dumb cradles.
There is a mystery—with whom relation°
Durst never meddle—in the soul of state,
Which hath an operation more divine
Than breath or pen can give expressure to.
205 All the commerce that you have had with Troy
As perfectly is ours as yours, my lord;
And better would it fit Achilles much
To throw down Hector than Polyxena.
But it must grieve young Pyrrhus° now at home,
210 When fame shall in our islands sound her trump,
And all the Greekish girls shall tripping sing,
"Great Hector's sister did Achilles win,
But our great Ajax bravely beat down him."
Farewell, my lord; I as your lover speak;
215 The fool slides o'er the ice that you should break.
                                        [*Exit.*]

Patroclus. To this effect, Achilles, have I moved you.
A woman impudent and mannish grown
Is not more loathed than an effeminate man
In time of action. I stand condemned for this;
220 They think my little stomach to the war
And your great love to me restrains you thus.
Sweet, rouse yourself; and the weak wanton Cupid
Shall from your neck unloose his amorous fold
And, like a dewdrop from the lion's mane,
Be shook to air.

225 *Achilles.*   Shall Ajax fight with Hector?

Patroclus. Ay, and perhaps receive much honor by
    him.

Achilles. I see my reputation is at stake.
My fame is shrewdly gored.°

199 *Keeps place* keeps up, runs parallel   201 *relation* open statement   209 *Pyrrhus* (Achilles' son, also called Neoptolemus)   228
shrewdly gored sorely wounded

Patroclus.   O, then, beware!
  Those wounds heal ill that men do give themselves.
  Omission to do what is necessary   230
  Seals a commision to a blank of danger;°
  And danger, like an ague, subtly taints°
  Even then when they sit idly in the sun.

Achilles. Go call Thersites hither, sweet Patroclus.
  I'll send the fool to Ajax and desire him   235
  T' invite the Troyan lords after the combat
  To see us here unarmed. I have a woman's°
    longing,
  An appetite that I am sick withal,
  To see great Hector in his weeds° of peace,
  To talk with him and to behold his visage,   240
  Even to my full of view.°

                    Enter Thersites.

                                    A labor saved!

Thersites. A wonder!

Achilles. What?

Thersites. Ajax goes up and down the field, asking
    for himself.°   245

Achilles. How so?

Thersites. He must fight singly tomorrow with Hector,
    and is so prophetically proud of an heroical cudgel-
    ing that he raves in saying nothing.

Achilles. How can that be?   250

Thersites. Why, he stalks up and down like a pea-
    cock—a stride and a stand; ruminates like an

231 *Seals . . . danger* i.e., binds one to confront unnamed danger
(royal officers sometimes carried blank warrants for arrest, already
bearing the commissioning seal of authority, which could be filled
in as necessary)   232 *taints* infects   237 *woman's* i.e., pregnant
woman's (?)   239 *weeds* apparel   240–41 *to behold . . . view*
(since in full armor Hector's face would have been hidden behind
the closed beaver of his helmet)   244–45 *asking for himself* (here
"Ajax" is probably a pun on a jakes, i.e., a privy)

hostess that hath no arithmetic but her brain to set
down her reckoning; bites his lip with a politic
255   regard,° as who should say, "There were wit in
this head an 'twould out"; and so there is, but it
lies as coldly in him as fire in a flint, which will not
show without knocking. The man's undone forever, for if Hector break not his neck i' the combat,
260   he'll break't himself in vainglory. He knows not
me. I said, "Good morrow, Ajax"; and he replies,
"Thanks, Agamemnon." What think you of this
man that takes me for the general? He's grown a
very land-fish, languageless, a monster. A plague
265   of opinion! A man may wear it on both sides like
a leather jerkin.°

Achilles. Thou must be my ambassador to him, Thersites.

Thersites. Who, I? Why, he'll answer nobody. He pro-
270   fesses not answering. Speaking is for beggars; he
wears his tongue in's arms. I will put on° his
presence; let Patroclus make demands to me, you
shall see the pageant of Ajax.

Achilles. To him, Patroclus. Tell him I humbly desire
275   the valiant Ajax to invite the most valorous Hector
to come unarmed to my tent, and to procure safe-
conduct for his person of the magnanimous and
most illustrious, six-or-seven-times-honored cap-
tain-general of the Grecian army, Agamemnon, et
280   cetera. Do this.

Patroclus. Jove bless great Ajax!

Thersites. Hum.

Patroclus. I come from the worthy Achilles——

Thersites. Ha!

285   *Patroclus.* Who most humbly desires you to invite
Hector to his tent——

254–55 *politic regard* expression of shrewd judgment   266 *jerkin*
close-fitting jacket   271 *put on* imitate

Thersites. Hum!

Patroclus. And to procure safe-conduct from Aga-
    memnon.

Thersites. Agamemnon?   290

Patroclus. Ay, my lord.

Thersites. Ha!

Patroclus. What say you to't?

Thersites. God b'wi'you, with all my heart.

Patroclus. Your answer, sir.   295

Thersites. If tomorrow be a fair day, by eleven of the
    clock it will go one way or other; howsoever, he
    shall pay for me ere he has me.

Patroclus. Your answer, sir.

Thersites. Fare ye well, with all my heart.   300

Achilles. Why, but he is not in this tune, is he?

Thersites. No, but out of tune thus. What music will
    be in him when Hector has knocked out his brains,
    I know not; but I am sure none, unless the fiddler
    Apollo get his sinews to make catlings° on.   305

Achilles. Come, thou shalt bear a letter to him
    straight.

Thersites. Let me bear another to his horse, for that's
    the more capable° creature.

Achilles. My mind is troubled, like a fountain stirred, 310
    And I myself see not the bottom of it.
                    [*Exeunt Achilles and Patroclus.*]

Thersites. Would the fountain of your mind were clear
    again, that I might water an ass at it! I had rather
    be a tick in a sheep than such a valiant ignorance.
                                              [*Exit.*]

305 *catlings* strings of catgut   309 *capable* intelligent

[ACT IV

Scene I. *Within Troy.*]

*Enter, at one door, Aeneas [with a torch;] at another,
Paris, Deiphobus, Antenor, Diomed the Grecian,
[and others,] with torches.*

Paris. See, ho! Who is that there?

Deiphobus.   It is the Lord Aeneas.

Aeneas. Is the prince there in person?
　　Had I so good occasion to lie long
　　As you, Prince Paris, nothing but heavenly business
5　　Should rob my bedmate of my company.

Diomedes. That's my mind too. Good morrow, Lord
　　Aeneas.

Paris. A valiant Greek, Aeneas; take his hand.
　　Witness the process° of your speech, wherein
　　You told how Diomed, a whole week by days,°
　　Did haunt you in the field.

10　*Aeneas.*   Health to you, valiant sir,
　　During all question of the gentle truce;°

IV.i.8 *process* gist, drift　9 *by days* day by day　11 *question of the
gentle truce* i.e., intercourse made possible by the truce

126

But when I meet you armed, as black defiance
As heart can think or courage execute.

Diomedes. The one and other Diomed embraces.
Our bloods are now in calm, and, so long, health!   15
But when contention and occasion° meet,
By Jove, I'll play the hunter for thy life
With all my force, pursuit, and policy.°

Aeneas. And thou shalt hunt a lion that will fly
With his face backward. In humane gentleness,   20
Welcome to Troy. Now, by Anchises'° life,
Welcome indeed! By Venus' hand° I swear,
No man alive can love in such a sort
The thing he means to kill more excellently.

Diomedes. We sympathize.° Jove, let Aeneas live,   25
If to my sword his fate be not the glory,
A thousand complete courses of the sun!
But, in mine emulous honor, let him die
With every joint a wound, and that tomorrow!

Aeneas. We know each other well.   30

Diomedes. We do, and long to know each other worse.

Paris. This is the most despiteful gentle greeting,
The noblest hateful love, that e'er I heard of.
What business, lord, so early?

Aeneas. I was sent for to the king; but why, I know
not.   35

Paris. His purpose meets you; it was to bring this
Greek
To Calchas' house, and there to render him,
For the enfreed Antenor, the fair Cressid.
Let's have your company; or, if you please,
Haste there before us. I constantly° do think—   40
Or rather call my thought a certain knowledge—
My brother Troilus lodges there tonight.

16 *occasion* opportunity   18 *policy* cunning   21 *Anchises* (Aeneas'
father)   22 *Venus' hand* (Diomedes was supposed to have wounded
Venus, Aeneas' mother, in the hand)   25 *sympathize* have the same
feeling   40 *constantly* firmly

Rouse him and give him note of our approach,
With the whole quality° wherefore. I fear
We shall be much unwelcome.

45 *Aeneas.*   That I assure you.
Troilus had rather Troy were borne to Greece
Than Cressid borne from Troy.

Paris.   There is no help.
The bitter disposition of the time
Will have it so. On, lord; we'll follow you.

50 *Aeneas.* Good morrow, all.   *Exit Aeneas.*

Paris. And tell me, noble Diomed; faith, tell me true,
Even in the soul of sound good-fellowship,
Who, in your thoughts, deserves fair Helen best,
Myself or Menelaus?

Diomedes.   Both alike.
55 He merits well to have her that doth seek her,
Not making any scruple of her soilure,
With such a hell of pain and world of charge;°
And you as well to keep her that defend her,
Not palating° the taste of her dishonor,
60 With such a costly loss of wealth and friends.
He, like a puling cuckold, would drink up
The lees and dregs of a flat tamèd piece;°
You, like a lecher, out of whorish loins
Are pleased to breed out your inheritors.
65 Both merits poised,° each weighs nor less nor more;
But he as he, the heavier for a whore.°

Paris. You are too bitter to your countrywoman.
Diomedes. She's bitter to her country! Hear me,
Paris—

44 *quality* occasion, explanation   57 *charge* cost   59 *Not palating*
insensible to   62 *flat tamèd piece* (1) cask of wine opened so long
that the wine has gone flat (2) woman so promiscuous that she can
no longer excite or be excited sexually   65 *poised* weighed   66
But he . . . a whore (1) but he, i.e., Menelaus, as heavy as his
small merit may be, plus the weight of the whore who is, after all,
his legal possession (?); (2) but he, whoever wins her, heavier
only by the weight of a whore (to be "light" was to be morally
loose) (?)

For every false drop in her bawdy veins
A Grecian's life hath sunk; for every scruple°   70
Of her contaminated carrion weight
A Troyan hath been slain. Since she could speak,
She hath not given so many good words breath
As for her Greeks and Troyans suffered death.

Paris. Fair Diomed, you do as chapmen° do,   75
Dispraise the thing that you desire to buy;
But we in silence hold this virtue well,
We'll not commend what we intend to sell.°
Here lies our way.   *Exeunt.*

[Scene II.   *Within Troy; Calchas' house.*]

Enter Troilus and Cressida.

Troilus. Dear, trouble not yourself; the morn is cold.

Cressida. Then, sweet my lord, I'll call mine uncle
    down;
He shall unbolt the gates.

Troilus.   Trouble him not;
To bed, to bed. Sleep kill° those pretty eyes,
And give as soft attachment° to thy senses   5
As infants' empty of all thought!

Cressida.   Good morrow then.

Troilus. I prithee now, to bed.

Cressida.   Are you aweary of me?

Troilus. O Cressida! But that the busy day,

70 *scruple* (the smallest possible unit of weight)   75 *chapmen*
hawkers of cheap wares   78 *We'll not . . . to sell* i.e., we'll not
practice the seller's tricks although you practice the buyer's (Paris
does not imply that Helen is for sale)   IV.ii.4 *kill* overpower   5
attachment seizure

Waked by the lark, hath roused the ribald crows,
10   And dreaming night will hide our joys no longer,
I would not from thee.

Cressida.   Night hath been too brief.

Troilus. Beshrew the witch! With venomous wights°
     she stays
As tediously as hell, but flies the grasps of love
With wings more momentary-swift than thought.
You will catch cold and curse me.

15   *Cressida.*   Prithee, tarry;
You men will never tarry.
O foolish Cressid! I might have still held off,
And then you would have tarried. Hark, there's one
     up.

Pandarus. (Within) What's all the doors open here?

20   *Troilus.* It is your uncle.

Cressida. A pestilence on him! Now will he be mock-
     ing.
I shall have such a life.

Enter Pandarus.

Pandarus. How now, how now! How go maidenheads?
Here, you maid, where's my cousin Cressid?

Cressida. Go hang yourself, you naughty mocking
25   uncle.
You bring me to do°—and then you flout me too.

Pandarus. To do what? To do what? Let her say what.
What have I brought you to do?

Cressida. Come come; beshrew your heart! You'll
     ne'er be good,
30   Nor suffer others.

Pandarus. Ha, ha! Alas, poor wretch! A poor capoc-

12 *venomous wights* malignant witches (or, simply, evil creatures)
26 *do* (used sometimes in obscene sense)

chia!° Hast not slept tonight? Would he not, a
naughty man, let it sleep? A bugbear° take him!

Cressida. Did not I tell you? Would he were knocked
    i' the head!   *One knocks.*
Who's that at door? Good uncle, go and see.   35
My lord, come you again into my chamber.
You smile and mock me, as if I meant naughtily.

Troilus. Ha, ha!

Cressida. Come, you are deceived, I think of no such
    thing.   *Knock.*
How earnestly they knock! Pray you, come in.   40
I would not for half Troy have you seen here.
        Exeunt [Troilus and Cressida].

Pandarus. Who's there? What's the matter? Will you
beat down the door? How now, what's the matter?

[Enter Aeneas.]

Aeneas. Good morrow, lord, good morrow.

Pandarus. Who's there? My Lord Aeneas! By my
    troth,   45
I knew you not. What news with you so early?

Aeneas. Is not Prince Troilus here?

Pandarus. Here? What should he do here?

Aeneas. Come, he is here, my lord. Do not deny him.
It doth import° him much to speak with me.   50

Pandarus. Is he here, say you? 'Tis more than I know,
I'll be sworn. For my own part, I came in late.
What should he do here?

Aeneas. Who!° Nay, then. Come, come, you'll do him
wrong ere you are ware. You'll be so true to him, to   55

31–32 *capocchia* simpleton   33 *bugbear* hobgoblin   50 *doth import*
is important to   54 *Who!* (an exclamation of impatience; sometimes as to call "stop!" to a horse)

be false to him. Do not you know of him, but yet
go fetch him hither; go.

Enter Troilus.

Troilus. How now, what's the matter?

Aeneas. My lord, I scarce have leisure to salute you,
60   My matter is so rash.° There is at hand
Paris your brother, and Deiphobus,
The Grecian Diomed, and our Antenor
Delivered to us; and for him forthwith,
Ere the first sacrifice, within this hour,
65   We must give up to Diomedes' hand
The Lady Cressida.

Troilus.   Is it so concluded?

Aeneas. By Priam, and the general state° of Troy.
They are at hand and ready to effect it.

Troilus. How my achievements mock me!
70   I will go meet them. And, my Lord Aeneas,
We met by chance; you did not find me here.

Aeneas. Good, good, my lord; the secrets° of nature
Have not more gift in taciturnity.
                    Exeunt [Troilus and Aeneas].

Pandarus. Is't possible? No sooner got but lost? The
75   devil take Antenor! The young prince will go mad.
A plague upon Antenor! I would they had broke 's
neck!

Enter Cressida.

Cressida. How now? What's the matter? Who was
here?

80 *Pandarus.* Ah, ah!

Cressida. Why sigh you so profoundly? Where's my

60 *rash* urgent   67 *general state* noblemen in council   72 *secrets*
most unknown parts

lord? Gone? Tell me, sweet uncle, what's the matter?

Pandarus. Would I were as deep under the earth as I am above!   *85*

Cressida. O the gods! What's the matter?

Pandarus. Pray thee, get thee in. Would thou hadst ne'er been born! I knew thou wouldst be his death. O poor gentleman! A plague upon Antenor!

Cressida. Good uncle, I beseech you on my knees,   *90* what's the matter?

Pandarus. Thou must be gone, wench, thou must be gone; thou art changed° for Antenor. Thou must to thy father and be gone from Troilus. 'Twill be his death; 'twill be his bane;° he cannot bear it.   *95*

Cressida. O you immortal gods! I will not go.

Pandarus. Thou must.

Cressida. I will not, uncle. I have forgot my father;
I know no touch of consanguinity°—
No kin, no love, no blood, no soul so near me   *100*
As the sweet Troilus. O you gods divine,
Make Cressid's name the very crown of falsehood
If ever she leave Troilus! Time, force, and death,
Do to this body what extremes you can;
But the strong base and building of my love   *105*
Is as the very center of the earth,
Drawing all things to it. I will go in and weep——

Pandarus. Do, do.

Cressida. —Tear my bright hair, and scratch my praisèd cheeks,
Crack my clear voice with sobs, and break my   *110*
heart
With sounding Troilus. I will not go from Troy.
                                                            Exeunt.

93 *changed* exchanged   95 *bane* poison, destruction   99 *no touch of consanguinity* no sense of relationship

[Scene III. *Within Troy; near Calchas' house.*]

Enter Paris, Troilus, Aeneas, Deiphobus, Antenor,
Diomedes.

Paris. It is great morning,° and the hour prefixed
  For her delivery to this valiant Greek
  Comes fast upon. Good my brother Troilus,
  Tell you the lady what she is to do,
  And haste her to the purpose.

5 *Troilus.*   Walk into her house.
  I'll bring her to the Grecian presently;°
  And to his hand when I deliver her,
  Think it an altar, and thy brother Troilus
  A priest there off'ring to it his own heart.

10 *Paris.* I know what 'tis to love;
  And would, as I shall pity, I could help.
  Please you walk in, my lords.   *Exeunt.*

[Scene IV. *Within Troy; Calchas' house.*]

Enter Pandarus and Cressida.

Pandarus. Be moderate, be moderate.

Cressida. Why tell you me of moderation?
  The grief is fine, full, perfect, that I taste,
  And violenteth° in a sense as strong

IV.iii.1 *great morning* broad daylight 6 *presently* immediately
IV.iv.4 *violenteth* rages

As that which causeth it. How can I moderate it?   5
If I could temporize with my affections,
Or brew it to a weak and colder palate,°
The like allayment could I give my grief.
My love admits no qualifying dross;°
No more my grief, in such a precious loss.   10

Enter Troilus.

Pandarus. Here, here, here he comes. Ah, sweet
ducks!

Cressida. O Troilus! Troilus!

Pandarus. What a pair of spectacles° is here! Let me
embrace too. "O heart," as the goodly saying is——   15
   O heart, heavy heart,
   Why sigh'st thou without breaking?
where he answers again,
   Because thou canst not ease thy smart
   By friendship nor by speaking.   20
There was never a truer rhyme. Let us cast away
nothing, for we may live to have need of such a
verse. We see it, we see it. How now, lambs!

Troilus. Cressid, I love thee in so strained° a purity,
That the blest gods, as angry with my fancy,°   25
More bright in zeal than the devotion which
Cold lips blow to their deities, take thee from me.

Cressida. Have the gods envy?

Pandarus. Ay, ay, ay, ay, 'tis too plain a case.

Cressida. And is it true that I must go from Troy?   30

Troilus. A hateful truth.

Cressida.   What, and from Troilus too?

Troilus. From Troy and Troilus.

Cressida.   Is't possible?

7 *palate* taste   9 *qualifying dross* moderating impurity   14 *spectacles* (a pun)   24 *strained* distilled, filtered   25 *fancy* love

Troilus. And suddenly, where injury of chance°
        Puts back leave-taking, justles roughly by
35   All time of pause, rudely beguiles our lips
        Of all rejoindure,° forcibly prevents
        Our locked embrasures, strangles our dear vows
        Even in the birth of our own laboring breath.
        We two, that with so many thousand sighs
40   Did buy each other, must poorly sell ourselves
        With the rude brevity and discharge of one.
        Injurious time now with a robber's haste
        Crams his rich thievery up, he knows not how;
        As many farewells as be stars in heaven,
45   With distinct breath and consigned kisses to them,°
        He fumbles° up into a loose adieu,
        And scants us with a single famished kiss,
        Distasted° with the salt of broken tears.

Aeneas. (*Within*) My lord, is the lady ready?

50 *Troilus.* Hark! You are called. Some say the Genius°
        Cries so to him that instantly must die.
        Bid them have patience; she shall come anon.

Pandarus. Where are my tears? Rain, to lay this wind,
        or my heart will be blown up by the root! [*Exit.*]

Cressida. I must, then, to the Grecians?

55 *Troilus.*   No remedy.

Cressida. A woeful Cressid 'mongst the merry Greeks!
        When shall we see again?

Troilus. Hear me, love. Be thou but true of heart——

Cressida. I true! How now! What wicked deem° is
        this?

60 *Troilus.* Nay, we must use expostulation kindly,

33 *injury of chance* injurious accident   36 *rejoindure* reunion   45
With distinct . . . to them with the words of each farewell and the
kisses which ratify each of them   46 *fumbles* wraps clumsily   48
Distasted the taste (of the kiss) ruined   50 *Genius* guardian spirit
59 *deem* thought

For it is parting from us.°
I speak not "be thou true" as fearing thee,
For I will throw my glove° to Death himself
That there's no maculation° in thy heart;
But "be thou true," say I, to fashion in   65
My sequent protestation:° be thou true,
And I will see thee.

Cressida. O, you shall be exposed, my lord, to dangers
As infinite as imminent; but I'll be true.

Troilus. And I'll grow friend with danger. Wear this
    sleeve.   70

Cressida. And you this glove. When shall I see you?

Troilus. I will corrupt the Grecian sentinels,
    To give thee nightly visitation.
    But yet, be true.

Cressida.   O heavens! "Be true" again!

Troilus. Hear why I speak it, love.   75
    The Grecian youths are full of quality;°
    They're loving,° well composed with gift of nature,
    And swelling o'er with arts and exercise.°
    How novelty may move, and parts with person,°
    Alas! A kind of godly jealousy—   80
    Which, I beseech you, call a virtuous sin—
    Makes me afeared.

Cressida.   O heavens, you love me not!

Troilus. Die I a villain then!
    In this I do not call your faith in question
    So mainly as my merit. I cannot sing,   85

60–61 *Nay, we . . . from us* we must be gentle in all remonstrance, for we are now saying good-bye 63 *throw my glove* give challenge 64 *maculation* taint, blemish (i.e., disloyalty) 65–66 *to fashion in . . . sequent protestation* as introduction for my own promise to follow 76 *quality* qualities 77 *loving* adept in the arts of love 78 *arts and exercise* talents both in theory and practice 79 *parts with person* specific qualities and talents, combined with personal charm

Nor heel the high lavolt,° nor sweeten talk,
Nor play at subtle games—fair virtues all,
To which the Grecians are most prompt and pregnant;°
But I can tell that in each grace of these
90 There lurks a still and dumb-discoursive° devil
That tempts most cunningly. But be not tempted.

Cressida. Do you think I will?

Troilus. No!
But something may be done that we will not;
95 And sometimes we are devils to ourselves
When we will tempt the frailty of our powers,
Presuming on their changeful potency.°

Aeneas. (*Within*) Nay, good my lord!

Troilus.   Come, kiss; and
let us part.

Paris. (*Within*) Brother Troilus!

Troilus.   Good brother, come
you hither;
100 And bring Aeneas and the Grecian with you.

Cressida. My lord, will you be true?

Troilus. Who? I? Alas, it is my vice, my fault.
Whiles others fish with craft for great opinion,°
I with great truth catch° mere simplicity;
105 Whilst some with cunning gild their copper crowns,
With truth and plainness I do wear mine bare.
Fear not my truth; the moral° of my wit
Is "plain and true"—there's all the reach of it.

[*Enter Aeneas, Paris, Antenor, Deiphobus and
Diomedes.*]

Welcome, Sir Diomed. Here is the lady

86 *the high lavolt* (the lavolt was a dance for two persons, requiring many high steps and bounds)   88 *pregnant* ready, fully able   90 *dumb-discoursive* articulate even in silence   97 *changeful potency* power which may alter to failure   103 *opinion* reputation   104 *catch* achieve; i.e., achieve a reputation for   107 *moral* maxim

Which for Antenor we deliver you.   110
At the port,° lord, I'll give her to thy hand,
And by the way possess° thee what she is.
Entreat° her fair; and, by my soul, fair Greek,
If e'er thou stand at mercy of my sword,
Name Cressid, and thy life shall be as safe   115
As Priam is in Ilion.

Diomedes.   Fair Lady Cressid,
So please you, save the thanks this prince expects.
The luster in your eye, heaven in your cheek,
Pleads your fair usage; and to Diomed
You shall be mistress, and command him wholly.   120

Troilus. Grecian, thou dost not use me courteously,
To shame the seal of my petition° to thee
In praising her. I tell thee, lord of Greece,
She is as far high-soaring o'er thy praises
As thou unworthy to be called her servant.   125
I charge thee use her well, even for my charge;°
For, by the dreadful Pluto, if thou dost not,
Though the great bulk Achilles be thy guard,
I'll cut thy throat.

Diomedes.   O, be not moved, Prince Troilus.
Let me be privileged by my place and message   130
To be a speaker free. When I am hence,
I'll answer to my lust;° and know you, lord,
I'll nothing do on charge. To her own worth
She shall be prized; but that you say "be't so,"
I speak it in my spirit and honor, "no."   135

Troilus. Come, to the port. I'll tell thee, Diomed,
This brave° shall oft make thee to hide thy head.
Lady, give me your hand, and, as we walk,
To our own selves bend we our needful talk.
        [*Exeunt Troilus, Cressida, and Diomedes.*]
                              Sound trumpet.

---

111 *port* gate (of the city)   112 *possess* inform   113 *Entreat* treat
122 *To shame the seal of my petition* to disdain the worth of my
charge and promise   126 *even for my charge* simply because I say
so   132 *answer to my lust* do as I please   137 *brave* boast

Paris. Hark! Hector's trumpet.

Aeneas.   How have we spent this
140   morning!
    The prince must think me tardy and remiss,
    That swore to ride before him to the field.

Paris. 'Tis Troilus' fault. Come, come, to field with
    him.

Deiphobus. Let us make ready straight.

145 *Aeneas.* Yea, with a bridegroom's fresh alacrity,
    Let us address° to tend on Hector's heels.
    The glory of our Troy doth this day lie
    On his fair worth and single chivalry.   *Exeunt.*

[Scene V. *The Greek camp.*]

*Enter Ajax, armed; Achilles, Patroclus, Agamemnon,
    Menelaus, Ulysses, Nestor, Calchas, &c.*

Agamemnon. Here art thou in appointment° fresh and
    fair,
    Anticipating time. With starting° courage,
    Give with thy trumpet a loud note to Troy,
    Thou dreadful Ajax, that the appallèd air
5   May pierce the head of the great combatant
    And hale him hither.

Ajax.   Thou, trumpet,° there's my
    purse.
    Now crack thy lungs, and split thy brazen pipe.
    Blow, villain, till thy spherèd bias° cheek
    Outswell the colic of puffed Aquilon!°

146 *address* prepare IV.v.1 *appointment* equipment and apparel
2 *starting* active, prompt 6 *trumpet* trumpeter 8 *bias* puffed-out
9 *the colic of puffed Aquilon* the north wind, distended as if by
colic

Come, stretch thy chest, and let thy eyes spout
   blood;   10
Thou blow'st for Hector.   [*Trumpet sounds.*]

Ulysses. No trumpet answers.

Achilles.   'Tis but early days.°

Agamemnon. Is not yond Diomed with Calchas'
   daughter?

Ulysses. 'Tis he, I ken the manner of his gait;
He rises on the toe. That spirit of his   15
In aspiration lifts him from the earth.

[*Enter Diomedes, with Cressida.*]

Agamemnon. Is this the Lady Cressid?

Diomedes.   Even she.

Agamemnon. Most dearly welcome to the Greeks,
   sweet lady.

Nestor. Our general doth salute you with a kiss.

Ulysses. Yet is the kindness but particular.°   20
'Twere better she were kissed in general.°

Nestor. And very courtly counsel. I'll begin.
So much for Nestor.

Achilles. I'll take that winter° from your lips, fair
   lady.
Achilles bids you welcome.   25

Menelaus. I had good argument for kissing once.

Patroclus. But that's no argument for kissing now;
For thus popped Paris in his hardiment,°
And parted thus you and your argument.°

Ulysses. O, deadly gall, and theme of all our scorns,   30

12 *days* in the day   20 *particular* single   21 *in general* (1) by
the general (2) universally   24 *that winter* i.e., Nestor's kiss
(cold from old age)   28 *hardiment* boldness   29 *argument* i.e.,
Helen

For which we lose our heads to gild his horns.

Patroclus. The first was Menelaus' kiss; this, mine.
Patroclus kisses you.

Menelaus. O, this is trim.

Patroclus. Paris and I kiss evermore for him.

35 *Menelaus.* I'll have my kiss, sir. Lady, by your leave.

Cressida. In kissing, do you render or receive?

Patroclus. Both take and give.

Cressida. I'll make my match to
live,°
The kiss you take is better than you give;
Therefore no kiss.

Menelaus. I'll give you boot;° I'll give you three for
40 one.

Cressida. You are an odd° man; give even, or give
none.

Menelaus. An odd man, lady? Every man is odd.

Cressida. No, Paris is not, for you know 'tis true
That you are odd and he is even with you.

Menelaus. You fillip° me o' the head.

45 *Cressida.* No, I'll be sworn.

Ulysses. It were no match, your nail against his
horn.°
May I, sweet lady, beg a kiss of you?

Cressida. You may.

Ulysses. I do desire it.

Cressida. Why, beg then.

---

37 *I'll . . . match to live* I'll bet my life 40 *boot* odds 41 *odd*
i.e., single and singular 45 *fillip* tap 46 *It . . . horn* your nail, in
tapping, would be no match for his hard cuckold's horn

Ulysses. Why, then, for Venus' sake, give me a kiss,
  When Helen is a maid again, and his.   50

Cressida. I am your debtor; claim it when 'tis due.

Ulysses. Never's my day, and then a kiss of you.

Diomedes. Lady, a word. I'll bring you to your father.
           [*Exeunt Diomedes and Cressida.*]

Nestor. A woman of quick sense.

Ulysses.   Fie, fie upon her!°
  There's language in her eye, her cheek, her lip;   55
  Nay, her foot speaks. Her wanton spirits look out
  At every joint and motive° of her body.
  O, these encounterers, so glib of tongue,
  That give a coasting welcome ere it comes,°
  And wide unclasp the tables° of their thoughts   60
  To every ticklish reader, set them down
  For sluttish spoils of opportunity°
  And daughters of the game.°

Flourish. Enter all of Troy [*Hector, Paris, Aeneas,
    Helenus, Troilus, and Attendants*].

All. The Troyans' trumpet.°

Agamemnon.   Yonder comes the troop.

Aeneas. Hail, all the state of Greece. What shall be
  done   65
  To him that victory commands? Or do you purpose
  A victor shall be known? Will you the knights
  Shall to the edge of all extremity
  Pursue each other, or shall they be divided°

---

54 *Fie, fie upon her!* (Ulysses' exclamation does not imply dis-
agreement with Nestor's observation; the following nine lines
elaborate "quick sense")   57 *motive* moving part   59 *a coasting
welcome ere it comes* a sidelong, flirtatious greeting before
being greeted   60 *tables* tablets   62 *sluttish spoils of opportunity* harlots who yield at every opportunity   63 *daughters of
the game* whores   64 *The Troyans' trumpet* (in the theater, this
line becomes a pun on "strumpet")   69 *divided* i.e., separated during the fight

70   By any voice or order of the field?
    Hector bade ask.

Agamemnon.   Which way would Hector have it?

Aeneas. He cares not; he'll obey conditions.

Achilles. 'Tis done like Hector; but securely° done,
    A little proudly, and great deal misprising
    The knight opposed.

75   *Aeneas.*   If not Achilles, sir.
    What is your name?

Achilles.   If not Achilles, nothing.

Aeneas. Therefore Achilles; but, whate'er, know this:
    In the extremity of great and little,
    Valor and pride excel themselves in Hector;
80   The one almost as infinite as all,
    The other blank as nothing. Weigh him well;
    And that which looks like pride is courtesy.
    This Ajax is half made of Hector's blood,°
    In love whereof half Hector stays at home;
85   Half heart, half hand, half Hector comes to seek
    This blended knight, half Troyan, and half Greek.

Achilles. A maiden° battle, then? O, I perceive you.

[*Enter Diomedes.*]

Agamemnon. Here is Sir Diomed. Go, gentle knight,
    Stand by our Ajax. As you and Lord Aeneas
90   Consent upon the order of their fight,
    So be it; either to the uttermost,
    Or else a breath.° The combatants being kin
    Half stints their strife before their strokes begin.
          [*Ajax and Hector enter the lists.*]

Ulysses. They are opposed already.

73 *securely* overconfidently   83 *Hector's blood* (see note to II.ii.77)
87 *maiden* bloodless (as of novices or men in training, who do
not intend to kill)   92 *breath* exercise

Agamemnon. What Troyan is that same that looks so
    heavy?°   95

Ulysses. The youngest son of Priam, a true knight,
    Not yet mature, yet matchless; firm of word,
    Speaking in deeds and deedless in his tongue,°
    Not soon provoked, nor being provoked soon
    calmed;
    His heart and hand both open and both free,°   100
    For what he has he gives, what thinks he shows;
    Yet gives he not till judgment guide his bounty,
    Nor dignifies an impare thought° with breath;
    Manly as Hector, but more dangerous;
    For Hector, in his blaze of wrath, subscribes   105
    To tender objects,° but he in heat of action
    Is more vindicative than jealous love.
    They call him Troilus, and on him erect
    A second hope as fairly built as Hector.
    Thus says Aeneas, one that knows the youth   110
    Even to his inches,° and with private soul°
    Did in great Ilion thus translate him to me.
                   Alarum. [Hector and Ajax fight.]

Agamemnon. They are in action.

Nestor. Now, Ajax, hold thine own!

Troilus.   Hector, thou
    sleep'st; awake thee!

Agamemnon. His blows are well disposed.° There,
    Ajax!   115

Diomedes. You must no more.   *Trumpets cease.*

Aeneas.   Princes, enough, so please
    you.

95 *heavy* heavyhearted   98 *deedless in his tongue* free of boasts
100 *free* generous   103 *impare thought* (1) ill-considered thought
(2) thought unequal to the dignity of his character   105–06 *sub-
scribes/To tender objects* grants merciful terms to the defense-
less   111 *Even to his inches* i.e., from head to toe   111 *with
private soul* in confidence   115 *well disposed* well aimed, well
placed

Ajax. I am not warm yet; let us fight again.

Diomedes. As Hector pleases.

Hector.   Why, then will I no
more.
Thou art, great lord, my father's sister's son,
120   A cousin-german to great Priam's seed;
The obligation of our blood forbids
A gory emulation 'twixt us twain.
Were thy commixtion° Greek and Troyan so
That thou couldst say, "This hand is Grecian all,
125   And this is Troyan; the sinews of this leg
All Greek, and this all Troy; my mother's blood
Runs on the dexter° cheek, and this sinister°
Bounds in my father's," by Jove multipotent,°
Thou shouldst not bear from me a Greekish mem-
ber
130   Wherein my sword had not impressure made
Of our rank feud. But the just gods gainsay
That any drop thou borrow'dst from thy mother,
My sacred aunt, should by my mortal sword
Be drained! Let me embrace thee, Ajax—
135   By him that thunders,° thou hast lusty arms;
Hector would have them fall upon him thus.°
Cousin, all honor to thee!

Ajax.   I thank thee, Hector;
Thou art too gentle and too free a man.
I came to kill thee, cousin, and bear hence
140   A great addition earnèd in thy death.

Hector. Not Neoptolemus° so mirable,°
On whose bright crest Fame with her loud'st
"Oyes"°
Cries, "This is he!" could promise to himself
A thought of added honor torn from Hector.

123 *commixtion* composition   127 *dexter* right   127 *sinister* left
128 *multipotent* of many powers   135 *him that thunders* i.e., Jove
(Zeus)   136 *thus* i.e., embracing him   141 *Neoptolemus* (this
name probably applies here to Achilles himself, and not to his
son, Pyrrhus)   141 *mirable* wonderful   142 *Oyes* cries beginning the proclamations of heralds or sessions of a court

Aeneas. There is expectance here from both the sides, 145
What further you will do.

Hector.   We'll answer it.
The issue° is embracement. Ajax, farewell.

Ajax. If I might in entreaties find success—
As seld° I have the chance—I would desire
My famous cousin to our Grecian tents. 150

Diomedes. 'Tis Agamemnon's wish; and great Achilles
Doth long to see unarmed the valiant Hector.

Hector. Aeneas, call my brother Troilus to me,
And signify° this loving interview
To the expecters of our Troyan part.° 155
Desire them home.° Give me thy hand, my cousin;
I will go eat with thee and see your knights.

[*Agamemnon and the rest approach them.*]

Ajax. Great Agamemnon comes to meet us here.

Hector. The worthiest of them tell me name by name;
But for Achilles, my own searching eyes 160
Shall find him by his large and portly size.

Agamemnon. Worthy all arms [*embraces him*], as wel-
come as to one
That would be rid of such an enemy—
But that's no welcome. Understand more clear,
What's past and what's to come is strewed with
husks 165
And formless ruin of oblivion;
But in this extant° moment, faith and troth,
Strained purely from all hollow bias-drawing,°
Bids thee, with most divine integrity,
From heart of very heart, great Hector, welcome. 170

147 *issue* result, outcome   149 *seld* seldom   154 *signify* expound,
explain   155 *the expecters of our Troyan part* those on our side,
the Trojans, awaiting news   156 *Desire them home* ask them to
go home   167 *extant* present   168 *all hollow bias-drawing* all
fruitless and tortuous dealings (in the course of the war, as in the
course given by the bias of a bowl in bowling)

Hector. I thank thee, most imperious Agamemnon.

Agamemnon. [*To Troilus*] My well-famed lord of
    Troy, no less to you.

Menelaus. Let me confirm my princely brother's
    greeting.
    You brace of warlike brothers, welcome hither.

Hector. Who must we answer?

175 *Aeneas.*   The noble Menelaus.

Hector. O, you, my lord? By Mars his gauntlet,
    thanks!
    Mock not that I affect th' untraded° oath;
    Your quondam° wife swears still by Venus' glove.
    She's well, but bade me not commend her to you.

Menelaus. Name her not now, sir; she's a deadly
180   theme.

Hector. O, pardon! I offend.

Nestor. I have, thou gallant Troyan, seen thee oft,
    Laboring for destiny,° make cruel way
    Through ranks of Greekish youth; and I have seen
        thee,
185   As hot as Perseus, spur thy Phrygian steed,
    Despising many forfeits and subduements,°
    When thou hast hung° thy advancèd sword i' th'
        air,
    Not letting it decline on the declinèd,
    That I have said to some my standers-by,
190   "Lo, Jupiter is yonder, dealing life!"°
    And I have seen thee pause and take thy breath,

177 *untraded* unusual, unfamiliar (Hector, apologizing for what
might appear to be an affected oath, gives his reason for using
it in the following line, in which he completes a satirical reference to Menelaus and Helen by alluding to the liaison between
Mars and Venus) 178 *quondam* former 183 *Laboring for
destiny* working in behalf of destiny, i.e., causing destined deaths
186 *Despising many forfeits and subduements* ignoring or disdain-
ing those already vanquished, whose lives were forfeit 187 *hung*
held suspended 190 *dealing life* dispensing life (as a god might
do by not causing death)

When that a ring of Greeks have shraped° thee in,
Like an Olympian wrestling. This have I seen;
But this thy countenance, still° locked in steel,
I never saw till now. I knew thy grandsire,°   *195*
And once fought with him. He was a soldier good;
But, by great Mars, the captain of us all,
Never like thee. O, let an old man embrace thee;
And, worthy warrior, welcome to our tents.

Aeneas. 'Tis the old Nestor.   *200*

Hector. Let me embrace thee, good old chronicle,
That hast so long walked hand in hand with time.
Most reverend Nestor, I am glad to clasp thee.

Nestor. I would my arms could match thee in conten-
    tion,
As they contend with thee in courtesy.   *205*

Hector. I would they could.

Nestor. Ha,
By this white beard, I'd fight with thee tomorrow.
Well, welcome, welcome. I have seen the time——

Ulysses. I wonder now how yonder city stands,   *210*
When we have here her base and pillar by us.

Hector. I know your favor,° Lord Ulysses, well.
Ah, sir, there's many a Greek and Troyan dead,
Since first I saw yourself and Diomed
In Ilion, on your Greekish embassy.   *215*

Ulysses. Sir, I foretold you then what would ensue.
My prophecy is but half his journey yet;
For yonder walls, that pertly front your town,
Yon towers, whose wanton tops do buss° the
    clouds,
Must kiss their own feet.

Hector.   I must not believe you.   *220*
There they stand yet, and modestly I think,

192 *shraped* trapped   194 *still* always   195 *grandsire* (Laomedon,
the builder of Troy)   212 *favor* face, features   219 *buss* kiss

The fall of every Phrygian stone will cost
A drop of Grecian blood. The end crowns all,
And that old common arbitrator, Time,
Will one day end it.

225 *Ulysses.*   So to him we leave it.
Most gentle and most valiant Hector, welcome.
After the general, I beseech you next
To feast with me and see me at my tent.

Achilles. I shall forestall thee, Lord Ulysses, thou!
230 Now, Hector, I have fed mine eyes on thee;
I have with exact view perused thee, Hector,
And quoted° joint by joint.

Hector.   Is this Achilles?

Achilles. I am Achilles.

Hector. Stand fair,° I pray thee; let me look on thee.

Achilles. Behold thy fill.

235 *Hector.*   Nay, I have done already.

Achilles. Thou art too brief. I will the second time,
As I would buy thee, view thee limb by limb.

Hector. O, like a book of sport thou'lt read me o'er;
But there's more in me than thou understand'st.
240 Why dost thou so oppress me with thine eye?

Achilles. Tell me, you heavens, in which part of his
       body
Shall I destroy him, whether there, or there, or
       there?
That I may give the local wound a name,
And make distinct the very breach whereout
245 Hector's great spirit flew. Answer me, heavens!

Hector. It would discredit the blessed gods, proud man,
To answer such a question. Stand again.
Think'st thou to catch my life so pleasantly°

232 *quoted* made exact mental note, scrutinized   234 *Stand fair*
stand openly, face me   248 *pleasantly* casually, merrily

As to prenominate in nice conjecture°
Where thou wilt hit me dead?

Achilles.   I tell thee, yea.   250

Hector. Wert thou an oracle to tell me so,
I'd not believe thee. Henceforth guard thee well,
For I'll not kill thee there, nor there, nor there;
But, by the forge that stithied° Mars his helm,
I'll kill thee everywhere, yea, o'er and o'er.   255
You wisest Grecians, pardon me this brag.
His insolence draws folly from my lips;
But I'll endeavor deeds to match these words,
Or may I never——

Ajax.   Do not chafe thee, cousin;
And you, Achilles, let these threats alone,   260
Till accident or purpose bring you to't.
You may have every day enough of Hector,
If you have stomach.° The general state,° I fear,
Can scarce entreat you to be odd° with him.

Hector. I pray you, let us see you in the field.   265
We have had pelting° wars since you refused
The Grecians' cause.

Achilles.   Dost thou entreat° me, Hector?
Tomorrow do I meet thee, fell° as death;
Tonight all friends.

Hector.   Thy hand upon that match.

Agamemnon. First, all you peers of Greece, go to my
     tent;   270
There in the full convive° we. Afterwards,
As Hector's leisure and your bounties shall
Concur together, severally° entreat him
To taste your bounties. Let the trumpets blow,

---

249 *prenominate in nice conjecture* name beforehand in detailed
conjecture   254 *stithied* forged   263 *stomach* inclination, relish
263 *general state* commanders in council   264 *odd* at odds, engaged in combat   266 *pelting* paltry, petty   267 *entreat* invite   268
fell fierce   271 *convive* feast   273 *severally* individually

275   That this great soldier may his welcome know.
          Exeunt [all except Troilus and Ulysses].

   Troilus. My Lord Ulysses, tell me, I beseech you,
    In what place of the field doth Calchas keep?°

   Ulysses. At Menelaus' tent, most princely Troilus.
    There Diomed doth feast with him tonight—
280 Who neither looks upon the heaven nor earth,
    But gives all gaze and bent of amorous view
    On the fair Cressid.

   Troilus. Shall I, sweet lord, be bound to you so much,
    After we part from Agamemnon's tent,
    To bring me thither?

285 *Ulysses.*   You shall command me, sir.
    But gentle tell me, of what honor was
    This Cressida in Troy? Had she no lover there
    That wails her absence?

   Troilus. O, sir, to such as boasting show their scars
290 A mock is due. Will you walk on, my lord?
    She was beloved, she loved; she is, and doth;
    But still sweet love is food for fortune's tooth.
                           Exeunt.

277 *keep* dwell

[ACT V

Scene I. *The Greek camp.*]

Enter Achilles and Patroclus.

Achilles. I'll heat his blood with Greekish wine to-
night,
Which with my scimitar I'll cool tomorrow.
Patroclus, let us feast him to the height.

Enter Thersites.

Patroclus. Here comes Thersites.

Achilles.   How now, thou cur
of envy!
Thou crusty batch° of nature, what's the news?   5

Thersites. Why, thou picture of what thou seemest,°
and idol of idiot-worshipers, here's a letter for thee.

Achilles. From whence, fragment?

Thersites. Why, thou full dish of fool, from Troy.

<hr />

V.i.5 *batch* (a mass of anything baked together, or baked without reheating the oven) 6 *thou picture of what thou seemest*
(i.e., who is nothing more than one glance sufficiently reveals)

10   *Patroclus.* Who keeps the tent now?°

Thersites. The surgeon's box or the patient's wound.°

Patroclus. Well said, adversity, and what needs these tricks?

Thersites. Prithee, be silent, boy; I profit not by thy
15   talk. Thou art said to be Achilles' male varlet.

Patroclus. Male varlet, you rogue! What's that?

Thersites. Why, his masculine whore. Now, the rotten
diseases of the south,° the guts-griping ruptures,
catarrhs, loads o' gravel in the back, lethargies,
20   cold palsies,° raw eyes, dirt-rotten livers, wheez-
ing lungs, bladders full of imposthume,° sciaticas,
lime-kilns° i'the palm, incurable bone-ache, and
the riveled° fee-simple of the tetter,° and the like,
take and take again such preposterous discoveries!°

25   *Patroclus.* Why, thou damnable box of envy, thou,
what means thou to curse thus?

Thersites. Do I curse thee?

Patroclus. Why, no, you ruinous butt,° you whoreson
indistinguishable° cur, no.

30   *Thersites.* No? Why art thou then exasperate, thou
idle immaterial skein of sleave silk,° thou green
sarcenet° flap for a sore eye, thou tassel of a
prodigal's purse, thou? Ah, how the poor world is

---

10 *Who keeps the tent now?* (Thersites can no longer taunt Achilles for refusing to leave his tent)   11 *The surgeon's . . . wound*
(from the play on "tent," a surgeon's probe for wounds)   18 *diseases of the south* i.e., venereal diseases   19–20 *gravel . . . palsies*
kidney stones, apoplectic strokes, paralysis of the limbs   21 *imposthume* internal abscess   22 *lime-kilns* psoriasis (burning red
patches covered with scales)   23 *riveled* wrinkled   23 *fee-simple of the tetter* chronic ringworm (?) ("fee-simple" implies unlimited possession)   24 *discoveries* (referring generally to—in
Thersites' opinion—such absurd monstrosities as Patroclus)   28
ruinous butt dilapidated cask   29 *indistinguishable* shapeless (here
suggesting mongrel)   31 *sleave silk* soft silk floss   32 *sarcenet*
(a fine silk taffeta)

pestered with such water-flies, diminutives of nature.   35

Patroclus. Out, gall!

Thersites. Finch egg!

Achilles. My sweet Patroclus, I am thwarted quite
    From my great purpose in tomorrow's battle.
    Here is a letter from Queen Hecuba,   40
    A token from her daughter, my fair love,
    Both taxing° me and gaging° me to keep
    An oath that I have sworn. I will not break it.
    Fall Greeks, fail fame, honor or go or° stay,
    My major vow lies here; this I'll obey.   45
    Come, come, Thersites, help to trim my tent;
    This night in banqueting must all be spent.
    Away, Patroclus!   *Exit [with Patroclus].*

Thersites. With too much blood and too little brain,
    these two may run mad; but if with too much brain   50
    and too little blood they do, I'll be a curer of mad-
    men. Here's Agamemnon, an honest fellow enough,
    and one that loves quails,° but he has not so much
    brain as ear-wax; and the goodly transformation
    of Jupiter° there, his brother, the bull, the primi- 55
    tive statue and oblique memorial of cuckolds°—
    a thrifty° shoeing-horn in a chain, hanging at his
    brother's leg°—to what form but that he is should
    wit larded with malice and malice forced° with wit
    turn him to? To an ass, were nothing; he is both   60
    ass and ox. To an ox, were nothing; he is both ox
    and ass. To be a dog, a mule, a cat, a fitchew,°

42 *taxing* censuring   42 *gaging* engaging to a promise   44 *or go
or* either go or   53 *quails* prostitutes   54–55 *transformation of
Jupiter* (i.e., into a bull, in which shape he seduced Europa)   55–
56 *the primitive statue . . . of cuckolds* (in having horns, the emblem or symbol of cuckoldry, although since Europa was not
married, the parallel to Paris' rape of Helen is "oblique")   57
thrifty stingy   57–58 *hanging at his brother's leg* (1) as Agamemnon's tool, appropriately enough a "horn," his pretext for
war (2) as being entirely dependent on Agamemnon   59 *forced*
stuffed, intermixed   62 *fitchew* polecat

a toad, a lizard, an owl, a puttock,° or a herring
without a roe, I would not care; but to be Menelaus!
65 I would conspire against destiny. Ask me not what
I would be, if I were not Thersites, for I care not
to be° the louse of a lazar,° so I were not Menelaus.
Hey-day, sprites and fires!

*Enter Agamemnon, Ulysses, Nestor, [Hector, Ajax,
Troilus, Menelaus,] and Diomedes, with lights.*

Agamemnon. We go wrong, we go wrong.

Ajax.   No, yonder 'tis;
There, where we see the lights.

70 *Hector.*   ·   I trouble you.

Ajax. No, not a whit.

Ulysses.   Here comes himself to guide you.

Enter Achilles.

Achilles. Welcome, brave Hector; welcome, princes
all.

Agamemnon. So now, fair prince of Troy, I bid good
night.
Ajax commands the guard to tend on you.

75 *Hector.* Thanks and good night to the Greeks' general.

Menelaus. Good night, my lord.

Hector. Good night, sweet Lord Menelaus.

Thersites. Sweet draught!° "Sweet," quoth 'a! Sweet
sink, sweet sewer.

Achilles. Good night and welcome both at once, to
80   those
That go or tarry.

63 *puttock* kite, a small hawk feeding on carrion 66–67 *I care not
to be* I wouldn't mind being 67 *lazar* leper 78 *draught* privy,
cesspool

Agamemnon. Good night.
> *Exeunt Agamemnon, Menelaus.*

Achilles. Old Nestor tarries, and you too, Diomed,
  Keep Hector company an hour or two.

Diomedes. I cannot, lord; I have important business,   85
  The tide° whereof is now. Good night, great Hector.

Hector. Give me your hand.

Ulysses. [*Aside to Troilus*] Follow his torch; he goes
    to Calchas' tent.
  I'll keep you company.

Troilus. Sweet sir, you honor me.

Hector.   And so, good night.   90
    [*Exeunt Diomedes, then Ulysses and Troilus.*]

Achilles. Come, come, enter my tent.
> *Exeunt [Achilles, Hector, Ajax, and Nestor].*

Thersites. That same Diomed's a false-hearted rogue,
  a most unjust knave; I will no more trust him when
  he leers than I will a serpent when he hisses. He
  will spend his mouth and promise like Brabbler   95
  the hound;° but when he performs, astronomers
  foretell it. It is prodigious, there will come some
  change. The sun borrows of the moon when Diomed keeps his word. I will rather leave to see°
  Hector than not to dog him. They say he keeps a   100
  Troyan drab, and uses the traitor Calchas' tent.
  I'll after—nothing but lechery! All incontinent var-
  lets!   [*Exit.*]

---

86 *tide* time   95–96 *Brabbler the hound* (a hunting hound who
would "spend his mouth" in barking while not on the scent would
be called "babbler" or "brabbler" by his master)   99 *leave to see*
miss seeing

[Scene II.   *The Greek camp.*]

Enter Diomed.

Diomedes. What, are you up here, ho? Speak.

Calchas. [*Within*] Who calls?

Diomedes. Diomed. Calchas, I think. Where's your
   daughter?

Calchas. [*Within*] She comes to you.

Enter Troilus and Ulysses; [after them Thersites.]

⁵ *Ulysses.* Stand where the torch may not discover us.

Enter Cressid.

Troilus. Cressid comes forth to him.

Diomedes.   How now, my charge!

Cressida. Now, my sweet guardian! Hark, a word with
   you.   [*Whispers.*]

Troilus. Yea, so familiar!

Ulysses. She will sing any man at first sight.

¹⁰ *Thersites.* And any man may sing her, if he can take
   her cliff;° she's noted.°

Diomedes. Will you remember?

Cressida. Remember? Yes.

V.ii.11 *cliff* clef (signifying the musical key; with an obscene
pun on "cleft")   11 *noted* reputed a loose woman (with a pun on
musical notes)

Diomedes. Nay, but do, then;
 And let your mind be coupled with your words.   *15*

Troilus. What shall she remember?

Ulysses. List!

Cressida. Sweet honey Greek, tempt me no more to
 folly.

Thersites. Roguery!

Diomedes. Nay, then——

Cressida.   I'll tell you what——   *20*

Diomedes. Foh, foh! Come, tell a pin. You are for-
 sworn.

Cressida. In faith, I cannot. What would you have me
 do?

Thersites. A juggling trick—to be secretly° open.

Diomedes. What did you swear you would bestow on
 me?

Cressida. I prithee, do not hold me to mine oath;   *25*
 Bid me do anything but that, sweet Greek.

Diomedes. Good night.

Troilus. Hold, patience!

Ulysses. How now, Troyan?

Cressida. Diomed——   *30*

Diomedes. No, no, good night; I'll be your fool no
 more.

Troilus. Thy better must.

Cressida.   Hark, a word in your ear.

Troilus. O plague and madness!

Ulysses. You are moved, prince; let us depart, I pray,

23 *secretly* privately, sexually

35 Lest your displeasure should enlarge itself
To wrathful terms. This place is dangerous;
The time right deadly. I beseech you, go.

Troilus. Behold, I pray you!

Ulysses.   Nay, good my lord, go off;
You flow to great distraction. Come, my lord.

Troilus. I prithee, stay.

40 *Ulysses.*   You have not patience; come.

Troilus. I pray you, stay! By hell, and all hell's tor-
ments, I will not speak a word!

Diomedes.   And so, good night.

Cressida. Nay, but you part in anger.

Troilus.   Doth that grieve thee?
O withered truth!

Ulysses.   How now, my lord!

Troilus.   By Jove,
I will be patient.

45 *Cressida.*   Guardian! Why, Greek!

Diomedes. Foh, foh! Adieu; you palter.

Cressida. In faith, I do not. Come hither once again.

Ulysses. You shake, my lord, at something. Will you
go?
You will break out.

Troilus.   She strokes his cheek!

Ulysses.   Come, come.

50 *Troilus.* Nay, stay; by Jove, I will not speak a word.
There is between my will and all offenses
A guard of patience. Stay a little while.

Thersites. How the devil Luxury,° with his fat rump

53 *Luxury* lechery

and potato° finger, tickles these together. Fry,   55
lechery, fry!

Diomedes. But will you, then?

Cressida. In faith, I will, la; never trust me else.

Diomedes. Give me some token for the surety of it.

Cressida. I'll fetch you one.   *Exit.*

Ulysses. You have sworn patience.

Troilus.   Fear me not, my lord;   60
I will not be myself, nor have cognition
Of what I feel. I am all patience.

                    Enter Cressida.

Thersites. Now the pledge! Now, now, now!

Cressida. Here, Diomed, keep this sleeve.

Troilus. O beauty, where is thy faith?

Ulysses.   My lord——   65

Troilus. I will be patient; outwardly I will.

Cressida. You look upon that sleeve; behold it well.
He loved me—O false wench! Give't me again.

Diomedes. Whose was't?

Cressida.   It is no matter, now I have't again.
I will not meet with you tomorrow night.   70
I prithee, Diomed, visit me no more.

Thersites. Now she sharpens.° Well said, whetstone!

Diomedes. I shall have it.

Cressida.   What, this?

Diomedes.   Ay, that.

Cressida. O, all you gods! O pretty, pretty pledge!

---

54 *potato* (potatoes were thought to be aphrodisiac)   72 *sharpens*
i.e., whets Diomedes' desire

75   Thy master now lies thinking on his bed
Of thee and me, and sighs, and takes my glove,
And gives memorial° dainty kisses to it,
As I kiss thee. Nay, do not snatch it from me;
He that takes that doth take my heart withal.

80   *Diomedes.* I had your heart before; this follows it.

Troilus. I did swear patience.

Cressida. You shall not have it, Diomed; faith, you
    shall not;
I'll give you something else.

Diomedes. I will have this. Whose was it?

Cressida.   It is no matter.

85   *Diomedes.* Come, tell me whose it was.

Cressida. 'Twas one's that loved me better than you
    will.
But, now you have it, take it.

Diomedes.   Whose was it?

Cressida. By all Diana's waiting-women° yond,
And by herself, I will not tell you whose.

90   *Diomedes.* Tomorrow will I wear it on my helm,
And grieve his spirit that dares not challenge it.

Troilus. Wert thou the devil, and wor'st it on thy horn,
It should be challenged.

Cressida. Well, well, 'tis done, 'tis past. And yet it is
    not;
I will not keep my word.

95   *Diomedes.*   Why then, farewell;
Thou never shalt mock Diomed again.

Cressida. You shall not go. One cannot speak a word
But it straight starts you.°

77 *memorial* in remembrance   88 *Diana's waiting-women* i.e., the
stars clustered about the moon   98 *straight starts you* immediately
makes you start angrily away

Diomedes.   I do not like this fooling.

Thersites. Nor I, by Pluto; but that that likes° not you
  Pleases me best.   100

Diomedes. What, shall I come? The hour?

Cressida.   Ay, come—
    O Jove!—
  Do come—I shall be plagued.°

Diomedes.   Farewell till then.

Cressida. Good night. I prithee, come.
                                  Exit [Diomedes].
  Troilus, farewell. One eye yet looks on thee,
  But with my heart the other eye doth see.   105
  Ah, poor our sex!° This fault in us I find,
  The error° of our eye directs our mind.
  What error leads must err. O, then conclude,
  Minds swayed by eyes are full of turpitude.   *Exit.*

Thersites. A proof of strength° she could not publish
    more,°   110
  Unless she said, "My mind is now turned whore."

Ulysses. All's done, my lord.

Troilus.   It is.

Ulysses.   Why stay we, then?

Troilus. To make a recordation to my soul
  Of every syllable that here was spoke.
  But if I tell how these two did coact,   115
  Shall I not lie in publishing a truth?
  Sith yet there is a credence in my heart,
  An esperance° so obstinately strong,
  That doth invert th' attest° of eyes and ears,
  As if those organs had deceptious° functions,   120
  Created only to calumniate.

99 *likes* pleases 102 *plagued* punished 106 *poor our sex* our
poor sex 107 *error* wandering (here, physically and morally)
110 *proof of strength* strong proof 110 *publish more* confess more
clearly 118 *esperance* hope 119 *attest* testimony 120 *deceptious*
deceiving

Was Cressid here?

Ulysses.   I cannot conjure,° Troyan.

Troilus. She was not, sure.

Ulysses.   Most sure she was.

Troilus. Why, my negation° hath no taste of madness.

125 *Ulysses.* Nor mine, my lord. Cressid was here but now.

Troilus. Let it not be believed for° womanhood!
    Think we had mothers; do not give advantage
    To stubborn critics, apt, without a theme,
    For depravation,° to square the general sex
130 By Cressid's rule.° Rather think this not Cressid.

Ulysses. What hath she done, prince, that can soil our
    mothers?

Troilus. Nothing at all, unless that this were she.

Thersites. Will 'a swagger himself out on's own eyes?°

Troilus. This she? No, this is Diomed's Cressida.
135 If beauty have a soul, this is not she;
    If souls guide vows, if vows be sanctimonies,
    If sanctimony be the gods' delight,
    If there be rule in unity itself,°
    This was not she. O madness of discourse,°
140 That cause sets up with and against itself:
    Bifold authority,° where reason can revolt

---

122 *conjure* raise spirits   124 *negation* denial   126 *for* for the sake of   128–29 *apt . . . For depravation* ready and eager to claim the depravity of women, but lacking examples   129–130 *square the . . . Cressid's rule* take the measure of womankind by Cressida's standard   133 *Will 'a . . . on's own eyes?* i.e., will he bluff himself out of trusting his own sight?   138 *If there . . . unity itself* i.e., if it is a true principle that one cannot be two (that Cressida may not be divided into two persons)   139 *discourse* reasonable sequence of thought   140–41 *That cause . . . Bifold authority* that case of principle wherein divided authority both supports and confutes the question

Without perdition, and loss assume all reason
Without revolt.° This is, and is not, Cressid.
Within my soul there doth conduce° a fight
Of this strange nature that a thing inseparate°   145
Divides more wider than the sky and earth;
And yet the spacious breadth of this division
Admits no orifex° for a point as subtle°
As Ariachne's broken woof° to enter.
Instance,° O instance, strong as Pluto's gates;   150
Cressid is mine, tied with the bonds of heaven.
Instance, O instance, strong as heaven itself;
The bonds of heaven are slipped, dissolved, and
    loosed,
And with another knot, five-finger-tied,°
The fractions of her faith, orts° of her love,   155
The fragments, scraps, the bits, and greasy relics
Of her o'ereaten° faith, are given to Diomed.

Ulysses. May worthy Troilus be half attached°
With that which here his passion doth express?

Troilus. Ay, Greek! And that shall be divulgèd well   160
In characters as red as Mars his heart
Inflamed with Venus. Never did young man fancy
With so eternal and so fixed a soul.
Hark, Greek. Much as I do Cressid love,
So much by weight hate I her Diomed;   165
That sleeve is mine that he'll bear on his helm;
Were it a casque° composed by Vulcan's skill,
My sword should bite it. Not the dreadful spout
Which shipmen do the hurricano call,

141–43 *where reason . . . Without revolt* where reason can rebel
without subsequent chaos, and loss of understanding assume the
appearance of reason without reason itself objecting   144 *conduce*
go on   145 *thing inseparate* that which is indivisible; i.e., Cressida
148 *orifex* opening   148 *subtle* finely sharp   149 *Ariachne's broken
woof* (Arachne was a Lydian woman who challenged Athene to
a weaving contest, but the goddess, angered, tore her work to
shreds and changed her to a spider)   150 *Instance* example, proof
(here, in the sense of "for instance")   154 *five-fingered-tied* (1) so
tied because Cressida's hand is now Diomedes' (?) (2) i.e., impossible to untie (?)   155 *orts* scraps, pieces (as of food)   157 *o'ereaten* eaten through, picked over (as a dog will eat the best pieces
first, the last scraps left over)   158 *half attached* i.e., half so much
affected (as it appears)   167 *casque* helmet

170   Constringed° in mass by the almighty sun,
     Shall dizzy with more clamor Neptune's ear
     In his descent than shall my prompted° sword
     Falling on Diomed.

     Thersites. He'll tickle it for his concupy.°

175 *Troilus.* O Cressid! O false Cressid! False, false, false!
     Let all untruths stand by thy stainèd name,
     And they'll seem glorious.

     Ulysses.   O, contain yourself;
     Your passion draws ears hither.

                    Enter Aeneas.

     Aeneas. I have been seeking you this hour, my lord.
180   Hector, by this, is arming him° in Troy;
     Ajax, your guard, stays to conduct you home.

     Troilus. Have with you,° prince. My courteous lord,
          adieu.
     Farewell, revolted fair; and Diomed,
     Stand fast, and wear a castle on thy head!

185 *Ulysses.* I'll bring you to the gates.

     Troilus. Accept distracted thanks.
                    Exeunt Troilus, Aeneas, and Ulysses.

     Thersites. Would I could meet that rogue Diomed. I
     would croak like a raven; I would bode,° I would
     bode. Patroclus will give me anything for the in-
190 telligence of this whore. The parrot will not do
     more for an almond than he for a commodious
     drab.° Lechery, lechery; still wars and lechery;
     nothing else holds fashion. A burning devil° take
     them!   *Exit.*

170 *Constringed* drawn together   172 *prompted* i.e., urged on, as
having its own motive   174 *He'll tickle it for his concupy* he'll
be well tickled for his concupiscence ("it" refers contemptuously
to Diomedes)   180 *him* himself   182 *Have with you* let's go
along   188 *bode* portend disaster   191–92 *commodious drab* serv-
iceable whore   193 *burning devil* venereal disease

[Scene III.   *Troy; Priam's palace.*]

Enter Hector and Andromache.

Andromache. When was my lord so much ungently
    tempered,
  To stop his ears against admonishment?
  Unarm, unarm, and do not fight today.

Hector. You train° me to offend° you; get you in.
  By all the everlasting gods, I'll go.   *5*

Andromache. My dreams will, sure, prove ominous
    to the day.°

Hector. No more, I say.

Enter Cassandra.

Cassandra.   Where is my brother Hector?

Andromache. Here, sister; armed and bloody in intent.
  Consort with me in loud and dear petition;
  Pursue we him on knees, for I have dreamed   *10*
  Of bloody turbulence, and this whole night
  Hath nothing been but shapes and forms of
    slaughter.

Cassandra. O, 'tis true.

Hector.   Ho, bid my trumpet sound.

Cassandra. No notes of sally, for the heavens, sweet
  brother.

Hector. Be gone, I say; the gods have heard me swear.   *15*

V.iii.4 *train* tempt   4 *offend* injure, insult   6 *ominous to the day*
omens applicable to this day

Cassandra. The gods are deaf to hot and peevish°
        vows.
    They are polluted offerings, more abhorred
    Than spotted° livers in the sacrifice.

Andromache. O, be persuaded! Do not count it holy
20   To hurt by being just. It is as lawful,
    For° we would give much, to use violent thefts,
    And rob in the behalf of charity.

Cassandra. It is the purpose that makes strong the
        vow;
    But vows to every purpose must not hold.°
    Unarm, sweet Hector.

25 *Hector.*   Hold you still, I say.
    Mine honor keeps the weather° of my fate.
    Life every man holds dear; but the dear° man
    Holds honor far more precious-dear than life.

                Enter Troilus.

    How now, young man; mean'st thou to fight today?

30 *Andromache.* Cassandra, call my father to persuade.
                        Exit Cassandra.

Hector. No, faith, young Troilus; doff thy harness,
        youth.
    I am today i' the vein of chivalry.
    Let grow thy sinews till their knots be strong,
    And tempt not yet the brushes° of the war.
35   Unarm thee; go, and doubt thou not, brave boy,
    I'll stand today for thee and me and Troy.

Troilus. Brother, you have a vice of mercy in you,
    Which better fits a lion than a man.

---

16 *peevish* brash, perverse   18 *spotted* i.e., spoiled   21 *For* because   24 *But vows . . . not hold* i.e., vows sworn indiscriminately
or to unlawful purpose should not bind the swearer   26 *keeps
the weather* i.e., maintains the position of advantage   27 *dear*
valuable, worthy   34 *brushes* encounters

Hector. What vice is that? Good Troilus, chide me for
   it.

Troilus. When many times the captive Grecian falls,   40
   Even in the fan and wind of your fair sword,
   You bid them rise and live.

Hector. O, 'tis fair play.

Troilus.   Fool's play, by heaven, Hector.

Hector. How now? How now?

Troilus.   For the love of all the gods,
   Let's leave the hermit pity with our mother,   45
   And when we have our armors buckled on,
   The venomed vengeance ride upon our swords,
   Spur them to ruthful° work, rein them from ruth.°

Hector. Fie, savage, fie!

Troilus.   Hector, then 'tis wars.°

Hector. Troilus, I would not have you fight today.   50

Troilus. Who should withhold me?
   Not fate, obedience, nor the hand of Mars
   Beck'ning with fiery truncheon° my retire;
   Not Priamus and Hecuba on knees,
   Their eyes o'ergallèd° with recourse° of tears;   55
   Nor you, my brother, with your true sword drawn,
   Opposed to hinder me, should stop my way,
   But by my ruin.

Enter Priam and Cassandra.

Cassandra. Lay hold upon him, Priam, hold him fast;
   He is thy crutch. Now if thou lose thy stay,°   60
   Thou on him leaning, and all Troy on thee,
   Fall all together.

48 *ruthful* i.e., to be pitied, woeful 48 *ruth* pity 49 *then 'tis
wars* that's what war is 53 *truncheon* (a kind of baton used by
the referee of a combat to signal the end of the fight) 55 *o'er-
gallèd* inflamed 55 *recourse* repeated coursing down, constant
flowing 60 *stay* support

Priam.   Come, Hector, come; go back.
　　Thy wife hath dreamt, thy mother hath had visions,
　　Cassandra doth foresee, and I myself
65　　Am like a prophet suddenly enrapt
　　To tell thee that this day is ominous.
　　Therefore, come back.

Hector.   Aeneas is afield;
　　And I do stand engaged to many Greeks,
　　Even in the faith of valor,° to appear
　　This morning to them.

70　*Priam.*   Ay, but thou shalt not go.

Hector. I must not break my faith.
　　You know me dutiful; therefore, dear sir,
　　Let me not shame respect,° but give me leave
　　To take that course by your consent and voice,
75　　Which you do here forbid me, royal Priam.

Cassandra. O Priam, yield not to him!

Andromache.   Do not, dear father.

Hector. Andromache, I am offended with you.
　　Upon the love you bear me, get you in.
　　　　　　　　　　　　　Exit Andromache.

Troilus. This foolish, dreaming, superstitious girl
　　Makes all these bodements.°

80　*Cassandra.*   O farewell, dear Hector!
　　Look, how thou diest; look, how thy eye turns pale;
　　Look, how thy wounds do bleed at many vents!
　　Hark, how Troy roars, how Hecuba cries out,
　　How poor Andromache shrills her dolors forth!
85　　Behold, distraction, frenzy, and amazement,
　　Like witless antics,° one another meet,
　　And all cry Hector! Hector's dead! O Hector!

Troilus. Away! Away!

69 *the faith of valor* a brave man's promise   73 *shame respect* i.e.,
disgrace the respect due to a parent   80 *bodements* evil omens
86 *antics* madmen

Cassandra. Farewell. Yet, soft; Hector, I take my
     leave.
  Thou dost thyself and all our Troy deceive.   *Exit.*   90

Hector. You are amazed, my liege, at her exclaim.
  Go in and cheer the town. We'll forth and fight;
  Do deeds worth praise and tell you them at night.

Priam. Farewell. The gods with safety stand about
     thee.   [*Exeunt Priam and Hector.*] *Alarum.*

Troilus. They are at it, hark. Proud Diomed, believe,   95
  I come to lose my arm, or win my sleeve.

                    Enter Pandar.

Pandarus. Do you hear, my lord? Do you hear?

Troilus. What now?

Pandarus. Here's a letter come from yond poor girl.

Troilus. Let me read.   100

Pandarus. A whoreson tisick,° a whoreson rascally
  tisick so troubles me, and the foolish fortune of
  this girl; and what one thing, what another, that I
  shall leave you one o'th'se days; and I have a
  rheum in mine eyes too, and such an ache in my   105
  bones that, unless a man were cursed, I cannot tell
  what to think on't. What says she there?

Troilus. Words, words, mere words, no matter from
     the heart;
  Th' effect doth operate another way.
                         [*Tearing the letter.*]
  Go, wind to wind, there turn and change together.   110
  My love with words and errors° still she feeds,
  But edifies another with her deeds.   *Exeunt.*

101 *tisick* cough   111 *errors* meanderings, i.e., underhanded tricks
(?)

[Scene IV. *The battlefield.*]

[*Alarum.*] *Enter Thersites. Excursions.*

Thersites. Now they are clapperclawing one another;
I'll go look on. That dissembling abominable varlet,
Diomed, has got that same scurvy doting foolish
young knave's sleeve of Troy there in his helm. I
would fain see them meet, that that same young
Troyan ass, that loves the whore there, might send
that Greekish whoremasterly villain with the sleeve
back to the dissembling luxurious drab, of a sleeve-
less° errand. O'the t'other side, the policy of those
crafty swearing° rascals—that stale old mouse-
eaten dry cheese, Nestor, and that same dog-fox,
Ulysses—is not proved worth a blackberry. They
set me up, in policy, that mongrel cur, Ajax,
against that dog of as bad a kind, Achilles; and
now is the cùr Ajax prouder than the cur Achilles,
and will not arm today. Whereupon the Grecians
begin to proclaim barbarism,° and policy grows
into an ill opinion.

Enter Diomedes and Troilus.

Soft, here comes sleeve, and t'other.

Troilus. Fly not; for shouldst thou take the river Styx,
I would swim after.

Diomedes.   Thou dost miscall retire.

V.iv.8–9 *sleeveless* futile, fruitless   10 *crafty swearing* craftily swearing, i.e., crafty to the extent of perjury   17 *proclaim barbarism*
i.e., recognize the authority of chaos (to replace policy)

I do not fly, but advantageous care
Withdrew me from the odds of multitude.°
Have at thee!

Thersites. Hold thy whore, Grecian! Now for thy
  whore,   25
  Troyan! Now the sleeve, now the sleeve!
          [*Exeunt Troilus and Diomedes, fighting.*]

Enter Hector.

Hector. What art thou, Greek? Art thou for Hector's
  match?
  Art thou of blood and honor?

Thersites. No, no, I am a rascal, a scurvy railing
  knave, a very filthy rogue.   30

Hector. I do believe thee; live.   [*Exit.*]

Thersites. God-a-mercy, that thou wilt believe me; but
  a plague break thy neck—for frighting me. What's
  become of the wenching rogues? I think they have
  swallowed one another. I would laugh at that mir-   35
  acle—yet, in a sort, lechery eats itself. I'll seek
  them.   *Exit.*

[Scene V.   *The battlefield.*]

Enter Diomed and Servant.

Diomedes. Go, go, my servant, take thou Troilus'
  horse;
  Present the fair steed to my Lady Cressid.
  Fellow, commend my service to her beauty;

22–23 *but advantageous . . . of multitude* care for my own advantage led me to avoid facing absurdly heavy odds

Tell her I have chastised the amorous Troyan,
And am her knight by proof.

5 *Servant.*   I go, my lord. [*Exit.*]

Enter Agamemnon.

Agamemnon. Renew, renew! The fierce Polydamas
    Hath beat down Menon; bastard Margarelon
    Hath Doreus prisoner,
    And stands colossus-wise, waving his beam,°
10 Upon the pashèd corses° of the kings
    Epistrophus and Cedius; Polyxenes is slain,
    Amphimachus and Thoas deadly hurt,
    Patroclus ta'en or slain, and Palamedes
    Sore hurt and bruised. The dreadful Sagittary°
15 Appals our numbers. Haste we, Diomed,
    To reinforcement, or we perish all.

Enter Nestor.

Nestor. Go, bear Patroclus' body to Achilles,
    And bid the snail-paced Ajax arm for shame.
    There is a thousand Hectors in the field;
20 Now here he fights on Galathe his horse,
    And there lacks work; anon he's there afoot,
    And there they fly or die, like scalèd sculls°
    Before the belching whale; then is he yonder,
    And there the strawy Greeks, ripe for his edge,°
25 Fall down before him, like a mower's swath.
    Here, there, and everywhere, he leaves and takes,
    Dexterity so obeying appetite
    That what he will he does, and does so much
    That proof° is called impossibility.

V.v.9 *beam* spear 10 *pashèd corses* battered corpses 14 *Sagittary* (a centaur [half man, half horse], who was a splendid archer and aided the Trojans) 22 *scalèd sculls* scaly schools of fish 24 *strawy . . . edge* i.e., Greeks who are like straw, ripe for the edge of the scythe 29 *proof* visible fact

Enter Ulysses.

Ulysses. O, courage, courage, princes! Great Achilles   *30*
   Is arming, weeping, cursing, vowing vengeance!
   Patroclus' wounds have roused his drowsy blood,
   Together with his mangled Myrmidons,
   That noseless, handless, hacked and chipped, come
     to him,
   Crying on Hector. Ajax hath lost a friend,   *35*
   And foams at mouth, and he is armed and at it,
   Roaring for Troilus, who hath done today
   Mad and fantastic execution,
   Engaging and redeeming of himself
   With such a careless force and forceless° care   *40*
   As if that luck, in very spite of cunning,
   Bade him win all.

Enter Ajax.

Ajax. Troilus, thou coward Troilus!   *Exit.*

Diomedes.   Ay, there, there.

Nestor. So, so, we draw together.   *Exit.*

Enter Achilles.

Achilles.   Where is this Hector?
   Come, come, thou boy-queller,° show thy face;   *45*
   Know what it is to meet Achilles angry.
   Hector, where's Hector? I will none but Hector.
                               Exit.

40 *forceless* casual, reckless   45 *boy-queller* boy-killer

[Scene VI. *The battlefield.*]

Enter Ajax.

Ajax. Troilus, thou coward Troilus, show thy head!

Enter Diomedes.

Diomedes. Troilus, I say, where's Troilus?

Ajax.   What wouldst thou?

Diomedes. I would correct him.

Ajax. Were I the general, thou shouldst have my office
5   Ere that correction.° Troilus, I say! What, Troilus!

Enter Troilus.

Troilus. O traitor Diomed! Turn thy false face, thou
        traitor,
    And pay thy life thou owest me for my horse.°

Diomedes. Ha, art thou there?

Ajax. I'll fight with him alone. Stand, Diomed.

10 *Diomedes.* He is my prize; I will not look upon.°

Troilus. Come, both you cogging° Greeks; have at
        you both!   [*Exeunt, fighting.*]

[*Enter Hector.*]

Hector. Yea, Troilus? O, well fought, my youngest
        brother!

V.vi.5 *correction* i.e., privilege to correct   7 *horse* (with a pun on
whore?)   10 *look upon* stand by   11 *cogging* deceitful

Enter Achilles.

Achilles. Now do I see thee, ha! Have at thee,
    Hector!   [*They fight; Achilles tires.*]

Hector. Pause, if thou wilt.

Achilles. I do disdain thy courtesy, proud Troyan;   15
    Be happy that my arms are out of use.
    My rest and negligence befriends thee now,
    But thou anon shalt hear of me again;
    Till when, go seek thy fortune.   *Exit.*

Hector.   Fare thee well;
    I would have been much more a fresher man,   20
    Had I expected thee.

Enter Troilus.

                    How now, my brother!

Troilus. Ajax hath ta'en° Aeneas! Shall it be?
    No, by the flame of yonder glorious heaven,
    He shall not carry him;° I'll be ta'en too,
    Or bring him off. Fate, hear me what I say!   25
    I reck not though thou end my life today.   *Exit.*

Enter one in armor.

Hector. Stand, stand, thou Greek; thou art a goodly
    mark.
    No? Wilt thou not? I like thy armor well;
    I'll frush° it and unlock the rivets all,
    But I'll be master of it. Wilt thou not, beast, abide?   30
    Why then, fly on, I'll hunt thee for thy hide.
                          Exit [*in pursuit*].

22 *ta'en* taken captive   24 *carry him* prevail over him   29 *frush*
smash

[Scene VII.   *The battlefield.*]

Enter Achilles with Myrmidons.

Achilles. Come here about me, you my Myrmidons;
Mark what I say. Attend me where I wheel.
Strike not a stroke, but keep yourselves in breath.
And when I have the bloody Hector found,
Empale him° with your weapons round about;
In fellest° manner execute° your arms.
Follow me, sirs, and my proceedings eye;
It is decreed Hector the great must die.

Exit [with Myrmidons].

5

Enter Thersites, Menelaus, Paris [the last two fighting].

Thersites. The cuckold and the cuckold-maker are at
it. Now, bull! Now, dog! 'Loo,° Paris, 'loo! Now,
my double-horned Spartan! 'Loo, Paris, 'loo! The
bull has the game;° 'ware horns, ho!

Exeunt Paris and Menelaus.

10

Enter Bastard [Margarelon].

Bastard. Turn, slave, and fight.

Thersites. What art thou?

Bastard. A bastard son of Priam's.

15

Thersites. I am a bastard too; I love bastards. I am bastard begot, bastard instructed, bastard in mind, bas-

V.vii.5 *Empale him* hem him in   6 *fellest* cruelest   6 *execute* use
10 *Now, bull! Now, dog! 'Loo* (Thersites compares the combat
of Menelaus and Paris to the baiting of a bull by a dog, as it was
done in such arenas as the Paris Garden)   12 *has the game*
wins

tard in valor, in everything illegitimate. One bear will
not bite another, and wherefore should one bastard? Take heed, the quarrel's most ominous to us.   20
If the son of a whore fight for a whore, he tempts
judgment. Farewell, bastard.

Bastard. The devil take thee, coward!   *Exeunt.*

[Scene VIII.   *The battlefield.*]

Enter Hector.

Hector. Most putrefièd core, so fair without,
   Thy goodly armor thus hath cost thy life.
   Now is my day's work done; I'll take my breath.
   Rest, sword; thou hast thy fill of blood and death.
                    [*Puts off his helmet, and
                    hangs his shield behind him.*]

Enter Achilles and Myrmidons.

Achilles. Look, Hector, how the sun begins to set,   5
   How ugly night comes breathing at his heels.
   Even with the vail° and dark'ning of the sun,
   To close the day up, Hector's life is done.

Hector. I am unarmed; forgo this vantage, Greek.

Achilles. Strike, fellows, strike. This is the man I seek.   10
                    [*Hector falls.*]
   So, Ilion, fall thou next! Come, Troy, sink down!
   Here lies thy heart, thy sinews, and thy bone.
   On, Myrmidons, and cry you all amain,
   "Achilles hath the mighty Hector slain!"   *Retreat.*
   Hark, a retire upon our Grecian part.   15

V.viii.7 *vail* sinking, going down

One Greek. The Troyans' trumpets sound the like, my
    lord.

Achilles. The dragon wing of night o'erspreads the
    earth.
    And, sticklerlike,° the armies separates.
    My half-supped sword, that frankly° would have
    fed,
20   Pleased with this dainty bait, thus goes to bed.
                         [Sheathes his sword.]
    Come, tie his body to my horse's tail;
    Along the field I will the Troyan trail.   *Exeunt.*

[Scene IX. *The battlefield.*]

*Enter Agamemnon, Ajax, Menelaus, Nestor, Diomed,
    and the rest, marching. [Sound retreat. Shout.]*

Agamemnon. Hark, hark, what shout is that?

Nestor.   Peace, drums!

Soldiers. (*Within*)   Achilles!
    Achilles! Hector's slain! Achilles!

Diomedes. The bruit° is, Hector's slain, and by
    Achilles.

Ajax. If it be so, yet bragless let it be;
5   Great Hector was as good a man as he.

Agamemnon. March patiently along. Let one be sent
    To pray Achilles see us at our tent.
    If in his death the gods have us befriended,
    Great Troy is ours, and our sharp wars are ended.
                              Exeunt.

---

18 *sticklerlike* like an umpire separating combatants, and ordering the field 19 *frankly* freely, abundantly V.ix.3 *bruit* rumor

[Scene X.   *The battlefield.*]

Enter Aeneas, Paris, Antenor, Deiphobus.

Aeneas. Stand, ho! Yet are we masters of the field.
  Never go home; here starve we out the night.

Enter Troilus.

Troilus. Hector is slain.

All.   Hector! The gods forbid!

Troilus. He's dead and at the murderer's horse's tail,
  In beastly sort, dragged through the shameful field.   5
  Frown on, you heavens, effect your rage with speed;
  Sit, gods, upon your thrones, and smile° at Troy.
  I say, at once let your brief plagues be mercy,°
  And linger not our sure destructions on.

Aeneas. My lord, you do discomfort all the host.   10

Troilus. You understand me not that tell me so.
  I do not speak of flight, of fear, of death,
  But dare all imminence that gods and men
  Address their dangers in.° Hector is gone.
  Who shall tell Priam so, or Hecuba?   15
  Let him that will a screech owl° aye be called
  Go in to Troy, and say there Hector's dead.
  There is a word will Priam turn to stone,
  Make wells and Niobes° of the maids and wives,

V.x.7 *smile* i.e., in derision   8 *let . . . mercy* be merciful in letting the plagues you send destroy us quickly   13–14 *But dare . . .
dangers in* but instead dare whatever imminent dangers gods and
men may be preparing   16 *screech-owl* (a bearer of ill omen)   19
Niobes (Niobe wept for her slain children until she was turned into
a column of stone, from which tears continued to flow)

20 Cold statues of the youth, and in a word
    Scare Troy out of itself. But march away.
    Hector is dead; there is no more to say.
    Stay yet. You vile abominable tents,
    Thus proudly pitched upon our Phrygian plains,
25 Let Titan° rise as early as he dare,
    I'll through and through you! And, thou great-sized
        coward,°
    No space of earth shall sunder our two hates.
    I'll haunt thee like a wicked conscience still,
    That moldeth goblins swift as frenzy's thoughts.
30 Strike a free march to Troy. With comfort go;
    Hope of revenge shall hide our inward woe.

                Enter Pandarus.

Pandarus. But hear you, hear you!

Troilus. Hence, broker, lackey! Ignominy and shame
    Pursue thy life, and live aye with thy name.
                        Exeunt all but Pandarus.

35 *Pandarus.* A goodly medicine for my aching bones! O
    world, world! Thus is the poor agent despised. O
    traders and bawds, how earnestly are you set
    awork, and how ill requited! Why should our en-
    deavor be so loved, and the performance so
40 loathed? What verse for it? What instance for it?
    Let me see.
        Full merrily the humble-bee doth sing,
        Till he hath lost his honey and his sting;
        And being once subdued in armèd tail,
45   Sweet honey and sweet notes together fail.
    Good traders in the flesh, set this in your painted
        cloths:°
    "As many as be here of Pandar's hall,
    Your eyes, half out, weep out at Pandar's fall;
    Or if you cannot weep, yet give some groans,

_____

25 *Titan* (Helios, the sun, one of the Titans) 26 *coward* i.e.,
Achilles 46 *painted cloths* painted cloth hangings, used in brothels,
sometimes bearing mottoes

Though not for me, yet for your aching bones."   50
Brethren and sisters of the hold-door trade,°
Some two months hence my will shall here be
    made.
It should be now, but that my fear is this,
Some gallèd goose of Winchester° would hiss.
Till then I'll sweat° and seek about for eases,   55
And at that time bequeath you my diseases.

                           [*Exit.*]

                  FINIS

---

51 *hold-door trade* prostitution   54 *gallèd goose of Winchester*
angry prostitute (the Bishop of Winchester had once held jurisdiction over the area of London called Southwark, where many brothels
stood; a prostitute—and sometimes a venereal disease—was called
a "Winchester goose")   55 *sweat* (a treatment for gout or rheu-
matism, as well as for venereal disease)

Textual Note

It is now generally believed that the 1609 quarto of *Troilus and Cressida* was printed from a transcript made from Shakespeare's original draft of the play. It omits about forty-five lines, the Prologue, and many stage directions that appear in the Folio, but on the whole contains a text that stands closer to Shakespeare's original than does that of the Folio. Since the compositors of the Folio apparently worked not only from the Quarto but from Shakespeare's autograph manuscript, it is surprising that they did not produce the better text; their readings are mainly inferior to those of the Quarto.

The relative values of the two texts (both of them, in different ways, stemming from Shakespeare's manuscript, and both of them, therefore, authoritative) depend on the nature of the copy used by the compositors, and the care and intelligence with which they worked. It is possible that the Quarto represents the play as it was shortened for performance, but more likely that the transcriber of the original manuscript was confused by Shakespeare's own second thoughts and deletions and failed to record some revisions and added speeches. On the other hand, although the compositors of the Folio probably had for reference and collation not only the Quarto but the original manuscript itself, their goal was speed and not always accuracy. While they added many lines omitted in the Quarto, they also introduced many mistaken readings; one compositor in particular evidently suited himself in interpreting difficult words and phrases, and made hash of most of them. Other portions of the Folio text were printed with greater care, however, and since the manuscript at hand may have been used in the playhouse, these portions include more complete stage directions and speech heads than appear in the Quarto. The Folio, therefore, supplies the fuller text; it should be used occasionally to emend the Quarto, but the earlier edition remains the better text. Its readings are frequently superior to those of the Folio, although, naturally, where the Folio prints speeches entirely omitted in the Quarto, these must be considered authoritative. Similarly, those readings in the Folio which introduce corrections on the basis of copy which was either Shakespeare's or very close to his should be followed.

The present edition is based on the Quarto but adds passages from the Folio. (These additions are recorded in the list of departures printed below.) Act and scene divisions (none are given for this play in Quarto or Folio) have been added in square brackets, along with simple indications of locale. Abbreviations have been amplified, spelling and punctuation have been modernized, and "and" is printed "an" when it means "if." The position of a few stage directions has been slightly altered when necessary. Other departures from the Quarto are listed below, the adopted reading first in italics, and then the original reading in roman. The adopted reading is most often from the Folio; when it is not, it is followed by (ed) to indicate that it is an editor's conjecture rather than an authoritative reading.

Dedicatory address   37 *state* (ed) states

Prologue (Q omits)   12 *barks* (ed; F has "Barke")   19 *Sperr* (ed; F has "Stirre")

I.i.78 *she were not* she were   80 *what care I* what I

I.ii.17 *they* the   35 s.d. *Enter Pandarus* (Q omits)   187 *Ilium* Ilion   212 *man's heart* man heart   249 s.d. *Enter Common Soldiers* (Q omits)   294 s.d. *Exit Pandarus* (Q omits)

I.iii.i. s.d. *Sennet* (Q omits)   13 *every* euer   31 *thy* the   36 *patient* ancient   54 *Returns* (ed) Retires   61 *thy* the   70–74 *Agamemnon. Speak . . . oracle* (Q omits)   75 *basis* bases   110 *meets* melts   159 *unsquared* vnsquare   195 *and discredit* our discredit   212 s.d. *Tucket* (Q omits)   214 s.d. *Enter Aeneas* (Q omits)   247 *affair* affaires   250 *whisper him* whisper with him   252 *the attentive* that

attentiue 256 *loud* alowd 263 *rusty* restie 267 *That seeks* And
feeds 276 *compass* couple 294 *one* no 298 *will tell* tell 302
youth men 305 *first* sir 309 s.d. *Exeunt. Manent Ulysses and
Nestor* (Q omits) 315 *This 'tis* (Q omits) 334 *his honor* those
honours 354–56 *which . . . the limbs* (F emended from "in his" to
"his"; Q omits) 390 *tarre* arre

II.i.11 s.d. *Strikes him* (Q omits) 14 *vinewed'st* (F:whinid'st)
vnsalted 18 *oration* oration without booke 18 *a prayer* praier
42–43 *Ajax . . . Do, do* (Q assigns to Thersites as one speech) 47
Thou scurvy-valiant you scuruy valiant 57 s.d. *Enter Achilles and
Patroclus* (Q omits) 58 *do you* do yee 74 *I* It 77 *I'll* I 104 *i,
he knock out* and knocke at 109 *your grandsires had nails on thei,
toes* (F emended from "their" to "your") their grandsiers had nailes
120 *brach* (ed) brooch 127 *fifth* first 141 s.d. *Exit* (Q omits)

II.ii.14–15 *surety, Surety* surely Surely 27 *father* fathers 33 ...
reasons of reasons 47 *Let's* Sets 64 *shores* shore 75 *truce* ttuce
86 *he* be 96 s.d. *with her hair about her ears* (Q omits) 104 *eld*
(ed; F has "old") elders 210 *strike* shrike

II.iii.23 s.d. *Enter Patroclus* (Q omits) 27 *wouldst* couldst 33 *art*
art not 49 *thyself* Thersites 57–62 *Patroclus. You . . . a fool*
(Q omits) 65 *commanded of Agamemnon* commanded 69
Creator Prouer 71 *Patroclus* Come Patroclus 72 s.d. *Exit* (Q
omits) 76–77 *Now . . . all* (Q omits) 81 *shent* (ed; F has "sent")
sate 82 *appertainments* appertainings 91 *A word, my lord* (Q
omits) 104 s.d. *Enter Patroclus* (Q omits) 132 *pettish lunes* (F
emended from "lines" to "lunes") course, and time 132 *as if* and if
134 *carriage of this action* streame of his commencement 143
enter you entertaine 143 s.d. *Exit Ulysses* (Q omits) 160 *I hate*
I do hate 193 *stale* (ed) staule 195 *titled* liked 205 *pash* push
214 *let his humor's* tell his humorous 222 *'A would . . . shares*
(Q gives to Ajax) 224 *He's . . . warm* (ed; Q and F give to Ajax)
225 *praises* praiers 244 *beyond, beyond all erudition* beyond all
thy erudition 250 *bourne* boord 251 *Thy* This 265 *cull* call

III.i. s.d. *Music . . . Servant* Enter Pandarus 24 *friend* (Q omits)
38 *that thou* thou 93 *your poor disposer's* your disposers 108
lord lad 115 *In . . . so* (Q omits) 118 *shaft confounds* shafts confound 150 *these* this 158 *thee* her

III.ii.1 s.d. *and Troilus'* Troylus 3 *he stays* stayes 3 s.d. *Enter
Troilus* (Q omits) 8 *Like* like to 10 *those* these 16 s.d. *Exit
Pandarus* (Q omits) 28 s.d. *Enter Pandarus* (Q omits) 34 s.d.
Exit Pandarus (Q omits) 38 *unawares* vnwares 68 *fears* (ed)
teares 82 *This is* This 94 *merit crown it. No perfection* merit
louer part no affection 101 s.d. *Enter Pandarus* (Q omits) 134
Cunning (ed) Comming 161 *aye* age 181 *Yet after* After 186
and or 194 *as wolf* or Wolfe 201 *pains* paine

III.iii. s.d. *Flourish* (Q omits) 4 *come* (ed) loue 102 *giver* giuers 128 *abject* obiect 140 *on* one 141 *shrinking* shriking 155 *one on* 158 *hedge* turne 160 *hindmost* him, most 161–63 *Or . . . on* (F emended from "neere" to "rear"; Q omits) 164 *past* passe 177 *give* (ed) goe 183 *Than* That 197 *every grain of Pluto's gold* euery thing 198 *th' uncomprehensive deeps* the vncomprehensiue depth 224 *a dewdrop* dew drop 251 *he* a 267 *ambassador to him* Ambassador 275 *most valorous* valorous 279 *Grecian army* armie 279–80 *Agamemnon, et cetera* Agamemnon 294 *God b' wi' you* (ed) God buy you

IV.i.4 *you* your 16 *But* Lul'd 36 *it was* twas 40 *do think* beleeue 50 s.d. *Exit Aeneas* (Q omits) 52 *the soul* soule 56 *soilure* soyle 76 *you* they

IV.ii.19 s.d. *Within* (Q omits) 22 s.d. *Enter Pandarus* (F places after line 20; Q omits) 51 *'Tis* Its 57 s.d. *Enter Troilus* (Q omits) 63 *to us; and for him forthwith* to him, and forth-with 72 *nature* neighbor Pandar 107 *I will* Ile 112 s.d. *Exeunt* (Q omits)

IV.iv.54 *the root* my throate 64 *there's* there is 76 *They're . . . nature* (Q omits) 79 *person* portion 139 s.d. *Sound trumpet* (Q omits) 144–48 *Deiphobus. Let us . . . chivalry* (F, with 144 assigned to Diomedes; Q omits)

IV.v.94 *Ulysses. They . . . already* (Q omits) 95 *Agamemnon* Vlises 98 *in deeds* deeds 131 *Of our rank feud* (Q omits) 132 *drop* day 164–69 *But that's . . . integrity* (Q omits) 177 *that I affect th' untraded oath* thy affect, the vntraded earth 187 *thy* th' 192 *shraped* (ed) shruped 205 *As they . . . courtesy* (Q omits) 254 *stithied* stichied 291 *she loved* my Lord

V.i.12 *these* this 14 *boy* box 19 *catarrhs* (Q omits) 23 *and the like* (Q omits) 48 s.d. *Exit* (Q omits) 55 *brother* be 57–58 *hanging at his brother's leg* at his bare legge 59 *forced* faced 61 *he is* her's 61–62 *dog, a mule* day, a Moyle 62 *fitchew* Fichooke 65 *ask me not* aske me 71 s.d. *Enter Achilles* (Q omits) 73 *good* God 79 *sewer* (ed) sure 80 *both at once* both

V.ii.4 s.d. *Enter . . . Ulysses* (Q omits) 13 *Cressida* Cal 38 *Nay* Now 39 *distraction* distruction 46 *Adieu* (Q omits) 54 *these together* together 56 *But will* Will 57 *la* (ed) lo 66 *Troilus. I . . . will* (Q omits) 67 *Cressida* Troy 78 *Nay . . . me* (Q, F assign to Diomedes) 82 *Cressida* (Q omits) 88 *By* And by 103 s.d. *Exit* (Q omits) 115 *coact* Court 120 *had deceptious* were deceptions 131 *soil* spoile 154 *fine* finde 164 *Much as* as much

V.iii.14 *Cassandra* Cres 20–22 *To hurt . . . charity* (F emended from "would count" to "would," and from "as" to "use"; Q omits) 23–25 *It is . . . sweet Hector* (Q assigns to Andromache) 29 *mean'st* meanest   58 *But by my ruin* (Q omits)   85 *distraction* destruction   90 *Exit* (Q omits)

V.iv.4 *young knave's* knaues   9 *errand* (F has "errant") arrant   9 *O' th'* Ath   17 *begin* (ed) began   18 s.d. *Enter Diomedes and Troilus* (Q omits)   27 *art thou* art

V.v.22 *scalèd* scaling   41 *luck* lust

V.vii.11 *double-horned* (ed) double-hen'd   12 s.d. *Exeunt* (ed) Exit   23 *Exeunt* Exit

V.viii.16 *One Greek* (F has "Gree.") One

V.ix.1 *what shout is that* what is this

V.x.2 *Never . . . night* (Q assigns to Troilus, and places his entrance before the line)   21–22 *But march away. Hector is dead* (Q omits)   23 *Vile* proud   32–34 *Pandarus. But hear you! . . . aye with thy name* (in F these lines appear as well after V.iii.112, concluding that scene)   33 *Ignominy and* ignominy   37 *traders* (ed) traitors   50 *your aching* my aking   51 *hold-door* hold-ore

A Note on the Sources of
"Troilus and Cressida"

There is no single source for *Troilus and Cressida*, but there are several works with which we can be certain Shakespeare was familiar, and which he probably used in composing the play. Modern editions of these are listed at the end of this note. Homer's poem, of course, stands behind the story of the war, and Shakespeare's Greek, while less than his small Latin, might have been sufficient to cope with it. He also used the first parts of Chapman's translation of the *Iliad,* published in 1598 (*Seaven Bookes of the Iliades* and *Achilles Shield*); Chapman's later work on Homer appeared too late for Shakespeare's use in this play. Certain details of characterization and action, however, indicate that he either consulted Homer directly or used one of the full Latin or French translations of the sixteenth century; some of these details, such as the characterization of Ulysses and the abuse of Hector's body, could not have resulted from hearsay or pseudo-Homeric versions. Other aspects of the camp scenes, both Greek and Trojan, stem from Lydgate's *Sege of Troye* (c. 1412–1420) or Caxton's *Recuyell of the Historyes of Troye* (1475). Both of these are derived ultimately from early pseudo-Homeric narratives, their more immediate source being the *Historia Troiana* (1287) of Guido delle Colonne; Guido had also provided one of the secondary sources for Chaucer's *Troilus and Criseyde.* Shakespeare also knew Arthur Golding's translation of Ovid's *Metamorphoses,* some parts of which touch upon the story of the Trojan war.

Shakespeare's major source for the love story was Chaucer's great narrative poem, *Troilus and Criseyde* (1382–1385), although one must qualify immediately the nature of his reliance upon it. The bones of the story, as Shakespeare knew it, and even some details of the action are from Chaucer, but it would be most misleading to assume that Shakespeare's treatment of the tale resembles Chaucer's. The qualities of the story that attracted Shakespeare, and to which he added much more specific action concerning the characters in the camp scenes, were not those emphasized—nor perhaps even recognized—by his most important predecessor in English literature. Chaucer's treatment of the story emphasizes the charm of the lovers and, while it lasts, the delight of their union. Pandarus is a warmhearted, benevolent courtier, himself a servant of love, though unsuccessful in his own amours. His humor is invariably genial, and although some of his jests are broad, they are never obscene. His main desire is the happiness of Troilus and Criseyde, and he is shocked into melancholy silence when he hears the news of Criseyde's betrayal. The heroine herself is a young woman of considerable dignity, imagination, and charm, with none of the coquetry or worldliness of Shakespeare's girl. She yields to Troilus only after long persuasion, and, befriended by Hector himself, enjoys a good reputation throughout the city. Chaucer's Troilus, like Shakespeare's, is a faithful and sensitive lover; but the affair is conducted in a vastly different manner in the two narratives. Pandarus, in Shakespeare's play, is glibly obscene, coarsely sentimental, and, frequently, hardly more than a leering *voyeur,* anxious for the lovers' happiness, but deriving from it what appears to be sexual pleasure for himself. In Chaucer's poem, the powers of love ennoble those who serve it, and the union of Troilus and Criseyde is set forth as an event of great beauty and cheer.

In Chaucer, the significance of Criseyde's fall is set against that of the great city itself, and both become part of a larger and more general sadness. Criseyde is shown to be confused and weak, but her lonely position in the Greek camp is also poignantly described. She becomes an instrument in the fortunes of both Troilus and Diomede, and some emphasis is thereby withdrawn from her faithless act itself. Her treachery is lamentable, but it is somehow overshadowed by the tragedy of Troy and the fate of mankind in general. Far from acknowledging in Criseyde an implicit harlotry, Chaucer sets forth, simply and with deep sadness, the tale of her loss. He is as moved by it as Pandarus, and seems to learn, with Troilus, that solace, if it can be found at all, is to be found in something more permanent than the life of this world. It should not be assumed that Chaucer's psychology was less subtle than Shakespeare's; it is derived in this poem, in fact, from the elaborate pattern of behavior defined in the code of courtly love—a code that could effect great beauty and delicacy of human feeling. Although Shakespeare's times —and ours—would describe such behavior pejoratively, as based in an adulterous relationship, no condemnation is implicit in Chaucer's work. It should be noted that his Criseyde is a widow when she first sees Troilus. His characters are capable of great strength and constancy, but Chaucer shows that the capricious movement of Fortune's wheel can crush what is beautiful and cause what is apparently constant to pass. His narrative is tragic in its treatment of the lovers' fall, comic to the extent that its characters are prone to folly and delusion.

By the time Shakespeare decided to write *Troilus and Cressida,* the story of the lovers had been retold many times, and the character of Cressida had been debased to that of a harlot. Chiefly responsible for this metamorphosis was Henryson's *The Testament of Cresseid,* which after 1532, when it was printed as Chaucer's in an edition of his works, was thought to be authentically Chaucerian. Henryson's poem is a sequel to the earlier narrative, beginning after Diomed, tiring of her, dismisses Cresseid. The girl rails against the gods in whom she had placed her trust, particularly Venus and Cupid, and in anger they transform her into a leper; she laments and goes upon her way, and finally dies—but not before Prince Troilus, upon his horse, passes her in the road and, not recognizing her transformed face, gives her alms. Henryson's tale treats the character of Cresseid sympathetically and with great human insight, although she is condemned for her faithlessness and especially for her great pride. Nevertheless, the Elizabethans read the piece entirely in the light of Cresseid's treachery, and it was not long before she became synonymous with all the evil qualities that the character in Shakespeare's play is willing to acknowledge if she prove false: "Yea, let them say, to stick the heart of falsehood, /'As false as Cressid'" (III.ii. 196–97).

There had been other dramatic renderings of the story before Shakespeare's, but all are lost; there is little doubt, however, that Cressida appeared in these versions as a strumpet. A surviving stage direction from the lost play by Chettle and Dekker (1599) reads, "Enter Cressida, with Beggars"—probably the company of lepers among whom, in Henryson's poem, she dies. References to Cressida as a whore abound in Elizabethan literature, and we may be sure that, just as the word for a base procurer stems from her uncle's name, her own became an equally common epithet.

The significance of this transformation should not be underestimated, although we may regret the violence it appears to do Chaucer and even Henryson. Shakespeare, in fact, may have been attracted to the plot, as I have suggested in the Introduction, because of its apparently unqualified statement of inconstancy. In this sense, his use of Homer (and Chapman's Homer), Lydgate, and Caxton, is much closer to our normal understanding of the word, "source," than is his reliance upon Chaucer. Although most of the details of the story are transformed, those relating to the camp and council scenes stand much closer to the originals than does his treatment of the love story.

Modern editions of major sources:

H. Bergen, ed. Lydgate's *Troy Book. Early English Text Society*, No. 97 (1906); Nos. 103, 106 (1908); No. 126 (1935).

Allardyce Nicoll, ed. *Chapman's Homer* (Bollingen Series XLI). 2 vols. New York: Pantheon Books, Inc., 1956.

F. N. Robinson, ed. *Troilus and Criseyde,* in *The Complete Works of Geoffrey Chaucer.* Boston: Houghton Mifflin Company; London: Oxford University Press, 1933. 2nd ed., 1957.

R. K. Root, ed. *The Book of Troilus and Criseyde by Geoffrey Chaucer.* Princeton, N. J.: Princeton University Press, 1945.

H. O. Sommer, ed. Caxton's *The Recuyell of the Historyes of Troye.* 2 vols. London: 1894.

Commentaries

W. W. LAWRENCE

from *Shakespeare's Problem Comedies*

With [the tradition of Chaucer and Henryson] confronting him, how could Shakespeare make the heroine of Chaucer's poem a sympathetic character for the men of his day. The story was too familiar to alter; its very popularity had stereotyped it. It is safe to say that the Elizabethans would have jeered at a pure and noble Cressida, just as the pit of an English theater today would jeer at a self-sacrificing and high-principled Guy Fawkes. It is true that in the seventeenth century Dryden ventured the experiment of redeeming the character of Cressida in his dramatic version of the story, but conditions in Restoration days were vastly different from those at the opening years of the seventeenth century. The theater was far less close to the people as a whole, and the tale of Troilus and Cressida had lost something of the popularity which it formerly enjoyed. Even had Shakespeare desired to do so, he could no more have whitewashed Cressida than he could have whitewashed Richard III, who was historically

From *Shakespeare's Problem Comedies* by W. W. Lawrence. New York and London: The Macmillan Company, 1931. Reprinted by permission of the Estate of W. W. Lawrence.

far from being the monster of Elizabethan tradition. He could not alter the well-known incidents of Cressida's career any more than he could have made Richard repent and die in the odor of sanctity. How impossible it would have been for him to introduce into his work the ideals of courtly love which underlie Chaucer's poem, even if he had understood them, may be realized if we reflect that according to those ideals it would have been proper for Cassio to make advances to Desdemona, for Emilia to encourage them, and ultimately, provided strict secrecy and the other rules were observed, for Desdemona to grant Cassio her love, as far as he desired. The social ethics of the Elizabethan stage were of a very different sort. . . . Cleopatra was never a byword for a loose and faithless woman, like Cressida. Sir Thomas North speaks of her "courteous nature" and her "noble mind and courage." To Chaucer she was one of the saints of Cupid, the first of the procession in the *Legend of Good Women*. Chaucer intended Helen, too, for one of Cupid's saints, a female martyr to love, but Shakespeare etches her portrait in these biting words:

> For every false drop in her bawdy veins
> A Grecian's life hath sunk; for every scruple
> Of her contaminated carrion weight
> A Troyan hath been slain.

The relation of Helen and Paris in Shakespeare's play are of much significance in judging those of Troilus and Cressida. The speech of Hector, in which he defends the laws of morality, is noteworthy:

> If Helen then be wife to Sparta's king,
> As it is known she is, these moral laws
> Of nature and of nation speak aloud
> To have her back return'd. Thus to persist
> In doing wrong extenuates not wrong,
> But makes it much more heavy.

There was no place in Elizabethan ethics for adultery. . . .

One of the strangest features of this strange play is its dénouement: Both of its plots terminate inconclusively. No poetic justice is meted out to Cressida, such as Henryson thought that she deserved, and such as had become, by Shakespeare's day, her traditional punishment. On the contrary, she is left, despite her faithlessness, in the full tide of her love affair with Diomedes. In Chaucer's poem and Heywood's play, the pain and disillusion of Troilus end in death; no such solution is found in Shakespeare. As far as we can see, Troilus is left to meet, with a broken heart, the futile continuance of the great struggle into which he had thrown his best energies. Again, the elaborate plan of the Greek chiefs to shame Achilles into action misses fire completely. Achilles is indeed resentful of the slights which have been put upon him, he is indeed moved by the reproaches of Ulysses and Patroclus, but instead of sending a challenge to Hector he merely dispatches Thersites to ask Ajax to invite the Trojans to his tent after the combat. When they do meet, Hector urges him to come into the field and fight, and Achilles promises to do so, but in the next scene he tells Patroclus that he is "thwarted quite" from his great purpose—he has received a letter from Hecuba and a token from Polyxena, his lady-love, "taxing and gaging" him to keep an oath which he has sworn—obviously not to do battle with Hector, Polyxena's own brother. He is finally roused to action by the killing of Patroclus, and contrives the death of Hector by a base trick. But he is not punished for his arrogance or for his inaction, and he is left in triumph after having compassed the death of the most brilliant and sympathetic hero in the play. Nor does the swollen vanity of Ajax meet any rebuff. The net result of it all is, in the words of Thersites, that "now is the cur Ajax prouder than the cur Achilles," and that all the policy of Ulysses and Nestor is "not prov'd worth a blackberry."

These inconclusive solutions are all the more striking when the generally skillful workmanship of the main part of the play is considered. The alternation of interest between the scenes in Troy and those in the Greek camp is deftly managed, and after the return of Cressida to the

Greeks, and the visit of Hector to the Greek camp, the two plots are interwoven with much dexterity. Moreover, the play shows the hand of the practiced writer in the balance between character and plot, and in the introduction of new material. The Troilus-Cressida theme is essentially undramatic. It is good stuff for a courtly romance like Boccaccio's or a psychological novel in verse like Chaucer's, but it is not well suited to the stage. Its interest lies mainly in character. In this regard it contrasts strikingly with *All's Well* and *Measure for Measure,* which are good stories, with plenty of action. Shakespeare wisely concentrated his energies, then, on the delineation of the emotions and characteristics of Cressida, Troilus, and Pandarus. Yet this left the play somewhat weak in plot-interest and suspense. Everyone knew the outlines of the love story, and of the tale of the Trojan War. So Shakespeare (or, possibly, the author of an earlier play upon which he worked) devised the ruse of Ulysses and Nestor, which immediately arrests attention, and provokes dramatic interest. How is it all going to end? Well, it does end very strangely, to be sure. Poetic justice is in no wise satisfied; there are neither the reconciliations of comedy nor the purifying calamities of tragedy to round out the action. "It is difficult," wrote Alden, "to exaggerate the dramatic futility of the whole effect."

Critics have objected vigorously, from the seventeenth century on; no subtleties of modern scholarship are needed to make this point plain. Dryden's remodeling of the play is instructive. It is unblushing, like his adaptations of Shakespeare in general, but it does achieve a vivid dramatic effect which the work of the greater master lacked. The plot is greatly altered. Cressida has really been true to Troilus, but has been forced by Calchas to pretend love for Diomedes, in order that they may the more readily escape from the beleaguered city. She gives to Diomedes Troilus's ring, and Diomedes asserts that she has yielded to his love. Cressida protests her innocence, and stabs herself as a final proof. Troilus slays Diomedes, but is slain by the Greeks. The big scene in the Fifth Act, in the grand manner, is dramatically effective, but it is not a fair illustration of how Shakespeare's Fifth Act might have been written, because it wrenches the whole framework of the plot so violently askew. Dryden was very pleased with it, however; he remarks with satisfaction, "The whole fifth act, both the plot and the writing, are my own additions." It was fortunate for him that the tale had faded sufficiently in popular consciousness to make such radical changes acceptable.

The easy way to account for the theatrically ineffective ending of Shakespeare's play is to blame the unknown writer of the spurious closing scenes. He is a convenient scapegoat. But we have to consider with some care whether this explanation is really satisfactory. These scenes would no doubt have been better written if Shakespeare had done them, but would they have been radically different in content? We know that his habit, in retelling old tales, was to leave their plots as they were, however unplausible or ineffective these might seem, and to strive to make them reasonable and plausible by skillful characterization. This practice was of course not invariable, but his tendency was always to fit his artistic conception to the plot as he found it rather than to remake the plot to fit a preconceived effect of his own. This general point has been frequently stressed in the pages which precede. If in *Troilus and Cressida* we suppose that he was revising an old piece, the final scenes of which were allowed to stand, his retention of an apparently anticlimactic end is comprehensible, though it still remains to be explained how he planned to make these final scenes harmonize with the earlier part of the play. If, on the other hand, we assume that the whole planning of the action was due to him, we still have to inquire whether it is not entirely possible that the closing scenes are in harmony with that design, and in accord with his intentions, though actually written by another hand. It must be remembered that division of authorship does not necessarily mean looseness of construction. As Wells remarks, "some of the most loosely constructed of Elizabethan plays, as *Old Fortunatus,* are apparently the work of one poet, while some of the best unified, as *The Maid's Tragedy,* and *Eastward Ho!,* are known to have been written by two or more poets." Why are we to conclude that the collaborator in *Troilus and Cressida* was ignorant of Shakespeare's design, or deliberately ran counter to it? Both Quarto and Folio texts agree in the final scenes, which were not reconstructed in the revisions which the play obviously suffered. Let us see, then, what is to be said for the piece as an artistic and coherent whole as it stands, and challenge Alden's statement that "the final scenes cannot represent Shakespeare's intention."

It will be clearest to consider the two parts of the action separately.

For the love story, only an unhappy ending was possible. The theme was so firmly established for an Elizabethan audience by tradition, as involving the separation of the lovers, the heartbreak of the one and the bad faith of the other, that no conventional happy ending could follow. But the Shakespearean ending is not unhappy enough to suit the critics. Both Tatlock and Rollins, in their long and elaborate analyses, conclude that Cressida ought to be punished. Rollins says:

It is almost incredible that, with his knowledge of Henryson, his preconceived ideas of the character of Cressid and the reward of her treachery, and his respect for what the public wanted, Shakespeare should have ended his play without at least punishing Cressid. How can the present ending have pleased his audiences? Even the groundlings, however much delighted with Thersites and Pandar, surely were dissatisfied when the play abruptly dropped the leading characters instead of carrying them on to the logical traditional *dénouement*. What American audience would care to see *Uncle Tom's Cabin* if no Little Eva appeared in the cast or if Eliza failed to cross the ice? Shakespeare, if he wrote all the play, wrenched the familiar story as violently in one direction as Dryden later did in another; neither version could have been satisfactory in 1602. . . . We could feel surer that Shakespeare was responsible for all of the play if he had punished Cressida—if in portraying her he had shown unmistakable bitterness and hatred.

Tatlock points out that in the *Iron Age,* and two other plays to which he has called attention, Cressida is punished, and in the *Iron Age* Troilus dies. "It is hard to fancy any skilled dramatist dropping his main threads without tying them up; and harder to fancy Shakespeare writing the end of the play and bringing the Achilles-motive to nothing."

To all this there seems to me a very simple answer. Shakespeare did no violence to tradition, for the reason that he did not carry the action to its ultimate end. He chose to end it, or to let someone else end it, with the beginning of the intrigue with Diomedes, just as Chaucer did. Why was he bound to carry it on to a later time, to the beggary and the leprosy, after the break with Diomedes? Why is it wrenching the familiar story to stop short of this? When we compare Heywood's play with Shakespeare's, we can see, as has already been pointed out, that Shakespeare omits material which Heywood introduced at the beginning. Why should he not also have omitted material at the end? Moreover, he had already filled a five-act play; I cannot see how he could have packed the desertion of Cressida by Diomedes and the smiting of Cressida with leprosy into a Fifth Act which had only just, in Scene ii, shown the love intrigue of Cressida and Diomedes for the first time. Could things be made to move as fast as that? Heywood got it all in, after a fashion, but he had ten acts to do it in. Even so, his treatment of Cressida's end is so sketchy that Rollins himself says that Heywood was "sure" that his audience could "finish out her story." If Heywood was sure of this, why not Shakespeare? Rollins's insistence that Cressida be punished is all the more remarkable in view of the fact that he thinks that Shakespeare dealt with her "so mildly," and says, "Certainly he has no apparent bitterness towards Cressida." Other Elizabethans made her more degraded, but I do not see how anyone can be in doubt as to what Shakespeare thought of her, and meant his audiences to think, after reading the famous scene in which she kisses the Greek chieftains all round, and the scorching comments of the clear-sighted Ulysses.

. . . What is important to recall is that the play, taken by itself as it stands, is clearly not one which would have pleased the groundlings at all, and that there are clear indications in its stage history that it did not. The hypothesis that it was originally written for a special audience, and not for the Globe Theater, remains highly plausible. If ever a play was caviar to the general, surely *Troilus and Cressida* was.

The ending of the camp scenes is in full accord with the inconclusive ending of the love story. The issue is again—failure. The Greek chieftains, with all the right on their side, with the shrewdest policy of their wisest leaders to guide them, are powerless, just like Troilus, before egotism, selfishness, and lust. The cowardly bully Ajax triumphs, and Achilles, at a word from his Trojan mistress, neglects his most imperative duties as a warrior and general. Here again the cause which engages our sympathies is defeated, and Achilles, who is as little heroic as Cressida, is left, like her, in a shameful triumph. The harmony between the two actions is complete. The ending of the subplot, like that of the main plot, is indeed both unsympathetic and ineffective theatrically. But we cannot blame all its shortcomings upon the unknown author of the spurious scenes in Act V (iv-x). The resolution of Achilles to continue his shameful inaction, for the love of Polyxena, is set forth in the opening scene of Act V, which is conceded to be Shakespeare's own work.

This fashion of ending the two actions affords a striking contrast to *All's Well* and *Measure for Measure*. In both those pieces, Shakespeare introduced a theatrically vivid climax, leading to a conventionally happy ending. Psychologically their fifth acts are weak; dramatically they are effective. This is due in part to the sources; Shakespeare followed essentially the same lines as Boccaccio and Whetstone, though with many elaborations. The last act of *Troilus and Cressida* affords a complete contrast; dramatically it is weak, psychologically it is strong. And here again the ending is in accord with the sources. No happy ending was possible for either part of the plot; everyone knew that the tale ended unhappily. Under these circumstances, what was Shakespeare to do? He could indeed have recast the whole play as tragedy, and deepened the poignancy of the climax. Why he decided not to do this, I shall not presume to say. But it seems clear that this was never his intention. While there is much in this play, in the relentless analysis of the darker sides of human passion, which recalls the great tragedies, there is not the intensity of emotion and violence of action which lead inevitably to a tragic climax. Try the experiment of reading the play, and imagining a Fifth Act in which Troilus is killed in battle, and Cressida left in the horrors of leprosy. Would that make of it a satisfactory tragedy? I do not think so; that is not the end to crown the work as Shakespeare wrought it. Perhaps the explanation lies in this: that the whole is too detached and too observant for tragedy. Shakespeare never quite seems to let himself go, to allow the action to sweep him on to an inevitable climax. Sir Edmund Chambers observes, "Comedy, in *Troilus and Cressida,* becomes critical." Richard Grant White called the play "Shakespeare's only piece of introspective work." We may question the word "only," perhaps, but not the rest of his verdict. And Barrett Wendell remarked, "It is a reflective, and so a bad play." There is plenty of reflection in the great tragedies, of course, but introspection does not control the action, even in *Hamlet.*

Like Chaucer, Shakespeare seems to have been deeply interested in analyzing the passion of an idealistic boy and an experienced coquette who, despite her shallowness, is touched for a moment with his own bright clear flame. But he was not free to make her in any degree sympathetic. She must be, to accord with the story as everyone in his day knew it, sensuous, calculating, temperamentally inconstant, if not worse. The purer love of Juliet is sensuous enough in some of its aspects, like normal human love generally; her speech "Gallop apace, you fiery-footed steeds" is a marvelous expression of this, but Shakespeare could not give to the soiled and scorned figure of Cressida the idealism of a Juliet, or the magnificent royal splendor which redeems the frank sensuality of Cleopatra. No other course was open to him than to treat Cressida realistically.

Romantic unreality may surround a Rosalind or a Hero or a Juliet, in spite of all the touches of reality which give them the breath of life, but it would never do for Cressida, any more than for Goneril or Regan or Lady Macbeth, or the Queen in *Hamlet*. Moreover, realistic plays were in fashion at the moment, and Shakespeare had written, or was writing, two "unpleasant" comedies, in which, despite their romantic plots, the treatment is in a high degree realistic. With all this the artificial mythological situation invented by Henryson accords very ill—Cressida's cursing of Mars and Venus, and her punishment in being stricken with leprosy. Mythology and realism are not good yoke-fellows.

The play ends in realistic and severely logical fashion. No concession is made to theatrical effect of the obvious sort, but a very definite impression is created of the futility and misery which come of loving a worthless woman. With this the earlier part of the play is in complete harmony. The whole background of the story is armed strife over another frail lady, Helen of Troy, strife which has become futile and dreary. Hector, the greatest of the Trojan heroes, is willing to continue it, despite its lack of moral justification, through a mistaken idea that Trojan honor demands it. Achilles, the flower of the Greek chivalry, throws honor to the winds because of an infatuation for a princess in the city of his enemies. The evil influence of love without honor, then, ends in the death of Hector, in the shame and the shameful triumph of Achilles in compassing his death, and in the complete disillusionment of Troilus. "Wars and lechery," says the Chorus Thersites, "nothing else holds fashion." And, in a less quoted passage, "What's become of the wenching rogues? I think they have swallowed one another. I would laugh at that miracle; and yet, in a sort, lechery eats itself" (Act V, Scene iv). The shadows deepen in the closing scenes. Like many a highly emotional boy with a strong sexual nature, Troilus suffers deeply in the very revulsion of his feeling. He is too heartsick at the faithlessness of his mistress to find harsh words for her, but he curses roundly the older man who has cynically taken advantage of his infatuation.

But Cressida, as Boas has emphasized, is to have her Nemesis, too, in the brutality of Diomedes. "The shallow coquette pays a heavy yet just price for her selfish levity, when she exchanges a chivalrous adorer for a harsh and imperious taskmaster." Dramatic justice lies in the future, not in the cheap and illogical solution of leprosy for Cressida and sudden death for Troilus, but in the realization, for both of them, that character and conduct bring inescapable consequences in life. The ending of the tale is in accord with the facts of human experience; life often settles nothing, it leaves the innocent to suffer, and the guilty to prevail. There is nothing else in Shakespearean comedy just like the spirit of these closing scenes; and their complete analogues cannot be found even in the tragedies. Whether Shakespeare himself or another man planned them, they carry steadily to the end the relentless logic of the play, the searching analysis of a reflective criticism of life.

. . . Something must now be said in regard to the often-expressed conclusion that *Troilus and Cressida* was written with satirical intent. No critic has made this more plausible than Boas, who perceives in it Shakespeare's manipulation of "the materials for a merciless satire of the high-flown ideal of love, fostered by the medieval cycle of romance, whence the tale had sprung. The absolute devotion of a gallant to his mistress, which this form of literature had glorified, is transformed into the delirious passion of a youth for a mere wanton. . . . The infatuation of Troilus is paralleled by that of Menelaus and Paris. . . . Helen and Cressida are made to figure in exactly the same light." The keynote of the play, which brings into harmonious relation the two plots, is, according to Boas, to be found in the words of Hector, " 'Tis mad idolatry to make the service greater than the god," which applies to Greeks and Trojans alike. "In both camps sentimental gallantry is the ruling motive, with disastrous results to true national interests."

But do not causes deeper and more universal than mere sentimental gallantry wreck the lives of these people? Was not Shakespeare rather analyzing life than satirizing chivalry? The weaknesses of the system of courtly love seem, in his analysis, of secondary rather than primary importance. This is very difficult to prove, since the whole action takes place in a society ruled by chivalric conventions. But certain reservations must be made. Shakespeare could not have portrayed Greek and Roman society, in view of the form which the story had assumed in his own day, excepting as subdued to those conventions. Moreover, a very different spirit from that of Cervantes seems to have gone to the making of *Troilus and Cressida*, though from Boas's summary one might not think so. Sir Edmund Chambers seems to have *Don Quixote* in mind when he writes of this play that "Shakespeare goes tilting at illusions." But surely Shakespeare's mood is very different from that of the satirist who "smiled Spain's chivalry away." His play is no genial exposure of absurdities, no shattering of the conventions of romance, but an earnest, concentrated, philosophical analysis of universal human passions in a corrupt society. He is not dissecting courtly etiquette, but lust, greed, selfishness, pride. Try the experiment of reading Chaucer's *Troilus* without making allowance for chivalric conventions; much of its significance is lost. But the passion of Shakespeare's Troilus, the faithlessness of Cressida, the arrogance of Achilles, the brutality of Ajax, the lust of Paris, the mistaken heroism of Hector need no such background to make them intelligible. Study of the form which medieval conventions had assumed in Shakespeare's day is essential because these conventions were inseparable from the tale as it then existed; but it does not force us to regard the whole as existing for the sake of those conventions. The experiences through which the Greeks and Trojans pass are common to every highly civilized age, no matter what its manners; they are experiences which will repeat themselves eternally, as long as the world endures. Depressing, unequal, and critical as *Troilus and Cressida* is, there is in it a universality which the more perfect masterpiece *Don Quixote* lacks.

Furthermore, is it *a priori* likely, despite the assertions of Ulrici, Schlegel, Rümelin, Fleay, and Furnivall, that

Shakespeare's intent was satirical at all? He had his flings at social absurdities and affectations, in dress, speech, and manners, but these are secondary; they do not determine the whole temper of any of his plays. Perhaps he comes closest to social satire in *Love's Labor's Lost* and in the portrait of Caliban in the *Tempest*. But the hits at court follies in the gay court comedy, and the remarkable anticipation of the effect of civilization upon the savage are neither of them such an attempt to "cleanse the foul body of the infected world" as *Troilus and Cressida* must be, if its chief intent be satiric. The general question is much like that which we have already considered in discussing *All's Well* and *Measure for Measure*. We cannot prove that satire does not exist in *Troilus and Cressida*, but we must be extremely cautious about assuming that it is present, and still more that it controls the spirit of the play. The old theory that it arises from the stage quarrel between Ben Jonson and the poetasters has long since been convincingly refuted.

If any one thing is plain in *Troilus and Cressida*, however, it is that Shakespeare's attitude is singularly detached and reflective. The great speeches of the Greek chieftains in Act I, those in the Trojan council in Act II, the interview between Ulysses and Achilles in Act III, are so closely packed with thought that their dramatic value is seriously impaired. I do not agree that two styles, reflecting two different periods of composition, are observable in the play; such differences seem to me rather due to the unlikeness of the two main actions. The debates among the chieftains obviously give more opportunity for philosophizing than does the love story, and require another sort of treatment, but it is to be observed that even the love scenes are handled in maturer and more reflective fashion than those in earlier plays. *Troilus and Cressida* appears to have been a dramatic experiment; not a wholly successful one, to be sure, but one which must remain of great significance for the understanding of the greater creative work of this period.

D. A. TRAVERSI

"Troilus and Cressida"

The close relationship between the values of love and war, which is one of the most marked features of *Troilus and Cressida,* corresponds to a conception of dramatic unity which, although its antecedents can be traced respectively to the sonnets and the historical plays, was, at the time of writing, new in his work. The novelty consists in uniting, in a manner mutually illuminating, a personal theme and its public, "social" extension. Instead of a political conflict objectively studied and commented on by a character (such as Falstaff) who stands, in a sense, outside it, we are presented with a personal issue— the story of two lovers of opposed parties—set in the context of the Trojan war. The situation of the lovers is variously connected with the cleavage between the warring parties to which they respectively belong; and the connection thus dramatically established is further strengthened by the pervasive presence of imagery which suggests disruptive tendencies barely contained within a common way of feeling. The result, in terms of poetic drama, is less a finished and coherent creation than a statement of emotional ambiguity, the reflection of an experience deprived of order and seeking clarification through its own expression.

The nature of this ambiguity, and more particularly its

From *An Approach to Shakespeare* by D. A. Traversi. 2nd ed. rev. New York: Doubleday & Company, Inc. (Anchor Books), 1956. Reprinted by permission of the author.

relation to the preoccupation with time, which we have already considered in the sonnets, is perhaps best studied in the passage in which Troilus takes leave of Cressida:

> *Cressida.* And is it true that I must go from Troy? . . .
> Is it possible?
>
> *Troilus.* And suddenly; where injury of chance
> Puts back leave-taking, justles roughly by
> All time of pause, rudely beguiles our lips
> Of all rejoindure, forcibly prevents
> Our lock'd embrasures, strangles our dear vows
> Even in the birth of our own laboring breath;
> We two, that with so many thousand sighs
> Did buy each other, must poorly sell ourselves
> With the rude brevity and discharge of one.
> Injurious time now with a robber's haste
> Crams his rich thievery up, he knows not how;
> As many farewells as be stars in heaven,
> With distinct breath and consign'd kisses to them,
> He fumbles up into a loose adieu,
> And scants us with a single famish'd kiss,
> Distasted with the salt of broken tears.
>
> (IV.iv. 30–48)

The verbal intricacy of this speech is highly characteristic of the play and helps to throw light upon the peculiar nature of its inspiration. The experience it reflects is, verbally at least, tremendously rich, endlessly elaborate, but the ordering of it is not equal to the complexity. The adverse action of time upon the parting lovers is represented by an astonishing number of verbs—"puts back," "justles roughly by," "rudely beguiles," "forcibly prevents," "strangles"—but the emotion does not *develop,* does not acquire added coherence in the course of its expression. It remains a long and acutely sensed effort to express a single moment of conflicting feeling. It belongs, in short, to a period in Shakespeare's development in which the keenness of his apprehension of certain elements of experience (already for the most part indicated in the sonnets) was not accompanied by a corresponding sense of order and significance. We shall see that order and significance gradually growing out of the increasing mastery of his art.

Nonetheless, though unsatisfactory, the experience behind *Troilus* is highly individual. In each of the verbs of parting which we have just collected there is an element, sharply and vividly realized, of harsh and hostile physical contact. This labored feeling is balanced by the poignant thinness of the positive love imagery which so inadequately accompanies it. Troilus, whose awareness of separation is so acute, so tangibly conceived, can only express his passion in images as intense as they are airy and essentially bodiless. Love is indeed "rich" in his estimation, fit to be mentioned with the "stars in heaven"; but it can only be expressed in "sighs" and "laboring *breath*," in the hurried breathlessness of "distinct *breath* and consign'd kisses," and in the intensely palated but transitory delicacy of "Distasted with the salt of broken tears." Opposed to this "airy," pathetic passion, the full brunt of the senses is felt in every phrase that stresses parting. "Rudely," "roughly," "forcibly," time and hostile circumstance undermine the tragic brevity of love, so that the "lock'd embrasures" which should normally convey the intensity of physical union are felt to be only an effort to snatch a moment's identity in the face of events which are forcibly drawing the lovers apart. The parting imposed by external circumstances, indeed, is subsidiary to a certain weakness inherent in passion itself. The ideal, which is perfect union, is desired intensely, but is as light as "breath" or "air"; and the bodies through whose coming together alone this intensity can be enjoyed are always, while they are united, "laboring" against a tendency to separate. Their "labor," irrevocably frustrated, issues in nothing tangible or permanent. Throughout *Troilus* the elements in love-making for separation are too strong for those which desire union, and "injurious time" is the process by which separation is born out of desired consummation.

Troilus and Cressida, then, insofar as it deals with the central pair of lovers, projects a metaphysical situation into the evocation of a personal relationship. The play is, in this as in other respects, the product of a profound uncertainty about the value of experience. The personal consequence of this uncertainty, as it affects more particularly the love poetry of Troilus, is the corruption of romantic sentiment. This is apparent in his first account of Cressida:

> I tell thee I am mad
> In Cressid's love; thou answer'st "she is fair";
> Pour'st in the open ulcer of my heart
> Her eyes, her hair, her cheek, her gait, her voice,
> Handlest in thy discourse, O that her hand,
> In whose comparison all whites are ink
> Writing their own reproach, to whose soft seizure
> The cygnet's down is harsh, and spirit of sense
> Hard as the palm of ploughman.
>
> (I.i.. 53–61)

The underlying convention here is clearly Petrarchan, romantically abstracted from common reality. It makes itself felt in the assertion that Troilus is "mad" for love, in the strained use of "pour'st" and "handlest" to describe Pandarus's speech, in the comparison of Cressida's hand to the "cygnet's down," and in the introduction of "ink" to bring out by contrast its superlative whiteness. But the conventional imagery is transformed, as it were, from within in a manner so closely bound up with the convention that it acts as a corrupting agent, intimately related to the surface sentiment. By giving deep sensuous value to the Petrarchan images, it conveys simultaneously an impression of intense feeling and an underlying lack of content. "Handlest in thy discourse" is, as I have said, a farfetched, literary image; but it brings with it a notable keenness of touch which is developed in the contrast between harshness and the "soft seizure" of the cygnet's down and in the almost unnatural immediacy of "spirit of sense." Yet the conventional note remains, and with it the feeling that Troilus's passion, for all its surface intensity, has an inadequate foundation, is vitiated by the strained self-pity which allows him to refer to "the open ulcer of my heart," and by the weakness to which he confesses in the course of the same speech: "I am weaker than a woman's tear."

It is important to realize why this weakness, which Cressida shares with her lover, does not produce a tragedy of character, but of situation. The tragedy indeed consists less in the personal suffering of the lovers than in the overriding influence exercised by time upon all human relationships and feelings. In *Antony and Cleopatra,* at least while the lovers are united by their feeling for one another, personal emotion has become strong enough to override mutability; in *Troilus,* the supremacy of time is never really questioned, and so a consistent status as persons inevitably eludes the lovers. Their weakness reflects the uncertainty of mood in which the play was conceived and to which they owe the peculiar poignancy, more than sentimental and less than tragic, with which they meet their personal fortunes. Antony and Cleopatra, as lovers, are fully drawn human beings because their love, while it lasts and within its own clearly defined limitations, is valid and confers upon their emotions a full personal value. Conversely, the complete realization in evil of Regan and Goneril in *King Lear,* with the sensual ferocity that characterizes it, proves that when he wrote that play, Shakespeare felt himself able to distinguish between the various elements in his moral experience without falling into ambiguity and confusion. Antony and Cleopatra, Regan and Goneril have full reality as characters precisely because they proceed from a clear understanding in their creator of the value of human emotion as distinct from the evil possibilities contained in it. *Troilus and Cressida,* however, with its intuition of passion as vain and transitory, is compatible with no such individuality of presentation; for time, as it is understood in this play, destroys personal values and makes them invalid.

This limiting observation can be applied with equal force to the behavior of both lovers, and through the entire action. Cressida's falseness does not spring from a deep-seated perversity or even from a strong positive attraction for Diomed, but from the mere process of events, from a flaw inherent in the human situation. Her tragedy, such as it is, derives from awareness of her helplessness. We feel it in her pathetic appeal when Troilus prepares to leave her after the night they have spent together:

> Prithee, tarry;
> You men will never tarry,
>
> (IV.ii. 15–16)

and in the moment of self-knowledge in which she tells him:

> I have a kind of self resides with you,
> But an unkind self that itself will leave
> To be another's fool.
>
> (III.ii. 149–51)

There is something in the expression of this uncertainty, half punning and conventional, which makes it difficult to conceive of Cressida as a fully realized being. At most she lives for us only in the mood of the moment, with barely a sign of that responsibility and consistency which is involved in the very conception of character. Any attempt to subject her inconsistency to a moral, of the kind which the medieval elaborators of this legend had in mind when they denounced her "faithlessness," is out of place because the spirit in which Shakespeare created her made it impossible for her to be shown as really responsible for her actions; and without responsibility there can be no moral evaluation. When she comments in the early part of the play on her refusal to reveal her feelings for Troilus:

> Yet hold I off. Women are angels, wooing;
> Things won are done; joy's soul lies in the doing,
>
> (I.ii. 298–99)

her aphoristic lines are not a revelation of wantonness, but simply an impression of the sense, which constitutes the only true tragedy of this play, of the impossibility, the meaninglessness of constancy in a world where time dominates human relationships and where attraction and separation seem necessary and connected aspects of a single situation.

This impossibility also dominates the poetry of Troilus himself and is there further developed from its original basis in romantic sentiment. Troilus's passion, even before it is faced with the necessity for separation, is strong only in anticipation. The intensity of its sensations is conveyed in a refinement of physical feeling, in an attempt to embody in terms of the senses an insubstantial and incorporeal emotion:

> I am giddy; expectation whirls me round.
> The imaginary relish is so sweet
> That it enchants my sense; what will it be,
> When that the watery palates taste indeed
> Love's thrice-repured nectar? death, I fear me,
> Swounding destruction, or some joy too fine,
> Too subtle-potent, tuned too sharp in sweetness,
> For the capacity of my ruder powers:
> I fear it much, and I do fear besides
> That I shall lose distinction in my joys ...
>
> (III.ii. 17–26)

The sensations of this passage are intense enough, but only on the palate and through the senses; like the corresponding emotions of Cressida, they scarcely involve any full personality in the speaker. Troilus's emotions are concentrated on "expectation," on "the *imaginary* relish," and he feels that the "watery palates" will be too weak to sustain the actual consummation. The whole speech turns upon this contrast between the refined intensity of feeling which he seeks, self-consciously and with a touch of indulgence, in "Love's *thrice-repured* nectar," and the giddiness, the "swounding destruction," which would follow its impossible consummation. The experience of love, it is suggested, is so fine, so "subtle-potent," that it surpasses the "ruder powers" of the body and remains an incorporeal aspiration which the senses strive vainly to attain.

Yet, by a strange contradiction, it is precisely because fulfillment in love is sought by Troilus exclusively on the sensual level that it proves unattainable. We can see now why the poetry of this play makes such extensive use of the imagery of taste, why Cressida, for example, says, before she leaves Troy for the Greek camp:

> The grief is fine, full, perfect, that I taste.
>
> (IV.iv. 3)

Taste is a sense at once luxurious, delicate, and transitory; also it can be connected, in gross opposition to Troilus's bodiless idealism, with digestion and the functioning of the body. For the weakness of Troilus's passion, as we have already suggested, implies that it is patent of corruption; and that corruption—it can now be added—is the logical consequence of an effort to extract from the refinement of the sensual a substitute for spiritual experience. Immediately before the speech just quoted there is a striking turn of phrase in his appeal to Pandarus:

> O, be thou my Charon,
> And give me swift transportance to those fields
> Where I may *wallow* in the lily-beds
> Proposed for the deserver.
>
> (III.ii. 10–12)

The ideal aspirations of Troilus remain abstract, intangible; such intensity as they achieve derives from their subjection to time, from their awareness of their own transitory nature. But this impermanence makes them bodiless, so that the sensual instincts, unable to associate themselves fully with the insubstantial ideal of union in a mutual passion, express themselves both weakly and basely, "wallowing" in what would be, if it were more forceful, a corrupt satisfaction.

This special use of the contrasted implications of sensual experience is extended in the course of the play from the personal to the public action, and contributes thus to the unity of its conception. The refined imagery of taste given to the Trojans, and especially to Troilus, reflects a bodiless ideal which becomes, in the mouths of the scurrilous Thersites and the Greek cynics, a series of clogged, heavy references to the digestive processes. Thersites has "majestic jaws," and Achilles calls him "my cheese, my digestion," while Agamemnon tells Patroclus that Achilles's virtues

> like fair fruit in an unwholesome dish
> Are like to rot untasted.
>
> (II.iii. 122–23)

In fact, the very sense which expresses the related intensity and lightness of Trojan passion becomes, in the Greeks, a symbol of inaction and distemper out of which issue the boils, "the botchy core," of Thersites's disgust.

In this way we pass from the individual to the public action, from the love of Troilus and Cressida to the war between the Greeks and Troy. This connection between the private and the public theme is indeed the most original feature of the play. The two parties, like the two lovers, are divergent within a common type of feeling. The Trojans share the fragile intensity of Troilus. They are deeply concerned with the value of "honor" and with a view of love which aspires to be idealistic, while Hector shows the virtues of war which are so noticeably absent from the bulky Ajax and the graceless Achilles. Typical of them is the speech in which Troilus explains the case for continuing the war:

> But, worthy Hector,
> She is a theme of honor and renown;
> A spur to valiant and magnanimous deeds,
> Whose present courage may beat down our foes,
> And fame in time to come canonize us.
>
> (II.ii. 198–202)

Yet the lightness and grace of this idealism covers a certain artificiality. It reads, at this stage in Shakespeare's development, like a survival from earlier plays set against

the contortions and involutions of so much of *Troilus*.
The impression is neither accidental nor isolated. Hector's
reasoning in the same scene shows clearly that the arguments advanced by Troilus are as flimsy in content as their
expression is tenuous. For all this "honor," for which
Troilus is ready to fight and, if need be, to die, is directed
to the defense of Helen, whose worth has been destroyed
by the manner in which she has been stolen from Menelaus. Even Paris can only plead that he

> would have the *soil* of her *fair* rape
> Wiped off in honorable keeping her,

and Troilus, conveying a slight but unmistakable twist to
conventional imagery, declares that Paris

> . . . bought a Grecian queen,
> whose youth and *freshness*
> Wrinkles Apollo's and *makes stale* the morning.

The juxtaposition of "fair" and "soil," "freshness" and
"stale," touches the basic weakness of Trojan idealism,
and points to the way in which that idealism is organically
connected in its expression with the sluggish inertia that
prevails in the Greek camp.

The true nature of this Trojan weakness is perhaps
most explicitly stated by Troilus when he sets forth, in an
attempt at reasoned expression, his argument for the continuation of the war:

> I take today a wife, and my election
> Is led on in the conduct of my will;
> My will enkindled by mine eyes and ears,
> Two traded pilots 'twixt the dangerous shores
> Of will and judgment: how may I avoid,
> Although my will distaste what it elected,
> The wife I chose? There can be no evasion
> To blench from this, and to stand firm by honor.
>
> (II.ii. 61–68)

Troilus's terminology is indefinite and the expression of

his argument, like so much of what passes for discussion
in this play, far more complicated than its content. There
seems at one point to be an opposition of "will," which
we may associate here with sensual impulse, and "judgment," by which this impulse should normally be restrained and directed; the opposition, in short, of sensuality and moral control, which became a little later the
central theme of *Measure for Measure*. In that play, however, the moral conflict is explicitly stated, and—what is
more important—takes shape in a dramatic clash of
clearly defined personalities; in *Troilus and Cressida* there
is only an uncertainty, a sense of uneasiness, which the
notable incoherence of the expression reflects. The conclusion reached by "judgment" is that affirmed by Hector
—"value dwells not in particular will," but rather in a
weighing of alternatives in the light of the principles of
reason—but the whole trend of Troilus's reply is to anni-
hilate, or at least confuse, the distinction between "will"
and "judgment" themselves, to show that "judgment" is
powerless and irrelevant once the sensual will has impelled
man towards action. In other words, the basis of Troilus's
"honor" is simply sensual impulse, and its weakness lies
largely in his unwillingness to recognize this fact, and in
the abstraction and lack of content which follow in the
train of this evasion.

Hector, indeed, is sufficiently outspoken on the subject
of Troilus's infatuation:

> Is your blood
> So madly hot that no discourse of reason,
> Nor fear of bad success in a bad cause
> Can qualify the same?
>
> (II.ii. 115–18,

The argument—though Troilus rejects it and Hector himself fails to follow it to its conclusion—once more binds
the personal love theme to that of the justification of public action. Troilus—and in this he is typical of the Trojans
—refuses to admit the weakness of his conception of
honor, which is, however, implied in the very situation

which brought the war into being: for the reality of Helen, as Hector points out, does not correspond to Troilus's embroidered and Marlovian conception of her:

> Brother, she is not worth what she doth cost
> The holding.
>
> (II.ii. 51–52)

But this same lack of solid foundation is apparent, as we have seen, in the undertones of Troilus's own poetry, where the unacknowledged sensual basis of his idealism refuses to be entirely suppressed. Underlying the "poetical" quality of Troilus's emotional flights, there is a distinct strain of coarseness and inertia. It appears in the references, so typical of this play, to the "soiled silks" and the "remainder viands" which are thrown away "because we now are full." Most typical of all, in the determination to hide its own weakness which it implies, is the Trojan reaction to reason:

> Nay, if we talk of reason,
> Let's shut our gates, and sleep: manhood and honor
> Should have hare hearts, would they but *fat* their thoughts
> With this *crammed* reason: reason and respect
> Make *livers pale* and lustihood deject.
>
> (II.ii. 46–50)

This insistence upon mental inertia and the obstruction of physical processes, as applied to reason, stands in significant contrast to the lightness and artificiality of Troilus's idealistic outbursts, but they are organically related to them. The Trojan devotion to honor, Shakespeare would seem to infer, is devotion to an abstraction that has no sufficient basis in reason, that is, in fact, no more than an empty justification of impulse; but—it is equally important to realize—to abandon honor for its lack of rational foundation is to expose oneself to the danger of lethargy, to a rooted disinclination to act at all.[1] Once more we are faced with the split between motive and im-

---

[1] The relation of this to *Hamlet*, and in particular to such a soliloquy as "How all occasions do inform against me" (IV. iv) is worth careful consideration.

pulse, moral *value* and sensual substitutes, which dominates this play, without a real glimpse of resolution.

The analysis of this important scene suggests how the contrast between the Greek and Trojan parties, which most critics have noted, is modified by significant points of contact. The Trojans, for all their concern to defend honor against the Greeks, are strangely related to their enemies. This relationship, of course, is openly "symbolized" in the combat between Hector and Ajax (IV.v), when Hector refuses to carry on the duel with his "cousin-german" and Ajax agrees to call a truce. But the contacts established through a common type of imagery are still more important for an understanding of the play. Where the Trojans reject reason in favor of ill-considered action, the Greeks accept it and are reduced to inaction. Agamemnon's very first speech, as the head and cornerstone of Greek unity, shows how inconclusive are the intellectual processes so painfully followed by the leaders who accompany him and how closely related they are to the views expressed by Troilus on "crammed reason":

> Princes,
> What grief hath set the jaundice on your cheeks?
> The ample proposition that hope makes
> In all designs begun on earth below
> Fails in the promised largeness; checks and disasters
> Grow in the veins of actions highest reared,
> As knots, by the conflux of meeting sap,
> Infect the sound pine and divert his grain
> Tortive and errant from his course of growth.
> Nor, princes, is it matter new to us
> That we come short of our suppose so far
> That after seven years' siege yet Troy walls stand;
> Sith every action that hath gone before,
> Whereof we have record, trial did draw
> Bias and thwart, not answering the aim
> And that unbodied figure of the thought
> That gave it surmised shape.

(I.iii. 1–17)

Agamemnon's thought proceeds not from point to point

according to a definite logical sequence, but by a series of
indeterminate digressions which illustrate his incapacity to
come to a conclusion. His labored illustrations destroy the
coherence of an argument which they do nothing to further; as so often in this play, there is no recognizable
development of thought to justify the complexity. The
repeated doublings of words—"checks and disasters,"
"tortive and errant," "bias and thwart"—all lay emphasis
upon obstruction, upon the speaker's struggle against obscure impediments which hinder the Greeks from successful action; and the use of unusual and unassimilated
Latinized words, such as "conflux" and "tortive," produces a similar sense of resistance and difficulty. More
significantly still, these obstructions are associated with
disturbances and interruptions in organic growth. The
prospect of hope "fails in the promised largeness," does
not grow to its anticipated stature. "Checks and disasters"
are intertwined with natural growth, and the very rising of
the sap in the "sound pine," which is so eminently a
natural process, produces infection and distortion in the
growth of the tree. Most important of all, because corresponding to the spirit expressed by Troilus, thought is
"unbodied" and its processes, separated from the actual
course of events, are equally cut off from the sensual
immediacy which finds irresponsible expression in the
comments of Thersites. The keen nervous quality so
noticeably lacking in the theoretical observations of the
Greek leaders breaks out significantly in Thersites's sweep-
ing affirmation of anarchy and disorder; in a similar manner, Troilus's disembodied idealism covers a sensual impulse which he refuses to recognize.

It is only natural that this discrepancy in the Greeks
between thought and action should be expressed in terms
of physical disorder; and here the link with the Trojans
becomes even more explicit. Thersites's boils and plague
spots are related to Agamemnon's laborious thoughts on
authority just as Troilus's contempt for "crammed reason"
and his insistent sense of soilure and physical obstruction
are connected with his abstract idealism. The vital point in
Shakespeare's presentation of the Greeks is this associa-

tion of continual ratiocination with a complete overthrow of "degree"; they are entirely unable to turn council into united action. The position in the Greek camp is briefly summed up by Thersites: "Agamemnon is a fool to offer to command Achilles; Achilles is a fool to be commanded of Agamemnon; Thersites is a fool to serve such a fool; and Patroclus is a fool positive" (II.iii). While Agamemnon, Nestor, and Ulysses scheme and discuss, Ajax and Achilles "fust" out of action; the hand that executes is out of touch with the *"still and mental* parts" that contrive the conduct of the war. Perhaps the point is most clearly made by Ulysses in his account of Achilles's pride:

> imagined worth
> Holds in his blood such swoln and hot discourse
> That *'twixt his mental and his active parts*
> Kingdom'd Achilles in commotion rages
> And batters down himself.
>
> (II.iii. 175–78)

The conflict in Achilles between personal pride and duty to the Greek cause is stated here in terms of "blood," of sensual passion; the implications of "swoln and hot," suggesting feverish disorder due to extreme intemperance, are unmistakable. The adjective "kingdom'd," like so many of the words which characterize the poetry of this play, is not fully explicit, but it clearly refers the personal issue back to the general theme of "degree." The individual warrior, like the Greek polity at war, should be a unity founded upon "degree"; and "degree" in the individual is an ideal correspondence between thought and action, impulse and control, "blood" and "judgment."[2]

On both sides this balance is profoundly disturbed. The "cunning" of the Greek leaders is manifestly out of touch with practical considerations and expends itself in an

2 Compare *Hamlet:*

> ... blest are those
> Whose blood and judgment are so well commingled
> That they are not a pipe for fortune's finger
> To sound what stop she pleases.
>
> (III.ii)

activity completely disproportionate to the desired end: "it will not in circumvention deliver a fly from a spider, without drawing their massy irons and cutting the web" (II.iii. 16–18). On the Trojan side the infidelity of Cressida finally undermines Troilus's faith in "honor" as a basis for action and leaves him dimly aware of the incompatible and contrary elements which underlie what he had assumed to be the indivisible simplicity of passion:

> Within my soul there doth conduce a fight
> Of this strange nature, that a thing inseparate
> Divides more wider than the sky and earth;
> And yet the spacious breadth of this division
> Admits no orifex for a point as subtle
> As Ariadne's broken woof to enter.
> Instance, O instance! strong as Pluto's gates;
> Cressid is mine, tied with the bonds of heaven:
> Instance, O instance! strong as heaven itself,
> The bonds of heaven are slipp'd, dissolved and
>   loosed:
> And with another knot, five-finger-tied,
> The fragments of her faith, orts of her love,
> The fragments, scraps, the bits and greasy relics
> Of her o'er-eaten faith, are bound to Diomed.
>
> (V.ii. 144–57)

All the characteristics of the love poetry of Troilus can be recognized here—its tenuous and unnaturally refined expression, its subtlety in dealing with distinctions within an apparent unity, its sensuous thinness balanced by the imagery of disgust and repletion which connects it with the verse given to the Greeks and indicates the unifying factor in this play. For the ambiguous attitude towards experience which so deeply exercised Shakespeare in many of his sonnets is the determining factor in his presentation of both parties. Proceeding from his sense of the disharmony introduced by their subjection to the temporal process into the love of Troilus and Cressida, it extends to embrace the two parties in their fantastic and unreasonable conflict. The Trojans follow a false idealism, which deceives itself with talk of "honor," but is really based on "blood" and ends in a pathetic and helpless realization of its own insufficiency; the Greeks elaborate endlessly a "judgment" that is out of touch with the instinctive sources of action, until Agamemnon's chaotic reasoning finds its proper counterpart in the distorted bitterness of Thersites's diseased sensibility.

The fundamental impulse of this play, and the link which binds personal cleavage to political disorder, is now clear. Ulysses's argument on "degree" reduces itself finally to an intuition of self-consuming passion:

> Then everything includes itself in power,
> Power into will, will into *appetite*;
> And appetite, an universal wolf,
> So doubly seconded with will and power,
> Must make perforce an universal prey,
> And last eat up himself.
>
> (I.iii. 119–24)

The speech is saved from the charge of abstraction by this relation of "degree" to the disorder introduced by passion or "appetite" into the human organism. This disorder, present on both sides in the conflict between Greeks and Trojans, is the real theme of the play. The Trojans seek to ignore the limitations of passion in a bodiless idealism; the Greeks, quite incapable of idealism, are weighed down by all that the Trojans try to forget. Both sides are bound together by the occasion of their quarrel; as Thersites says: "All the argument is a cuckold and a whore." Troilus, in one magnificent phrase, sums up the crux from which the varied contradictions of the play draw their interest:

> This is the monstruosity in love, lady, that the will is infinite and the execution confined, that the desire is boundless and the act a slave to limit.
>
> (III.ii. 82–85)

The infinity sought by the will is the idealistic love of Troilus, which neglects the wearing action of time and the related inability of passion to live up to ideals of love and honor which can only be redeemed from abstraction by an adequate spiritual integration; and the very boundlessness of the desire, when it encounters the limits imposed by time and the body to which, in the absence of such an integration, it feels enslaved, turns to the clogged inertia of Achilles and the endless self-scrutiny of the Greek camp.

S. L. BETHELL

from *Shakespeare and the Popular Dramatic Tradition*

Troilus and Cressida is a consciously philosophical play. Normally Shakespeare's philosophical notions are incarnated in character and action; and his poetic thought, always concrete and image-filled, relates to character and action directly, and only indirectly to whatever general truths may be implied. The "Tomorrow, and tomorrow" speech (*Macbeth* V.v.) expresses directly Macbeth's re-action to his wife's death, and merely implies the atheism ("dusty death," "Signifying nothing") which has resulted from his gradual hardening in crime. In *Troilus and Cressida*, on the other hand, the thought, only partially embodied in character and action, flows over into the dialogue, which, though usually concrete enough and full of imagery, is frequently developed almost independently of the situation to which it refers. Ulysses' great speech on "degree" (*Troilus and Cressida* I.iii.75) begins and ends with Troy, but is much more concerned with generalities of political philosophy than with the Trojan war: in *Troilus and Cressida* the story is an excuse for thought rather than the embodiment of thought. The metaphysical problems of the tragedies must, from the

From *Shakespeare and the Popular Dramatic Tradition* by S. L. Bethell. London: Staples Press, 1944; Durham, North Carolina: Duke University Press, 1945. Reprinted by permission of Staples Press.

first, have presented themselves to Shakespeare in terms
of concrete experience; but in *Troilus and Cressida* he
pursues philosophical abstractions with the impassioned
eagerness of Donne. Problems of time and value and
their mutual relations are thrust forward for the audience's
attention:

> Time hath, my lord, a wallet at his back,
> Wherein he puts alms for oblivion.
>
> (III.iii. 145)

As in Donne, philosophy is usually apprehended in terms
of sense experience, but occasionally even the bare bones
of abstract thinking appear, e.g. in Troilus' crucial but
awkward query: "What is aught, but as 'tis valued?"
(II.ii. 52).

In such a play it is no wonder to find characters with
something of a "morality" flavor. As Thersites recalls the
old Vice, so Ulysses conveys some suggestion of an abstract Worldly Wisdom. Most of the characters in *Troilus
and Cressida* express themselves philosophically, but
Ulysses has an especially large share of such speeches,
including the famous "degree" speech and the speech on
Time. With him even more than the others, what he says
is infinitely more important than why he says it, and at
times even his behavior is hard to interpret on naturalistic
grounds. When Cressida arrives in the Grecian camp,
Agamemnon receives her with a kiss:

> Our general doth salute you with a kiss,
>
> (IV.v. 19)

says Nestor. Ulysses comments with a pun:

> Yet is the kindness but particular;
> 'Twere better she were kiss'd in general.
>
> (IV.v. 20–21)

The others act upon this advice, and Cressida is kissed
in turn by all the Greek leaders. When his own turn

comes, however, there is a short wit-battle in which Ulysses insultingly rejects the kiss that Cressida is presumably willing to give:

Ulysses. May I, sweet lady, beg a kiss of you?

Cressida. You may.

Ulysses.   I do desire it.

Cressida.   Why, beg, then.

Ulysses. Why then for Venus' sake, give me a kiss,
        When Helen is a maid again, and his
        [i.e. Menelaus'].

Cressida. I am your debtor, claim it when 'tis due.

Ulysses. Never's my day, and then a kiss of you.

When Diomedes leads Cressida away, Ulysses bursts into denunciation:

> Fie, fie upon her!
> There's language in her eye, her cheek, her lip,
> Nay, her foot speaks; her wanton spirits look out
> At every joint and motive of her body.
> O, these encounterers, so glib of tongue,
> That give accosting welcome ere it comes,
> And wide unclasp the tables of their thoughts
> To every ticklish reader! set them down
> For sluttish spoils of opportunity
> And daughters of the game.

(IV.v. 54–63)

Speaking naturalistically, we should admire this moral rectitude more heartily, if Ulysses had not himself initiated the general kissing. Taken conventionally, however, the incident is central to the Troilus-Cressida theme. The handing over of Cressida to the Greeks is the handing over of Troilus' ideal love to the sullying of the world: we are to be prepared for his betrayal, and our knowledge of Cressida's character must be so established that no psychological doubt remain to befog the philosophical issue. Ulysses, at least during this incident (episodic intensification again!), represents an impersonal Wisdom, whose judgment we must accept. He devises a test for Cressida which sufficiently reveals her character and the character of those she has come among; and his own refusal to kiss her sets him apart from the others, in judicial aloofness, so that we are prepared to accept the verdict which he pronounces after Cressida is led away. The whole passage is in rhyme and full of wordplay: this not only emphasizes the tone of badinage and flirtation, but also serves to distance or frame the whole incident, which thus appears in a sort of vocal italics to draw attention to its symbolic function. To condemn Ulysses' conduct as ungentlemanly would be to attribute to the character a representational quality which the passage seems to disallow. There is a suggestion of deity about Ulysses: we must accept his moral judgments, but we must not search the morality of his own conduct, which is, as it were, an Olympian setting of the stage for human conflict. As the embodiment of wisdom, he is to be praised or blamed solely in reference to that one quality. It is only at times that this hint of allegory appears in the action and dialogue of Ulysses: Shakespeare's reversion to an older technique is probably unconscious; but it is none the less interesting on that account.

Troilus and Cressida, as probably the most intellectual of Shakespeare's plays, reveals an unusually high degree of conventionalism in the presentation of character; examples can be found of most of the conventions discussed in this chapter and the last. Thersites, whose relation to the Vice has already been mentioned, might perhaps best be classed as a "humor," his predominant characteristic being cynical and prurient wit. Lechery is his favorite theme:

> Nothing but lechery! all incontinent varlets!
> (V.i. 102–03)

He does duty also as a scurrilous chorus upon the futility of war—a role comparable to that of Falstaff in the battle scenes of *Henry IV, Part I.* His remark above occurs significantly at the end of a scene, and the next scene closes with a similar but even more emphatic outburst:

> Lechery, lechery; still, wars and lechery; nothing else holds fashion: a burning devil take them!
>
> (V.ii. 192–94)

To close two successive scenes of the fifth act in this way is surely to commend the opinion of Thersites to our very serious attention. Ajax and Achilles are practically humors: senseless vanity and strength in Ajax; selfish pride and strength in Achilles. Helen is also a humor: in the one scene in which she appears, her only characteristic is a weak and silly sex obsession:

> Let thy song be love: this love will undo us all. O Cupid, Cupid, Cupid!
>
> (III.i. 111–12)

Professor Wilson Knight is surely mistaken in considering her to be a worthy object of Trojan idealism.[1] This scene, which is almost central in position, is certainly central at any rate to one theme of the play: the theme of "fair without and foul within," which I shall later treat more fully. The Helen whose face had launched a thousand Marlovian ships is subjected to a remorseless Shakespearean "debunking"; in a few lines the real Helen is revealed, the inadequate object of so much misplaced idealism. Other characters in the play are more complex, though none is seen very clearly in the round. . . .

Action as well as character may be symbolic, even action which is not represented on the stage. Paris' request that Helen should "help unarm our Hector" (III.i. 149) clinches the Helen scene and assures its central position. The outward show of chivalry is there; but we know Hector to be the worthiest of the Trojans, and

---

[1] So at least he implies, in speaking of this scene: "the strains of music," he says, "herald the entry of Helen, queen of romance" (*The Wheel of Fire*, p. 67).

Helen a worthless strumpet. That Hector should yield to
fight in such a cause is the undoing of himself and of
Troy: that Helen should play the role of his "fair lady"—
a Helen who can be so much at home with Pandarus—is
the height of Shakespearean irony. In the play's last act,
action and character mingle in what is unique in Shakespeare—a direct allegorical presentation of his dramatic
theme. Hector, despite the entreaties of Andromache, and
the prophetic warnings of Cassandra, joins the battle,
as his honor bids him. The usual battle confusion is presented in what modern editors unnecessarily divide into
a series of short scenes. Near the end of Scene vi there is
a stage direction which reads, in our modern editions,
Enter one in sumptuous armor. In the Quarto and Folios,
it is simply *Enter one in armor,*[2] but Malone's addition
of "sumptuous"[3] merely underlines Shakespeare's obvious
intention, for Hector cries out to this anonymous figure:

> Stand, stand, thou Greek; thou art a goodly mark:
> No? Wilt thou not? I like thy armor well;
> I'll frush it and unlock the rivets all,
> But I'll be master of it: wilt thou not, beast, abide?
> Why, then fly on, I'll hunt thee for thy hide.
>
> (V.vi. 27–31)

At the beginning of Scene viii, we find Hector presumably
standing over the mysterious person, whom he has now
slain, and saying:

> Most putrefied core, so fair without,
> Thy goodly armor thus hath cost thy life.
> Now is my day's work done; I'll take good breath:
> Rest, sword; thou hast thy fill of blood and death.
>
> (V.viii. 1–4)

At this point *"Enter* Achilles *and* Myrmidons," and Hector

2, 3 *Troilus and Cressida,* in *The Cambridge Shakespeare,* ed. William
Aldis Wright (Macmillan, 1894), p. 159, note to l. 27.

meets his death unarmed at the hands of the cowardly hero and his pack. We hear from Troilus, two scenes later, that

> He's dead; and at the murderer's horse's tail,
> In beastly sort, dragg'd through the shameful field.
>
> (V.x. 4–5)

Shakespeare took the incident of the "one in sumptuous armor" from Lydgate's *Troye Boke*,[4] but seems to have given it a wider significance. The crucial question here is, "Why 'putrefied core'?"[5] There is nothing in Lydgate to explain this remarkable apostrophe. What did Shakespeare intend by it? The "one in sumptuous armor" was surely not dead when he first entered, and he had had no time to putrefy after being killed. Or does it mean that he was old, or diseased, or infirm? In any event, Hector had won the armor which he coveted, so why this apparently embittered comment? I do not see any naturalistic explanation. What I suggest is that Shakespeare saw in the incident in Lydgate an allegory similar to the "whited sepulcher" of Holy Scripture: "a sumptuous armor" stands for the "outward show" which covers an inner corruption. Perhaps with the scriptural passage in mind, Shakespeare rendered his symbol complete by adding the "putrefied core," although the reference is

---

[4] *Vide*, a note of Steevens, in Malone's edition of Shakespeare (pub. 1821), vol. viii, p. 437:

"This circumstance is taken from Lydgate's poem, p. 196:

'—Guido in his historic doth shew
By worthy Hector's fall, who coveting
To have the sumptuous armor of the king, etc.
So greedy was thereof, that when he had
The body up, and on his horse it bare,
To have the spoil thereof such haste he made
That he did hang his shield without all care
Behind him at his back, the easier
To pull the armor off at his desire,
And by that means his breast clean open lay,' etc.

This furnished Shakespeare with the hint for the following line:

'I am unarm'd; forego this vantage, Greek.' "

Malone obviously borrowed the epithet "sumptuous" from Steevens' quotation or its original.

[5] The word is "core," not "corse," and implies a metaphor from rotten fruit.

incapable of natural explanation, and must be taken by the audience on an entirely different plane from the rest of the play. The "sumptuous armor" with its "putrefied core" thus becomes a symbol of all the play presents to us, an allegorical enactment of the theme of "fair without, and foul within," which is applicable almost everywhere in the Troy and Troilus stories as Shakespeare rewrites them. It applies to the war, with its false chivalry and inadequate aim; to Helen, to Cressida, and a good many more of the personages involved; and it applies, lastly, to the death of Hector, with which it is so closely linked in presentation. Hector was the best of the Trojans, and better than the best of the Greeks: he saw, most clearly of them all, the essential evil of the war, waged to keep Helen from her lawful husband:

> . . . 'tis mad idolatry
> To make the service greater than the god,
>
> (II. ii. 56–57)

he said. And yet he concluded for the continuation of the war:

> For 'tis a cause that hath no mean dependance
> Upon our joint and several dignities.
>
> (II.ii. 192–93)

Later, he ignored Andromache and Cassandra, in order to fulfill the supposed duties of a false conception of honor. Unworthy aims are bound to tarnish the most chivalrous nature: and so Hector himself, a few moments before he is brutally murdered, so far loses his chivalric courtesy as to call out "beast" after the "one in sumptuous armor," and then: "I'll hunt thee for thy hide"— the least worthy of motives. His death and the shameful treatment of his corpse are perhaps punishment in excess of his swerving, but they point sharply to the previous degradation he had suffered. Even in the *Troye Boke*, there is at least a suggestion that Hector's death was in some sense a consequence of his greed. Shakespeare elaborates the incident, places it at the climax of his play, and removes all possibility of natural explanation, so that he surely meant it to bear the extended significance which I have suggested. Otherwise there seems no point in his choice of this particular incident when so many important happenings in the Troy story are necessarily omitted, and absolutely no point in the further complication of the "putrefied core."

Troilus and Cressida is thus a play which especially calls for the exercise of multi-consciousness. In addition to the usual dual consciousness of play world and real world, and of past and present time, there is the dual consciousness of story and philosophy, since the two are not wholly merged; there is the dual consciousness of character as representative and as allegorical; and, further, there must be a dual consciousness of certain incidents in their naturalistic and their allegorical significances. . . .

I. A. RICHARDS

"Troilus and Cressida" and Plato

"In *Troilus,* all Chaucer's characters are debased, even Pandarus, hard as the task may seem. Cressida is a wily profligate, Troilus a whining babbler." This judgment from Jusserand[1] may serve us as an excellent warning against reading the views of our own day into Shakespeare. We are a long way now from Jusserand, but equally exposed to this danger—and more exposed to the worse risk of supposing that the meanings we may rightly find in the work are to be limited by what we can conjecture to have been Shakespeare's intentions. These Notes, on what *Troilus and Cressida* may say to readers who have recently gained an acquaintance with the *Iliad* and the *Republic* (in a General Education program, for example), try to dodge between these dangers. Shakespeare's works are the offspring of Language and Tradition—of English in a peculiarly inflamed state and of a meander of the tradition which proved to be more than ordinarily fertile. We may reasonably find meanings in the plays without attributing them to Shakespeare himself; remembering that we have to find them and not plant them there ourselves.

Jusserand will remind us of another danger—the conventional wrenching of the detached line. "Even in his

From *Speculative Instruments* by I. A. Richards. Chicago: University of Chicago Press; London: Routledge & Kegan Paul, Ltd., 1955. Originally published in *The Hudson Review* (1948). Copyright I. A. Richards, 1948, 1955. Reprinted by permission of the author, *The Hudson Review*, and University of Chicago Press.

1 *A Literary History of the English People,* Vol. III, p. 253.

most hastily composed plays . . . just as we were about
to revolt, to protest against a puppet show, behold, the
magician emerges from his torpor, life circulates, and
the wooden doll of a moment ago now utters words that
no ages can ever forget."[2] In a footnote: "Example: to
Ulysses, a mere puppet through most of the play, is
given the famous line: 'One touch of nature makes the
whole world kin.'" This is indeed a famous line. In
spite of many protests, it will continue to be quoted as
if the "one touch of nature" were something like "one
impulse from the vernal wood" and not an ignoble
slavery to fashion:

That all with one consent praise new borne gaudes.

More lessons lie here than can be enumerated. We have
to try to take them to heart.

In this case both the fame and the wrenching seem
more than usually explicable. In moods of general benevo-
lence, to think of the whole world becoming kin is
agreeable and relieves anxiety. And it seems particularly
appropriate that this should happen through "one touch
of nature," as though nature were some sweet recreative
influence restoring us to an original innocence. The *kin-
kind* pun becomes active perhaps. In contrast, the specify-
ing line is unflattering, painfully true, pointing to things
that goodhearted folk would rather not think of. Worst
still, *this* "touch of nature," which unites us in such a
humbling bond, seems (if we stress *one* as I think we
should) to be set over against other touches of nature
apt to seal us all up "in will peculiar and self-admission."

These estimates of *Troilus and Cressida* and of its
characters seem to be still widely received. I have heard
highly accredited opinion voice a doubt whether the play
deserves a place in a General Education course even as
a sequence to Homer and Plato. I hope here to give
some reasons for thinking that conventional views under-

2 *Op. cit.*, p. 310.

estimate the play; that its scenes are among the most summoning of Shakespeare's glances at life, that they have at least an affinity with and an elective power of reflecting Plato at his height; in particular that Troilus is as little a "whining babbler" as Ulysses is a "wooden doll," and in general that current interpretations misread the play as badly as the tag-quotation mistakes the famous line.

Our conception of Troilus himself will, of course, be the key to the rest of the argument. But since Ulysses is the source of a major piece of testimony about Troilus we may well consider the Prince of Ithaca a moment. His great speech on order (I.iii. 75–137) has received deserved attention. Less has been paid to his aspect as head of an Intelligence Service. As he himself claims to Achilles (III.iii. 201):

> There is a mystery—with whom relation
> Durst never meddle—in the soul of state . . .
> All the commerce that you have had with Troy
> As perfectly is ours as yours, my lord.

In this mystery Ulysses is a master. He proves it at point after point in the play—with Achilles throughout, with Ajax (II.iii. 86), with Cressida (IV.v. 54–63), with the movements of Diomede (IV.v. 278–82; V.i. 88) and all through Act V, Scene ii. He is the supremely well qualified man to describe Troilus to Agamemnon:

> The youngest son of Priam, a true knight;
> Not yet mature, yet matchless; firm of word,
> Speaking in deeds and deedless in his tongue;
> Not soon provok'd nor, being provok'd, soon calm'd:
> His heart and hand both open and both free;
> For what he has he gives, what thinks he shows;
> Yet gives he not till judgment guide his bounty,
> Nor dignifies an impare thought with breath:
> Manly as Hector, but more dangerous;
> For Hector, in his blaze of wrath, subscribes
> To tender objects; but he, in heat of action
> Is more vindicative than jealous love.

> They call him Troilus; and on him erect
> A second hope, as fairly built as Hector.
> Thus says Aeneas; one that knows the youth
> Even to his inches, and with private soul
> Did in great Ilion thus translate him to me.

Shakespeare might almost have had Jusserand's opinion —"a whining babbler"—in mind when he wrote these lines. Unless there is evidence in Troilus' actual behavior and speeches that Ulysses is utterly wrong here, we should not set such testimony aside. And when we remember that Shakespeare, here, as so often, is following his sources closely, there is less reason for minimizing its weight.

Let us look then at what Troilus does and says. In the first scene, he indulges in some most elegant rhetorical sighs. That he blames himself for his passion it would be unfair to use against him; but it may be admitted that these early scenes do little to prepare for what is coming. They do not point forward to philosophic action. With the Trojan War Council (II.ii), however, his stature is changed. He becomes the reflective apologist of Honor, a theme and cause (Homeric with a difference) in which he easily triumphs over Helenus:

> You are for dreams and slumbers, brother priest,
> You fur your gloves with reasons

and even over Hector himself, who at the end cries out:

> I am yours
> You valiant offspring of great Priamus.

The argument of this scene is the mainspring of the play and will, I believe, repay as much examination as any reader has time to give to it. In line 52 comes Troilus' great question—which Act V, Scene ii is to force him to rethink:

> What is aught but as 'tis valued?

Hector's answer can be read, I suggest, with profit, as a comment on Troilus' own later struggle with this truly central problem of all philosophy: value and fact, the ideal and the actual, or however we care to phrase it.

> But value dwells not in particular will;
> It holds his estimate and dignity
> As well wherein 'tis precious of itself
> As in the prizer. 'Tis mad idolatry
> To make the service greater than the god;
> And the will dotes, that is inclinable
> To what infectiously itself affects,
> Without some image of the affected merit.

Each sentence here, and every word (especially the small ones, the "as well," the "of itself" and the "in") deserves the fullest imaginative study. Troilus is to face his own "mad idolatry," to measure the service with the god in the instance of Cressida—driven to it by the sharpest case of jilting in literature—and, above all, to watch the division and reunion of will and reason in himself under the severest testing that they can perhaps be given. He has a long way to go before this and here he replies to Hector chiefly in terms of fidelity—with a marriage figure:

> How may I avoid
> Although my will distaste what it elected,
> The wife I chose? There can be no evasion
> To blench from this and to stand firm by honor.

He is not announcing his marriage (see IV.ii. 71); he is simply using the image most present to his mind. In his next speech, the lines:

> We may not think the justness of each act
> Such and no other than event doth form it,

are again premonitory and perhaps exculpative.

Hector praises these speeches but quotes Aristotle's echo of the *Republic* (539) and finds them superficial.

He then in the spirit of Plato's great analogy (matrimony apart) parallels the individual will with that of the state:

> Nature craves
> All dues be render'd to their owners . . .
> If this law
> Of Nature be corrupted through affection

(a pivotal word in the play)

> And that great minds, of partial indulgence
> To their benumbed wills, resist the same,
> There is a law in each well-order'd nation
> To curb those raging appetites that are
> Most disobedient and refractory.

Then suddenly, in spite of "these moral laws of nature and of nations" and though

> Hector's opinion
> Is this, in way of truth,

he veers. With an infirmity of purpose which supports Ulysses' judgment of him and with a feckless gallantry matching the poor strategy of his "roisting challenge" (1. 208), he joins Paris and Troilus:

> My sprightly brethren, I propend to you
> In resolution to keep Helen still;
> For 'tis a cause that hath no mean dependance
> Upon our joint and several dignities.

The contrast between this inconsequence and the policies of "that same dog-fox Ulysses" is one of many which make the play an exercise in meditation on the sources of power.

The Orchard scene (III.ii) shows us a Troilus in whom I see no ground to doubt his own description:

> I am as true as truth's simplicity
> And simpler than the infancy of truth.

Truth, as he sees it, is indeed in its infancy here. It is to grow up swiftly. That he prefaces these lines with an "Alas!" and something very like a determination to be deaf to certain doubts about Cressida, does not in the least impare them.

How we see Troilus here depends in a measure upon how we conceive Cressida. I like to make her very young —almost with her finger in her mouth still—a little actress through and through, trying out her powers without caring or knowing much about the roles she picks up or drops. Something of this sort fits both the giddy speed of her transitions (rather than betrayals) and these queer forebodings in Troilus both here and in the farewell scene at dawn. Poor Cressida. Truly she has

> an unkind self, that itself will leave,
> To be another's fool . . .
> I know not what I speak.

To such a natural putter-on of possible passions Shakespeare can give language of great power:

> Time, force and death,
> Do to this body what extremes you can;
> But the strong base and building of my love
> Is as the very center of the earth
> Drawing all things to it.

> (IV.ii. 103–07)

Troilus (III.ii. 180) simply said, "as earth to the center." This young novice Cressida is an experimentalist in feelings, curious and sparing as a wine taster, though exuberant in expression:

> *Pandarus.* Be moderate, be moderate.
> *Cressida.* Why tell you me of moderation?
>   The grief is fine, full, perfect, that I taste,
>   And violenteth in a sense as strong
>   As that which causeth it: how can I moderate it?
>   If I could temporize with my affection . . .

> (IV.iv. 1–6)

Neither Cressida, nor Troilus in his following speech, know what they are saying. Only the audience—or the close rereader with the whole play in mind—can see what is happening or into what examples their words will turn them. The fashion in which Cressida can temporize (intemperately) with her affection will be Troilus' punishment for the words he now utters. With Arachne and Niobe coming later in the play (and in Troilus' own mouth) it is hard to suppose that the ensuing specimen of *hubris* is accidental. "What a pair of spectacles is here!" as Pandarus cries, with more reason than he knows. (I must in passing protest against the traditional excess of contempt[3] for this tenderhearted and fanciful snob. He has laid aside, it is true, the oath-breaking bow of the *Iliad* to play Cupid. He has, no doubt in a superior degree, the vicarious eroticism of the matchmaker, but the insult I have quoted from Jusserand is unfair to Chaucer and to Shakespeare as well as to Pandar. It is letting his name take over the offices of perception and judgment.) "How now, lambs!" he says.

> *Troilus.* Cressid, I love thee in so strain'd a purity,
>   That the bless'd gods, as angry with my fancy,
>   More bright in zeal than the devotion which
>   Cold lips blow to their deities, take thee from me.
>
> *Cressida.* Have the gods envy?
>
> *Pandarus.* Ay, ay, ay, ay; 'Tis too plain a case.

It is truly. And for this blasphemy they *will* take his goddess from him, farther than to the Greek camp.

> *Troilus.* Hark! you are call'd: some say the Genius so
>   Cries 'Come!' to him that instantly must die.

This Genius, however he got here, comes from the *Republic:* "And Lachesis sent with each, as the guardian of his life and the fulfiller of his choice, the genius that

---

3."... The filthy, prurient, self-appointed tool, who revels in garbage of words and garbage of deeds ..." The Arden Shakespeare, 1906. *The Interpretation of Dreams* came into English in 1913.

he had chosen." (X, 620E). Its business is to see that we do not escape the life plan we have selected from among those cast before us. It is the same Being which Shakespeare put into *Julius Caesar* II.i.:

> *Brutus.* Between the acting of a dreadful thing
> And the first motion, all the interim is
> Like a phantasma or a hideous dream:
> The genius and the mortal instruments
> Are then in council, and the state of man,
> Like to a little kingdom, suffers then
> The nature of an insurrection.

These lines share two things with *Troilus and Cressida:* this Genius, so unlike the others in Shakespeare; and the image of the state of man in insurrection, also derived, ultimately, from the *Republic:* [4]

> Kingdom'd Achilles in commotion rages
> And batters down himself.
>
> (II.iii. 177–78)

We will pass now to the Betrayal Scene (V.ii) where the strength of the government in Troilus is tested. With Ulysses at his elbow and Thersites (another sort of connoisseur in human nature) suitably prone in the other wing as observers and chorus, Troilus has to watch Cressida, at the mouth of Calchas' tent, *palter* (It is Diomede's word) with her new lover. He has to see the sleeve he gave to her as a love token, "five-finger-tied" (I think) to Diomede's helmet.

Before considering the crisis speeches, it is well to consider what sort of shock Troilus is undergoing:

> *Ulysses.* You shake, my lord, at something: will you go?
> You will break out.

and with what measure he is attempting to meet it:

---

[4] I have written elsewhere, in *How to Read a Page* (p. 74) of the Platonic echoes in I. iii. 116–24.

Troilus. She strokes his cheek!

Ulysses.   Come, come.

Troilus. Nay, stay; by Jove, I will not speak a word:
There is between my will and all offenses
A guard of patience.

As Cressida goes to fetch the sleeve, Ulysses, with his hand—thought-readerwise—on Troilus' shoulder, says:

You have sworn patience.
Troilus.   Fear me not, sweet lord.
I will not be myself, nor have cognition
Of what I feel: I am all patience.

Such unnatural self-control cannot last. This guard of patience, though reinforced, as it is, *seven* times in the Scene (whether through the Language or the Tradition, it came from the *Republic*) cannot be expected to hold down forever a city in such turmoil.

Never did young man fancy
With so eternal and so fixed a soul.

It is "as true as Troilus"; and this man, as we know from Ulysses,

in heat of action
Is more vindicative than jealous love.

Something has to happen. We have to consider, as we watch it happening, what it is, and by what canons this behavior is exemplary.

Socrates. Poetry copies men: acting either under force or of their own free will; seeing themselves in the outcome to have done well or ill; and, in all this, feeling grief or joy. Is there something in addition?
Glaucon. Nothing.
Socrates. Is a man of one mind with himself in all this?

Or is there division and fighting with himself—as there was when in vision he had opposite opinions at the same time about the same things. . . . Our souls at any one time are attacked by endless opposite views. There was one thing, however, we didn't say then which has to be said now.

Glaucon. What was it?

Socrates. We said then, I believe, that a good man who is ruled by reason will take such blows of fate as the loss of a son or anything very dear to him less hardly than other people. . . . So, because there are two opposite impulses in such a man at the same time about the same thing, we say there are two things in him. One of them is ready to be guided by the law which, I take it, says that it is best to keep quiet as far as possible when griefs come and not to cry out, because we are not certain what is good and what is evil in such things, and to take them hardly does not make them any better. Reason says that nothing in man's existence is to be taken so seriously, and our grief keeps us back from the very thing we need as quickly as possible in such times.

Glaucon. What is that?

Socrates. To take thought on the event; and, as we order our play by the way the cards fall, to see how to order our acts, in view of what has come about, in the ways reason points to as the best. Don't let us be like children when they have had a fall, and go on crying out with a hand on the place. Look after the wound first and pick up what has had a fall, and make grief give place to medical help.

(*Republic*, 603–04)

Or consider again:

Socrates. And don't the best things undergo the least changes and motions that come to them from other things . . . For example, the body is changed by meat and drink and work, and every plant by the light of the sun and the wind. . . . But isn't the change least in the plant or body that is healthiest and strongest? So of the soul. It will be the bravest and wisest soul which is least moved and changed from without.

(*Republic*, 381)

Again, it may be through Language or Tradition (and we may separate or combine these with the greatest of ease) that the conception of the self-governing soul controls this scene. Now we watch it meeting a storm which could readily break the heart or overthrow the reason of a less healthy or weaker being than Troilus.

> *Ulysses.* All's done my lord.
>
> *Troilus.* It is.
>
> *Ulysses.*   Why stay we, then?
>
> *Troilus.* To make a recordation to my soul
>   Of every syllable that here was spoke.

His impulse to disbelieve is going to make him forget what he has seen and heard—unless he forestalls it— much as Darwin is said to have made *immediate* note of discrepant facts. By the next line but one:

>   Shall I not lie in publishing a truth?

the cleavage is beginning. The old faith and hope, and new evidence and despair, are too strong for one another:

>   Sith yet there is a credence in my heart
>   An esperance so obstinately strong,
>   That doth invert the attest of eyes and ears
>   As if those organs had deceptious functions,
>   Created only to calumniate.

Something has to give way; who was it at the mouth of Calchas' tent?

> *Troilus.* Was Cressid here?
>
> *Ulysses.*   I cannot conjure, Trojan.
>
> *Troilus.* She was not, sure.
>
> *Ulysses.*   Most sure she was.
>
> *Troilus.* Why, my negation hath no taste of madness.

He carries this far enough to make Thersites wonder:

"Will he swagger himself out on's own eyes?" But the two truths are so equal that this is no way out. Something must break and it is Cressid who divides:

> this is, and is not, Cressid.

"What is aught but as 'tis valued?" When the valuations become irreconcilable and insuperable, the thing splits and the thinker (or thinger) then has to remain *one* (if he can) himself:

> *Troilus.* This she? no, this is Diomede's Cressida.
> If beauty have a soul, this is not she,

(That which he loved in her was not this)

> If souls guide vows, if vows are sanctimony,

(Two certainties, if "vows" and "sanctimony" are understood aright)

> If sanctimony be the gods' delight,

("*Socrates:* Do the gods love sanctimony because it is sanctimony? Or is it sanctimony because the gods love it? . . . What is this art of serving the gods, Euthyphro? What is the great result of it? The care of the soul?")

> If there be rule in unity itself,
> This is not she.

(The very thing which holds him together and keeps the universe from shaking to pieces must make this separation in her)

> O madness of discourse,
> That cause sets up, with and against itself,
> Bifold authority!

(In this consists a spirit, that it is self-reflective.)

The two in Troilus that correspond to the two Cressids change place: reason, the very rule in unity itself, safely throwing off its own authority, and that very perdition (which is also loss of one of the Cressids) taking up the rule:

> where reason can revolt
> Without perdition, and loss assume all reason
> Without revolt.

This is language become itself a translucent instance of what it would describe; it both *says* what it means and illustrates it. Troilus, absorbed now in the mystery of how

> this is and is not Cressid,

seems to draw from the stroke itself the resolution. The opposites are all before him

> more wider than the sky and earth

and yet they come together and are indistinguishable— as Ariadne's clue and Arachne's web are merged in "Ariachne's broken woof." (As escape from a labyrinth containing a devouring monster, with an ensuing betrayal; a penalty for *hubris* with a horrible transformation.) With that "broken," however anguishingly it echoes, we know that it applies not to his heart but to whatever held him to Cressid—some fabric of gossamer texture. And as the last waves of this earthquate subside we can compare the hard darkness of:

> strong as Pluto's gates

with an airy brightness:

> strong as heaven itself

and feel the expansion and reunion occurring already in this suddenly restored lover. The bonds of heaven, that

seemed so strong, are dissolv'd. We see through Troilus'
eyes what it is that

> with another knot, five-finger-tied

Diomede has gained:

> orts of her love
> The fragments, scraps, the bits and greasy reliques
> Of her o'er-eaten faith.

And discerning Ulysses here speaks for us when he asks,

> May worthy Troilus be half attach'd
> With that which here his passion doth express?

Troilus' reply shows us that he knows how to deal with
that half-attachment. In Coleridge's words, "having a
depth of calmer element in a will stronger than desire,
more entire than choice . . . the same moral energy is
represented as snatching him aloof from all neighborhood
with her dishonor." It is like Shakespeare to give the
summing-up to his almost monstrously detached and avid
observer, the sick artist.

> *Thersites.* He'll tickle it for his concupy.

When Aeneas arrives seeking him, this "whining babbler"
is almost whole again.

> *Troilus.* Have with you prince. My courteous lord, adieu.
>   Farewell, revolted fair! and Diomede,
>   Stand fast, and wear a castle on thy head.
>
> *Ulysses.* I'll bring you to the gates.
>
> *Troilus.* Accept distracted thanks.
>
>
> *Troilus.* The bless'd gods as angry with my fancy
>   . . . take thee from me.

Cressida. Have the gods envy?

Troilus. If sanctimony be the god's delight . . .
    This is not she.

Socrates, in puzzling Euthyphro—a very Deuteronomic
sort of young man—with questions about the service and
the god and the outcome of the service, is keeping well
within that self-confident theologian's intellectual reach,
almost within his grasp. But Plato was to give Socrates
other questions which were to empty such inquiries as:

        If sanctimony be the god's delight.

In the more than sunlight of the Idea of the Good, "which
gives true being to whatever deep knowledge is of, and
the power of knowing to the knower" (*Republic*, 508)
all contrasts between the things the gods value and their
valuings fade out. "What is aught but as 'tis valued?" is
a dangerous question, as Hector pointed out, when applied
to "particular will." But it is other words for the Idea
of the Good if the valuing is that of knowledge. And
"Have the gods envy?"—which Homer's Achilles could
ask as literally as any child—turns, on reflection, into
a deep inquiry about

        degree, priority and place,
    Insisture, course, proportion, season, form
    Office, and custom, in all line of order.
                                        (I.iii. 86–88)

Troilus does misplace his adoration. And to do that *is*
to offend the jealous gods. Indeed the more closely we
read the two Council Scenes, the more closely knit

        If there be rule in unity itself,

this "most hastily composed play" will be found. Even in
what may seem no more than Agamemnon's preliminary
prosing:

> which are indeed naught else
> But the protractive trials of great Jove,
> To find persistive constancy in men

even in these

> there is seen
> The baby figure of the giant mass
> Of things to come at large.

This is not unusual in Shakespeare—though this play, with *Julius Caesar,* is unwontedly thick with premonitions and echoes. What is exceptional, to my mind, is the degree to which its central thought seems to accord with Plato's. Others have wondered whether "the strange fellow" who had written to Ulysses (III.iii. 95) might not have been Plato. I find a strange fellowship throughout. And perhaps the strangeness is the condition of the fellowship:

> For speculation turns not to itself
> Till it hath travel'd, and is married there
> Where it may see itself.

REUBEN A. BROWER

from *Poetic and Dramatic Structure in Versions and Translations of Shakespeare*

The typical "heresy" among critics of poetic drama two generations back was to analyze the experience in terms of dramatic "form"—plot, character, rising and falling action. The typical heresy of the present generation has been to reduce the well-made play to the well-wrought urn. *King Lear* is no longer a bad play, but a supreme lyric poem on order and disorder in nature. Both extremes of interpretation betray the same defect, the assumption that the play as poem and the play as drama are separable entities. Although every critic "knows better," acting better is another matter. Whether we are formalists in the old sense or the new, what we lack is not principles, but control of critical discourse, mastery of a critical style for describing the experience of drama, a style that will continually acknowledge the claims of the poetic and the dramatic. This paper attempts to move in the direction of creating such a style by exploring in a new setting the connection between poetic and dramatic structures. The "new setting" offered is comparison of versions and translations of Shakespeare's plays.

The aim of this study was first suggested by T. S. Eliot's admirable remark in his essay on *Poetry and Drama:* " . . . when Shakespeare, in one of his mature plays, introduces what might seem a purely poetic line or passage, it never

From *Poetics*, Polska Akademia Nauk, Instytut Badan Literackich, Warsaw, 1961. Reprinted by permission of the author and the editor.

interrupts the action, or is out of character, but on the contrary, in some mysterious way supports both action and character." Another point of departure was Roman Jakobson's paper, *Linguistics and Poetics*. In his analysis of Antony's funeral oration from *Julius Caesar*, Jakobson showed that by starting from the simplest uses of language one could see that "The main dramatic force of Antony's exordium . . . is achieved by Shakespeare's playing on grammatical categories and constructions." It should be noted here that I am approaching the problem of the poetic and the dramatic not as an expert in linguistics but as a literary critic, not with the aim of making "censorious verdicts," but rather with the Arnoldian purpose of preparing for "the judgment which almost insensibly forms itself in a fair and clear mind, along with fresh knowledge." Like many English and American critics since the Richardsian revolution, I am concerned with interpreting works of imaginative literature, "imaginative" in the sense of offering experiences of a high degree of interconnectedness. (And we shall dine at journey's end with Coleridge and with Arnold.) Such works may be described as both "poetic" and "mimetic." "Poetic" structure is of the first importance: that is, language is being used to direct attention to the words as *heard* events and to produce "parallels" or "similarities." They are also "mimetic" in the sense that resources of language are being exploited in order to "mime," to represent men in action. In drama, obviously enough, all verbal resources, nonpoetic as well as poetic, are subdued to the mimetic function.

Translations offer most useful examples for exploring the connection between the two kinds of design because of the two necessary yet conflicting purposes of the translator. (1) He attempts to give the reader the same dramatic experience as that offered by the original (e.g., the experience of the voice, the role, the attitudes that equal *Hamlet*). (2) He attempts to produce this identity of effect through a different verbal medium, in another language. What happens when he undertakes this impossible task? What can we learn from his attempt about the nterconnection of the poetic and the dramatic? (May I remind the reader that my aim is not to judge the transations, though judgments will now and then insensibly orm themselves.) . . .

Dryden's *Troilus and Cressida* is a more respectable example of Restoration "improvement" than Tate's *Lear*, and his transformations are also much more instructive. The blank verse is not despicable, and there is evidence that Dryden had a clear understanding of much that Shakespeare was doing. He is equally clear about the necessity of "correcting" Shakespeare's style, a necessity imposed by the state of the language, which he contrasts with that of Greek in the age of Aeschylus, when ". . . the Greek tongue was arriv'd to its full perfection. . . ." Consider the application of this doctrine in the reworking of Ulysses' great speech on "degree":

> *Ulysses.* Troy had been down ere this, and Hectors Sword
>   Wanted a Master but for our disorders:
>   The observance due to rule has been neglected;
>   Observe how many Grecians Tents stand void
>   Upon this plain; so many hollow factions:
>   For when the General is not like the Hive
>   To whom the Foragers should all repair,
>   What Hony can our empty Combs expect?
>   O when Supremacy of Kings is shaken,
>   What can succeed: How cou'd Communities
>   Or peacefull traffick from divided shores,
>   Prerogative of Age, Crowns, Scepters, Lawrells,
>   But by degree stand on their solid base!
>   Then everything resolves to brutal force
>   And headlong force is led by hoodwink'd will,
>   For wild Ambition, like a ravenous Woolf,
>   Spurd on by will and seconded by power,
>   Must make an universal prey of all,
>   And last devour it self.

The essential points in the Shakespearean argument are reserved, and key lines are kept or intelligently parahrased. The case is clinched by the striking metaphor of the "ravenous Woolf"; but somehow the final line seems tame: we hardly feel that this beast will bite, let alone "devour itself." Comparison with Shakespeare's text shows why the metaphorical climax works so much better there than here. The whole speech—too long for quotation —has built up a highly particularized definition of "degree" as illustrated in different orders of society and in the cosmos, the disturbance of degree being expressed in violent metaphors of storm and disease (with *related* imagery of feeding). The final paradox has behind it a peculiar structure:

> Strength should be lord of imbecility,
> And the rude son should strike his father dead;
> Force should be right; or rather, right and wrong,
> Between whose endless jar justice resides,
> Should lose their names, and so should justice too,
> Then everything includes itself in power,
> Power into will, will into appetite;
> And appetite, an universal wolf,
> So doubly seconded with will and power,
> Must make perforce an universal prey,
> And last eat up himself.

(I.iii. 114–24)

Not only is "eat up himself" a cruder idiom; it is the summing up of a metaphorical and grammatical pattern. In substituting "ambition" for "appetite" Dryden shows that he had not felt the way in which this image of self-cannibalism is prepared for. We have a whole series of grammatical "ingorgings" in which we hear one verbal mass, one name, being eaten up, included, within another: right in force; "right and wrong" in an "endless jar"; right, wrong, and justice "lose their names," absorbed in "everything"; "everything includes itself in power"; "power into will"; "will into appetite" (and perhaps also will and power become seconds, substitutes for appetite). Finally we hear the universal eater consumed by the universal eaten (since appetite by eating everything has become everything eaten). Appetite has been verbally self-consumed a half-dozen or more times before the final paradox released. Dryden's version is a perfect example of poetic excitement diminished by the loss of a peculiar grammatical figure. But the dramatic loss is equally great. In the Shakespearean original we get a special sense of a mind thinking and feeling its way through the process of moral and social decay that is only *named* by the argument from degree. The fine intelligence projected by the poetic progression, by the complexity of its grammatical unfolding, largely disappears in the lines by Dryden. His Ulysses is a pronouncer of clear and distinct platitudes, much nearer to the public speakers of *Julius Caesar* than to the tortured thinkers of this most metaphysical play. "Character" in this speech of Shakespeare is as much grammar as metaphor.

The reduction in style in this crucial passage of *Troilus and Cressida*—one that presents the key metaphor of "degree" in imagery that recurs throughout the play—has its effect much later in the main dramatic crisis, Troilus' discovery of Cressida's falsity:

[*Troilus.*] Was Cressid here?

Ulysses. I cannot conjure, Trojan.

Troilus. She was not, sure.

Ulysses. Most sure she was.

Troilus. Why, my negation hath no taste of madness.

Ulysses. Nor mine, my lord; Cressid was here but now.

Troilus. Let it not be believed for womanhood!
  Think we had mothers. Do not give advantage
  To stubborn critics, apt without a theme
  For depravation, to square the general sex
  By Cressid's rule; rather think this not Cressid.

Ulysses. What hath she done, prince, that can soil our mothers?

Troilus. Nothing at all, unless that this were she.

Thersites. Will 'a swagger himself out on's own eyes?

Troilus. This she? No; this is Diomed's Cressida.

If beauty have a soul, this is not she;
If souls guide vows, if vows be sanctimonies,
If sanctimony be the gods' delight,
If there be rule in unity itself,
This is not she. O madness of discourse,
That cause sets up with and against itself!
Bifold authority! where reason can revolt
Without perdition, and loss assume all reason
Without revolt. This is, and is not, Cressid!
Within my soul there doth conduce a fight
Of this strange nature, that a thing inseparate
Divides more wider than the sky and earth;
And yet the spacious breadth of this division
Admits no orifex for a point as subtle
As Ariachne's broken woof to enter.
Instance, O instance! strong as Pluto's gates:
Cressid is mine, tied with the bonds of heaven.
Instance, O instance! strong as heaven itself:
The bonds of heaven are slipped, dissolved and loosed,
And with another knot, five-finger-tied,
The fractions of her faith, orts of her love,
The fragments, scraps, the bits and greasy relics
Of her o'ereaten faith are given to Diomed.

                                    (V.ii. 122–57)

The "revolt" of reason is expressed here not by sensuous imagery, but by mad "discourse" in which the same logical and grammatical routines repeat and repeat that "is" and "is not" are equal. Dryden's reduction shows that as in ritual, belief in nonsense depends largely on suggestive repetition:

Troilus. Was Cressida here?

Ulysses. I cannot conjure Trojan.

Troilus. She was not sure! she was not.
   Let it not be believ'd for womanhood:
   Think we had Mothers, do not give advantage
   To biting Satyr, apt without a theme,
   For defamation, to square all the sex
   By Cressid's rule, rather think this not Cressida.

Thersites. Will he swagger himself out on's own eyes!

Troilus. This she! no this was Diomedes Cressida.
  If beauty have a Soul, this is not she:
  I cannot speak for rage, that Ring was mine,
  By Heaven I gave it, in that point of time,
  When both our joys were fullest!—if he keeps it,
  Let dogs eat Troilus.

But the elimination of logical and grammatical hypnosis
has a further effect. The great culminating metaphor,

The bonds of heaven are slipped, dissolved and loosed;

cannot be reached, the cosmic overtones disappear, and
the connection of Troilus' personal chaos with the social
and moral chaos described in Ulysses' speech and dramatized in the war scenes, utterly disappears. (It is not
surprising that the accompanying imagery of foul feeding
is also lost.) The bonds of metaphor are loosed, and with
them the Shakespearean vision of the link between war
and lechery is also broken. Not only do we lose a thematic
design, but the large philosophic meaning of Troilus' act
is lost, and it becomes a much smaller thing. The disturbance in the mind of Shakespeare's hero opens up into
a vision of irrationality not only in the history of his love,
but in the human mind and the cosmos. Again we find
ourselves talking about losses in dramatic as well as
philosophic meaning. Dryden's Troilus is less disturbed
by the revolt of reason than by seeing his ring on Diomede's hand. Shakespeare's hero has been transformed
from a Proustian dialectician with a heroic accent into
an angry young man. In correcting grammar Dryden
"corrected" a great deal else. Although we sometimes
talk of plot and character as surviving in translation
while poetry is lost, we must observe that if poetry is
completely lost, plot and character tend to become un-
recognizable. . . .

R. A. FOAKES

"Troilus and Cressida" Reconsidered

There are almost as many opinions about the nature of Shakespeare's *Troilus and Cressida* as there are critics; and each critic can fortify his argument by referring to the inability of the play's first editors to see eye to eye about it. In particular if he wants to claim it as comedy, he can cite the preface of the Quarto of 1609, for whoever wrote that praised the play as "passing full of the palme comicall"; and if he prefers to deal with it as tragedy, he can point to the first plan of the editors of the Folio of 1623, who meant to place it after *Romeo and Juliet*. To add to the confusion, the Folio text seems to contain two endings to the play, for Troilus's last dismissal of Pandarus is there printed twice, in V.iii, and in V.x. Shakespeare clearly conceived at some time a bitter or "tragic" ending, culminating in Troilus's fine speech in V.x; after one false ending, omitted in the Quarto,

> But march away.
> Hector is dead; there is no more to say,

Troilus utters his last threats, and closes by inviting all present to leave the stage,

From *University of Toronto Quarterly*, XXXII (January, 1963), pp. 142–54. Reprinted by permission of the author and the editor.

> Strike a free march to Troy; with comfort go;
> Hope of revenge shall hide our inward woe.

This is a characteristic final couplet, reminiscent of other endings, like that, for instance, of *Julius Caesar*:

> So call the field to rest, and let's away
> To part the glories of this happy day.

The actual ending, which brings on Pandarus to speak a bawdy epilogue and finish in less solemn vein, evidently supplied some of that "edge of witte" that the writer of the Quarto preface found in the play. It would seem, then, that Shakespeare himself can be called as witness by those who see the play as comedy, and by those who claim it as tragedy. I propose to argue that these endings are not opposed, but complementary, and together establish an "open" ending; and, further, that in order to understand the play and its ending, we should, in this special instance, use our external knowledge of the events it describes.

It will be useful to glance first at the action of the play, in order to see in what way its development looks forward to the ending. The confusion of opinions among early editors, and the variations in the text do not give the critic license to fit the play into any category he chooses. Textual scholars agree that the comic ending represents Shakespeare's final thoughts; and if the play had enough somber coloring to encourage the editors of the Folio to include it among the tragedies in 1623, so, too, had *Cymbeline*. The play itself bears out the inferences of the scholars, and while it does not altogether support the discovery in it of a "comprehensive comic purpose,"[1] it positively forbids a reading of the play as tragedy.[2]

The prologue promises a tale of war, but the first line spoken by Troilus,

> Call here my varlet, I'll unarm again,

displays him in the conventional posture of the courtly
lover, prostrate, like Orsino in *Twelfth Night,* and able
only to bewail his fate. As Pandarus implies in his opening words, "Will this gear ne'er be mended?" Troilus has
for some time been more concerned over the war in his
heart than his country's strife, and more anxious to avoid
being a "traitor" to Cressida, by thinking constantly of
her, than troubled by his failure to serve Troy well. He
claims to be "mad/In Cressid's love," constantly fortify-
ing himself in the pose of an impassioned lover. The
extravagant rhetoric of his speeches is thrown into relief
against the kitchen imagery of Pandarus, who knows he
can make the cake for Troilus, and manipulate the whole
affair; and Troilus's overearnestness, his yearning to turn
the business into high romance, to make her bed India,
and his adventure for her wild and dangerous, becomes
comic against the facts of the situation as Pandarus reveals them. By the end of the scene he manages, after all,
to put her from his mind, and goes off to the "sport
abroad" (l. 119), the game of fighting.

If Troilus becomes comic in his posing, the extrava-
gance of his passion, Cressida is comic in her jesting;
we laugh at him and with her. If he is too serious, she
is too light, too flippant in her attitude to the war, to the
court, and to him. In I.ii. Pandarus contributes much to
the tone, and to our impression of Cressida, who listens
to his bawdy jests about Helen, and matches her wit
against his. The procession of returning warriors becomes
finely entertaining as Pandarus fails to recognize Troilus
after praising him highly; so his attempt to sell Troilus
to her is revealed to Cressida as, partly at any rate, a
pose, and she turns on him with the words "Peace, for
shame, peace!" (I.ii. 238). At the end of the scene she
shows that her flippancy, too, is partly a pose, in the
couplets which mark her soliloquy as coming from the
heart; for here, like Helena in *All's Well That Ends Well*
(I.ii.), and Beatrice in *Much Ado about Nothing* (III.i.),
she confesses her love in rhyme, which marks her serious-
ness. It is, nevertheless, cool verse, too full of common-

places and sententiae (three lines are marked by inverted commas in the Quarto) to be convincing. She may love, but her love is within her control; "Yet hold I off," she cries, in contrast to Troilus's "I am mad/In Cressid's love."

There are, of course, wider implications in these first scenes; the war is "sport" to Aeneas as well as to Troilus, and the attitude of Pandarus to the rape of Helen hardly suggests that the Trojans take this seriously either. The flippancy of Cressida matches the bawdy of Pandarus, and establishes something of the atmosphere of Troy, where the image of adultery, of a woman lying with a man, is familiar, and sanctioned by the presence of Helen and Paris; perhaps Cressida's casual acceptance of the idea takes her halfway to the deed itself. However, the predominant tone of these scenes is one of comedy, and this tone is maintained in the scenes that follow in the Greek camp.

Polonius, for all his prolixity, knows that

> to expostulate
> What majesty should be, what duty is,
> Why day is day, night night, and time is time,
> Were nothing but to waste night, day and time.
>
> (*Hamlet*, II.ii)

The Greeks, in their council scene, come close to doing this in their empty flatteries and resounding commonplaces, which culminate in Ulysses's lecture on what majesty should be. Their big words express general truths, but bear little relation to their deeds, to the petty trick that is to be practiced on Achilles; and because their actions do not measure up to their words, the words remain empty. Their concern is with immediate policy, not with degree. The hollowness of their high talk is exposed by Aeneas, who interrupts the conference to bring a challenge from Hector, and asks to be told which of the princes is Agamemnon, how he is to know "those most imperial looks" from those of other mortals? How indeed? "I ask," he says,

> that I might waken reverence,
> And bid the cheek be ready with a blush
> Modest as Morning when she coldly eyes
> The youthful Phoebus.
> Which is that god in office, guiding men?
> Which is the high and mighty Agamemnon?
>
> (I.iii. 227–32)

Agamemnon suspects for a moment that "This Troyan scorns us," but passes it off as courtesy. Yet if Agamemnon were a "god in office," Aeneas would not have had so much difficulty in picking him out; and his address exposes the earlier flattery of Nestor and Ulysses in such phrases as,

> With due observance of thy godlike seat,
> Great Agamemnon, Nestor shall apply
> Thy latest words.
>
> (I.iii. 31–33)

The godlike Agamemnon, and the great warriors Achilles and Ajax, dwindle further in the next scene, when Thersites displays his venom and his wit at their expense.

The deliberations of the Trojans in council are more straightforward; II.ii is the first scene without humor, perhaps because the basis of discussion is ethical, and concerned with the motives and justice of the war, in contrast to the Greek discussion, which was political, and concerned with the conduct and order of the war. The Trojans are no better than the Greeks; for if the Greeks pursue policy in defiance of rule, the Trojans pursue honor in defiance of the laws of nature and of nations. However, the play's serious oppositions and concern with values are still subdued beneath the general comic tone, and only take control of the action, so to speak, after the end of Act III. The fine talk of honor by Troilus and Hector in council receives a crushing comment in the following scenes; to them Helen is "a theme of honor and renown," but when we see her in III.i. she is relaxed in the sensual atmosphere of a high-class brothel, an atmosphere cloying in the heady sweetness of "Love, love, nothing but love, still love, still more," to cite the opening line of Pandarus's song. The conversation is at once ceremonious and bawdy, overlaying with its repeated adjectives, "sweet," "honey-sweet," "fair," the hot blood, hot thoughts, and hot deeds of a luxurious palace. Helen hardly inspires Paris to deeds of honor; he is like Troilus at the play's opening, "I would fain have arm'd today, but my Nell would not have it so." Not that she is simply a "whore," as Thersites calls her, for she is shown as sharing a security of affection with Paris that enables them mutually to tease Pandarus into comically parodying himself.

The predominantly comic tone is maintained in the process by which Ajax is persuaded into such a good opinion of himself that he thinks he is taking over the wisdom of Nestor, and asks, in all simplicity, "Shall I call you father?" It is apparent, too, in the meeting of Troilus and Cressida. Troilus, absorbed in an "imaginary relish" of sexual enjoyment, acts out his romantic extravaganza to the last moment, crying to Pandarus as he stands outside her door, at most a few yards away from her,

> I stalk about her door
> Like a strange soul upon the Stygian banks
> Staying for waftage. O, be thou my Charon,
> And give me swift transportance to these fields
> Where I may wallow in the lily beds
> Propos'd for the deserver! O gentle Pandar,
> From Cupid's shoulder pluck his painted wings,
> And fly with me to Cressid!
>
> (III.ii. 7–14)

His knowledge that he is by her door gives way to extravagant and absurd fantasy, with an undertone of irony in its image of himself as a dead soul, and of Pandarus as the grim and morose Charon; but Pandarus pulls him, and us, back to the matter in hand with his short reply, "Walk here i' th' orchard, I'll bring her straight." He has no need of wings, as he pushes them into each other's arms. For Troilus, the sweetness of love lies in the imagined consummation, "the will is infinite, the act a slave to limit"; for her, it lies in the holding off. He shows a rapture beyond the occasion, while she displays "more craft than love," and they swear their absurd bargain of truth in front of the gloating Pandarus, whose scene this is, as we see him carry out "the making of the cake, the heating of the oven, and the baking" that he had spoken of in I.i. It is his triumph to bring them to a bed where Troilus may "wallow" comfortably, and talk of truth and virtue without seeing that he is a lecher, and Pandarus a bawd.

After this the tone changes, as Cressida is delivered to the Greeks, Ajax and Hector fight, and Diomedes easily wins over Cressida; humor almost disappears; those who had been playing roles, like Troilus, suddenly discover the gap between fantasy and reality, and the war, which had been a sport to the Trojans and a political game to the Greeks, becomes earnest indeed. Troilus cries pathetically to Cressida as he parts from her, "be thou true of heart," but truth has had little to do with their compact; if she is now a "daughter of the game," in the phrase of Ulysses, Troilus brought her to it. It is bitter, nevertheless, for him to see clearly now what she is like, as he watches her talking with Diomedes, and he would still delude himself that "Cressid is mine, tied with the bonds of heaven," when the only bond heaven recognizes is that of married love.

Troilus is watched here by Ulysses, and all are spied on by Thersites, as Cressida teases her new lover in the accents of Helen in the Trojan court, calling Diomedes "Sweet honey Greek." The best and the worst in Trojan and Greek are juxtaposed in this scene. Troilus, who, for all his loyalty and truth, has no sense of moral perspective, and Ulysses, who, for all his insight and common sense, is petty-minded, stand between Cressida and Thersites; Cressida plays with Diomedes the free game of love or lust that Helen with Paris, Polyxena with Achilles, and she with Troilus, have taken for granted, and Thersites strips away glamor, honor, and truth in his bitter railing, to leave nothing but "Lechery, lechery! still wars and lechery!"

The war, like love, does indeed turn sour at the end, though never reduced to the level of animality suggested by Thersites. To Hector, as to Troilus, war is noble and honorable inasmuch as it may bring fame, and offers the opportunity for magnanimous deeds; to Achilles and the Greeks, apart from Nestor and Ulysses, war is a matter for dispatch through intrigue and craft. Hector is right in obvious ways, but wrong in putting personal honor before moral law; Achilles is wrong in obvious ways, as he is petty, selfish, and cruel, but he is right, too, in his vision of war as a nasty and brutish business. Hector goes into battle at the end because he is "i' th' vein of chivalry," and refuses to listen to Cassandra's pleas, although he had expected Troilus to take note of her "high strains of divination" in the council scene earlier. He shows his nobility in refusing to fight with Thersites, since he is not "of blood and honor," and in allowing Achilles to breathe; yet we see him also chase a Greek in sumptuous armor as if he were a beast, crying "I'll hunt thee for thy hide." The contraries in him are displayed here; he can spare his man being down, and yet hunt another for his gold armor. He is at last butchered when unarmed, but there is some justice in his death; it is the supreme irony of the play that the Trojans, who possess more romantic, more evidently attractive qualities than the Greeks, should be the ones to refuse an offer to end the war, and should prolong it for a dubious notion of personal "honor." As Hector is chiefly responsible for this, so he suffers for it.

Hector's values are false to the situation, as Thersites describes it and Achilles acts upon it; the values of Thersites and Achilles are false to human nature as we hope we may finally describe it. So the play moves to its double ending; first comes Troilus's passionate outburst of rage and grief, which is appealing because it is grounded in his love and loyalty, although it issues in a cry for revenge, and secondly, Pandarus's double-edged jesting with the audience as all bawds together, which is appealing because it is rooted in the comic element in the play. Troilus's honor and Pandarus's practicality suggest two poles of human nature, which are here indissolubly tied, for Troilus employed Pandarus in what he thought of as a virtuous and enduring affair of love. These two parts of the ending also link with the two scales of time operative in the play, time as projected by the idealizing Troilus, and time as acted out in daily business; so Troilus dismisses Pandarus with the impassioned wish that ignominy may "live aye" with his name, while Pandarus dismisses the audience with a promise to return in two months:

> Till then I'll sweat and seek about for eases,
> And at that time bequeath you my diseases.

As love and war are discussed, contemplated in the abstract, or ritualized in the approach of Troilus to Cressida, and the duel of Hector and Ajax, the envisaged truth of the one, and the promised glory of the other, are related to a scale of time projected by the characters; they think of the events in which they are engaged as celebrated in the future, when lovers may "approve their truth by Troilus," and warriors may look back on the Trojan heroes as canonized by "fame in time to come." As love and war are worked out in earnest, the characters are seen to be involved in lust, in politic scheming, and in the brute necessities of the battlefield; and they provoke the commentary of Thersites, who sees what they are doing as a temporary lapse into "wars and lechery. Nothing else holds fashion."

So, when the rich comedy of the first three acts gives way to the unpleasantness of lust in action and the fury of war, it is not that there is any failure of continuity in the action, only that we see differently as the game of love and the sport of war have to be played in earnest. Something of that comic tone persists; the play unfolds in time, and the weight of the first three acts bears on the ending, and makes the acted effect of Thersites's sardonic remarks more comic than it may seem in the reading. The final effect of the play is not simply comic or tragic; and it is not to be explained as satire, or understood as a debate ending in disillusionment and futility.[3] The open ending, with its two complementary yet opposed attitudes represented by Troilus and Pandarus, is a unique kind of conclusion among Shakespeare's plays, in that very little is concluded; the play begins in the middle of things, and it ends a little further on, but still in the middle of things. Hector is dead, and Cressida proved false, but the war goes on.[4]

Nevertheless, *Troilus and Cressida* ends fitly. An action has been completed, and the double ending seems proper. I think we can perhaps understand this better by considering further aspects of the play's concern with time, and its place in time. Its emphasis on time is another characteristic of the play that makes it unique among Shakespeare's dramas, but it has been chiefly studied in the famous speech of Ulysses to Achilles. There has been much discussion of time as the destructive element, "envious and calumniating Time," on the inconstancy of time in relation to Fortune, and, more subtly, on time as the unknown factor that interposes "between aim and achievement, between the ideal and its realization," mocking the transience of human achievement, although the impulse to achieve endures.[5] Because Ulysses himself stresses what is true to man's common observation of his society, the continual change of habit and fashion, the readiness to

> give to dust that is a little gilt
> More laud than gilt o'erdusted,
>
> (III.iii. 177–78)

he seems to be summing up a truth about human nature, so that it is possible to regard his comments on time, like his account of degree, as a general statement sanctioned by Shakespeare. In fact he offers a shoddy and partial attempt to prod Achilles into action. He talks of "good truth, deliberately confusing several kinds of value in his deeds," of "honor" as a large, general concept ("Perseverance, dear my lord, /Keeps honor bright"), when he is really advising Achilles to keep his name before the

public; he lists virtue, love, friendship, and charity as subject to time, as if these are in the same category as
fashion, reputation, and "vigor of bone." Human existence, as he depicts it, is a universal rat race, in which,

> if you give way,
> Or hedge aside from the direct forthright,
> Like to an enter'd tide they all rush by
> And leave you hindmost;
> Or, like a gallant horse fall'n in first rank,
> Lie there for pavement to the abject rear,
> O'er-run and trampled on.
>
> (III.iii. 157–63)

In this ruthless competition, good deeds are "devour'd/As
fast as they are made," virtue looks for remuneration, and
love is soon forgotten.

However, the play offers another vision of time, and
an equally valid one. It is that looked forward to by
Troilus and Cressida when they swear their truth to one
another, their eternal love, looking to that memory which
remains

> When time is old and hath forgot itself,
> When waterdrops have worn the stones of Troy,
> And blind oblivion swallow'd cities up,
> And mighty states characterless are grated
> To dusty nothing.
>
> (III.ii. 186–90)

Here is implied an idea of time as sifting deeds and values,
and registering finally what is true and worthwhile. In this
perspective, the truth of Troilus is rescued from his faults,
and the greatness of Hector's magnanimity outweighs his
rejection of the moral law; Achilles survives for his
strength and soldiership, Ulysses for his wisdom, Helen
for her beauty, and Cressida's curse on herself has been
fulfilled—her falsehood has become proverbial. Shakespeare knew, when he made his lovers prophesy about
their future reputations, that his audience would have in-
herited ideas about these and other characters in the play.

This perspective of time has a special importance here because this is the only play Shakespeare wrote on the theme of one of the great Western epic myths. Many among Shakespeare's audience knew the "story" of the various history plays, but these plays show the whole story, and, as far as the principal figures are concerned, depart very little from the representation of them by Tudor historians, so that no clash of perspectives is brought into play. Perhaps the Roman plays, *Julius Caesar* and *Antony and Cleopatra,* approach more nearly the peculiar nature of *Troilus and Cressida;* but in them, again, the story is completed, in that the full history of the civil war, and of Antony's destruction, is shown. There is some clash between Shakespeare's portraits of Antony, Cleopatra, and Octavius, and their depiction by contemporary historians, but *Troilus and Cressida* is unique in enacting only a small part of a story that was very well known, and in its frequent appeal to the legend as established by time in the consciousness of the audience. The action is incomplete in the sense that, as a literate audience would know, the war went on, and that, before it ended, in the fall of Troy, most of the play's characters, including Troilus, Paris, and Achilles, were dead; and I think it is impossible for an audience not to relate what the play shows to the rest of the story as they know it.

The story of Troy had a meaning for the age of Shakespeare that it has now lost, and perhaps its outlines were more generally familiar then than they are now. In the same year that saw the publication of the Quarto of *Troilus and Cressida,* there appeared Thomas Heywood's *Troia Britannica,* which narrates the progress of the Trojan war, and ends by tracing the ancestry of James I back to Brutus, a grandson of Aeneas who gave his name to Britain, and founded Trinovantum, New Troy, later known as London, or Lud's Town. The legend was popular; it was related pithily in George Warner's *Albion's England* (1584), Spenser made his Prince Arthur read an account of his Trojan ancestry in the chronicles called "Briton Monuments" that he finds in the Castle of Alma

(*Faerie Queene,* II.x.), and Michael Drayton gave a full account of it in his *Polyolbion* (1612); the verses describing "My Britain-founding Brute" in Song I of this long poem are accompanied by an elaborate defense in prose of the story. These poets were all celebrating the famous origins of Britain, and the ancestry of Queen Elizabeth, as these were described in the common histories and chronicles of the age, including those of Raphael Holinshed and John Stow.[6] The Queen even quartered the arms of a mythical Trojan in one version of her official coat of arms,[7] so acknowledging the antiquity of her line.

The Brutus legend flourished in popular literature, and afforded material for plays at the public theaters,[8] so it may have some relevance to what Shakespeare did in *Troilus and Cressida.* The two famous survivors of the war of Troy, Ulysses and Aeneas, are neutral figures in the play, not directly involved in the main action;[9] there is no sign that Shakespeare was concerned with the link between Troy and Britain, or that he had more sympathy for the Trojans than the Greeks, unless he showed it in making the Trojans the repository of romantic and heroic attitudes. At the same time, I think that the complex of national sentiment about Troy, and the common knowledge of the outcome of the war, affected the way Shakespeare wrote of it. He could assume this sentiment and knowledge in his audience, and could expect them to complete what remains incomplete in his play. This extra knowledge no doubt affected reaction to the play at first, and our extra knowledge affects our critical attitude to the play. If we are addicted to the glamor of the heroic legend, we may find *Troilus and Cressida* harsh and unpleasant; if we retain a traditional sympathy for the Trojans, we may emphasize their honor and generosity as against the practicality of the Greeks; if we see the conflict as a representative one, we may read the play as a philosophical debate; in any case, we interpret the play in some measure by what we know of the characters and events outside the play. The open ending, the play's incompleteness, has helped to foster a variety of opinion

about it, but this incompleteness is not merely a factor in
the play's rich complexity; it also, properly understood,
affords a guide to a balanced assessment of it.

Both Trojans and Greeks are displayed in their virtues
and faults; all are imperfect, and are confined, whatever
their pretensions, within that day-to-day "emulation" in
living which Ulysses describes to Achilles. The Trojans,
or rather Troilus and Hector, occasionally think of a
larger dimension of time, and so do some of the Greeks,
as Ulysses, in his speech on degree, attacks precisely that
"emulation," that "envious fever" (I.iii.133), which later
he regards as a norm; and Nestor, that

> good old chronicle,
> That hast so long walk'd hand in hand with time,
> (IV.v. 201–02)

provides us with an image of Hector as the vista of history
finally shows him, his faults winnowed away, the noblest
soldier of them all:

> I have, thou gallant Troyan, seen thee oft,
> Laboring for destiny, make cruel way
> Through ranks of Greekish youth; and I have seen thee,
> As hot as Perseus, spur thy Phrygian steed,
> Despising many forfeits and subduements,
> When thou hast hung thy advanced sword i' th' air,
> Not letting it decline on the declin'd;
> That I have said to some my standers-by
> "Lo, Jupiter is yonder, dealing life!"
> And I have seen thee pause and take thy breath,
> When that a ring of Greeks have hemm'd thee in,
> Like an Olympian wrestling. This have I seen;
> But this thy countenance, still lock'd in steel,
> I never saw till now. I knew thy grandsire,
> And once fought with him. He was a soldier good,
> But, by great Mars, the captain of us all,
> Never like thee. O, let an old man embrace thee;
> And, worthy warrior, welcome to our tents.
> (IV.v. 182–99)

Nestor is here almost the figure of Time himself, looking back through generations to discover none as great and worthy as Hector, finding fit comparisons for him only with the god Jupiter, or with one of the sons of Zeus, Perseus, and looking forward to his future reputation, seeing him labor "for destiny." This is the view that time outside the play confirms. Hector himself cannot see this, nor does any of the characters know how time will judge him, but we do; we have an advantage Shakespeare relied on us to use, and stand in the place of "that old common arbitrator, Time," to whom Hector refers the future. We can see that the Trojans and the Greeks fail to bring the two perspectives of time within the play, the two scales of values, the ideal and the practical, the absolute and the daily necessity, into a satisfactory relationship; but we also measure their failure against their permanent standing in a great historical myth.

In other words, the play presents its characters and events realistically in the sense that they are reduced to the common human level; weakness, folly, mental blindness betray the good intentions and ideals of all. Shakespeare is not being cynical,[10] but merely showing the muddle in which most people move, approving the good, but too often following the bad; and if he reduces the accepted stature of the heroes of Greece and Troy by making them succumb to an idea of time as "envious and calumniating," he does it securely in the knowledge that we will have in mind the legend that has descended from Homer, via Virgil, with medieval accretions that added the story of Troilus and Cressida, and the fiction of the Brutus who founded London, and has survived all additions and modifications to maintain still the ready image of Hector and Achilles as types of great warriors, Helen as a type of beauty. This vision modifies our attitude to the play, so that we see constantly beyond the "extant moment," and know, as Achilles does not, "What's past and what's to come." The stress on time in the play is designed to enforce this double awareness, and to remind us that the heroism, magnanimity, wisdom, truth, love, and charity displayed only fitfully by the characters yet remain to grace them through all time, as far as we can imagine it. The play does not damage the larger myth; it is the myth that modifies the play, which does not belong within the accepted categories of tragedy or comedy. It might be called, perhaps, an heroic farce,[11] in which the comedy and satire finally reinforce those noble values envisaged in the action.

NOTES

1. Alice Walker, in her Introduction to the New Cambridge edition (1957), xvi.

2. As by Harold Wilson, in his *On the Design of Shakespearian Tragedy* (1957), or by Brian Morris, "The Tragic Structure of *Troilus and Cressida*," *Shakespeare Quarterly*, X (1959), 481-92.

3. The conflict of views about the play can best be studied in the New Variorum edition, ed. H. N. Hillebrand and T. W. Baldwin (1953). The main attitudes have been noted above; the most important recent defenders of the play as comedy and tragedy have been Alice Walker and Harold Wilson, and the latter has behind him the authority of E. K. Chambers, in his "Shakespeare: An Epilogue," *Review of English Studies*, XVI (1940), 400. G. Wilson Knight's reading of the play in *The Wheel of Fire* (1930) was also close to a tragic one. O. J. Campbell saw the play as satire ending in futility in his *Shakespeare's Comicall Satire* (1943), and W. W. Lawrence, in *Shakespeare's Problem Comedies* (1931), stressed the "philosophical" aspect of the play, finding in it "the searching analysis of a reflective criticism of life" (169), an approach which has been developed by Donald Stauffer and L. C. Knights.

4. In spite of its title, this is a play as much about the Trojan war, about Hector, Achilles, Ulysses, Ajax, and a host of others, as *Julius Caesar* is a play about Rome, and Brutus, Cassius, Antony, and a host of others.

5. See A. S. Knowland, "*Troilus and Cressida*," *Shakespeare Quarterly*, X (1959), 353-65.

6. The whole business is documented in T. D. Kendrick, *British Antiquity* (1950); see especially 39 ff. William Camden's attack on the legend in *Britannia* (1586) led to the scholarly dismissal of it in the later seventeenth century, but the first edition of the *Britannia* in English did not appear until 1610.

7. Kendrick, 35–36.

8. For instance, the Admiral's Men paid John Day and Henry Chettle for a play, or perhaps two plays, on the theme of Brutus in 1598; see *Henslowe's Diary*, ed. R. A. Foakes and R. T. Rickert (1961), 96, 98, 100, 102.

9. I think this is basically true of Ulysses; his big speeches have little effect on others, and the trick he plays on Achilles does not work; nevertheless, he has been regarded as the hero and the villain of the play. For a summary of critical opinions about him, see W. B. Stanford, *The Ulysses Theme* (1954), 164–65.

10. It is a common view of the play that it shows us a disillusioned, cynical, or disgusted Shakespeare; see the New Variorum edition, 536, 538–39, 541, 543, for representative comments.

11. To alter the phrase "tragic farce," coined, I think, by Eugene Ionesco to describe his play *The Chairs*.

Suggested References

The number of possible references is vast and grows alarmingly. (The *Shakespeare Quarterly* devotes one issue each year to a list of the previous year's work, and *Shakespeare Survey* —an annual publication—includes a substantial review of recent scholarship, as well as an occasional essay surveying a few decades of scholarship on a chosen topic.) Though no works are indispensable, those listed below have been found especially helpful.

1. Shakespeare's Times

Byrne, M. St. Clare. *Elizabethan Life in Town and Country.* Rev. ed. New York: Barnes & Noble, 1961. Chapters on manners, beliefs, education, etc., with illustrations.

Joseph, B. L. *Shakespeare's Eden: The Commonwealth of England, 1558–1629.* New York: Barnes & Noble, 1971. An account of the social, political, economic, and cultural life of England.

Schoenbaum, S. *Shakespeare: The Globe and the World.* New York: Oxford University Press, 1979. A readable, handsomely illustrated book on the world of the Elizabethans.

Shakespeare's England. 2 vols. London: Oxford University Press, 1916. A large collection of scholarly essays on a wide variety of topics (e.g. astrology, costume, gardening, horsemanship), with special attention to Shakespeare's references to these topics.

Stone, Lawrence. *The Crisis of the Aristocracy, 1558–1641,* abridged edition. London: Oxford University Press, 1967.

2. Shakespeare

Barnet, Sylvan. *A Short Guide to Shakespeare.* New York: Harcourt Brace Jovanovich, 1974. An introduction to all of the works and to the dramatic traditions behind them.

Bentley, Gerald E. *Shakespeare: A Biographical Handbook.* New Haven, Conn.: Yale University Press, 1961. The facts about Shakespeare, with virtually no conjecture intermingled.

Bush, Geoffrey. *Shakespeare and the Natural Condition.* Cambridge, Mass.: Harvard University Press, 1956. A short, sensitive account of Shakespeare's view of "Nature," touching most of the works.

Chambers, E. K. *William Shakespeare: A Study of Facts and Problems.* 2 vols. London: Oxford University Press, 1930. An invaluable, detailed reference work; not for the casual reader.

Chute, Marchette. *Shakespeare of London.* New York: Dutton, 1949. A readable biography fused with portraits of Stratford and London life.

Clemen, Wolfgang H. *The Development of Shakespeare's Imagery.* Cambridge, Mass.: Harvard University Press, 1951. (Originally published in German, 1936.) A temperate account of a subject often abused.

Granville-Barker, Harley. *Prefaces to Shakespeare.* 2 vols. Princeton, N.J.: Princeton University Press, 1946–47. Essays on ten plays by a scholarly man of the theater.

Harbage, Alfred. *As They Liked It.* New York: Macmillan, 1947. A long, sensitive essay on Shakespeare, morality, and the audience's expectations.

Kernan, Alvin B., ed. *Modern Shakespearean Criticism: Essays on Style, Dramaturgy, and the Major Plays.* New York: Harcourt Brace Jovanovich, 1970. A collection of major formalist criticism.

————. "The Plays and the Playwrights." In *The Revels History of Drama in English,* general editors Clifford Leech and T. W. Craik. Vol. III. London: Methuen, 1975. A book-length essay surveying Elizabethan drama with substantial discussions of Shakespeare's plays.

Schoenbaum, S. *Shakespeare's Lives.* Oxford: Clarendon Press, 1970. A review of the evidence, and an examination of many biographies, including those by Baconians and other heretics.

————. *William Shakespeare: A Compact Documentary Life.* New York: Oxford University Press, 1977. A readable presentation of all that the documents tell us about Shakespeare.

Traversi, D. A. *An Approach to Shakespeare*. 3rd rev. ed. 2 vols. New York: Doubleday, 1968–69. An analysis of the plays beginning with words, images, and themes, rather than with characters.

Van Doren, Mark. *Shakespeare*. New York: Holt, 1939. Brief, perceptive readings of all of the plays.

3. Shakespeare's Theater

Beckerman, Bernard. *Shakespeare at the Globe, 1599–1609*. New York: Macmillan, 1962. On the playhouse and on Elizabethan dramaturgy, acting, and staging.

Chambers, E. K. *The Elizabethan Stage*. 4 vols. New York: Oxford University Press, 1945. A major reference work on theaters, theatrical companies, and staging at court.

Cook, Ann Jennalie. *The Privileged Playgoers of Shakespeare's London, 1576–1642*. Princeton, N.J.: Princeton University Press, 1981. Sees Shakespeare's audience as more middle-class and more intellectual than Harbage (below) does.

Gurr, Andrew. *The Shakespearean Stage: 1579–1642*. 2d edition. Cambridge: Cambridge University Press, 1980. On the acting companies, the actors, the playhouses, the stages, and the audiences.

Harbage, Alfred. *Shakespeare's Audience*. New York: Columbia University Press, 1941. A study of the size and nature of the theatrical public, emphasizing its representativeness.

Hodges, C. Walter. *The Globe Restored*. London: Ernest Benn, 1953. A well-illustrated and readable attempt to reconstruct the Globe Theatre.

Hosley, Richard. "The Playhouses." In *The Revels History of Drama in English*, general editors Clifford Leech and T. W. Craik. Vol. III. London: Methuen, 1975. An essay of one hundred pages on the physical aspects of the playhouses.

Kernodle, George R. *From Art to Theatre: Form and Convention in the Renaissance*. Chicago: University of Chicago Press, 1944. Pioneering and stimulating work on the symbolic and cultural meanings of theater construction.

Nagler, A. M. *Shakespeare's Stage*. Trans. Ralph Manheim. New Haven, Conn.: Yale University Press, 1958. A very brief introduction to the physical aspects of the playhouse.

Slater, Ann Pasternak. *Shakespeare the Director*. Totowa, N.J.: Barnes & Noble, 1982. An analysis of theatrical effects (e.g., kissing, kneeling) in stage directions and dialogue.

Thomson, Peter. *Shakespeare's Theatre*. London: Routledge and Kegan Paul, 1983. A discussion of how plays were staged in Shakespeare's time.

4. Miscellaneous Reference Works

Abbott, E. A. *A Shakespearean Grammar*. New Edition. New York: Macmillan, 1877. An examination of differences between Elizabethan and modern grammar.

Bevington, David. *Shakespeare*. Arlington Heights, Ill.: A. H. M. Publishing, 1978. A short guide to hundreds of important writings on the works.

Bullough, Geoffrey. *Narrative and Dramatic Sources of Shakespeare*. 8 vols. New York: Columbia University Press, 1957–75. A collection of many of the books Shakespeare drew upon, with judicious comments.

Campbell, Oscar James, and Edward G. Quinn. *The Reader's Encyclopedia of Shakespeare*. New York: Crowell, 1966. More than 2,600 entries, from a few sentences to a few pages, on everything related to Shakespeare.

Greg. W. W. *The Shakespeare First Folio*. New York: Oxford University Press, 1955. A detailed yet readable history of the first collection (1623) of Shakespeare's plays.

Kökeritz, Helge. *Shakespeare's Names*. New Haven, Conn.: Yale University Press, 1959. A guide to the pronunciation of some 1,800 names appearing in Shakespeare.

———. *Shakespeare's Pronunciation*. New Haven, Conn.: Yale University Press, 1953. Contains much information about puns and rhymes.

Muir, Kenneth. *The Sources of Shakespeare's Plays*. New Haven, Conn.: Yale University Press, 1978. An account of Shakespeare's use of his reading.

The Norton Facsimile: The First Folio of Shakespeare. Prepared by Charlton Hinman. New York: Norton, 1968. A handsome and accurate facsimile of the first collection (1623) of Shakespeare's plays.

Onions, C. T. *A Shakespeare Glossary*. 2d ed., rev., with enlarged addenda. London: Oxford University Press, 1953. Definitions of words (or senses of words) now obsolete.

Partridge, Eric. *Shakespeare's Bawdy*. Rev. ed. New York: Dutton, 1955. A glossary of bawdy words and phrases.

Shakespeare Quarterly. See headnote to Suggested References.

Shakespeare Survey. See headnote to Suggested References.

Shakespeare's Plays in Quarto. A Facsimile Edition. Ed. Michael J. B. Allen and Kenneth Muir. Berkeley, Calif.: University of California Press, 1981. A book of nine hundred pages, containing facsimiles of twenty-two of the quarto editions of Shakespeare's plays. An invaluable complement to *The Norton Facsimile: The First Folio of Shakespeare* (see above).

Smith, Gordon Ross. *A Classified Shakespeare Bibliography 1936–1958.* University Park, Pa.: Pennsylvania State University Press, 1963. A list of some twenty thousand items on Shakespeare.

Spevack, Marvin. *The Harvard Concordance to Shakespeare.* Cambridge, Mass.: Harvard University Press, 1973. An index to Shakespeare's words.

Wells, Stanley, ed. *Shakespeare: Select Bibliographies.* London: Oxford University Press, 1973. Seventeen essays surveying scholarship and criticism of Shakespeare's life, work, and theater.

5. *Troilus and Cressida*

Alexander, Peter. "*Troilus and Cressida,* 1609, *The Library,* Ser. 4, 9 (1928), 267–86.

Bayley, John. "Time and the Trojans," *Essays in Criticism,* 25 (1975), 55–73.

Bradbrook, Muriel C. "What Shakespeare Did to Chaucer's *Troilus and Criseyde,*" *Shakespeare Quarterly,* 9 (1958), 311–19.

Brooke, C. F. Tucker. "Shakespeare's Study in Culture and Anarchy," *Yale Review,* 17 (1928), 571–77.

Campbell, Oscar J. *Comicall Satyre and Shakespeare's "Troilus and Cressida."* San Marino, Calif.: Huntington Library; London: Oxford University Press, 1938.

Chapman, John Jay. *Selected Writings,* ed. Jacques Barzun. New York: Doubleday & Company, Inc. (Anchor Books), 1959.

Charlton, H. B. "The Dark Comedies," *Bulletin of the John Rylands Library,* 21 (1937), 78–128.

Coleridge, Samuel Taylor. *Coleridge's Writings on Shakespeare,* ed. Terence Hawkes, introd. Alfred B. Harbage. New York: G. P. Putnam's Sons (Capricorn Books), 1959.

Ellis-Fermor, Una. *The Frontiers of Drama.* London:

Methuen & Co., Ltd., 1945; New York: Oxford University Press, 1946; rev. ed., 1948.

Gérard, Albert. "Meaning and Structure in *Troilus and Cressida*," *English Studies*, 40 (1959), 148–51, 156–57.

Harrier, R. C. "Troilus Divided," *Studies in the English Renaissance Drama in Memory of Karl Julius Holzknecht*, ed. Josephine W. Bennett et al. New York: New York University Press, 1959.

Kaula, David. "Will and Reason in *Troilus and Cressida*," *Shakespeare Quarterly*, 12 (1961), 271–83.

Kendall, P. M. "Inaction and Ambivalence in *Troilus and Cressida*," *English Studies in Honor of James Southall Wilson*, ed. Fredson Bowers. Charlottesville, Va.: Alderman Library, University of Virginia, 1951.

Kimbrough, Robert. *Shakespeare's "Troilus and Cressida" and its Setting*. Cambridge, Mass.: Harvard University Press, 1964.

Knight, G. Wilson. *The Wheel of Fire*. New York and London: Oxford University Press, 1930; 5th rev. ed., New York: Meridian Books, Inc., 1957.

Knights, L. C. "*Troilus and Cressida* Again," *Scrutiny*, 18 (1951), 144–57.

Muir, Kenneth. "*Troilus and Cressida*," *Shakespeare Survey*, 8 (1955), 28–39.

Nowottny, Winifred M. T. "'Opinion' and 'Value' in *Troilus and Cressida*," *Essays in Criticism*, 4 (1954), 282–96.

Rabkin, Norman. "Troilus and Cressida: The Uses of the Double Plot," *Shakespeare Studies*, 1 (1965), 265–82.

Reynolds, George F. "*Troilus and Cressida* on the Elizabethan Stage" *Joseph Quincy Adams Memorial Studies*, ed. J. G. McManaway, G. E. Dawson, E. E. Willoughby. Washington, D.C.: Folger Shakespeare Library, 1948.

Rollins, Hyder E. "The Troilus-Cressida Story from Chaucer to Shakespeare," *Publications of the Modern Language Association*, 32 (1917), 383–429.

Spencer, Theodore. *Shakespeare and the Nature of Man*. New York: The Macmillan Company, 1942.

Tillyard, E. M. W. *Shakespeare's Problem Plays*. Toronto: University of Toronto Press, 1949; London: Chatto & Windus, 1950.

Walker, Alice. *Textual Problems of the First Folio*. New York and London: Cambridge University Press, 1953.

© **SIGNET CLASSIC** (0451)

The Signet Classic Shakespeare

*Prices slightly higher in Canada
